PRAISE FOR *BREAKING SKY*

"An action-packed thrill ride that smashes through all kinds of barriers at a Mach 5 pace."

—Carrie Jones, *New York Times* bestselling author of the Need series

"A nonstop thrill ride…will keep you reading at the speed of sound. *Breaking Sky* is one of the most exciting reads of the year."

—Thomas E. Sniegoski, *New York Times* bestselling author of The Fallen series

"Had me in its grip from takeoff to landing. Chase is a kick-butt female and the swoon-worthy flyboys kept me up way past my bedtime."

—Joy N. Hensley, author of *Rites of Passage*

"*Breaking Sky* ticks all the boxes: love, war, friendship, action, and danger—I was left wanting more, more, more!"

—Jessica Shirvington, author of *One Past Midnight*

"Replete with fighter pilot jargon, plausible science fiction elements, and nerd-friendly literary allusions, this taut, well-crafted novel should have broad appeal, for fans of everything from Roth's *Divergent* to Wein's *Code Name Verity*."

—*The Bulletin for the Center for Children's Books*, Starred Review

"Strong characterizations, action, adventure, and emotion combine to produce a sci-fi novel that is more than just the sum of its parts."
—*School Library Journal*, Starred Review

"Smart, exciting, confident—and quite possibly the next Big Thing."
—*Kirkus Reviews*

"McCarthy puts her characters in increasingly tense situations, testing them to the breaking point and giving what could have been merely a popcorn thriller sudden gravity. This crazy-cool story should soar."
—*Booklist*

"McCarthy deploys breath-stopping depictions of high-stakes piloting with enviable ease, and the in-your-face personal confrontations are nearly as taut."
—*Publishers Weekly*

BREAKING SKY

CORI MCCARTHY

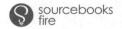

Copyright © 2015 by Cori McCarthy

Cover and internal design © 2015 by Sourcebooks, Inc.

Cover design by Sammy Yuen

Cover art by Sammy Yuen

Sourcebooks and the colophon are registered trademarks of Sourcebooks, Inc.

All rights reserved. No part of this book may be reproduced in any form or by any electronic or mechanical means including information storage and retrieval systems—except in the case of brief quotations embodied in critical articles or reviews—without permission in writing from its publisher, Sourcebooks, Inc.

The characters and events portrayed in this book are fictitious or are used fictitiously. Any similarity to real persons, living or dead, is purely coincidental and not intended by the author.

Published by Sourcebooks Fire, an imprint of Sourcebooks, Inc.

P.O. Box 4410, Naperville, Illinois 60567-4410

(630) 961-3900

Fax: (630) 961-2168

www.sourcebooks.com

The Library of Congress has cataloged the hardcover edition as follows:

McCarthy, Cori.

  Breaking sky / Cori McCarthy.

    pages cm

  Summary: In the year 2048 Chase Harcourt, call sign "Nyx," is one of only two pilots chosen to fly the experimental "Streaker" jets at the junior Air Force Academy, but few know the pain and loneliness of her past or the dark secret about her father, and as the world tilts toward war, Chase cracks open a military secret.

  (hard cover : alk. paper) [1. Air pilots--Fiction. 2. Secrets--Fiction. 3. Science fiction.] I. Title.

PZ7.M47841233Br 2015

[Fic]--dc23

2014036355

Printed and bound in the United States of America.

VP 10 9 8 7 6 5 4 3 2 1

For Maverick Archer,
my wingman

"There is an art, or rather, a knack to flying.
The knack lies in learning how to throw yourself at the ground
and **miss**.*"*

—Douglas Adams, *Life, the Universe and Everything*

◄ DELTA ►

The lake held up a mirror to the sky's razor-blue, and Chase heard glass cracking in that color. An icy wind dried the blood on her chapped hands. She made a fist and her knuckles split.

She had killed him.

His body drained a red thread into the faint waves, blooming, fading, and pulling deeper into the water. She said his name in a whisper. Then a scream. She said it as if the word might let her keep him, but his name only echoed once over the lake and then died.

The government would take that name. Stamp it onto some monument, and he'd be nothing more than the first casualty of the war. The world war that had started moments ago.

Oh God.

All her senses were misfiring. Her jet was in three pieces and half-sunk against the shore. Chase stared at its crumpled body as the wind turned on her, pitching black smoke at her face. She squeezed her eyes, but the blue world stabbed inward.

Everything was fracturing, and it had been ever since she chased *Phoenix* out of the sky.

1

SOUND BARRIER

Break It, Baby

Speed turned her on.

The other cadets talked about the thrill of flying, but Chase didn't relate. Her love was more specific. She flew for the high-g press of ten times the weight of gravity. For the throttle thrust forward, the roar-rev of the engines, and then, the mach rush.

Chase was in the atmosphere—flying so fast she felt like solid muscle. Her thoughts were a dance of impulse as she backed off the speed and looked through the tempered glass canopy. The earth knelt before her like she was holding court over the whole damn planet.

She smiled.

"I don't suppose you see a gas station." Pippin sat a few feet behind her, but his voice was closer, a direct link from his mask to her helmet's headphones. "Nearing bingo fuel, Nyx."

"Give me two minutes." Chase smelled a challenge. Or she imagined one. Anything to prolong the hop and do something *fun*.

She pulled back on the stick, pointing the nose of her jet straight at the midday sun.

Brilliance charged the crystal dome.

"Tower to Nyx. Come in, Nyx," Pippin mocked. "My sense of mortality insists I ask if we're coming down anytime soon. As much as I wanted to be an astronaut when I was five, *Dragon* isn't a starship. Where are we going exactly?"

"Somewhere. Anywhere." The sun blinded through her smoky visor, but she kept her eyes ahead. "Up."

"Yes, I was going to point out that *somewhere* feels like *up* today. Sylph is already halfway home."

"Good." Chase gripped the throttle, and the leather of her gloves gripped back. "We don't need Sylph sniffing around for this."

Moments scratched by, and Pippin cleared his throat. Twice.

"We got to get high, Pip. Real high. Otherwise, we'll smash into the ground before we can break the sound barrier in a downward spiral."

"WHAT? WHY?"

Her reasons stacked. Because the training runs were tedious. Because Sylph, the pilot of the other experimental Streaker jet, had never and would never try such a stunt. And because Chase was Nyx, and with that title came certain wild expectations.

And the cherry on top? Because Chase needed to prove she *could* do it.

When they were nearly thirty miles up, about to leave the stratosphere, she turned the jet toward the curve of the earth's surface and let them freefall. Gravity took hold, and she steeled herself to punch through it.

"Wait, Nyx. I'm all for fun, but this is—"

The engine howl took over. They blazed at the blue-on-blue planet, the green smatterings coming into focus. She felt the mach tuck, the air trying to slow her down, just as the sound barrier broke.

The sonic **boom** was lost behind them, but a pearly halo erupted in their wake.

She crowed.

Chase Harcourt, call sign "Nyx," had broken the speed of sound at absolute zero sink rate. The other cadets could put that on her headstone.

Speaking of, she was about to die.

"Nyx!" Pippin yelled. "We're not going to pull up in time!"

The earth was growing larger fast.

Too fast.

Chase reeled in the speed, but the jet resisted. Pippin panic-hummed "Ode to Joy," and Chase's arm muscles shook. Land filled the cockpit glass. They were going to slam into it. Houses came into focus.

Trees.

People even.

Chase caught an updraft at the last second. They soared into the sky, leveling above the blush of wispy clouds. Pippin ripped off his mask to gasp, while Chase's eyes stuck a little too wide. Far below, the humped back of South America led to the arm of Panama, rising fist-up through the Caribbean Sea.

Chase let go of the throttle slowly, her fingers stiff. "Christ. That was fun."

"Balls of fi—"

A flash of shining silver cut Pippin off. Cut everything off. *Dragon* flipped. Chase fought to frame the horizon, but what she saw next iced her blood.

A Streaker. A twin to the prototype she sat in.

It was like walking by a mirror she didn't know existed. It made her jump, defensively jinking her wings. The other pilot looked her way right before jet-washing *Dragon*. Chase and Pippin spun through the fiery engine wake. Long seconds passed before she won the stick back and blinked the red out of her vision. By the time *Dragon* had stabilized, nothing but the other Streaker's contrail remained. A white highway.

Chase exploded after it.

"Time for a conference call, Nyx." Pippin's tight voice belied his mocking. "What in the blazes was that?"

"A bogey."

"That looked like Sylph."

"Sylph's almost home. You said it yourself. That was someone else."

Pippin didn't bother to agree. He was into his controls in a desperate way. After all, he was her RIO, her radar intercept officer. The sky was his ingrained map, and it was his job to make sure the air was clear around them, like a human satellite. "That bird has no signal," he finally said, a hint of wonder in his voice. "How could it have no signal?"

"No signal *and* it's headed for U.S. soil." Chase's pulse picked up. Her muscles went tight as she leaned into the pursuit. This wasn't like the stunt she'd just pulled. This was what she was trained for, and she left safe speeds way behind.

"What are you going to do if we catch it? We're not armed, Nyx."

"Track it. See where it lands." *Make sure it isn't a sneaking spy from China,* she added to herself.

They passed Mach 3.

Chase grinned so fiercely from the pressure that she felt crazed. "There. You see him?"

Far below, metal winked over the serpentine glisten of the Mississippi. She pulled lower, closer to the blue-ferocity of the engines—dual engines that reached under each narrow wing and married together at the back like the infinity symbol. Just like *Dragon*'s engines.

Chase dove under the jet. God, it was *blinding* fast. The pilot tilted into her space, their wings nearly kissing. She'd never gotten remotely this close to Sylph's bird in the air...it made her laugh out loud and test how much closer she could get. The other pilot's bloodred helmet shot a look her way, and she had the funniest feeling *he* was laughing too.

"Pip, look at that helmet—"

Dragon's emergency low fuel alarm pierced the cockpit. She slapped at the control board to turn it off, but her speed died as the engines defaulted to reserve levels. The other jet broke east toward the indigo muscles of the Great Lakes.

Chase had just enough time to read the sharp military stenciling along its side:

PHOENIX

2

DRONE

An Enemy without a Face

Pippin wanted that jet to be Sylph. He wouldn't let it go. "The Star could be trying out some new music or a block. Maybe they fuzzed my radar to see how close Sylph could get."

"Sylph doesn't have the lady balls to fly that fast," Chase said. *Dragon* was far west now, above Seattle, and headed due north. The clouds evaporated, revealing a jagged coastline. "Pip, I saw *red*."

"No, surely not." He checked his sarcasm with a growling sigh. "You went feral flyboy. You would have followed that contrail straight across the d-line if it had headed that way."

"*Red helmet*." She touched her black standard-issue helmet. Chase wasn't technically in the Air Force yet, but as a top-ranked cadet, she had fought for the opportunity to pilot one of two Streaker prototypes.

One of *three*…

"Are you scanning for drones?" Chase's voice pitched, betraying her standard cool. Pippin grunted a confirmation. They were only a few hundred miles from the demarcation line, the invisible boundary that split the Pacific Ocean and kept the Second Cold War so chilly.

She pulled her mask from her face only to reattach it. Bingo fuel meant autopilot, and autopilot meant that *Dragon* was flying at tricycle pace. In the meantime, Chase drilled her emotions, set up each worry like a toy soldier. Where did that bird come from? Who knew about it? And more importantly, who *didn't* know about it?

"Did you see its name, Pip? That bird had *Phoenix* stenciled on its side."

"*Phoenix* looks a lot like Sylph's *Pegasus*. Seven letters. Begins with *P*."

"Except for the fact that they're different words."

"Different mythological beasts, in fact."

"That wasn't Sylph, *Henry*." She hoped using his real name might emphasize her point. "Why do I feel like you're trying to convince me to drop it?"

"Because I'm smarter than you. *Chase*."

"You're smarter than everybody."

"My cross to bear."

Chase's impatience held down her smirk. She drummed her fingers on the cockpit. Most canopies were made of thick plastic, but *Dragon*'s was crafted from tempered glass, the strongest in the world. "That *Phoenix* had the same crystal canopy. The same blue-silver skin."

In Chase's mind, the Streakers stood apart in the sky and in aviation history. Light, sleek, and fueled by rip-roaring twin engines. They were hybrids of the older manned jets with HOTAS controls—hands-on throttle and stick—and the popular aerodynamic drones of the early twenty-first century.

"You saw it," she said a little harder.

"Maybe it's a backup," Pippin tried. "The Air Force's dirty little secret. Or hey, maybe the Navy academy has a Streaker we don't know about."

"Bite your tongue," Chase grumbled. "The Streakers are the Air Force's babies. Kale promised me that much."

"I forgot. You think the brigadier general is all *hand to God*."

"Hey, now," she said. "You're supposed to warn me before you snark that hard."

He chuckled, and that alone was worth the bickering. Pippin needed a laugh these days like most two-year-olds needed a nap. Not that Pippin was the only one struggling. Chase, the other cadets, the airmen at the Star—everyone needed a break from the strangling tension of the Second Cold War. Chase's thoughts plunged as she watched the beach below run a white scar toward the horizon. She couldn't stop herself from imagining World War III. Battleships crowding the West Coast. The black rain of missiles falling.

America on fire.

The blaze she imagined was a collage of crimson. Red drones. Ri Xiong Di's bleeding flag. And that maroon-helmeted pilot. Could *Phoenix* have come from the New Eastern Bloc? Did the Asians steal the design? Build their own Streaker?

No. That would be impossible. *Catastrophic.*

"You think Kale is fuming in the tower right now?" Chase asked. "No doubt they caught that near collision on the satellite feed."

"By design, *Dragon* comes up as little more than a speeding blip on their radar. If we didn't, the bad guys would have crossed the line and taken us down two years ago."

"Don't say 'bad guys,'" Chase said. "That makes them feel like a joke."

"I prefer when they feel like a joke." He added under his breath, "So do you." Pippin sprinkled everything with cynicism.

"We could radio in," she tried. "Let Kale know about the phantom Streaker."

"Nyx, that bird wasn't armed. It's not an immediate threat. Kale wouldn't want you to risk opening up our signal to anyone waiting to shake us down." Pippin said *anyone*, but he meant Ri Xiong Di. Spying jerks, they were always listening, always sending out code viruses that could cripple navigation, misfire missiles, or worst of all, crash jets kamikaze-style into civilian areas. *Bam.*

So the Streakers flew off the grid, which necessitated a two-man team and radio silence. But Ri Xiong Di's cyber superiority affected more than just airpower. Any time they wanted to take over a TV station or satellite, they did. Even the U.S. military's network had been hacked in the past.

Nothing was safe.

Chase leaned into the canopy glass. They crossed the Canadian border, skirting a never-ending white-on-woods landscape.

Canada was rumored to be as depressed as America these days. No one could say for sure—the borders had been closed since 2022—and communication wasn't permitted between America and other countries.

The U.S. had been on its own for twenty-six years, which meant constant vigilance and a raw state of survival. Chase felt that responsibility through her hands, her gloves, her throttle and stick. Straight to the titanium bones of the beautiful bird she called *Dragon*.

"Kale needs to know about that Streaker, Pip. ASAP. I'm going to break autopilot."

"We only have enough fuel to keep this speed. Besides, we're almost there." His subtext was *wait*. After all, the cold war was purely that: endless waiting.

In poli-sci, Chase had learned that Ri Xiong Di had spread through Asia during the 2010s like a quiet cancer. The continent solidified under the anti-democratic political faction, and the new superpower took a stand by toppling the old one. They limited America's global trade and scared away natural allies like Canada with fleets of red drones.

Chase had to be proud of what happened next. It was the reason she was only a junior and yet flying a multibillion-dollar jet. Congress enacted the Youth Services Charter, establishing junior military academies to rescue the nation's brightest teens from the country's bleak poverty. At the same time, the Air Force began to experiment with manned fighter jets that might someday best the red drones. The latest secret hope was the Streakers—jets so fast they required teen pilots in top physical form with impulse-swift reflexes.

Banks Island came into view as the sky darkened. From the air, the ice-covered archipelago was shaped like a tousled T-shirt, complete with river wrinkles and a star structure where the chest pocket would be.

The United Star Academy.

The place glittered with life, serving as both a full-functioning Air Force base *and* the junior military academy. Chase traced the six triangular buildings fanned around a hexagonal center as the blue blink of the runway greeted her like a string of Christmas lights. The Star always welcomed, which never felt small after her smoking hole of a childhood.

Chase stole the jet from autopilot and sped into the landing, letting down with a shriek of tires and engines. The fuel gauge hung like a broken arm, and she kept off the brakes as she headed across the landing apron toward the hangar.

"Care to slow down?" Pippin asked. "We're going to get pulled over, and I think you've been drinking."

"Be serious for a sec, Pippin."

"Okay. Seriously slow down."

"Can't. Might stall out."

Pippin did that annoying thing where he knew what she was thinking. "Kale's not going to react when you tell him about Mr. Red Helmet. Not the way you want him to."

Her RIO's continued dismissal of the phantom Streaker finally hit her too hard. She unhooked her harness and turned around in her seat to face him. *Dragon* jerked off course, and they headed for the side of the hangar, still taxiing fast.

"How can you think we should drop this?"

Pippin unstrapped his mask and flipped up his visor. "Remember when Crowley said he saw drones over Florida? They put him on the Down List before he'd finished filing the report. Also"—he pointed forward—"there's a wall there."

"You're really not curious?"

"I'm really not worried. There could be three Streakers instead of two. Wall. The military is a labyrinth of lies. Wall."

"Interesting career choice you've made."

"Wall, Chase! WALL!"

"All right!" She swung around and turned too fast. *Dragon* careened through the hangar doors and scattered ground crew like pigeons before sliding into a neat stop beside the other Streaker, *Pegasus*, with a light bump of wing against wing.

Chase popped off her helmet. "I need you on my team, Pippin."

"Do I get a Team Nyx T-shirt?"

"I'm serious."

"As a bullfight." Pippin unstrapped his harness and flipped up his visor. Their eyes met the way they always did after a long hop. With relief and exhaustion and whatever was on the shadow side of trust. Chase thought it scanned like regret, but whatever it was had been rooted throughout their friendship. What they did, they did together. Hands down.

"I know you're serious," Pippin said, giving the word its full meaning for once. "I'll back you up."

She swatted his helmet affectionately and opened the canopy. Densely cold air sunk into the cockpit, but she took a deep, leveling breath. She was home.

3

COLORFUL ACTIONS

Safety Is Overrated

Chase spent the next five minutes getting chewed out by the deck officer. Irresponsible. Show-off. Reckless. Maverick. He spent all the standard criticisms so fast that she couldn't help being impressed. All that for a slightly rushed parking job—he didn't even know about the stunt she'd pulled in the air.

A couple of freshman ground crew waited by the fuel tanks, chatting up Pippin. They gave her thumbs-ups from behind the officer's back. Chase knew her fan club by sight, but she hadn't bothered to learn their names. That might have seemed flyboy elitist like everything else at the Star, but she really just wasn't the kind of girl to focus on anyone or anything outside of *Dragon*.

When the officer finally stomped away, Chase strode over with her helmet under her arm. She couldn't keep back a smile. She loved riling up an officer—putting on a show. It was better than being overlooked, and it also kept people at a manageable distance.

"You flew *Dragon* to her vapors, Nyx," one of the freshmen said.

He had a zit the size of Mount Vesuvius on his forehead, but his eyes were headlight bright. "What happened? Red drones?"

"You know I can't answer that." Chase dropped her helmet into his outstretched hands. She rubbed the now cold sweat through her short hair and respiked her fauxhawk.

"So what happened?" a girl asked. She had acne too. Working in the grease mist of the hangar wreaked havoc on skin. "Did you *almost* die?"

"Would you say twice?" Chase asked Pippin.

"Counting the wall? Three." Her RIO was sweatier than normal after their garden-variety flights, and when she tried to catch his eye, he rubbed the back of his neck and looked elsewhere.

"Sweet." The freshman cradled Chase's helmet. He started to talk a little too fast about a secret party that he was throwing in his barracks that weekend. Chase wasn't really listening until the girl broke in.

"Don't ask her. She's just going to say no." The last name on the girl's jumpsuit was *HELENA*. "Flyboys never hang out with the ground crew."

Her comment was aimed at Chase, but Helena was sending missiles at the wrong bogey. Chase wasn't the one who set the rules. Flyboys kept their own company. Ground crew kept theirs. Add to that the divisions of the grades… These guys were not only ground crew but freshmen to boot. They were circles away.

"Thanks for the invite, Jameson, but I'm busy with train—"

"See?" Helena broke in. "Told you, *Stephens*. She doesn't even know your name."

Stephens didn't seem to care. He was giving Chase I-want-to-hug-on-you eyes. She redirected. "I need Kale. Is he in the tower?"

Helena said yes while Stephens said no. Chase left them to debate, taking off at a tired jog and weaving a path through the cavernous hangar with Pippin at her heels. They both knew that when they finally stopped moving, really stopped, they'd knock out. Flight was exhausting; non-flyboys never quite got that. A few hours in the air and she was beat—and that was at lower speeds. The faster she flew, the harder the strain on her body to fight the extra gravity. Kale said it was the equivalent of running a half marathon every time she broke mach speed for more than five minutes.

It didn't help that the hangar was a lesson in cold, sinking ice fingers into her muscles. The building was cement-floored with four-story-high ceilings. Chase jogged around planes, jets, and helicopters in a range of working order. There were even a few older, now obsolete drones. Some birds stood under huge tarps like veiled dinosaur bones while others were shiny and fueled, ready to fly far and fast in case someone turned up the burner on the Second Cold War. The pilots stationed here lived at the ready.

"You could have said you'd try to make it." Pippin jogged faster to catch up. "Let them dream a little."

"Hope is sugar. Truth is protein," she said, unwittingly quoting her father.

"Cheers, Gandhi."

"Come on. A freshman ground crew party in the barracks? It'll be broken up in fifteen minutes, and I don't know about you, but I don't need any more demerits."

"It couldn't hurt to have a few more friends, Chase. Even out your reputation a little."

"Not my concern," she said, ignoring his jibe. There were a little more than a thousand cadets at the Star, and while everyone seemed to know Chase because of her status as a Streaker pilot, she only knew the flyboys she interacted with daily—and the ones she singled out for a little fun.

Chase flung open the door to the tower and took the steps two at a time. "You're one to talk, Pip. I don't see you socializing with anyone outside of Baggins or Skywalker during free hour."

At the top of the stairs, she entered a circular room bustling with airmen and lined with windows. Outside, the sky lapsed into navy twilight while the green mist of the northern lights shone down.

The academy and the Air Force base, known jointly as the Star, lay within view of Canada's glacial rolls and epic forests. Banks Island was formerly a Canadian National Park, a forgotten little piece of ice that the U.S. had purchased decades back, right before Ri Xiong Di took over. It was an "out of sight, out of mind" kind of location. A pain in the butt to get to for those people who didn't have military aircraft at their disposal. It was also strategically located just east of Alaska—a likely invasion point if Ri Xiong Di stormed through Siberia.

A set of older fighter jets took off on the runway below. They roared and sent vibrations through the tower and straight into

Chase's chest. Those birds were probably impressive in their day, but now they wouldn't last half a minute against a red drone. Too many things felt that way. Great, but dated. Chase had been born in a country stuck in survival mode, and when she read about America's recent history of prosperity, she had to squint. What did that look like?

Chase elbowed toward the busy center of the tower. Pippin was with her, although he hung back. She knew her RIO better than he liked to admit, and something about that phantom Streaker had spooked him. Well, Chase was spooked too.

She cleared her throat twice before a staff sergeant swung around in his chair. The name above the chest pocket on the digital tiger stripe pattern of his Airman Battle Uniform was *MASTERS*.

"Pippin and Nyx. My lucky day." Masters was young and hawkish in nature with narrow-close eyes and a nose that skewed beak-like. "Cadets can't be in the tower. Out."

"But, sir—"

"Out!"

"Do you mean 'shouldn't be in the tower?'" Pippin asked. "Because we are clearly able to be in the tower, thus disproving the use of *can*, its verb root being 'to be able to.'"

"Pippin, I suspect that semantics are not the staff sergeant's strong suit."

"Truth." Pippin's smirk was all in his eyes, mischief in a brainy-gone-cute way.

Masters practiced a cold scowl. Clearly, he imagined himself to be a general. Too bad he looked like he was about to squawk. "You two think you're so untouchable. You might be Kale's pet, Harcourt, but your RIO is just a RIO. How would he like some demerits?"

Chase turned to Pippin. "Is it 138?"

"142 last time I tested."

Chase smiled at Masters. "His IQ is 142, sir. Just how badly do you think the military wants him here and happy?"

Masters leaned back in his chair, making it groan. "I don't have time to pal around with you two. And I can't help you do whatever it is you're up to."

"Now that use of *can* I do believe to be accurate," Pippin said.

"Where's Kale? We have business that concerns the whole goddamn military." Chase pointed to the blipping radar screen. "You saw that I had company up there."

"I saw nothing." Masters folded his arms. "Are you imagining things? Should I let the academy psychiatrist know that *Dragon*'s team is cracking up? Is Nyx finally washing out?"

Chase leaned in. Her body tensed like gravity was about to triple. "You—"

Her RIO took her arm and led her out of the tower just as her fist readied to plant itself into the staff sergeant's face. The door clamped shut behind them, giving way to the dense cool of the stairway and its concrete-encased quiet.

"I'm all for lipping pompous officers, but violence is only going to get you on the Down List." Pippin took hold of her shoulders and peered in close. She looked away. He knew how to haul her out of her red zone like no one else, and she wasn't always pleased about it. Anger was like speed—it gave her direction.

She shook out her fists. "I know. This all feels really weird. Don't you sense it?"

"Yes. Very weird. That staff sergeant was told not to talk to us, Chase."

"How could you tell?"

"Because he looked way too happy to say he didn't see anything. Either that or…" Pippin ran out of words. It wasn't like him. His calm was something Chase piled her recklessness on. That way, no matter how wrong she was—and she was wrong quite a bit—she always had the bedrock of his self-assurance.

"What?" she asked.

"Or…maybe they really didn't see anything." Pippin looked older than seventeen when he was this tired, and yet his face had a forever-young quality. Chase called it "boyishly boyish good looks" when she was trying to get him riled. But right now, with his hair sweat-sticky and his eyes red, he looked older than the staff sergeant she'd almost hammered.

Chase buzzed with the last of her energy. "So you didn't see that jet on your radar, and the tower might not have seen it on the satellite. Is that even possible?"

"I don't know." Pippin was stumped as often as he was grave.

And he was suddenly both.

Chase took off toward the administration offices and Kale with a corkscrew feeling deep in her stomach. A secret jet without a signal didn't smell like a backup Air Force bird. It reeked of Ri Xiong Di. Of sabotage.

4
BRIGADIER GENERAL
One Serious Star

Kale's office smelled like coffee. A pot always burbled in the corner, and shelves lined every inch of wall space, sagging under the weight of old books, sad-armed plants, and military paraphernalia from centuries past. Chase knocked on the doorjamb, waiting for the brigadier general, the head of the Star, to invite them in.

He didn't.

His head was bowed over a book on his desk, his gray hair looking soft. His shoulders, on the other hand, were hard and straight—the kind you could balance a country on. Although Chase loved to fly and the academy was home, there were days when she wondered how she'd stay in the military as a career. Then she'd see Kale in his uniform and she'd scrape around in her imagination, wanting to picture herself weathered and proud and in charge.

"General?"

Kale waved her into silence. She waited a few moments while he licked his thumb and flicked through a few pages. "General, I..."

Kale snapped a look that made both cadets stand at attention and clip their hands to their foreheads. "I need a word with Harcourt," he said. "Donnet, you're dismissed."

Pippin backed into the hall and whispered, "Watch yourself. Don't say too much."

Chase mocked a sneer at her RIO, but Pippin wasn't joking. He had that too-serious look on his face again. "*What?*" Chase mouthed.

"Harcourt," Kale commanded. Chase stepped into his office, suddenly nervy without Pippin at her back. She couldn't fly without him, and that feeling often permeated her time on the ground.

Kale shut his book. "Let me tell you about my night, Harcourt. Here I was, peacefully trying to eat my dinner, only to get a call from the tower. Do you know what they said?"

"No, General."

"*Dragon* is crashing."

Kale stood up, and something in Chase's chest sat down. "So I ran to the tower only to hear it was a *stunt*. You broke the speed of sound at absolute zero sink rate over *civilian airspace*."

"But we saw—"

"Do I look finished?" Kale was livid with hints of disappointment. He hadn't come down this hard on her in—well—a few weeks, but it still turned her over to feel like she'd blown his approval. Again. "You give new definition to 'colorful actions.' We don't even have demerits for that kind of recklessness. Plus, my eggs got cold." He motioned to a plate of now fossilized scrambled eggs and toast. "You can't eat cold eggs, Harcourt. They taste like socks."

There it was. An encouraging spark at the corner of his eye.

"You eat breakfast for dinner, General?"

"You're not the only one who enjoys doing things your own way." He sat down and motioned for her to do the same. "So here's my real problem. You won't follow rules. Sylph won't break them. I don't know which one of you is worse. We hoped that between the two of you we would be able to figure out exactly what the Streakers can do, but I swear you won't be happy until you send *Dragon* back to the taxpayers in a box of parts."

The two of you… Did Kale really not know about the third Streaker?

She ran her hands over the cracked leather of the armchair. Wispy stuffing stuck through like white hair. "General, we have a problem… I saw another jet up there today. I sort of chased him."

Kale leaned halfway over his desk, his face unreadable. "Another jet?"

"Another Streaker. I know it sounds crazy. I checked the tower." She drank in his reaction, but it was empty. No lifted eyebrow. No brightness in his gaze. "They didn't see anything on the satellite," she continued. "And Pippin didn't pick it up on his controls."

"So it was a ghost. You probably saw your own reflection in a cloud pool." His tone was final, but it made her dive into the memory of the pearly blue flash. Chase picked up a rusty bayonet off the edge of his desk and rolled it between her palms.

"There are only two Streakers, Harcourt. *Dragon* and *Pegasus*."

And *Phoenix*, she added to herself.

So Kale knew. If he wasn't genuinely curious—if he pretended like he didn't believe her—he knew. What then? Pippin was right; the military wasn't exactly forthcoming with hard facts, but Chase had always trusted Kale—and he appeared to trust her.

She sat taller and put the bayonet down with a sharp thump. "Is it a secret bird? A backup? I just need to know if it's American. If Ri Xiong Di stole the plans—"

"You didn't see anything, Harcourt." He shot her a look that snapped her back to attention. To being a cadet at the academy and not the star pilot kicking back in her favorite commander's office. It stung.

"It's the trials, isn't it?" he added a little gruffly, a little late. "They're getting to you."

"I'm *not* cracking up!" She stood, her chest as tight as a fist.

"Of course not." He waved for her to sit back down. "But we're three months to January. It'd be natural if you were feeling the pinch."

Chase glared at the worn tile. It was a low blow to bring up the pressure of the trials. Kale must have really wanted to distract her from the mystery Streaker.

It worked.

"Pinch," she muttered. That was like calling a bullet wound a copper-coated splinter. In the air, she could face anything, but the upcoming government trials over whether the U.S. would fund a fleet of Streakers made her flinch outright. The question would come down to her flying—and Sylph's. And if they failed? If they couldn't prove the Streakers could beat a red drone? No more *Dragon*. No more reaching hope for the U.S.

Kale crossed the room and sat on the edge of the desk before her. "Harcourt, 2049 will be a revolutionary year for the U.S. For the world. I'm not worried."

"That makes me feel so much more relaxed." Chase's sarcasm was as good as her helmet visor. She could flick it down when she didn't want anyone to know where she was looking. But now her words turned flat, the mask of her confidence slipping. "Sylph will give the government board what they want to see. She can run all the standard maneuvers backward and forward."

"But not half as fast as you." Kale's stare was polished brown stone. "And you know it's not about having jets that can fly. It's about jets that can outfly those drones."

Chase couldn't hold his gaze. She stared at the sound edge of his left shoulder, at the single shining star, and wondered if she really was cracking up.

"I keep thinking about those reds we saw over the d-line last month." The memory flared. Chase had risked a maneuver only a few miles from the demarcation line and glimpsed a scarlet hive: red drones, all of them missile toting. She prickled like a wasp had set down on her nose. "Seems like the border is bulking up for something big."

"The New Eastern Bloc is nervous because we've been quiet. And they should be, shouldn't they? No doubt they're dying to catch one of those speeding blips on their satellites. We're close,

Harcourt. I can taste the U.S. as a world protector again." His chin was set at the best angle. "We'll reset the balance. Put an end to human rights violations and help all those people in Ri Xiong Di's stranglehold. We'll resurrect the standard of American lives."

He paused, and she thought he might be waiting. This was her chance to say something equally poetic and patriotic.

"We'll do…that," she managed. "No problem." Good Lord.

Kale laughed, a lifting sound. His salt and ash hair shook. It was always a little longer than regulation and seemed to prove that he was the only person who could head a military academy full of teens who spent as much time battling each other as keeping their eyes on the horizon of a very real war. "Sylph is a fine, clinical pilot, but she doesn't have the spirit to outthink those drones. You're the one who's going to prove that a mind will always beat a machine."

Chase touched the side of her head as though she needed to make sure her brains were really in there.

Kale's eyes held a renewed spark. "Just be yourself, Harcourt. Well, be a less impulsive version of yourself."

She nodded.

"Go get out of that zoom bag. Get some rest." He sat back in his desk chair and his voice went soft. "You gave me a serious scare with that stunt, but—and I'll deny it if you relay this to anyone else—it was a fine maneuver." He bent his head over the book he had been reading when she entered. "Dismissed, cadet."

She tried not to grin—and failed.

5

KNIFE FIGHT IN A PHONE BOOTH

Getting Too Close to Sylph

Chase loved the Green. The crisp scent of trees filled each breath while the clip of her boots on the brick path sounded a strong beat.

Banks Island rubbed elbows with the Arctic shelf, but the center of the Star was a glass-ceilinged greenhouse designed to feel like a campus in temperate zones. The trees were too straight, however, lining up every few steps for the length of two football fields. Pippin called them "planted soldiers poised for battle." She wished he were wrong. But it seemed like the threat of war was everywhere, even in the landscaping patterns.

Chase's muscles were beyond tired, but she kicked into a jog and then a full-out run. Her dog tags *thwopped* against each other on her chest, the rubber silencers depriving them of their traditional metal clink.

Get some rest, Kale had said. People always suggested it like it was easy. Just lie down. Relax. Take a load off.

No way.

If Chase stopped, the world rushed in. She'd long since learned how to escape the hardest truths. Before the Star, she'd outrun her father's shadow and her mother's neglect—literally. She could sprint nearly two miles by the time she was twelve. That stamina helped her get on the Star's radar, and now her endurance and evasive tactics made her an excellent pilot. And, if she were being honest, kind of a crappy person.

What people never understood—not even Pippin—was that Chase wasn't blind to her reputation. She just needed her tunnel vision more. Needed direction. Pippin didn't really get it. He was more concerned with literature and music than any one element of the real world. Maybe it was a perk to having a genius level IQ, but he got by swimmingly in the military with his nose stuck in a fantasy and some Mahler tune pounding through his headphones. Chase sometimes wondered if he was constantly trying to distract himself from where he was.

The overhead sunlamps flickered like runway lights as she ran, her footsteps hammering the brick. No one was around. It was a little late, and she had classes early the next morning. Still, she couldn't head back to her room. Not yet.

Something sat at the edge of her mind and waved a red helmet, and even though she felt like the bull eyeing the cape, she couldn't resist. First, Pippin had gotten weird about what they'd seen. Then, the tower had denied her. Practically called her crazy. Add to that that Kale had been an odd mixture of reproachful and distracting. Something was up.

There had been one other flight team in the sky. Maybe Sylph had seen something.

Of course, that meant going after Sylph.

Chase was delighted by the sudden challenge. It would be easier to ask Sylph's RIO, Riot—after all, they had a *thing* going on—but confronting Sylph was always like hitting the throttle hard. Yes, please.

The recreation room buzzed, filled with the academy's after-hours mayhem. It was as dim as a bar and smelled just as grimy. Cadets mingled around pool tables, gaming machines, and flight simulators. Arguments cracked in every direction, but tonight's main attraction was in the back corner where two pilots sparred with thick foam gloves on the roped-off gym mat.

Chase pushed forward, fielding enthusiastic greetings from freshmen and seniors, flyboys and ground crew alike. The rec room really was the great leveler at the Star. Everyone, every specialty and class, mingled here. Chase had heard that before Kale was in charge, only a year before she had started, the room was reserved for flyboys. It was a smart move on the brigadier general's part; Chase wouldn't know a single cadet outside of her circle if she didn't frequent the rec room as often as she did.

"Nyx!" someone yelled, followed by a volley of several more cadets chanting her call sign. She waved and pounded some fists without taking in faces. Her attention was glued to the central fight.

The boxers were really going at it. The taller of the two was a girl who Chase knew all too well. Leah Grenadine.

Better known by her call sign, Sylph.

Sylph's thick blond braid whipped like a stinging tail with each punch she threw. Her toned arms were scaled with sweat, but she showed no sign of tiring, which sucked because she was simply destroying the other fighter. He was also all too familiar.

Asian American. Adorable. Tanner Won.

Chase found herself swearing on a loop. *Not again.*

One of Tanner's eyes was swollen, and his shoulders folded in to protect his chest. Sylph slammed him over and over until he fell to his knees, coughing for breath. She adjusted her gloves like she had a few more rounds left in her, and Chase ducked under the rope and stood between them.

"If it isn't Nyx." Sylph wiped her forehead with her arm. "You here to fight?"

The crowd went ballistic. Chase could already hear the chatter at breakfast tomorrow: *The Streaker pilots beat the snot out of each other. They're cracking under the pressure!*

"No more fighting." Chase nudged Tanner with her knee. "Your work is done here."

"It's *done* when he stops running his mouth about my RIO," Sylph said.

Chase felt like she'd stepped in a bucket of ice water. Of course. This was about Riot. And Chase.

Chase and Riot.

"*Tanner,*" she said like a curse.

"So you know my name again. Convenient." Tanner glared past

her, aiming his murder eyes at the ceiling. Blood trickled from a cut on his eyebrow. He'd been so sweet when they were doing… whatever they had been doing…but since then, Tanner's attitude had woken like a pissed-off dragon.

He spat. "I don't need your pity assistance, Nyx. If you really want to help me, tell everyone you're screwing Sylph's RIO." *Oh hell.* "So she can stop calling me a liar."

Chase heard Tanner's voice, but she leaped over his words like a broken step. It was harder than usual. She waved over a couple of freshman cadets, some of her ground crew fan club. They dragged Tanner beneath the rope. Chase turned back to Sylph. "I mean it. This is done. You have a problem with him again, you take it up with me."

"Gladly," Sylph said. Man, the girl could grin daggers, but the look was only a stunning preamble to the left hook she aimed at Chase's face.

Sunburst of pain, and the crowd sung a cheer.

Chase fell to one knee. Her lower lip pulsed, but she forced a smile. Somehow her adrenaline found a hidden reserve and zapped it through her veins. "Sylph, how are we ever going to fall in love if you keep hitting me?"

Sylph's glare sharpened. "You better strap in, Nyx. We have business."

Chase hopped up. "Look, there are bigger things going on than Riot and me."

"You know that's not what I mean. I'm talking about that ridiculous stunt you pulled today. *How could you?*" Sylph's anger made her seem more human than her chilled-marrow demeanor usually allowed. Chase shrugged and her shoulders felt like concrete.

Sylph stood back and called out to quiet the room. "Nyx here decided to do a suicidal maneuver over land today. Where people live. She could have crashed into someone's house. Killed their kids."

Chase wasn't that surprised by Sylph's deliberate cruelty. She was always this hard. A competitor. Merciless. It made Sylph a precise pilot and the furthest thing from a friend that Chase could imagine, although Kale seemed to think they were buds.

She could see where he misread the situation. Sylph and Nyx had been on each other's tails since the brigadier general announced the Streaker project freshman year. They'd battled in tandem through rigorous competition in order to gain top cadet rank and win the chance to pilot *Dragon* and *Pegasus*. Now every hop, every class… wherever Chase was, Sylph wasn't far behind. And vice versa. But the bottom line was that it had nothing to do with Sylph. Chase didn't have auxiliary friends. She had Pippin, and he was enough.

"If the move was so suicidal, how come she's still alive?" Tanner yelled over the ugly quiet. He stood against a pool table with an ice pack over one side of his face. Chase couldn't decide if it mattered that Tanner must hate Sylph more than he hated her.

Chase touched her bottom lip, still aching from Sylph's rather impressive left hook. She stepped closer to Sylph's model-class beauty. The hum of eyeing her down felt like Chase was back in the air. Engines burning and wind locked around her wings.

She gripped Sylph's gloves in case the blonde was thinking about throwing another punch. "Forget the stunt and listen to me. Did you see anything today…anything up there?"

Sylph's velvet brown eyes narrowed. "You're really a piece of work, you know that? To fake out the whole base. To make everyone think you were crashing."

Chase gave up. "Where's Riot? Maybe he'll listen."

"I *hope* he's getting checked for STDs." Sylph's look was full-out exasperation. "You really are hooking up with him. Couldn't leave my RIO alone, could you?"

Chase didn't have to answer.

"Nyx!" Riot bounded through the rec room. He leaped over the rope and wrapped Chase in a crush of a hug. "I went to your room to catch you. Pippin said you were in Kale's office." His face pressed to hers in a way that made her want to pull away, but she gave him a quick squeeze instead. "We thought you guys were going to die," he said. "Didn't we, Sylph?"

Chase let go. "Not even close," she lied.

Riot was the tallest in their class but on the thin side for flight crew. He had an annoying habit of putting his chin on the top of her head, and yet he was quirky cute with kissable, full lips. "We tried to fly back out to you, but—"

Sylph elbowed him out of the way. "Keep it in your pants, Riot." She used her teeth to peel off the Velcro that fastened the boxing gloves over her wrists. "Let's go."

"I need him for a few minutes," Chase said.

Riot glanced between them with a small smile. "Now, ladies, not another knife fight."

"Remember who won last time," Sylph said. Chase flashed to a few days ago—their Streakers in an elbow-rubbing dogfight. Chase had been in the lead until Sylph wore her down into making a stupid turn and claimed missile lock on *Dragon*. That flight had been thrilling, but compared to her latest hop with *Phoenix*, it was nothing.

"Yeah. Right." Chase searched for the fastest way to wrap this up, wanting to shake Riot for answers and maybe a little something extra. She got an arm around his waist, and he stared down with make-out eyes. Sometimes the boy was too easy. Okay, he was always too easy.

Even Sylph's scornful expression had a polished air. "Wash him up before you send him back."

The crowd of cadets was still waiting, watching.

Chase leaned forward and planted a smack of a kiss on Sylph's mouth.

"Eh!" The blonde wiped her face with the back of her hand and ducked under the ropes, cursing all the while. The crowd howled, and Riot raised Chase's fist and proclaimed her the winner.

Beyond the faces, Chase caught sight of Tanner's back as he trudged out of the room. This time her heart lurched like she'd missed a step and nearly fallen down a flight of stairs.

ⓘ④ⓘ

The boys' locker room was deserted. Chase followed Riot to the back by the sinks and showers. She'd been here before. With Riot. With other guys. It didn't feel too good to remember, so she didn't.

"That look on Sylph's face when you kissed her was..." Riot sighed. "Kick-ass."

"Great." Chase dismissed that one fast. "Today in the air...what happened on your end?"

Riot ripped off a paper towel, wet it, and held it to her bottom lip. The cool water felt good against the slight swelling. "We got the speed records at one hundred thousand feet and headed back. Boring as ever."

Chase's whole body frowned. "Have you heard anything about a secret bird?"

"Nope. Don't know anything about any Streaker jets," he mocked and tickled her neck with a kiss. She slid out of his hold and wondered, not for the first time, exactly what she was doing with him. Was this about angering Sylph? No. Maybe.

"We saw something up there today."

"A drone?" Riot's face turned too serious too fast.

"It was a jet. A manned jet."

"There are lots of those." He wrapped his arms around her hips. Chase thought about asking if Sylph had ever said anything about a third Streaker, but before she could, Riot yanked her into the shower and pinned her under the nozzle. Her thoughts took off like a flock of dark birds.

Oh yes. *That's* what she was doing with him.

"Kiss me?" His face was close. She stared at his lips but pressed her own together, shaking her head while trying not to smile. If she grinned, he'd kiss her, and although it was fun to tongue wrestle with Riot, the pregame was always better than the match.

He gripped the showerhead. "Kiss me or you're getting doused."

"You wouldn't," she dared.

He spun the handle. Icy water covered them. She screamed and he roared, but then the water began to flow warmer and everything started to heat up. He kissed her, and Chase's mind hummed like she was revving *Dragon*'s engines. It had little to do with Riot though. She liked him, but what she liked best was the distraction. When she was tangled up with him, there were no trials to fret about. No demarcation line or Second Cold War.

The water seeped through her clothes, bringing a full body rush, and yet the image of *Phoenix* flew through her mind. Where did it come from? Why did it appear? Why didn't Kale want her to know about it?

"We saw another Streaker," she said into his hair.

Riot was too busy kissing her neck. "Never realized how much I liked you until I thought you were going to die. I think I love you."

"That's crazy." She skipped over his declaration as though it were a mud puddle. "Why did you think I was going to die?"

Riot frowned. "Why is it crazy for me to love you?"

"Because you don't know me."

"I know you like this." He pressed his hands on her hips and kissed her neck as though that was all the proof he needed.

"What's my favorite color, Riot?"

"Huh?"

"Exactly." Chase grabbed his hair, hauling his face from its desperate mission toward her cleavage. "Tell me why you thought we were dying."

"They screamed over the emergency radio that you were crashing, but we didn't have enough fuel to get back out to you. Sylph panicked."

"Wait. Sylph was *worried* about us?"

"Jet Fighter Barbie has a heart after all." He tried to kiss her again, but she held back.

"So…you were called to save me? The tower broke radio silence? What did they say?"

"Kale was yelling over and over, '*Get to* Dragon*! Dragon is going down!*' They wanted us to get to you, although I'm not sure what we could have done except guard the crash site. Maybe call in your parachute if you had time to punch out."

Chase's mind turned over slowly. "They called you by name? I mean, they called *Pegasus*? Did they say, '*Pegasus, get to Dragon?*'"

Riot blew out a frustrated breath. "Who else would they be talking to?" He pulled her close and kissed the top of her head, which made her want to knock him away and fix her hair. Only she didn't.

The pieces were lining up.

Dragon *is going down!*

That's why the third Streaker had appeared. *Phoenix* wasn't an enemy. It had been tuned into the same emergency frequency.

That pilot had answered the call to rescue them.

6

NO JOY

Loss of Radio or Visual Contact

Pippin was in their small room, looking bone-tired and sprawled across the lower bunk. He pulled off huge headphones when Chase came in, and classical music thumped through them. "What happened with Kale?"

"He wouldn't say anything, but by my powers of deduction, I figured out that whoever *Phoenix* is, he's a friendly. The tower called out to him. They thought we were crashing."

"How could they make that mistake?" Pippin snarked.

Weariness rolled over Chase. Flying was one thing, but handling people's emotions—even Pippin's—took more out of her than she liked to admit. This was delicate. Pippin was being distant and tight-lipped about something important. She knew she should proceed with caution, but when he tried to disappear beneath his headphones, she sat on him instead.

"You've been weird since we saw the third Streaker."

"You're all wet!" He pushed her off.

"Incident in the showers."

Pippin lifted his eyebrow, throwing a secret sort of guilt at her. He was the only one who could do that, and she didn't like him for it. "Riot? Or are we on to someone new these days?"

"It was Riot, but thanks for that." She unlaced her boots so she wouldn't have to look at Pippin. The adrenaline drive that had kept her moving from Kale's office to the rec room to the boys' locker room was draining fast. Stillness crept in. "I caught Sylph trying to hollow out Tanner's face in the ring. He's talking trash about Riot and me."

"Tanner's going to wash out if he doesn't get under control," Pippin said. "Is that what you're worried about?"

Chase nodded. Could she have hurt Tanner so much that he'd drop out of the academy? She scrubbed her face. "Feels like watching him crash and burn."

"It is, in a way." Pippin's eyes were on her, hard and bleak. "You shouldn't have played with him. He had real feelings for you."

"I *wasn't* playing, but I do feel like I'm stuck on a Ferris wheel. Same problems over and over." Guilt dumped on her like an avalanche. "Riot said he loves me. Ugh."

"And you told him he doesn't know you?"

"How do you…"

"That's what you always tell them. Say, I got an idea. Why don't you *let* him know you?"

"I don't trust him." She waited for Pippin's snappy answer, but it didn't come. "Maybe I just have to. To escape the pressure of the trials and whatnot. Kale understands."

"I assure you Kale does not understand your romantic conquests." Pippin turned a page in his notebook. "And your 'have to' moments are getting worse." Maybe he meant Tanner or Riot, but it felt like he was saying more.

"Pip, today…you didn't think we were going to *die*, did you?" Riot had sounded stupid when he said it, but now Chase saw her stunt from Pippin's perspective. The ground so close. The fall seemingly irreversible…

He plopped the headphones over his ears instead of answering. The marching base of "Ode to Joy" leaked through, and she flashed to his frantic humming as they careened toward the earth. She'd frightened him. That's why he was being so weird.

"Sorry," she forced, but it didn't help. Maybe the word was broken.

"I *am* sorry," she tried again. Pippin jotted in his notebook like he couldn't hear her. She tried to peek. "You know there are already words to 'Ode to Joy.' German words."

"They're lyrics, not words. And I hold to the observation that this song is not about joy."

"What's it about then?"

"Apology accepted, Chase." He folded the notebook across his chest. "You're not interested in my music. You're pretending because you feel bad." He waved his hand like a wizard. "I release you of your guilt."

His gesture might have worked if he didn't immediately cross the room to sit at his desk. She settled back on his pillow, glancing over his family pictures stuck between the bars of the bunk above.

Dozens of snapshots of his three younger brothers, his padded-hipped mother. Even one of his father, a man who he defined as "straight as a flagpole."

Chase's thoughts flew by her own pre-academy memories. Loneliness shifted in like a cloud. It'd been years since she'd seen Janice, but Chase still smelled smoky hair and heard the tap of glossy nails when she thought about her mother. The woman was a waitress, an addict, an all-around failure of a human. The day Kale showed up at their door with an invitation to the Star was the best moment of Chase's life. Well, second best. The first time she hit the sky in *Dragon* was never going to be surpassed.

When Chase arrived at the Star, she realized how strange Kale's in-person summons had been. The brigadier general hadn't shown up on everyone's doorstep.

Just hers.

When she asked him about it, he said he knew her father, and she avoided the rest of the subject as though it were radioactive. But not before Kale added, "It's good you have your mother's last name. It'll be best if the other cadets never find out who your father is." Chase believed Kale. The truth of her parentage was a secret so well guarded that even Pippin had been warned off of ever broaching the subject.

She found herself tracing the stitched letters of her last name above her chest pocket. *HARCOURT*. The name still felt strange. Slightly alien. She'd only had it for a couple of years.

Chase sat up, desperate for other thoughts. *Phoenix* appeared like a brilliant flare shot into a dark sky. Flying with him—why did she keep calling him *him*?—felt like a tease. A flirt. She remembered how they'd popped Mach 3 in tandem, their jets tearing high unlike any flight she'd shared with Sylph as her wingman.

"Who is he?" Chase muttered. She imagined that red helmet, stripping it off in her thoughts with a flourish. She swapped skin tones and features onto an unknowable face, each one bearing a smirk. He was cocky. She got that much from how he skirted close when he flew. How he jet washed her like it was nothing more than a playful bite to the shoulder.

"Pip, why a secret third Streaker? Why can't I know about him?"

"Drop it, Chase. Remember what I said about Crowley? They'll take your wings if you keep this up. Even if you're Kale's favorite." He twirled his headphone cord. "There isn't anything worse than a pilot without wings, but I'm pretty sure you would cease to be a person altogether."

Chase ignored him. "That pilot has to be young, right?"

Pippin rubbed his eyes. "No. He just has to be in top shape. It's possible he's in his twenties, like some Olympic athletes. The Streakers need strong bodies. Massive endurance." He paused. "Wait, why are we calling the pilot *him*?"

"I keep asking myself the same question. Five bucks says he's a guy."

Pippin groaned. "Chase, you don't have the hots for the *Phoenix* pilot. Say you don't. He could be a robotic lizard beneath that helmet."

"So you admit he exists!"

They laughed together, but it phased into silence a little too fast.

"You have to admit it was pretty hot how fast we flew, wing under wing…"

Pippin pointed his pencil at a folded note on her bunk. "You got another summons from Ritz."

"Damn Crackers." Chase balled it up without reading it.

Pippin took out his digital atlas and the screen lit up. "You can't keep ignoring the psychiatrist. You're way overdue for an eval. Do me a huge favor. *Don't* bring up the phantom Streaker."

"Ritz'll have to catch me first."

"You delight in evading that woman far too much."

"Pleasure in the small things." Chase tossed the ball of paper across Pippin's desk. It bounced through a hologram of mountains, and he swept it into the trash can. His headphones were over his ears again.

"Back into the secret cave of Pippinland."

"Dwarf doors are invisible when closed." He was really gone now. When the Tolkien dialogue came out, her genius RIO had retreated to inaccessible depths. Chase peeled off the top of her damp flight suit and let it hang from her hips. Ordinarily, she changed in their small bathroom out of courtesy, but she wasn't feeling polite. She unhooked her bra and slingshot it at him. He caught it and tossed it over his head. No blush. No break in concentration.

"No joy," she said and sat on the edge of the bunk.

"I love you, Chase, really I do, but I have a geography test tomorrow."

"You know more than Professor Davis. Besides"—she scraped up a pile of clothes beneath the bed and her father's words from somewhere much darker—"love is pointless."

Pippin threw something at her over his head, so he didn't see when she dropped all her clothes to catch it.

Chase squeezed the little plastic pterodactyl and remembered her first moments at the Star. She had shivered in the hangar, surrounded by the other incoming freshmen who were waiting while the military police checked their possessions for contraband. The new cadets—fresh out of eighth grade—reviewed one another awkwardly, ready to judge, sort, and label. But the lanky boy beside Chase eyed the inspection as though one of the bags was about to explode.

"Did you pack your bomb by mistake?" she asked in a whisper.

"I'm more concerned about the pterodactyl." The kid was a natural deadpanner.

"A dinosaur?"

"Pterosaur. Dinosaurs did not have wings." He cursed. "My mom packed it to be cute. Any chance people will forget?"

"Not before graduation."

An MP with curly-haired forearms extricated the plastic toy and held it up like it might contain drugs. "Whose is this?"

The lanky kid's blush went maroon at the hairline.

"Mine," Chase said. She took it from the MP. "Got a problem with pterosaurs?"

"Watch your attitude, cadet," the MP snapped. The group

laughed at Chase. She took the fun out of their teasing by playing it up, perching the toy on her shoulder like a pet. She was sure this behavior would make her fellow cadets steer clear; she worked best on her own anyway.

Not even an hour later, the pterodactyl incident saved her from the disastrous fate of an assigned roommate. A girl with a mighty blond braid took one look at Chase and demanded to trade rooms.

A few minutes later, the lanky boy dropped his bag on the lower bunk. "Did you see those prototype jets in the hangar? I bet those engines could pop Mach 4 with a strong pilot. Maybe more."

"I want to fly them."

"Me too. Did you test into pilot range?"

"I did. You?"

"I'm leaning toward navigation, but I got a pass for any position I want." He tapped his head, and it was a wonder the move didn't come across as bragging. Maybe it was because it seemed a little forlorn. "The military wants my critical thinking skills. Bar none."

"That's pretty cool."

He shrugged. "My call sign will be Pippin."

"That's…different. Why did you pick it?" she asked.

"Pippin was shanghaied into the Fellowship."

"I seriously don't understand half of that."

Chase had to admit that three years later, she still didn't understand Pippin as well as she wanted.

Despite her exhaustion, Chase spent the night after her encounter with *Phoenix* trudging in and out of sleep. Blasted by explosions, the black sky of her dreams lit up with gunfire.

In the morning, she struggled free from her reoccurring nightmare. It felt like belly crawling beneath barbed wire, which was in fact what she'd done all those years ago. The back of her right arm stung, and she kneaded the scar tissue with her fingers. Chase had long since given up hope that it would someday cease to feel like a wound.

She hopped down from her bunk and stretched. On her way to class, she took the hallway corner too fast and smacked into Dr. Ritz, the academy's pocket-sized psychiatrist.

The woman grabbed Chase by both arms to steady herself. "Chase Harcourt. Just the person I was hoping to run into. Although, not literally. You could have knocked me down."

"I'll try harder next time."

Dr. Ritz narrowed her eyes. "Do you mean you'll try harder to knock me down next time or harder *not to*, Chase Harcourt?"

Chase maneuvered around the psychiatrist. The woman's braided bun on top of her head was nearly as large as her head itself. "Why do you always use my whole name? It isn't natural. You don't see me yelling out, 'Hey, Eugenia Ritz Crackers' every five seconds."

"I've asked you repeatedly not to call me 'Crackers.'"

"Force of habit." Chase popped her knuckles while Ritz adjusted her glasses.

A good, old-fashioned standoff.

Freshman year, Chase had been duped into thinking that Ritz cared. She'd opened up about Janice and her solitary childhood—until the psychiatrist started to report that Chase was "emotionally unstable." There were talks about putting Nyx on the Down List, and Chase vowed not to give the woman another ounce of truth. Which pretty much meant she'd been dodging Crackers ever since.

"Well, *Chase*..." Ritz looked pained in having to use half her name. "You're ignoring my summons, so I'll have to tell you right here. I've been asked to speak to you by Brigadier General Kale. He believes you are seeing imaginary jets in the sky."

Chase, who had been trying to sneak away, stopped. It was a full-bodied brake that she felt in her chest like her harness had been pulled too tight. "Kale did not say that."

He wouldn't. She had flown side by side with *Phoenix*. Kale could command her not to talk about what she saw, but he could not expect her to pretend it didn't exist.

To say that she had *imagined* it...

Chase was frozen from her eyes to her knees, and she was sure the shock showed on her face. She trusted Kale. He trusted her. Would he really sell her out like that? Was Chase about to get kicked off the Streaker project? The blood rushed to her face in a way that brought way too much breathing and a sudden headache.

Before Ritz could pipe back in, the bell rang and the hallway swarmed with cadets. "If the pressures of this arrangement are getting to you, Chase Harcourt," Ritz yelled over the crowd, "there are options that—"

"Option this." Chase turned her back. She blended into the uniformed crowd, a sudden firestorm in her veins. There *was* a jet up there. A friendly that was as fast as *Dragon*. Maybe faster. "And when I catch it," she muttered to herself, "I'll drop it off in Crackers's office."

7

MAYDAY

Dear God, Help Me

Chase sat in *Dragon's* cockpit. She shoved her leather gloves between each finger and spun with thoughts. It should have gotten better. It all should have been cleared up by now, but it wasn't. She'd skipped her classes and gone after Kale, and what had he done?

Walked off into a cadet-restricted section of the base, calling out "Things happen the way they need to happen."

Well, Chase couldn't let things happen in a way that would drag her down. Pippin had brought up Crowley's story as a warning to keep her mouth shut. Crowley had "imagined" spotting red drones over Florida, so they took his wings. He washed out. But Chase had made out with that boy a few times—enough encounters to know he wasn't creative enough to fabricate such a sighting. He'd seen something, and the Air Force had sold him out. That would not happen to her. She wouldn't say a word—she would *show* them. Somehow.

Pippin dropped into his seat behind Chase and fastened in. "Where've you been?"

"Thinking." Chase closed *Dragon's* canopy.

"Sounds ominous."

Pegasus left the hangar slowly, and *Dragon* was stuck behind her, rolling toward the runway a foot at a time.

Chase muttered a few choice curses. "God, Sylph makes flying look like a job."

"Hey there, Bad Mood," Pippin said with slight care. "Want to vent a little before you launch us into the death grip of the sky?"

The shortwave radio popped, and Chase opened the channel. "Get in the air, Sylph!"

Sylph's voice jabbed through. "Better stay with me, Nyx. I hear you've been *seeing things*."

Chase snapped. "Yeah, well, how are we ever going to get up there if you take five years to get to the runway?" She punched the radio link off. "How does she know?"

"Small community. Big gossip. And to think the boys' locker room isn't such a discreet place…" Pippin sighed. "We could park *Dragon* in Riot's mouth if he held it still long enough."

"It's not just Sylph," Chase admitted, with what felt like gravity swelling all around her. "Kale told Crackers that I imagined sighting a Streaker. Crackers hinted that I'm cracking up."

"Christ on a bike, Chase." He swore. A heavy, four-letter, rhymes with duck kind of swear. "I thought Kale was smarter than that."

"Smarter than what?"

He ignored her. "I told you to let it go. Now it's probably already on your record. They could give *Dragon* to one of the runner-up pilots for the trials."

Was that true? Did Chase already ruin her chances to keep her spot with *Dragon*? If Sylph knew, the whole Star knew—maybe it *was* too late. Her face burned as her thoughts zoomed to the red helmet. *Phoenix* was the answer. She had to find a way to fly with him again. Tail him back to his base. Unmask him.

Prove he was real. That she belonged at the Star. She did… didn't she?

She hadn't realized she'd stopped *Dragon*. Ground crew looked up from where they held the huge hangar doors open, no doubt wondering what had made her stall out in the middle of the entryway.

"Nyx." Pippin strapped his mask on. His voice came loud and clear through her helmet. "Push past it for now. We have to fly. You all in?" He said it like he was worried that she was cracking up too.

"I'm going after *Phoenix*."

Pippin's voice was urgent. Desperate. "No, Chase. Revealing the third Streaker to the Star will open up intel about it to the world. Kale doesn't want that. They're not ready. We'll know more after the trials."

"*Wait*." A red-hot spark lit in her chest. "You know about this, don't you? You knew about the third Streaker even before we saw him. Didn't you?"

"I put some pieces together. Parts logs always showed three sets. It seemed off, so I asked Kale about it last year."

"*Last year?* And you never said anything?"

"He ordered me not to say anything. Besides, he didn't give me any real answers." Pippin's tone hung with panic. He knew Chase too well not to know that this wasn't going well. He knew her too well to say what he said next. "Let it go. This is much bigger than the Nyx Show."

She punched the throttle as they rolled onto the runway. *Dragon* sped around *Pegasus*, cutting off Sylph. This was Chase's life. Her wings. Wasn't that what Kale was always telling her? Fly from the gut. Use your fear. Trust your instincts. Well, all three of those things were telling her to risk it all. Prove *herself*.

Dragon blasted down the runway only to spin out and turn back around. She directed them at *Pegasus*. She tasted the same kind of blind resolve that had sent her into the landmine obstacle course when she was twelve, trying to prove to her father she was as tough as his recruits. She'd failed that time, emerging muddied, heartbroken, and slick with her own blood. But she wouldn't fail today.

"Are we playing chicken with Sylph? Because that's not really a contest." Pippin was trying to joke. To reach her.

No joy.

Sylph was already trying to get out of the way, but Chase turned toward her and kicked up the speed.

"You should have told me, Pippin," she said through her teeth. "I thought we trusted each other."

"Chase…"

"And Kale should know that if he's going to make me look crazy, I'm going to act crazy." Chase accelerated so fast that Sylph had to turn awkwardly to avoid collision. *Pegasus* slid out on the ice and rammed a ground crew supply shack.

Chase shot *Dragon* into the air.

"You took out Sylph!" Pippin yelled.

"Oops," she said flatly. Chase headed past Canada, toward America, her plan in action and her thoughts blind to everything else. Kale tried to reach her on the emergency feed, and Pippin pleaded, but she ignored all of it and flew—nothing but the ever-blue air and the promise of seeing *Phoenix* lighting up her veins.

۞ ④ ۞

"I'm sorry," Pippin said for maybe the fiftieth time. "Whatever you're about to do to get back at me, I'm sorry!"

Chase ignored him. Her whole body was concentrating on flying. They were approaching the Grand Canyon at Mach 2, and the area was appropriately deserted for what she wanted to do. "Get ready to call Mayday, Pip."

"What?!"

"We're going to crash. Or look like we're crashing. Then they'll send help, just like last time, and because Sylph is grounded..."

"They'll send *Phoenix*," Pippin finished for her. "God almighty, Nyx."

"Exactly."

Pippin started to swear as *Dragon* dropped into the earth's great rift. The rust and toast-colored striations zipped past like the jet was entering warp speed.

"Let's make it look good, shall we?" Chase spun *Dragon* toward the sun before flipping them to face the ground. A strange thrill overtook the fall, and it matched the buzzing out-of-control spin of her mind.

Pippin hit the emergency radio with very real fear. "Mayday, Mayday, Mayday!"

A few hundred feet before they crashed, Chase pulled on the stick. She dragged in the speed, dropping the landing gear at the last second. They came to a smashing stop, the struts bouncing off the hard-sand bottom. *Dragon's* tires let out with a pop and a scream.

Wheezing air filled the sudden silence.

"All right back there?"

Pippin groaned. "I think I just lost forty IQ points."

"You have enough to spare." A bit of the insane red was leaving her vision. She might really be on the Down List after this stunt, but she didn't regret it. "I had to," she said before Pippin could ask.

"Yeah, well." He sounded more resigned than angry. "You always do."

"You're not mad?"

"Team Nyx," he said, and she felt his honesty like an embrace. "Maybe you'll finally get me sent home this time."

"Knock it off." Nothing got under her skin faster than when Pippin joked about wanting to leave the Star. "You're stuck with me whether you like it or not."

"If you tell me you're in love with me, I'll have to point out that you don't know me." Pippin's line had all the appearance of a joke without the tone. Chase made a note to mull that one over later. For now, she scanned the sky for their rescuer.

She didn't have to wait long.

8

BOARDS OUT

Speed Brakes Extended

A jet screeched overhead.

Phoenix looped into the canyon, the right wing a little higher than the left. The pilot set down like Chase often did, hard and tight and *not* like Sylph. There was nothing careful or overly rehearsed in his maneuvers, almost like he was making it up as he went.

She burned to know what else they had in common, and she had to hold herself back from flipping the canopy open and jumping out to greet him. Instead, she played dead and ordered Pippin to do the same.

Phoenix taxied over. The third Streaker *was* identical to the other two, except it didn't bear any standard markings. No Air Force symbol. Not even the Navy's—which she had prayed it wouldn't. Nothing worse than dealing with the TOPGUN know-it-alls. But then, where did the Streaker come from? Why all the mystery and hush-hush?

The bird's nose turned just to the right of *Dragon*'s, sidling them cockpit to cockpit.

And there he was: Mr. Red Helmet.

Only a few feet away.

He could have been anyone behind his mask and visor. A robotic lizard, Pippin had suggested, but Chase didn't see a tail. What she saw was a large, gloved hand pressed to his canopy as he peered close. She saw shoulders like Kale's and arms that made Riot's look like pencils.

"I owe you five bucks," Pippin said. "Looks like a boy to me. The RIO too."

"I want to meet them," Chase said.

"And how do you propose—"

"Easy. Let's follow them home." Chase unsnapped her mask and showed *Phoenix*'s team a wide smile. "*Got you*," she mouthed.

The pilot's head panic-swung left and right before he launched *Phoenix* into the air. Chase shot after them, mangling the takeoff on her popped tires.

"Bad idea, Chase! Way worse than your first one." If Pippin had given up on her call sign, he really was desperate, but she was so far beyond coming down. She smelled a challenge, and she wasn't wrong. *Phoenix* should have been long gone by the time *Dragon* hit the sky, but she found him right away.

He was waiting for her.

Dragon slid under *Phoenix* as they left the canyon behind. Flying low, *way* too low, they clipped across the barren desert—right before the other pilot punched the throttle with such ferocity that she screamed when she mimicked his move. She left her old speed record way behind while they raced wildly. Chase's body was all pressure and heat, but her mind danced, delighted.

Phoenix wasn't trying to escape. She felt like he was playing, flirting, and she found herself teasing him right back. Before the spotted green edge of the Gulf of Mexico, he stole the lead, and she executed a double cross so close that Pippin whooped with joy or terror—or more likely both.

When the bingo fuel alarm went off, Chase overrode it and kept after *Phoenix*. He was heading northeast, the same direction he had escaped during their last flight.

"Nyx, no gas for this," Pippin said.

"Yeah, but double or nothing says he knows where there's a gas station close by." She could feel *Dragon*'s limits. They were going much slower now but still too fast, still burning through their limited fuel. And yet she couldn't disengage. Where was he going? What did he look like? And why did she so desperately need to see him?

The right engine went out.

Dragon's wings shook as *Phoenix* crossed the Hudson Bay and set down on a hiccup of an island.

"Wait." Pippin's voice trembled. "This is bad, Nyx! Turn around! Turn around while you still have altitude!"

"I can't." Her voice was cool, but her mind was blazing. "I'm going to land behind him. He's a friendly, remember?"

Pippin didn't buy her forced calm. "This is bad, bad, bad. That's not U.S. soil. Remember the Declaration of No Assistance?"

She did. Shit.

Too late.

The left engine flickered and died. She managed a fast coast of a landing, skidding sideways on popped tires while metal squealed against the pavement.

Boards out.

☉④☉

Dragon shook when it finally stopped, and Chase noticed the runway for the first time: military green.

"Pippin." She prickled with nerves. "This apron is camouflaged. Did we just land on some secret Ri Xiong Di base?"

"We're in Canada."

"Canada?" She forced a laugh. "Oh man, you really freaked me out for a sec."

"We shouldn't be here." No snark. No sarcasm.

"Yes, I know that, but we'll be gone in five. What're the odds that Ri Xiong Di is monitoring this tiny speck of an island at this exact second?"

"The odds are never in America's favor, Nyx. That's what this cold war has been all about."

She switched the canopy latch and unstrapped her harness. *Phoenix* was so close, and about a mile away, a small hangar door opened and people poured out. Many people. "Let's go make friends before that crowd sends us packing."

"Chase! Listen to me!" Pippin yelled.

Chase jumped from *Dragon*, the deep fall sending a jolt through her knees. She hadn't set down outside of the Arctic in so long that the mild lake breeze took her by surprise. "It's too late," she called up to her RIO. "We're all in now."

She popped her helmet off and messed the sweat through her fauxhawk into a more pleasing look. "Will it make a difference if we go say hi?"

"I don't know," he called out.

"Don't you want to meet them?" She fought the edge of a smile as Pippin de-helmeted, swore, and scrambled down from *Dragon*.

"You're crazy, Nyx."

"Yeah, but I'm not cracking up." They jogged to *Phoenix* together. "Come down!" she yelled at the two figures in the cockpit.

Phoenix's canopy lifted, and the pilot and RIO leaped out. Chase stepped back, bumping into Pippin. *Phoenix*'s team was a lot bigger than they appeared in the air. Both of them were over six feet tall with swimmer's shoulders.

"Think you owe *me* five bucks," Pippin muttered. "Those aren't boys. They're men."

The RIO took his helmet off first—and threw it. He was the sort of wide-broad guy that could pass for fifteen or twenty-five. Still, he was cute—if you didn't mind the caveman-worthy brow ridge.

Before Chase could put a greeting together, the RIO charged. He hit Pippin like a linebacker, tossing him to the pavement. Chase threw herself on the guy's back. She got her elbow around his neck and was about to choke him when the pilot lifted her off like she weighed nothing. He tossed her down and hauled his RIO away from Pippin.

"You've ruined everything!" the RIO shouted as his pilot dragged him to a safer distance. His voice cramped with a French accent.

"He didn't fly us into this!" Chase yelled back. "I did!"

"I don't hit girls." The RIO pointed at Pippin. "That little one I can take."

"How noble." Chase pulled Pippin to his feet. His face was cranberry and he gasped unevenly. "You all right?"

He slapped his chest and gave her a thumbs-up.

Chase set her eyes on the pilot. His face was all but hidden behind his visor, and his red helmet was adorned with a white maple leaf above a stenciled call sign: *ARROW*. So the third Streaker was from the Royal Canadian Air Force? Weird. But even weirder, the pilot was grinning at her.

"You. Arrow." She wanted this moment to be better, but she was running low on time. The crowd approaching from the hangar was much closer, and the way they hustled unnerved her. "Afraid to show yourself?"

Arrow ducked out of his helmet, rolling it under his arm in a slick move.

Whatever Chase had been imagining, he wasn't it. He was young, with a heated blush that lit up his cheekbones and underscored playful blue eyes. His black hair was long—a sweaty mess, half contained in a ponytail at the back of his neck.

He was also *laughing* at her.

"What's funny?"

"You. You're so serious." Arrow stepped closer, and his humor faded into a smirk. He *was* cocky; she had been right on that score. But Pippin was wrong to call them men just because they were big. Arrow didn't have the manly swagger she'd been expecting. He seemed lighthearted and easygoing, like a guy standing before a particularly awesome arcade game. Like someone who'd never been hungry or scared or left to bleed beneath a patchwork of barbed wire. Chase had been expecting her equal. What she'd found was another boy.

She had plenty of those already.

He held his hand out to shake, but she didn't take it.

Arrow registered his disappointment with a tilt of his head, reminding her of his slanted wings in flight.

"Why..." Chase felt the pressure to ask a real question before they were interrupted by what looked like half of the Royal Canadian Air Force. "Why do *you* have a Streaker?"

Arrow's eyes sharpened, the laughter fading fast. She'd hit a nerve. Good.

"We shouldn't be talking to them, Arrow," his RIO said from behind him.

"Agreed," Pippin added.

Arrow spoke without taking his eyes off Chase. "After what we did in the air, I think a little polite greeting is in order." He was still holding his hand out, still daring her to take it, and his words hinted at the feelings she'd had when flying with him. The tease and flirt. The tangle and stamina. The mach charge.

Chase held his gaze and shook his hand.

His leather gloves gripped hers, tugging all the way to her backbone as he hauled her a step closer. His eyes reminded her of the sky at high altitudes. No. It was more like that glint of blue in the bottom of a flame.

"Nice to meet you, Chase Harcourt." He said her name with authority, like he'd said it many times before.

Her shock came with a stomach plunge. "How do you know who I am?"

"You kidding me?" His smile returned. Brash and brilliant. "I've been dying to meet Nyx for years."

What?

They were pushed apart before she could stutter a response. The crowd of Royal Canadian airmen had reached the two Streakers, and Chase was all but wrestled back to her jet.

The sky dimmed as the ground crew rolled out a huge camouflage canopy to cover up *Dragon* while they immediately changed her tires and pumped her full of fuel from a truck. Chase marveled at the crowd's swiftness. By the time she looked back to Arrow, he was being escorted toward *Phoenix*.

He popped his helmet on and threw a smirk at her that made her want to flick him off.

So she did.

72

And he mock-saluted.

An officer with a white mustache got in her face, herding her toward ramp stairs that had been rolled up to *Dragon*'s cockpit. He spoke through the dense fug of coffee breath. "You are to fly back to the Star. Immediately."

"You can't give me orders," Chase said, a little dazed by the speed with which everything was changing. *Phoenix*'s canopy was down, and Arrow was rolling toward the hangar at a solid clip. Would she ever see him again? She told herself she didn't care.

The officer thrust a piece of paper into Chase's hand. "These orders aren't from me. They're from Brigadier General Kale."

She looked down at the note, and her whole body tensed.

Home now. You face expulsion.

9

TURBULENCE

Feel It; Don't Fight It

Chase couldn't sit down. She swept through Kale's office, touching the waxy-leafed plants and fingering the bowl of old bullets.

Expulsion. The word was a vicious crosswind, tossing her from question to question. Why did the Canadians have a Streaker? Why did Arrow know her name? And more importantly, would Kale make her leave?

She had nowhere to go. He knew that; he'd met Janice.

Chase knew she was in the wrong. She'd broken orders, engaged *Phoenix*, and set down outside of the Star. All things she could rightly get expelled for, but everyone was acting like the situation was worse. Like war had been declared. When *Dragon* slid into its spot in the hangar, Kale and a number of senior officers had been waiting. Kale took Pippin by the elbow in one direction while an MP escorted Chase to the brigadier general's office.

To wait forever, apparently.

She'd been there for over two hours with nothing to go on except her worst thoughts. The MP guarded the door the whole time, making sure she stayed put but otherwise refraining from giving her a single answer. She'd already nicknamed him Sergeant Pillar Face.

Chase tossed herself into her favorite leather chair and balled the small piece of paper with Kale's message on it. That note, in and of itself, was a huge question. What was Kale doing in contact with the Royal Canadian Air Force? What huge secret had she stumbled upon?

Pippin had brought up the Declaration of No Assistance, but that felt more uncomfortable than ominous. Ri Xiong Di had hundreds of declarations, but most of them were empty threats. This one was about countries aiding the U.S.—Chase paid attention long enough in history class to know that much—but could Ri Xiong Di really be pissed about her landing in Canada for ten minutes? That did not constitute "aid."

Chase remembered the story of a British cargo fleet that had tried to fly in medicine during an influenza outbreak years back. Those birds had been hacked and crashed kamikaze-style into the Atlantic by Ri Xiong Di. Now *that* was the Declaration of No Assistance. She shivered, her body near exhaustion from flying. Her face and neck were covered in dried sweat, and she itched all over. Something bigger was going on, and it had everything to do with *Phoenix* and that pilot.

Arrow. His call sign was too simple. Too straightforward. It was too good, that's what it was. He had been so smug about saying her name. How in the blazes did he know her?

"Chase Harcourt?"

Oh no. Chase had been waiting for Kale. Not Crackers.

Dr. Ritz walked in and sat behind Kale's desk. "Brigadier General David Kale asked me to check in on you."

"So I'm not the only person you go full title on," she muttered.

"What was that?" Ritz asked.

"I said, 'Great to see you!'"

Ritz touched the corner of her glasses. "I know you're under a lot of pressure. The trials in January are important."

"Dive right in, why don't you." When she didn't respond, Chase added, "No, really?"

"More than you seem to understand. What you did today was appalling. The Canadians might not have manpower equal to the Star, but JAFA is just as essential to eventual victory."

"Jaff what?"

"The Royal Canadian Junior Air Force Academy. JAFA."

Chase popped her knuckles. "Didn't know its name. So wait, if you know about it, tell me why they have a Streaker."

Ritz's tight expression proved she knew more than what she was saying, but the crafty woman switched directions. Had they been maneuvering in the air, Chase might have been impressed. "If those jets are as capable as their reputation suggests, the Second Cold War could be coming to an end. Depending on *you*."

Missile lock.

"Christ, Crackers." Heat scorched up Chase's neck. "Why would you…are you *trying* to make me crumble under the pressure? I'm aware of what's at stake."

"Are you?" Ritz asked. "Because I'm having trouble believing that the military's best option is putting our future in the hands of young cadets. In *your* hands."

"And Sylph," Chase said fast. Kale acted the same way, like even though she was one half of the Streaker project, she was the half that mattered. "Why don't you go give Sylph this little pep talk?"

"Because Leah Grenadine is a model student. She completes her homework on time and visits me regularly to discuss the trials. *She* doesn't use study sessions to break the tender hearts of other students."

Chase's blush went viral. "Didn't realize that you're also a love doctor, Crackers."

"I've been summoning you over the past few weeks to talk about Tanner Won. He's been in to see me following your romantic encounter."

"You should thank me. Tanner now knows he shouldn't let emotions sucker punch him. There's practically a war on." It was a bold lie to say that she'd helped Tanner. She'd hurt him. That's what she'd done, but Chase suppressed that knowledge under the idea he would come out of this stronger. "Whatever doesn't kill you, right?"

A clock ticked loud seconds. Ritz didn't respond. Chase was swept up into asking her real question. "Is Kale working on my expulsion?"

The psychiatrist frowned. "I think he's fighting to keep you. Does that surprise you?"

"Fighting with who?" Chase shouldn't have asked that question.

She shouldn't have let the words—followed by the very real possibility—enter her world. Kale answered to few people, all higher-up generals without direct authority over the Star. With one exception. The highest of them all who had a say in everything. Five stars to Kale's solitary one.

The General of the Air Force.

Chase tucked in her limbs, made herself tight and tiny against the idea that Kale was arguing with *him*. The very person whose existence reminded her that she did not belong at the Star.

Her father.

Ritz made a *tsk* sound. Apparently being a psychiatrist did not entitle her to an understanding of body language. Either that or the woman wanted to poke Chase when she was down. "What made you believe you could engage in such a reckless flight with so little regard for the consequences?"

"I proved I'm not crazy," Chase said. "I wasn't imagining that Streaker."

"And in the process you've endangered Canada. And America. You do see that."

"I didn't start this!" Chase couldn't stop herself from yelling. "If I had been told about that Canadian Streaker, none of this would have happened. I should have been trusted."

"You're supposed to trust your superior officers." Kale's voice came through the room like a gale. It blew Ritz to her feet and sent her out the door. He closed it behind her. "You risked your life, your RIO's life, and the lives of Streaker Team *Phoenix*. Not to mention what you did to *Pegasus*. You don't deserve to keep your wings beyond this conversation."

"General, I…" Chase couldn't breathe. "I had to prove I wasn't going crazy like Crowley."

"Cadet Crowley? What does he have to do with this?" Kale sat behind his desk before he caught up with the reference. "Oh, I see. You thought…" He cleared his throat. "Your RIO just spent an hour explaining your actions. Donnet insists it was our fault for daring you. He turned that brain on me and said I should have known better, since I claim to know you so well. He got six demerits for his cheek." Chase made a mental note to give Pippin's big brain a kiss the next time she saw it. Kale's voice slid low. "So. You feel swindled. Is that it?"

She answered with silence.

Kale's hair was wild, like he'd been tugging on it. "Deception and misdirection have always been tools in the military, Harcourt. That doesn't mean I'm making excuses. I detest it. I wish I had a way around it, but there are certain ways things must be done in the business of the nation's safety. Your RIO might have a point, but I had to report to General Tourn all the same. I'm waiting for his decision now."

Chase stood, but inside she was falling—straight through the tile. Through the earth's crust and into its liquid-burning core. "You can't leave it up to him. He'll throw me away."

Tears strode down her cheeks, but she didn't bother to wipe them.

Kale looked hard in the other direction. "You didn't leave me a choice."

The phone rang, and Kale answered using his sharpest tone. Chase trembled when she heard her father's voice over the line, aligning commands like a ripple of thunder. She touched the back of her right arm as memory-pain lit up her scar like lightning.

"Yes, General. Every satellite. We'll have warning if they launch an airstrike." Kale's scowl deepened with each new order. Chase knew full well what that felt like.

"Of course, but she'll want to speak with—" A clapping order cut Kale off. Chase sat down, shaking. Her father would ship her back to Michigan where Janice was scratching out a living. Tourn wouldn't care if she starved or had to fight off one of Janice's drunken boyfriends in the dead of the night.

He'd left her to that life once before.

"I'll give her the message." Kale hung up and sat back in his desk chair. He scrubbed his face with both hands until Chase thought she might detonate from the silence.

Finally, Kale sat tall. "To cut to it, you're not expelled. You retain your wings. General Tourn believes you are too vital to the Streaker project to lose in light of the upcoming trials. You are, however, on restricted duty for the rest of your life. Hear me?"

Relief slid around her like a lava flow, painfully measured. "What else did he say?" She held herself back from adding, *Did he tell you I shouldn't be here?*

"He said he believes it's time for action." Kale blew out a long breath. "It doesn't matter to him that we're not ready to face Ri Xiong Di's forces. He's ready for the cold war to *heat up*. That's actually what he said. The man's a warmonger." Kale's expression released. "That was out of line. Forgive me."

Chase nodded, ready to do anything for him. "He is, General. You don't need to tell me that."

"Of course you know what he's like." Kale's tone had gone warm—he was trying to make her feel better. Build her up. Chase knew this wasn't over. She might have only spent one summer with her father, but it was long enough to know the man was never finished until he'd punched her with his words.

"What was his message?"

Kale hesitated. "This is Tourn's message, not mine."

"Understood."

"He said, 'If she breaks orders again, I'll come there personally and take her wings in front of the whole academy.'"

Chase imagined it down to the crisp smell of the Green. Her father would stand over her, striking her with insults before steel-straight lines of her uniformed peers. Then everyone would know she was the daughter of *the* general—the only five-star general designated in the Air Force since the 1980s—Lance Harold Tourn.

Always those three names together. Like the assassin he was.

Chase squeezed her knuckles until they hurt, and her secret fear found voice. "General Kale, if the other cadets knew he's my father, they'd say he got me in here. That I didn't earn my wings. Wouldn't they? That's why you told me not to tell anyone during my first week."

"If they said that, Harcourt, I'd say you've proven them wrong.

You tested to the head of your class and then the head of the academy. You learned how to fly a Streaker when a dozen of your peers washed out. You did that. Tourn can't take that from you."

Kale was detached enough from his teenage years to believe that gem. Good for him. Chase knew the truth. The rest of the academy was filled with cadets who had spent years—and their families' savings—on the training and tests in order to be selected. With the exception of Pippin, whose IQ planted him in the military's line of sight like a neon flag.

Her classmates would burn her in effigy on the Green. And she wouldn't blame them.

Kale cleared his throat. "I shouldn't have to tell you to keep your discovery about *Phoenix* to yourself, but I will. Not a word to the other cadets, including Sylph." Chase nodded, and Kale added, "Don't forget. Restricted duty. You're dismissed."

She stood and held on to the back of the leather chair. "I have a question, General."

"I imagine you have many, and I bet I can't answer a single one of them," Kale said. Chase began to leave, but his voice stopped her at the door. "Ask your question, cadet."

"How did that pilot know me?" Thinking about Arrow made all her father feelings evaporate sharp and fast. "He knew my call sign. My name. He knows the way I fly like he's studied me."

Kale lifted an eyebrow, and she didn't need an answer.

She'd crashed into the truth all on her own.

10

HOOK SLAP

Catching on in a Big Way

After her morning classes, Chase headed to the weight room. Restricted duty meant she could train and run through her schedule—but no free time. No rec room. No fun.

So it was a good thing Kale didn't know how much she enjoyed the bench press. There was something about being pinned beneath the weight, fighting to control the plunge before sending the bar up with a grunt—a little like being locked under a dare.

Chief Master Sergeant Black waved her in and handed her a pair of weightlifting gloves before barking at a trio of freshmen who were manhandling the medicine balls. Chief Black ran trainings like boot camp, but Chase kind of liked him for it. His clipped way of speaking reminded her of her father, and not in ways that made her shrink like a smacked child.

Pippin was late. Chase loaded the bench press, and the first few reps were nothing. Images of *Phoenix* and its laid-back pilot zoomed through her thoughts. She was being too tough on Arrow, maybe, but she couldn't help it. He'd come on so strong with the laughing and the showing off that he knew her name.

Chase's left arm wobbled beneath the weight, then her right lost integrity. The bar sunk on her chest and pinched the breath out of her lungs. She knew better. She'd been in physical training forty hours a week since she started at the Star. Flyboys had to be all-over strong to fight high-g. Every limb needed to be squeezed solid so that her blood made it to her brain despite the multiplied pressure and weight of gravity. G-LOC was a pilot's worst nightmare. The "LOC" standing for "loss of consciousness."

Lights out meant life out.

Black spots popped into her vision as she did her best to get the situation back under control. No luck. Pippin appeared, grabbed the bar, and lifted it onto its supports. Chase sucked in air. Her head spun, especially because Pippin reeked of the caustic soap they used in the kitchen's industrial-sized dishwashers.

"Did you…you…"

"Aerate, Chase. You're purple." Pippin sat beside her on the bench.

She breathed deeply and closed her eyes. The weight room's sounds and smells trickled in. The clank and whirl of machines. Metal and salt in the air. When she lifted her head, the world felt lighter. Straighter.

"Working off those demerits?" she asked. "Kale told me you gave him cheek."

"Just finished," he said.

This was where she should say thanks. Thanks for standing up to Kale on her behalf. Instead, she looked up and gave him a guilty half-smile. He thumped her on the back like he knew what she was thinking. But did he? His teasing in the canyon—about her not knowing him—came back like a bad taste at the back of her throat.

"Next time, I insist you pull some of those Nyx strings and get me on hangar cleanup. Kitchen duty is frightful. The cook told me I had a cute butt." Pippin looked truly horrified, but Chase couldn't stop a snicker.

On the other side of the room, freshmen dropped a payload of weights on the floor, and Chief Black threatened their lives in a way that made everyone in the room stifle laughs.

"I've been thinking." Chase paused for emphasis. "He watched our flight tapes. That's how he knew us." It took Pippin a few moments to catch that she had switched to discussing *Phoenix*. "Maybe the government hired them to run some sort of combat test during the trials. How long will it really be before Ri Xiong Di copies the Streaker engines and we're fighting our equivalents up there. Right? We need to prove we can take down other manned jets."

Pippin pushed her off the bench and fixed his weightlifting gloves. "Drones are one thing, but I don't like the idea of missile locking on other pilots. No matter what side they're on."

"But it makes sense, doesn't it?"

Pippin executed five smooth reps before his neck strained and a red blotch lit up old acne scars. "So this Arrow and…what's his RIO's call sign?"

Chase kept two fingers of each hand on the bar until he finished. "The caveman? He threw his helmet before I could read it."

"Would we call him a caveman?" Pippin was upside down, but he still looked weird. Angry maybe. She'd never seen Pippin riled about something outside of Middle Earth.

Chase turned her head sideways to get a better look at him. "That was a brow ridge to best all other brow ridges. You didn't notice?"

"Not when he was standing on my face, no."

Chief Black walked by with a freshman tucked in a head-lock beneath his bulging, hairy arm. "Harcourt. Donnet. Don't forget to work your back with your chest." He demonstrated on the freshman, bending him into a hunchbacked creature. "See? That's too much back, not enough chest work." The chief made the freshman puff out his chest like…well, like Sylph. "Too much front, not enough back. Never neglect inverse muscles."

Chase waited until the sergeant was a safe distance away. "What I can't figure out is, why Canada?"

"Hey. Declaration of No Assistance," he said lowly. "Drop it."

She leaned in to whisper, "I still don't know how that applies to this situation."

"They're obviously working with us on the Streaker project. And if the New Eastern Bloc finds out, they'll label Canada an 'active enemy.' That'll get ugly fast." He made a noise like a dozen explosions going off at once.

"They'll be destroyed." Chase thought about Arrow with his wavy, black hair and his kickback attitude. "Their Air Force is ill-equipped."

"That's grossly naive, Chase, but it's true they wouldn't last long. No one would. That's the point of the declaration. No joining forces against the New Eastern Bloc. Our landing in Canada was probably the first satellite-visible interaction between our two countries in twenty years. And you can bet your wings that Ri Xiong Di saw it."

"That's why everyone was upset?"

"That's why."

"Christ." Chase pinched her leg hard enough to make her nerves shriek. "But if Ri Xiong Di saw, we'd be at war already. So they didn't see."

He shrugged. "That's what no one knows."

Riot entered the weight room with a grimy towel over his shoulder. "Sylph's looking for you, and I mean that as a life or death warning." He sauntered toward the free weights.

"I still haven't run into Sylph since I took out *Pegasus*," Chase explained to Pippin. "I have a strong feeling it's not going to go well."

Pippin didn't say anything, and Chase was suddenly more than muscle tired. Facing down Sylph meant acknowledging how crazed Chase had been when she was on the hunt for *Phoenix*.

On the other side of the weight room, Riot grunted through bicep curls while watching himself in the mirrored wall.

"What a winner." Pippin shook his head. "The whole academy to choose from and you've landed on that one."

"I know, right?" Chase fixed her gloves. "Whatever. He's decent. He's around. He doesn't mind my reputation."

"That's because he thinks he'll get laid. Boy, is he in for a disappointment. Sylph will kill you if this tryst follows established patterns."

"Sylph should realize that her RIO can make out with whoever he wants."

"You'd be mad if someone broke my heart," Pippin said.

"What hearts? There are no hearts involved. Just some lips and skin. I've pretty much told Riot that." She shoved Pippin's shoulder with her own. "Besides, you would have to show interest in a girl before hearts could be broken."

Pippin positioned himself under the bench press. "Not till God makes women out of some other metal than earth."

"English translation?"

"Indeed."

Chase let Pippin be Pippin. She eyed Riot and thought about Streaker Team *Pegasus*. It didn't feel right that they were out of the loop. "I kinda wish Sylph knew about *Phoenix*."

"Kale said shut up, so we shut up."

"Donnet!" Chief Black shouted. He stood beside an upside-down freshman who was hanging from the ceiling bar by his feet. "You've got a family call. Hustle to."

Pippin disappeared so fast that Chase felt his wake like a pass of engine heat. She couldn't blame him. Up in the near-Arctic and so dependent on the military, she often felt like there was no one else. After all, Chase didn't have a family waiting on her calls. But Pippin did, and they loved him and missed him.

Chase lay back under the bench press and forced herself through a chest ache that had nothing to do with her muscles.

☉ ☉ ☉

Kale often called Chase a glutton for punishment. She didn't deny it.

After her arms were jellied with muscle fatigue, she set off in search of Sylph. It was time to take another pounding. One she deserved.

She found Sylph in the hangar. The cold seeped through the concrete walls, making Chase wish she were wearing the uniquely light insulation of her zoom bag. She held her chest over her T-shirt, bit the ball chain of her dog tags, and jogged around the old planes, drones, and helos. When she arrived at the Streakers, her arms fell to her sides. Her mouth hung open.

Chase hadn't realized it was this bad.

The engineers had completely dismantled *Pegasus*'s right wing while *Dragon* sat on blocks, her landing gear stripped down to its nuts and bolts and struts. Chase left Sylph standing with her back to her beneath *Pegasus* and went to *Dragon* first. She put her hand on the jet's nose. The metal skin was always a little warmer than the chilled air in the hangar, which made it feel alive.

"I'm sorry," she told her bird. An airman cast her a dirty look, but she kept touching *Dragon*, pressing her face to the jet and whispering her regrets. There were so many.

Sylph grabbed Chase and spun her by the shoulders. Chase

fell backward onto her butt. Her palms burned from hitting the concrete floor so hard.

"You reckless, stupid, *stupid* girl!" The blonde raised a fist destined for Chase's face but then stopped. They both had tears stinging at the corner of their eyes. They both noticed it. "You don't care about anything or anyone."

Chase looked past Sylph to the beautiful, broken Streakers. "That's not true."

"Prove it next time." Sylph's fist reared back some more, and Chase was going to let her plant one on her nose, eyes, mouth—whatever the girl needed to hit to make them square again. But Sylph's hand dropped instead. Chase stared at her loose fingers. "You don't even understand what you did wrong."

"I do," Chase muttered. If anyone was acutely aware of her failings, her callousness, and her tunnel vision, it was Chase.

"You're not worth the bruised knuckles." Sylph stomped away.

Now Chase knew another truth: the only thing worse than getting punched in the face was not getting punched in the face when you deserved it.

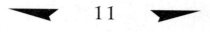

11

TAG THE BOGEY

Sighting the Enemy

Pippin was still talking to his family when Chase entered the barracks hall. At the far end, a tiny closet of a room was set up for video calls. It didn't have a door—most likely to dissuade dirty talking—but that also meant Chase couldn't get by without Pippin's family seeing her in the background.

"Nyx!" his littlest brother, Andrew, called out. "Nyx! Nyx!"

Chase leaned on the doorjamb and crossed her arms. "Hey there, Andy. Still bulking up to turn flyboy?"

"Yeah, look!" The ten-year-old showed off his biceps.

"Impressive." Chase tried to look at Andrew's eyes when she talked to him. Tried not to stare at how filthy and skinny he was or how patched his clothes were. Andrew yelled at Pippin's other two brothers off camera, and Pippin said something about one of their ticklish ears. Andrew dove off screen. A wrestling match ensued until one of them kicked the camera and the screen fuzzed before it went black.

Pippin stood up, the tiny folding chair creaking with relief.

"I'm beginning to doubt if they know any other way to hang up." His voice was stiff. "There's water rationing in Trenton. Can you believe that?"

"Yes," Chase said.

"I know." He drummed his fingers on his chest. "A bit deluding living up here with all the food we can eat and regular showers, clean clothes." Pippin looked guilty.

Chase picked at her sleeve. "Janice doesn't need my living stipend, Pip. I wish you'd let me route it to the Donnet clan. I want to."

"My dad wouldn't take it. He doesn't even like taking my money, but at least he does." Pippin messed up his hair. It was trying to be curly and settling for fluffy. He really was boyishly cute. "Besides, they're not starving. They're just not very clean." He took the hallway at a pace that proved he needed to be alone for a little while.

Chase slouched in the folding chair. The Second Cold War snuck up on them in weird ways. At the Star, they talked about battles and bombings. They lived right up against the border of invasion from Siberia, and yet they were protected from what Ri Xiong Di's trade embargoes did to the U.S. America wasn't just banned from taking military action with other countries. The U.S. was being "punished for a century of self-centered extravagance"—or so the infamous declaration read. No real trade was permitted, which meant the country had been forced to become self-sustaining. However, it wasn't doing so hot. Not in matters like education and medicine.

And water, it seemed.

Kale kept explaining that one concrete military advantage could upset the standoff and make the New Eastern Bloc back down. That was the hope of the Streakers. The only things standing in the way were the government trials—and Chase's famed recklessness.

She dialed her mother's number. The screen lit up with the pale purple wall in Janice's living room, ringing and ringing. The color matched Janice's always-polished nails, and Chase remembered being tiny and trying to hold her mother's hand to cross the street. Trying and failing.

The machine asked if she wanted to leave a message.

"Sure." After the beep, Chase sat taller. "What's up, Janice? You're probably out. Want to hear a laugh? I got Tourn's attention the other day by being an idiot." It wasn't funny, not even in the jovial way she was trying to say it. Chase had screwed up big-time. Enough to jeopardize the cold war ceasefire, but what felt so much worse was she didn't know how to stop herself from doing the same thing again. Maybe she *should* lose her wings...

Her focus blurred. Why was she reaching out to Janice anyway?

Because Janice knew that Tourn was her father, and that made her one of three people who knew the truth. That's why.

Kale and Pippin were the other two. Dr. Ritz knew as well, but Chase easily discounted the woman—she'd simply read it in Chase's file. Pippin had gotten the secret out of her one night during freshman year after she'd beat the snot out of two of her classmates. She had caught them discussing "Tourn the Mass Murderer" and had turned feral until Pippin pulled her off. He'd proven his best friend–hood that moment by taking a solemn oath to act like he didn't know for the rest of eternity.

Chase swallowed, her throat sticky. That memory never made sense. Her father had killed people. Admittedly. Why in the world would she defend him? And the academy was her home now. Pippin was her family. She should just forget about Michigan and Janice. And Tourn.

Easier said than done. Her parents were a gray cloud she couldn't shirk.

Chase deleted the message like all the others, feeling as unanswered as her mother's line.

$$\textcircled{1}\textcircled{4}\textcircled{1}$$

The hangar filled with screams. Shouts. Cries.

Chase dropped her tools. She'd been helping the engineers rebuild *Dragon*'s landing gear, but all that was forgotten as the red alarm light blared.

Something had happened.

Chase rushed into action, gasping. It was only now with everyone yelling that she realized she'd been holding her breath since Pippin explained what her landing in Canada could mean: Ri Xiong Di retaliation.

She waited before the hangar doors with the rest of the airmen while her father's words shook her thoughts. The Second Cold

War *was* heating up. Tourn would be so pleased. She pictured him lording over some base. Kale had mentioned Texas once, but Chase only wanted to know where it was so she didn't fly over it.

The hangar doors peeled open, blasting Arctic wind and spitting ice flecks. Chase buried her face in her sleeve and pushed toward the action. An older fighter jet, an Eagle, taxied in. Hoses dumped white foam on its smoking engines.

Below the cockpit, a jagged hole bled greasy liquid and a streak of red that could be nothing other than blood.

"Get that canopy open!" someone yelled. "Get Erricks out! Get him out!"

Ramp stairs were pushed up to the cockpit, and ground crew pressed in. They hammered at the canopy joint with crowbars, but it was wedged shut from the damage to the body. An engineer called for a welding torch, and Chase ran back to retrieve the one they had been using on *Dragon*. She handed it to the airman, and he cast a cold look at her. "Get out of here, cadet! You're in the way."

Chase stumbled back, a little too blown by the situation to register the insult. They finally wrenched the canopy open and strapped the pilot to a stretcher. He was making terrible animal sounds and grabbing at his leg, which had gotten splintered into the wreckage. It didn't look like a leg anymore. More like meat smashed up with a zoom bag.

They ran him toward the infirmary.

Chase choked on the smoke still pouring from the Eagle. A cadet tugged on the back of Chase's uniform, pulling her away from the scene of destruction. She went with him, too overwhelmed to register anything outside of what she had just witnessed.

"What happened?" she asked blindly. A familiar voice answered, but not the kind of familiar that eased her nerves.

"That's red drone damage," Tanner said. "The Eagle was running surveillance over the North Pole. Trying to spy from the backyard. Can't believe they thought that'd work."

A greenish bruise still highlighted his eye, reminding Chase of the pummeling he took from Sylph two weeks ago. "We should get out of here before they suspend our flight privileges." His voice was matter of fact, in a tone that always felt like a personality trait.

They walked together, which felt as strange as it should. Chase bridged the gap from the smoke of the real war to the internal fight she felt when she looked at Tanner. Last semester, he had tutored her in history when she couldn't get her head around which country Ri Xiong Di bought first. And when his cute Asian-American features stirred up some cultural curiosity, she'd started doing the same things with him that she now did with Riot.

"Will it mean war?" Chase asked. "Put us over the edge?"

"No. The bastards knew what they were doing. They didn't kill the pilot, did they? They let him limp back here to show us a taste of what they're capable of. It's probably just retaliation. They're flexing their muscles at us."

Retaliation for Chase's landing in Canada?

Her breath went tight. This had to be her fault. Had Ri Xiong Di attacked the Canadian base too? Did Ri Xiong Di find a way to knock *Phoenix* out of the sky? All of a sudden, the long-haired image of Arrow didn't make her want to roll her eyes.

Was he okay? He had to be.

They had to fly together again.

She came out of her thoughts slowly. "What?"

Tanner was eyeing her as though he had asked something important. "I said, why Riot?"

"Are you serious? After what we just saw…that stuff doesn't matter."

"It matters to me." Tanner's expression pegged her, and he leaned a little closer, reminding her of his pressing, small kisses. "I might not be on a Streaker team, but I'm better than Riot. Riot blabs to the whole academy every time you hook up. I actually like you."

"But you don't know…" Chase's voice trailed off as she remembered Pippin's ribbing—that this had become more of a standard answer than a real response. "Why?" she asked instead. "Why do you think you like me?"

He stood a little taller. "It's a gut reaction. I look forward to seeing you."

"But that's just you. It has nothing to do with me, you know? And seriously, Tanner, I've been terrible to you." She stopped herself from adding, *on purpose.* Tanner was smart and sweet, a pilot with extracurricular talents. He was ten times the boy Riot was, and as soon as Chase realized that, she'd cut him off. He didn't deserve to get tangled up with the Nyx.

"Find someone else." Her words ended up sounding so much harsher than she intended, but it was too late. Tanner left.

Chase stood in the glass tunnel that connected the hangar to the Green. Outside, a snowstorm pressed on the navy sky. She wondered if *Phoenix* was up there somewhere. If Canada had been attacked too. *Dragon* would be fixed soon, she hoped. And then she'd look for Arrow—catch him in the sky where no satellite could hang onto their signal for long. She had to make sure he'd made it through.

Arrow didn't deserve the hazardous wake of her bad decisions either.

12

ZERO DARK THIRTY

After Midnight, Before Sunrise

The night had gone past that zone of sleeplessness and into vulgar awake. Chase flipped in bed so often that Pippin put his headphones on to drown out the creaks of the bunk frame. The tramping bass of some classical tune trickled up through the silence.

She closed her eyes, only to remember the hangar and Captain Erricks's mangled leg. Guilt seized her and threw a bag over her head.

"Pippin!"

He shot up. "I'm—what?" He yawned lionlike. "Did I miss something?"

"Was the attack on the Eagle my fault?" she asked.

Pippin didn't say anything. Maybe he shrugged. Or nodded. She couldn't see him. She hung her head over the bar to look down on him. "Was it retaliation for landing in Canada?"

He took his headphones off. "I don't know, Chase."

Coming from a bona fide genius, this answer felt stark.

"Guess then."

"No."

"Please, Pip."

"I meant, no, it's not your fault. Probably not. There are many cogs turning. You're only one of them—not a small one, but only one. Make sense?" When she didn't answer, he added, "We're under enough pressure. Guilt is overkill at this point. Trust me."

Chase did. That trust was one of the best things in her life, and she held on to it as she buried the scene in the hangar and begged sleep. Her nightmare was waiting.

Chase crawled on her belly through a black night. The mud sucked her hands past the wrists with each move. She stifled grunts—her father was watching from the tower with his men, and she didn't want him to hear.

One more hill, topped with a barbed-wire net, remained between her and the finish line. The recruits were supposed to jump it; she'd watched many times. They were supposed to expose themselves to rubber bullets, duck and dive. But she was smaller, no real muscles yet, and definitely no boobs. She scurried under the wire and crested the hill. Panic made her careless.

The barbed teeth bit into her shirt.

Explosions. *They were only flash burns, but she still screamed. Her right shoulder caught, ripping a stinging line down her arm. Another blast. Another. She knew this part; the longer she took to get to the finish, the closer the explosions would get.*

Mud rained and detonations illuminated the red gush from her arm…

A pounding through her room slashed her nightmare.

Pippin sprang to answer the door. A technical sergeant thrust a note in his hand and ran down the hallway.

Chase leaped from the top bunk. "A drill?" Her heart was beating to the tune of her nightmare, adrenaline kicking through her veins.

Pippin watched the sergeant sprint. "They don't run that fast for a drill." He unfolded the paper. "Emergency. We've got to get in the air." He dropped the note and stepped into his G-suit.

Chase pulled on her own zoom bag while she tried to read the note, but it was in code followed by a set of coordinates. RIO speak. "An attack?"

"Yes."

Her pulse was a mess as she zipped up and dug her helmet out of a pile of laundry. Within moments, they were jogging down the hall, meeting Riot and Sylph along the way.

"Drill?" Riot asked hopefully.

"Don't think so. Those tend to feel—"

"Smoother." Sylph cut Chase off. She was tying her hair back in a braid.

"No hard feelings," Chase said to Sylph, startling the whole group into slowing down. "Well, we might have to fight together up there. We're on the same side, right?"

Sylph sneered. "I won't punch you out of the sky, if that's what you're worried about."

"Leah…" Riot warned, but she shot him a look that silenced him. They crossed the Green at a jog but began to run when they hit the buzz of the hangar. Airmen sprinted in every direction, and several of the old jets rolled out the door and into the black sky.

"Definitely not a drill," Pippin murmured as Kale met them by the Streakers.

"Inbound airstrike?" Chase asked. "Red drones?"

"No drones." Kale's voice was hoarse, probably from shouting commands. "There's been an internal bombing. High casualties. We're sending reinforcements, but they won't get there fast enough. If you push it, you'll get there with a chance."

Chase's anxiety was mounting. "A chance of what?"

"Of helping survivors. If there are any flight-capable birds left, lead them back here. We can't afford to radio our position. Stay completely off the grid. Don't even use the shortwave. And *do not* land."

Sylph and Riot were already cresting the ramp stairs and sinking into *Pegasus*'s cockpit. Pippin slid into his seat in *Dragon* and strapped in.

Chase's thoughts swirled. "General, I—"

Kale grabbed her leg and hoisted her up. She swung over the edge and into the cockpit, still unable to phrase her fear.

"Open up her speed, Harcourt," Kale said. "This is your chance."

☽ ☾ ☽

The night was deep. Veiled stars and nothing beyond the silver streak of her bird around her. She hit Mach 3 in a hurry, knowing

Sylph would fall behind. Sylph could fly as fast as Chase, but she wasn't strong enough to hold the speed for as long.

Pippin was busy with his controls, mapping out coordinates. "Balls to blackout flying," he complained. "Can't sense a thing. We need to bounce our position off a satellite. We need like two seconds of radar."

"Kale said to keep off the grid, Pippin. We're on our own."

"So what do we do if a commercial plane comes at us?"

"Duck." She punched the throttle and crested past Mach 4. More than two thousand miles an hour. They had been going southeast for too long, and although she was no geographical genius like her RIO, she could tell they were headed toward the Hudson Bay. And JAFA.

"Do you think..." Chase swallowed her words. The horizon was orange, not from sunrise but from the reach of high flames. "JAFA," she whispered. "Where's *Phoenix*?"

"Maybe he didn't get out in time," Pippin said. "The roofs are blown outward. Must have been an inside job. Spies. That must be what Kale meant by *internal bombing*. Nyx, there could be bogies in the sky. I'm going to be a busy bee keeping lookout."

"Buzz away." Chase reined in her speed and pulled closer to the burning buildings.

Fire groped the night. The hangar was the only building not fully ablaze, but smoke poured out of broken windows. Chase couldn't see anyone on the ground. No one fleeing or fighting the fire. Kale's had spoken about survivors, but...

105

"There's no one," she murmured.

"Sylph will be here in five minutes," Pippin announced.

"This'll be over in two." Chase bit back anger. Sylph should be faster. JAFA shouldn't be burning. She should *do* something. Chase eyed the hangar door. A blue fiery blast lit up the inside. Chase knew that color. Jet engine flashes. She dropped even closer, peering through the smoke-blackened windows.

Faces peered back. Dozens of them.

"There are *people* stuck in there!" Chase set down on the runway before Pippin could object, taxiing toward the hangar door too fast.

"What're you...Nyx!" He knew her too well. "We're not a battering ram!"

"*Dragon* is fortified titanium. She's stronger than whatever that is, right?" Chase didn't wait for a response. People were dying a few yards away. The least she could do was try. She hit the throttle and drove at the sealed door, crossing her fingers that the people inside saw her coming.

That they moved back.

She smashed into it, screeching metal on metal, and pushed all the way to the front edge of the cockpit. When she rolled back, a frame of wreckage hung from *Dragon*'s nose, but the door was punctured. Smoke chugged out of the gaping hole.

"Come on!" she whispered.

The platform of ramp stairs appeared on the other side of the hangar door. People began to jump from the stairs and through the

Breaking Sky

hole, helping each other down. They were young. Cadets just like at the Star.

"Nyx, we won't be able to take off with that scrap stuck to us. And we need to get out of here."

"I have to help them." She hit the canopy switch and leaped out, hitting the pavement hard enough to fall and mangle her knees through her G-suit. She shook out the stinging pain and ran.

Older airmen and officers appeared among the survivors, directing everyone toward the woods beside the runway. Chase helped a few cadets out of the fiery hangar, all the while searching for a sign of Streaker Team *Phoenix*.

Arrow was among the last. She met his eyes with soft shock— relief and something else. He stood on the ramp stairs, helping an elderly woman in a white lab coat through the hole. When the woman was through, he leaned out and yelled to Chase. "I'm going to get my bird out. Clear back."

The last of the survivors ran into the woods beyond the runway.

Chase headed to *Dragon*, tugging at the metal frame on her jet's nose. It was too heavy. She pulled, only budging it a few inches. Any second, *Phoenix* was going to slam blindly out of the hangar doors—and right into her. They'd all be dead in a flash of scorching jet fuel.

"Pippin! Help!" Her words were lost in the roaring collapse of a nearby building. Chase went back to the scrap and pulled with everything she had. This was going to end badly. Both Streakers would be blown up. Both teams would die because she had to break orders. Had to land.

107

She yanked harder, choking on swears, but suddenly, her hands weren't alone. Her arms were a pair among many as shoulders pushed into her own. The group pulled as one, and the piece screeched as it slid off *Dragon* and smashed on the ground.

Before anyone could speak, *Pegasus* flew by with a shriek of furious speed. Arrow threw out a protective arm that slammed into Chase's chest.

"That's just Sylph," Chase yelled over the fire's destruction. She loosened his grip on her chest and pushed him away with both hands. "She's on our side."

"Mostly," Pippin croaked. Arrow's RIO laughed at that—a desperate sound amid the chaos.

"Come on. I'll lead you—" she started, but Arrow cut her off.

"We're forgetting something." His eyes searched the runway, his demeanor slightly frozen. Black smears ran down his face and into his long hair. Finally he pointed.

The fuel truck was mere feet from one of the burning buildings. Chase watched as the ground underneath it began to burn.

"Down!" Arrow yelled. He was on top of her so fast, over Pippin and his RIO too, shielding them with his body.

The sky lit up like daylight.

The explosion shook the air and speared his hearing.

Moments later, they were all standing, staring. Dazed. *Pegasus* flew by again, but this time Arrow was struck still. Chase gripped the shoulders of his T-shirt and yelled his call sign into his face. The orange blare of fire danced over his blue eyes, but they were static.

108

She shouted at his RIO. "Help him!"

The RIO smacked Arrow. Hard. "Tristan!" he yelled. "Snap to. We've got to get out of here."

Arrow pulled at his ears and worked his jaw like the blast had taken out his hearing.

She took hold of his shirt again. "Tristan." His eyes locked on hers. Unlike his call sign, his name was a link straight through to him. "Get in your bird. Follow me home."

He nodded.

Chase and Pippin climbed into their Streaker while *Phoenix*'s team returned through the hole in the smoking hangar. In a few rasping breaths, she'd flung *Dragon* up into the night. Pippin held on to her shoulder while they circled what was left of JAFA.

"You think they'll make it?" His question was barely out when the hangar roof began to collapse.

"Come *on*," Chase whispered.

As if he didn't want to make her wait, the rest of the building flew apart as *Phoenix* broke through the flames and into her sky.

BRAVO

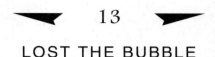

LOST THE BUBBLE

Which End Is Up?

The syrup was a golden brown lake spreading across Chase's plate. Her French toast was a raft to nowhere.

"Hey, Ender, come back to the starship," Pippin said from across the table.

"I hate when you call me Ender." She skewered her fork through the starchy stack. "And what does that even mean?"

"It means I'm worried about you."

"Wasn't Ender the boy the military used to beat all those bugs?"

"It's just a story," Pippin said. "What I wouldn't give to be battling swarms of crickets instead of Ri Xiong Di."

Crickets? What was happening? Chase's ears still hummed from the roar of collapsing buildings, her throat stung from the smoke, and yet it was French toast morning in the chow hall. "This doesn't feel right." She motioned to the crowd of cadets elbow-jostling over vats of syrup. "Everything seems normal."

Six hours ago, the flight back to the Star had been the tensest experience of Chase's life. Her fists had stayed tight, her body hunched forward—all the while expecting red drones to drop in at her, missiles hot. Her still-depleted adrenaline levels left her feeling like her head was sliding off her neck.

Chase skewered her stack with her fork. "Surely we're at war after last night."

"The whole thing'll be classified." Starchy globs rolled around Pippin's mouth with each word. She knew better than to try to talk to him now; he was serious about breakfast.

"So many people died," she murmured. It couldn't be swept under the rug. And what about Streaker Team *Phoenix*? As soon as they landed at the Star, Kale and a handful of other officers had swept the Canadians into the cadet-restricted section of the base. Chase might not see Tristan again until they faced off at the government trials in two and a half months.

Tristan. She couldn't think of him as Arrow. Not after the way they had blown into each other through the explosions and flames.

There had to be aftermath. Not the least of which might be that she'd broken direct orders in landing on JAFA's runway, *and* she'd rammed that hangar door open. Would Kale call Tourn again? Would her father appear to discipline her? She could only imagine what Tourn would say if he found out that she used a multibillion-dollar jet as a battering ram…

When she looked up, Pippin had paused mid-chew. Stunned. "Can we help you?" he asked.

Sylph sat down beside Chase, nearly on top of her. The blonde's tray banged into Chase's, knocking her fork across the table. "The enemy of our enemy is our friend."

"Come again?" Pippin asked.

Riot put his tray down beside Pippin and gave Chase a smile that she glanced away from.

Sylph sighed. "It means—"

"I know what it means, Sylph," Pippin said. "Do *you*?"

"We need to stick together." Sylph took Chase's shoulder, violating their long-standing "no touching unless assaulting" policy. "That third Streaker team is our enemy."

"For the trials," Chase amended.

"For everything. We have to win, and we'll last longer if we gang up on them." Sylph looked around the table like she was about to give an executive command. "We're going to take *Phoenix* down. I don't know what they're playing at, but I'm. Not. Going. To. Lose. Especially not to Canadians."

Chase shifted under Sylph's glare. Before last night she might have had a similar drive, but things had changed when she'd worked with Tristan and his RIO to get the wreckage off *Dragon*'s nose. "So your plan is what exactly?"

"Step one is discussing our weaknesses. I'll tell you what you do wrong, and then you share how you think I might improve."

"That sounds like it will go well," Chase muttered.

Pippin started choking on a muted laugh.

Sylph wasn't budging for humor. "We're going to best them *before* the trials. Learn their weaknesses and exploit them."

115

Chase fetched her fork and reskewered her breakfast. "Sylph, we probably won't even see them again until January. No doubt they're on the other end of North America by now."

"Lesson one." Sylph turned Chase's head by her chin, aiming her attention to a table overflowing with cadets. Tristan and his RIO were seated among them. *Laughing.* The image hit her all wrong. After last night, what in the world could they find funny?

"You have no peripheral vision, Nyx. It's how I've outmaneuvered you like ninety percent of the time."

Chase shrugged out of Sylph's hold at the same time Tristan eyed her across the room. He got up immediately and began to cross the distance between them, RIO in tow.

"Game on," Sylph whispered in Chase's ear. Chase swatted her away just as Streaker Team *Phoenix* stopped before them.

Riot broke the silence. "Hi…guys. How are we liking our stay at the Star? Looks like you've already made some ground crew friends. A little tip? Flyboys don't hang out with them."

Chase caught herself rolling her eyes on that point. After last night, she had trouble imagining how it could possibly matter who hung out with whom. They could all be at war by tomorrow. She was just about to tell Riot to shut up when Tristan maneuvered first.

He stuck out a hand to Sylph much like he'd done to Chase when they first met, an easy smile on his face. "You must be Sylph. I'm Tristan Router. Lovely flyby last night."

Sylph ignored his hand, stood, and swept her long braid behind her shoulder. "I'm aware of who you are. Don't daydream that I'll celebrate it." She faced the group. "Kale ordered us to report to the conference room next to his office for debriefing at oh eight hundred. All of us." Her whole body seemed to go ice-hard as she shouldered past Tristan and his RIO. More so than she ever did around Chase.

Sylph headed for the door, and Riot and Pippin stood to empty their trays.

Riot banged his tray over the trash can and chatted up *Phoenix*'s RIO. "I'm Riot. This is Pippin."

"Really, I'm Henry," Pippin said. "You remember me. You stood on my face."

"Sure, I remember," the broad-shouldered man-boy said. "No hard feelings?"

"'Course not," Pippin said.

"I'm Romeo."

Pippin seemed like he'd gotten conked in the head. Chase wondered if he was about to execute some revenge for getting stomped on, but that's not what came out. "Do you bite your thumb at us, sir?"

It was a weird moment. Even Riot was dumbfounded, or at least he looked dumber than usual.

Romeo clapped Pippin's shoulder. "*La loi est-elle de notre côté, si je dis oui?*"

"*Non.*" Pippin laughed real hard at that, and it got right under Chase's fingernails.

117

"That's great. There's a RIO trio now," she said to herself, enjoying the rhyme. She watched the boys walk toward the door and a scowling, cross-armed Sylph. "What was all that about anyway?"

"They just had a Shakespeare moment," Tristan said. "In French. Romeo loves that stuff. He thinks it helps him win favor with the ladies."

"Pippin loves that stuff too," Chase said. "Guess that means he'll forgive your RIO for the bashing the other day."

She had to sidestep Tristan to put her tray on the conveyor belt. While she plopped her silverware into the sudsy tub, a group of freshmen surrounded Tristan. She recognized Stephens and Helena from her ground crew fan club.

"Arrow, have you seen the rec room yet? We could meet you there tonight. Show you around," Stephens said.

Tristan said he would meet them. And then he said goodbye to half of them by name, apologizing to the three he didn't know yet.

The laid-back, overly friendly attitude Chase had hated the moment she met Tristan was back. Once more, he reminded her of someone who'd never known a second of crap in his whole life. But now she knew that wasn't true—it couldn't be after last night.

Chase took in every angle and curve of his profile as they walked toward the conference room. The insanely heroic boy who'd shielded her from a fuel blast *with his body* had to be under that civil expression. So where was he? What was this act about?

"You're off to a running start, Arrow," she said.

"I have a feeling I'm going to be here for a while. Might as well make friends."

She grunted.

"You're not very pleasant considering what happened."

"And you're too pleasant"—she paused—"*considering*. Aren't you the least bit upset about last night?"

Tristan stopped, turned sideways in the hall like he'd forgotten where he was going. Where he was. His face had the exact same washed-blank look that he had after the fuel truck exploded. Like everything he loved had just burned...

Oh God.

"I'm sorry." Chase touched his arm, but he didn't move. "I'm a jerk. You'll see. No one really likes me, except for Pippin, but I think he's been stuck with me for too long. Stockholm syndrome, you know?"

Tristan looked down at the spot where she held his sleeve. She let go. Chase's heart was beating faster than it should. What in the blazes had she just said? It was like she'd sneezed truth all over the front of his uniform.

His voice came up from somewhere deep. "I'm fine, Chase."

"People call me Nyx."

He smiled, but it wasn't the polite, all-purpose look from before. This was a little sad. A little...beautiful. He pulled his hair into a ponytail and eyed the conference room door. "I think we're about to find out what happened last night."

"Or that we're not a high enough rank to merit answers," she said.

"We figure out what they're hiding by the way they try to hide it, Chase. Isn't that how you tracked me down?" He opened the door for her.

14

CHECK SIX

Watch Your Back

Chase hadn't considered the fact that Tourn might be there. That he might have flown in during the night to attend this meeting. But those were her immediate thoughts when she entered the room overflowing with officers.

The Canadian uniforms were a lighter shade of blue than Kale and the other U.S. officers' deep navy, but otherwise they were very much the same. She went shoulder by shoulder, looking for the circle of five stars that denoted her father's elite position. She didn't check faces, unwilling to make eye contact without warning.

But he wasn't there.

Kale ushered the Streaker teams to sit around a grand oak table along with a white-haired civilian, who had pencils stuck through the worn holes of her lab coat like safety pins. Tristan sat beside her, speaking into the woman's ear, and Chase was surprised to recognize her as one of the survivors Tristan had escorted through the hole in the hangar door.

When he caught Chase watching him, he stared back, and she

could sense the lingering pain she'd evoked in the hallway. He was messed up about what had happened at JAFA—and why shouldn't he be? If Chase lost the Star, she had no doubt that the whole sky would fall. But she couldn't help wondering why he was so interested in pretending like it *didn't* bother him.

Sylph elbowed Chase so hard, so sharp, that she let out a gasp. "Eyes on your own paper," the blonde muttered.

Kale stepped closer and put a hand on Chase's shoulder. The other officers were finishing their individual conversations, passing stacks of forms around. Kale stayed close to her back, and what felt like favoritism turned into a distinct warning when he started to speak.

"You're here to be debriefed about the events of last night." Kale pressed a button on the console at the center of the table, and a screen emerged, buzzing with static. "General Tourn, we are all present."

Her father's face was *there*. Clipped gray hair and a uniform with such sharp lines that it already felt like it was cutting her. The room hummed with people responding to her father—the way rooms always went electric because of his name.

Kale squeezed her shoulder. "He can't see us," he whispered.

The image of her father grunted, followed by a voice that sounded like an avalanche of gravel. "On October 28, 2048, the Royal Canadian Junior Air Force Academy was bombed from within. Casualties are estimated at eighty-seven. Two spies associated with Ri Xiong Di are in custody."

The rest of the room probably thought he was reading a prepared

122

statement because he sounded so unemotional. Chase knew better. He always sounded collected. Arranged. He lived and breathed orders and assignments. "Honed detachment," she called it. It'd been one of his genetic gifts to Chase, although it was failing her now. Failing big-time.

She began to shake, and Kale's other hand clamped down on her shoulder.

Tourn continued. "It is our understanding that Ri Xiong Di is aware of the events of five days ago when a U.S. cadet pilot interacted with a Canadian pilot, breaking the Declaration of No Assistance." Chase glanced to Tristan, but his gaze was locked on the grain of the wood table. "Neither Canada nor the U.S. has received an official message from the New Eastern Bloc, and we have decided not to release the news of the bombing to the public. JAFA's destruction will be attributed to a fire. You will all sign confidentiality documents."

Kale handed out a sheet of paper to everyone seated, and Chase looked down at the blur of words. Her father was *there*. Sitting at the center of the table like a Roman bust. Did he have any thoughts about her? Anything at all?

"Now. What I'm about to tell you is top secret and will not leave this room." He cleared his throat again, and she might have been the only person to understand that he meant it as a sort of sigh. "An American-Canadian Alliance is beginning to emerge. We hope the public news of this arrangement will coincide with the government boards' favorable decision on the Streaker models. As a united front, and with advanced airpower, we will stand a chance at breaking the Second Cold War standoff.

"In the meantime, the Canadian cadets designated as Streaker Team *Phoenix* will continue training at the United Star Academy in anticipation of the trials in January. Is Dr. Adrien present?"

The elderly woman sat forward, speaking with an accent that, like Romeo, belied her French Canadian heritage. "I am, General Tourn."

"Will you be able to continue your work from the Star?"

"Yes."

"Good. You are all dismissed as soon as you have signed the documentation."

The cadets bent over the sheets of paper, signing without reading. Chase squeezed her capped pen, distracted. More military secrets like the third Streaker—except this time Chase was on the side of those who knew. It was a slight shock to realize that knowing wasn't any better or easy. Secrets were still secrets. She listened to the scratch of signatures—and before she was ready, everyone was standing. Leaving. She hurried to catch up, but she wasn't fast enough.

"Cadet Harcourt, remain," Tourn said. "Everyone else is dismissed."

Her heart took off in too many directions. People sifted out of the room. Sylph cast a look back at her that was tinted with curiosity. Tristan paused at the door until Romeo tugged him along by the shoulder. Pippin hadn't moved. Chase had avoided looking at him throughout the whole meeting. Her RIO was in a unique position to understand how painful it was for her to see her father, and that made Chase completely unable to make eye contact with him.

There were very few things in the world she was worse at dealing with than pity.

Kale took Pippin's paper and pointed toward the exit. Pippin went, and she caught a glimpse of his panic. The door shut loudly, and for a second, Chase thought Kale had left too. But the brigadier general stood by the door, chin raised in a sort of defiant pride. He held a finger to his lips and motioned for her to speak.

"I'm here, General Tourn," she managed.

"You acted to assist those people." For a heartbreaking moment she thought he was going to give her a strand of praise. "That is *the only* reason you are still a pilot. Understood?"

"Yes, General Tourn."

His watery gray eyes stared hard into the camera, but they were so unseeing that it made her feel transparent. The picture fuzzed and then blanked. He'd hung up.

Chase made a guttural, wounded sound. She'd been so prepared for his harshest words that the brevity of the ones he'd given her smashed her to pieces.

$$\odot \, \textcircled{4} \, \odot$$

A half hour later, Chase was still in the conference room. Kale had stayed. He sat next to her and kept quiet while she bled tears as though she were twelve years old all over again.

When she didn't have anything left, Kale finally spoke. "Get some rest. And have a little fun where you can find it. You're off restricted duty. Your father might not share my outlook, but I believe you showed bravery and good judgment when you aided *Phoenix*'s escape and rescued those people in the hangar."

Chase took a breath that was supposed to steady her but made her shake instead.

"We'll get you back in the air as soon as possible." Kale knew her so well. She needed *Dragon*. Direction and speed.

"Thank you for staying. I know how ridiculous this is."

"Ridiculous?"

"I've spent so long not caring about him." She scrubbed at the tears on her cheeks. "But this looks an awful lot like caring."

"I wouldn't judge. He made me cry once."

Chase choked on a laugh. "You're lying, General."

"No. He beat me senseless. It was my first semester at the academy. He was older, overseeing a drill, and I dropped behind during a running exercise and gave up. When he came back to find me, I was sitting on the edge of the road with my head between my knees." Kale paused. "I was in the infirmary for two nights after he was finished with me."

Chase stood and it wasn't so bad. She opened the door. "So my father's always been an asshole, is that it? Sometimes I hope that… after what he did…maybe that changed him into the Tourn he is today. Maybe he was once human."

Kale looked strained. No doubt he didn't want to talk about

Tourn's nuclear history. "I'll tell you this, Harcourt. I've never given up midstride again."

Chase left wondering if Kale was implying there was a method to her father's madness—but her thoughts stalled there. Tristan was on the hallway floor, his arms over his knees and his head back against the wall. He looked like a strange mixture of lost and found.

He looked like he had been listening the whole time.

"The pilot who dropped that bomb. Who killed all those Filipinos…"

She stumbled, trying to walk away fast, but the hall was a tunnel and his voice was strong.

"He's your *father?*"

Chase should have stopped. Turned back. She should have sworn him to secrecy with some massive bribe or threat. She should have done something, but her fear dawned blindingly. And she ran.

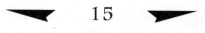

15

MISSILE LOCK

Oh, F@ck

Chase hadn't been in the embrace of the sky for a week. Not since the night flight to JAFA and back again. She missed *Dragon*. She missed mach speed and all its glorious direction. She missed being able to think about something—anything—other than the fact that Tristan Router knew the secret of her parentage.

She kept reliving that moment when she'd stepped into the hall. The very focused yet resigned look on Tristan's face. The way he had seemed small, folded up on the floor even though he was nearly a foot taller than her.

What had he been doing there? Waiting? Eavesdropping?

Her anxiety wrestled with the memory, smacked it down only to feel it flip into anger. It almost made her want to catch Tristan and threaten the breath out of him, but her fear held even those more Nyx-like aggressions in check. She was in new territory, and it was like waking up in a room that she hadn't fallen asleep in.

It didn't help that Tristan had assumed an ambitious social agenda, gallivanting around the Star, making friends with everyone.

He was already liked and trusted, and if he told one person, just *one*, she would no longer be the elusive celebrity pilot but *the* black sheep. The girl who didn't deserve to be at the Star.

Chase lay across her bunk like roadkill, exhausted from frustration, when Pippin came in. She rolled over, half falling off the mattress. "How's the library?"

"Wasn't at the library," he said.

"Where've you been?"

"Out."

"No shit, Sherlock. Out where?"

Pippin sat down and scribbled in his notebook. "I haven't been with anyone."

"Wow, that wasn't even my question. What's going on?" He didn't answer, so she added, "I'll tell you what's going on with me."

Pippin eyed her wearily. "Will you?"

"Um…" Chase braked. She hadn't told him about her talk with Tourn—or that Tristan knew about her dad. That would mean *discussing* it. No way. Pippin might be her only real friend at the Star, but she had limits.

"I just…I need a hop. I feel so meandery without flight in my veins."

"Evocative. Also incorrect. Adding a *y* to the end of word doesn't make you a creator of neologisms. It makes you ignorant." Pippin put his pencil down. He closed his eyes like he had to force himself to be civil. "They won't send us skyward until the terror threat is lowered back to reasonable levels. It should only be a few more days. Unless Ri Xiong Di decides to do to us what they did to JAFA."

She rolled the rest of the way off the bunk and landed so hard that Pippin jumped and gripped his notebook against his chest. Chase held her hand out. "All right, give them to me. You know you're not supposed to take your asshole pill twice in one day."

"Me? You've been paranoid all week. I know you're worried *Phoenix* will take *Dragon's* spot in the trials, but take a breath. There's nothing we can do while grounded."

"What?"

They stared at each other.

"Don't tell me you haven't figured that out." He sighed. "Now that they can't surprise *Phoenix* on us at the trials, they really only need two jets to face off. Three is overkill. Sylph is going ballistic over the fact. She should. She's the slowest. They'll probably run a few hops to suss out the worst candidate and ground him or her."

Chase's mouth was hanging open. *Phoenix* could replace *Dragon* or *Pegasus*?

Pippin cocked his head. "If that's not what's bothering you, what is?"

"Nothing," she lied. "I've just got a lot on my mind right now."

"Spill."

"You first."

"Touché."

Chase bit off the edge of a hangnail while Pippin went back to scribbling. She hadn't told her RIO a thing, and yet he'd picked up on her anxiety all the same. Maybe she should tell him. Would it help? She felt newly close to giving it a try. After all, if she couldn't talk to Pippin, then she couldn't talk to anyone.

Baby steps, she thought.

"Pip, how about a change of scenery? Let's go down to the hangar and see *Dragon*." She moved a little closer, and he snapped his notebook shut.

"The jet is not a grandma in a home. It doesn't need visitors."

Whoa. She stepped back. Pippin didn't usually dismiss *Dragon*, although Chase had to admit he didn't love the Streaker the way she did. He didn't love anything at the Star the same way. And suddenly, the fact that he wouldn't even tell her where he'd just been proved that she couldn't possibly talk to him about what Tristan knew.

Anger twisted down her arms. Her fists closed tight. "Are you thinking about quitting again? Do I have to remind you about the trials? Christ, I need you up there!"

"Stop yelling. I'm not going to quit." He spit the words. "I *can't*, if you haven't noticed. Not unless I want my brothers to starve."

She made herself lower her voice. "Look, I'm feeling it too. I don't want the Star to get leveled like JAFA or to lose *Dragon*, but—"

Pippin laughed so hard that she took another step back. "I'm sorry," he said, wiping bizarre tears from his eyes. "You're so far off the mark that it's funny."

"Yeah. Hilarious."

He reached for his headphones, but she was faster. She flung them across the room, and they hit the wall before flopping onto his bed. He met her gaze coolly. "Do you want to fight?"

"No. Do you want to fight with me?"

A knock sounded on the door, followed by Riot's voice. "Nyx. Food."

They continued to stare at each other while the moment released slowly. Too slowly. She'd never fought with Pippin before. They snarked and rubbed elbows sometimes, but this felt so strange. Borderline hostile. When Chase forced herself to speak again, her voice cracked. "We're going to the chow hall. Come with us?"

"Not hungry." He returned to his notebook.

"Eat. Let's go," Riot called sluggishly.

"What a dreamboat," Pippin mocked. She could tell he was pressuring himself to sound normal too. "How do you contain yourself?" Chase play-punched his shoulder, and Pippin grabbed her hand, a hint of wild right behind his eyes. "I'll talk to you later, but you have to share too. Deal?"

She braked again. She couldn't help it. "Yeah…right."

Pippin must have heard the taillights in Chase's tone. He let go of her hand with a frown and went back to his notebook, scribbling so hard his pencil went off the side of the paper and he wrote across the desk.

Riot and Chase got their lunches to go and sat beneath the largest tree on the Green. The sunlamps shone a very brilliant orange-yellow, but Chase looked beyond, past the glass ceiling to the navy sky tinged with flame blue. The color reminded her of Tristan's eyes reflecting JAFA's blaze.

The fire was so high...

Her imagination hacked her consciousness. She saw red drones overhead. Missiles falling hard and fast. Her world turned to fire and screams and broken glass. Is that what it had been like for Tristan? Is that what it would be like if this face-off opened itself to another world war?

Her mouth had gone thick and dry, near-panic leaning over her like cloud shadow. She tossed her sandwich to Riot.

"Where's Pippin?" Sylph sat cross-legged in the grass beside them, flipping her braid over her shoulder. "We need to discuss our anti-Canadian strategy for the trials."

"He's busy."

"Busy with what?" Riot asked.

"With whatever he wants to do," Chase said, trying not to give away the fact that they'd been arguing. Just thinking about how they'd snapped at each other made her feel red—both aggravated and embarrassed. Truth was, Chase wasn't used to fighting with anyone. Whenever she disagreed, she cut and ran. It was a policy that had kept her from having scores of friends but also from all the suffocating drama at the Star.

A policy that had just failed.

"Pippin's not with us." Sylph produced an inch-thick folder.

Chase peered over at the stream of notes. *OFF-THE-CUFF* was written across the top in intensely red ink. "A collection of your thoughts on my flying?"

Sylph eyed her coolly. "We'll get to that soon. More importantly, we need to discuss our major weaknesses. And your primary one is that Pippin is irreversibly contaminated. He's been hanging out with the *Phoenix* team."

"Pippin hasn't been with the Canadians," Chase said, instantly wondering if he had been.

"He has. In the rec room. Every night." Riot shoved her sandwich into his mouth like a dog bent on swallowing something whole. What was she doing with him again?

"Why don't you know where he's been? Or wait"—Sylph's eyes gleamed—"you sent him to spy on them. Didn't you?"

"What?"

Sylph went back to her notebook. "Disappointing. But we'll work around it."

Chase popped her knuckles one by one. Pippin was hanging out with Tristan and Romeo?

"Speak of the devils," Sylph said as Tristan and his RIO set their bags down at the foot of a tree a few yards away. "I can't believe everyone is so infatuated with them. *Exchange students*," Sylph said. "What a euphemism. Like Ri Xiong Di would even allow us to have an exchange program. I suppose they can't hide the big one's French accent."

135

"They're survivors, Sylph," Chase found herself saying. "They've been through a lot."

"Yeah. They look it."

Chase couldn't argue with her. Tristan and Romeo certainly didn't act like they'd escaped with only their lives a week ago. Four underclassmen girls stood in a semicircle around them. Their titters and body language proved they were all in love with Tristan. Romeo, seemingly oblivious, kept trying to engage one of them in a thumb-wrestling match.

"Maybe we should be working with them to make the trials look amazing, not scheming behind their backs, Sylph."

"The government board wants combat and skill. Not an American-Canadian alliance. No matter what General Tourn said. *You* are my wingman. They are the enemy. That's the setup of the trials from what I've gathered from Kale. We have to outfly them, Nyx."

Chase eyed Sylph. "Why do you hate them so much?"

"Hate implies emotional investment, of which I have none." Sylph shut the folder and stood.

"Pippin said that one of us might get booted from the trials. That they only need two jets."

Sylph acted as though she hadn't heard Chase. "Fifteen minutes to class. Don't be late. If you get put on restricted duty again, we'll never have time to figure this out." Sylph left.

Chase shook her head. "Sometimes I worry she's not all there."

"You struck a nerve, that's all." Riot reclined in the grass with his hands behind his head. "She's scared. She doesn't like them because they're faster than she is."

"Everyone's faster than she is. She slows down every time she has to pull a maneuver. Maybe that's what I should tell her when we're 'exchanging weaknesses.'"

"Please don't. I like your face better without bruises." He tried to take Chase's hand, but she leaned back. Across the way, Romeo was hanging upside down from a tree branch. That RIO was a helpless, crazed flirt; she'd gathered that much. Tristan was harder to pin down. She stared at his dark hair, his easygoing everything. It felt like a front, but it was hard to say. She'd only glimpsed a few flashes of the more serious and driven side underneath.

Enough to want to see more.

The fear came back with her curiosity. He had so much power over her, and he probably didn't even know it. All Tristan had to do was tell one person that she was the spawn of the military's angel of death…

Why, why, *why* had he been waiting in the hall?

Tanner walked across the Green. He paused to talk to Tristan like they were old friends. *Boy, this day just keeps getting better.*

"Hey." Riot pinched her ankle. "Want to meet up tonight? Boys' locker room?"

"*Ugh*, no." She couldn't stop herself. "I think we're played out, Riot."

Riot sat up. "What're you upset about?"

Chase had answers to that, but none that had to do with Riot.

"Do you tell people when we hook up?" she asked, remembering Tanner's disclosure in the hangar, back before JAFA burned and her whole world turned Canadian.

"Are you asking if I brag? Of course I brag. You should like that." Riot's frown zapped all the cute out of his face. "This is about the stupid *Phoenix* team. Everyone loves Arrow and *Romeo*. You too, I bet."

"I don't." Chase was still staring at Tristan. Busted. She looked away in a hurry, catching Riot's doubt. "I'm keeping an eye on them for Sylph."

"Don't be a skank, Nyx," he yelled. He left, and every cadet on the green, including the Canadian contingent, was looking at her. She put on a small smile and lay back in the grass with her arms behind her head.

What a morning. The emotions that had been so new earlier—like waking up in a strange room—now made her feel like being stranded on a different planet. She'd fought with Pippin, found out that the trials might be reorganized, pissed off Sylph, and dumped Riot.

Then there was the X factor: she still hadn't figure out what to do about Arrow.

To make matters worse, the loneliness that she hadn't felt since before she'd come to the Star trickled over her. She wasn't supposed to feel this here. She was supposed to be surrounded by peers, flying in one proud direction and striving for an end to the Second Cold War. Tears sprang forward, and she made herself whistle "Another One Bites the Dust"—that crazy old song Pippin loved to sing after one of her affairs flamed out.

Her faux nonchalance was heavy and hard to maintain.

And it crashed in a heartbeat.

Beneath the nearest tree, Tristan and Tanner watched Chase as one. Tanner appeared to be mid-swear, his back hunched sourly like a gargoyle. Chase sat up. They were talking about her. Clearly.

Tristan must have just told Tanner about her dad.

16

LETHAL CONE

Left Vulnerable

Chase wasn't nearly as swift on the ground as she was in the sky, but she knew how to maneuver. She caught Tristan's arm when he bent to tie his boots and hauled him so hard and fast through a door that the cadets he'd been walking with didn't even notice.

Once she was inside, she lost speed. She'd thought the room was a closet. Nope. It was a classroom. A big one. At least it was empty, although that just meant it echoed the slam of the door a little ominously.

"Hello, Chase," Tristan said, rubbing the arm she'd manhandled him by. "Let me guess, you want to talk to me?"

Her mouth was suddenly dry, but she twisted the front of his uniform in both fists and pressed him to the wall. "What did you tell Tanner?"

"What?"

"I saw you talking to him. You were looking at me. I'm not an idiot. I know what you told him." Tears spotted her eyes, but Chase only tightened her hold on his shirt.

Tristan looked even more boyish close up. "I didn't tell him anything. He was telling me about you."

"Wha…why?"

"Because I asked."

Chase let go but not without a small shove. "Why would you do that?"

"Because you saved my life a week ago, and now you won't make eye contact with me. It's a little strange."

Chase stared down his blue eyes pointedly, and something tightened in her chest. "Happy now?"

"Not really," he said. "You look like you're going to clock me."

"Well, you can't tell anyone…" She dug for the words but only succeeded in feeling the tears again. "What you heard…you can't just tell people…" Oh God, was he going to make her say it?

"I wouldn't." Tristan straightened his uniform. "I know a life-altering secret when I hear one."

"Um, all right." She wrapped her arms around her chest. Could she believe him? "Tell me why you were eavesdropping in the hallway after the JAFA debriefing."

"I wasn't eavesdropping on purpose. I was waiting for you." He unhooked his ponytail and finger-combed his hair. Chase thought it looked a lot softer than normal boy hair.

"Why were you waiting?"

"I wanted to talk to you. I didn't know then just how hard that is." Tristan showed his frustration a little, gritting his teeth when he swore. Chase found it strangely endearing that she'd gotten under his nerves. "I wanted to ask you not to tell anyone about how I kind of…went catatonic in the hallway. Remember?"

"I do."

He pushed his hands through his hair, and Chase wondered why that was supposed to be sexy. It looked reckless. Like he needed to get a hold on himself and every other part of his body was unsteady.

"Oh. I know why you're worried," Chase said, blinking hard as if the sun were dawning over the SMART Board and right into her eyes. "You think they'll take your wings. It's an act, isn't it? You want everyone to think you're nice so you don't get put on the Down List. That's why you're befriending everyone."

"I happen to think I am *nice*, at least under normal circumstances. When I'm not mourning the death of some of my best friends." Whatever light had come with understanding Tristan went out. He was warning her off, carefully choosing his words. "Maybe it's cliché to claim revenge, but I won't fail before the trials. I want my chance to face down Ri Xiong Di."

Chase nodded. She could understand vengeance. "I won't say anything, and I'll even help you hide it from Sylph. She's the person who you should be worried about. In exchange, you won't say anything about my—about Tourn. Do we have a deal?"

His eyes narrowed in a way that made her look away. "You think we need to use something against each other?"

"I think it's a smart way to play this. We're opponents." She paused and made herself look at him again. It was surprisingly hard. "I won't say a word. And I hope you do the same. No matter how much you want to beat me in the trials."

Chase started to leave, and he walked after her.

"Is that how someone would beat you?" he asked. She swung around, and the teasing smile he aimed her way was a bit of a surprise. "I was just planning to outfly you."

She twisted the front point of her hair. "I'd like to see you try, Tristan Router."

Chase paused at the door. Her plan had been to threaten Tristan and leave him too scared of her to tell anyone about Tourn. Now they were what? Flirting?

"We have class," she mumbled, surprised she was holding the door open for him and even more surprised that she was apparently inviting him to walk with her.

On the way, she began to talk about the Star. She couldn't seem to stop herself. "This class is for pilots in all the grade levels. We watch fighter flight tapes from as far back as World War I. It's cool."

"How many pilots are there?" Tristan asked. He walked as fast as she did, and she wanted to like him for it. Even Pippin couldn't keep up with her went she hit optimum hallway speed.

"About a hundred. A tenth of the cadet population. The rest are in specialized training. Engineers, navigators, ground crew, what have you. Flyboys are in the minority. We try to stick together."

When the conversation slipped away, Chase found herself close to a strange edge.

Ordinarily, she liked being around boys because they made

her darker thoughts vanish. But she wasn't getting that vibe from Tristan. He reminded her of JAFA—of her father's dismissive words—and yet he was still looking down at her with an easygoing smile. Weird.

They passed through one of the glass tunnels that connected the buildings to the Green. Outside, the snow whirled like the wind was blowing three ways at once. Chase began to patch together a question that ordinarily she wouldn't bring up—to ask Tristan if he worried about the other shoe dropping. About what might happen if Ri Xiong Di turned its foul intentions on the Star. Or her real question. The big one: did he blame her for what happened to JAFA?

But before she could put it all together, she remembered that tormented look she'd gotten out of him in the hallway, and she couldn't.

When they entered the Green, a group of her fellow juniors walked by and said hello to Tristan. Nothing to Chase, although one of them chanted her call sign. It had the effect of insinuating that Tristan was now *with* Chase…of course.

"Aren't you the star of the Star?" She winced at her lameness. "How do you find the energy?"

"I'm not as popular as you," Tristan said. "Nyx is a big deal. Everyone knows you."

"Everyone *thinks* they know Nyx," she corrected, a little stumped as to why she'd take the time to set the record straight.

"They like you a helluva lot better than Sylph."

"That's not a fair comparison. I'm pretty sure not even Sylph likes Sylph."

"Maybe not. Although, no one seems to know anything about you. You're a mystery," he said. "For example, when I asked people what part of the country you're from, I got three different answers."

"That's because I don't answer that question. They only know what I want them to know." Chase lost her amusement, remembering Tristan's tandem dark look with Tanner. She could only imagine what Tanner would say. Actually, she could imagine *exactly* what he would say. "I'm the heartbreaker. Is that what you're hearing?"

"I believe Tanner Won used the term *love vampire*."

"*Jesus Christ.*"

Tristan smiled, not that genial look he tossed to everyone, but a genuine smirk. She liked it a little too much, and it encouraged her to give him just a little more. "It's a bad habit at this point. I say I want to fool around. The crush in question agrees, but then they want more…"

Chase let him think she meant sex. Most of the time, her hookups *did* want sex, which she didn't mess around with. Pregnancy, STDs—no thanks. Of course with Tanner, sex wasn't what he wanted. "I'm not into more," she added a little late.

"Tanner said you forgot who he was. Walked right past him like he wasn't there." Tristan whistled. "That's tough stuff. He seems like a worthy sort of guy."

"He was different." Chase started to walk slower, feeling herself defocus. She remembered lying on Tanner's bed and telling him to kiss her, only for him to stare at her with eyes that stirred in warmth. He asked about where she came from. About her family and dreams. It wasn't until she started to want to answer him that she had to cut him off.

Chase had walked past Tanner in the hall, avoided his smiles, then his scowls, and then his heartbreaking glances. She had fed tears to the shower and ached to explain. Instead, she found the opposite of Tanner: Riot. A boy whose needs were upfront, like the kind of restaurant where the ketchup and mustard are always out on the table.

When she blinked back to Tristan, she couldn't quite tell how much she'd said aloud. He had that affect on her. And his eyes put Tanner's to shame. The blue was so focused. It was worse than warm; it was acceptance. But then maybe Tristan did this to everyone. Maybe that's why people liked him. After all, he'd already proved he was a social chameleon.

"You do realize this is the first real conversation we've ever had." She paused. "Why are we talking about my exes?"

"You brought it up."

A few freshmen passed, and Tristan bumped fists with two of them.

She was annoyed all over again, and it was much more familiar than being honest. "You think you know me because you watched my tapes at JAFA. But you only know how I fly. You don't know anything about me on the ground. Besides the fact that…"

She couldn't say it. Couldn't bring up her father.

Tristan eyed her. "I bet you think you know me because you've seen me fly a few times."

"I know you're—" Chase's voice cut off because they'd turned the corner. The auditorium door was open, and Riot stood cross-armed in the entrance. He looked from Chase to Tristan, and his face twitched.

"You stood me up last night." Riot was angry, but he forced a smile, which made her want to punch him.

"We already talked about this, Riot."

"Are you breaking up with me?"

"Did you think we were together? Wouldn't that involve dates or hand-holding or anything vaguely romantic?" Riot looked more hurt than she had intended, and she was overly aware Tristan was listening. "We're friends. Just no more...you know."

"Nyx," he said. Chase tried to pass him, but he tugged on her bag. She checked the desire to throw him off, not wanting to embarrass him. To make a Tanner of him. "I knew you were a tease when we started this, but—"

Tristan stepped closer. She expected to see some variety of testosterone overkill, but he was wearing that polite I-love-everyone look.

"Riot. I thought you were a RIO. I hear it's pilots only for this class."

Chase pushed Riot. "He's leaving."

Riot's eyes lit up for a fight. "You fuc—"

Sylph flew out of the auditorium. She got Riot by the ear and dragged him down the hallway. "Everyone can hear you blabbering at Nyx. Get your head together and get to class!" She shoved him and stomped back toward the door. "You," she snapped at Chase. "You fix him ASAP." Her braid swung as she whipped into the auditorium.

"Wow," Tristan said. "You guys definitely have more fun than we did at our academy."

"How's that?" Chase felt a creeping blush. "You guys didn't mess around?"

"There were thirty-four cadets at JAFA. Eleven girls. We were close like a family. I think it would have been like dating my cousins. I mean, consider the breakups…yikes."

Chase felt judged. No doubt Tristan was hearing that her breakups always ended badly. Tanner was among the worst, but others had become favorite stories in the rec room. There was Killian, who became a booze-in-his-water-bottle drunk. And Meg, who bitched Chase out so loud in the chow hall that even Ritz had overheard, spawning a super awkward conversation about "alternative sexualities."

The flash of heat in her face was giving away her embarrassment, which only brought about an even deeper flush. This was why she didn't like to talk to people. It was a steep fall from telling someone nothing—to everything. She had to push him back beyond her walls and out of her way.

Chase was shaking her head without realizing it. "I'm glad I'm American then. JAFA sounds like it would have been way too small for me."

"Good thing I'm no longer stuck there." Tristan's expression darkened. The recollection that his academy—his world—had burned came a little late. Chase saw the deeper side of him in that moment. The hard as steel pilot. Right before he blew it with a Sylph-quality insult. "I hear you'd find someone no matter the situation."

He was over the wall all right. He was light-years away in a blink. But then she'd known since that first moment she saw him that he knew how to hit the gas. Nonetheless, something dense sunk inside as she scrounged up a retort.

"True. I hook up with everyone. Except Canadians."

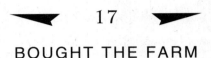

BOUGHT THE FARM

Killed in Action

The overhead lights were already off in the auditorium, and the only light came from the projector screen on the stage.

Chief Master Sergeant Black fussed with the media equipment while every pilot at the Star sat tall in flip-down chairs. Chase took a spot toward the back, more than a little aware that Tristan settled in her row, two seats over. She got the feeling that although they had just traded barbs, he still wanted to be pals with her.

No way.

Sylph sat a few rows down and threw a threatening look over her shoulder. Chase felt the girl's glare like a laser scope. Riot was now a problem. A problem that came with Sylph. He had been fun because she had assumed he wasn't like Tanner. He wasn't sweet or innocent. He wasn't trying to make her his girlfriend—but apparently he had been. How could she keep missing these signs?

"What are we going to watch today, Chief Black?" Baron, the Star's token idiot, yelled. "More Soviet MiGs? They were fun."

A few people laughed, but the chief ignored them as the screen turned a solid blue-green, what the ocean looked like from the onboard cameras beneath a wing.

Chase felt a chill she couldn't place.

"Today we're watching Taiwan in 2020," Black finally said.

The flyboys went mute; the room deadened. The Battle of Taiwanese Independence could do that—strike a whole room of jock pilots into silence. After all, it was the most infamous dogfight in the history of military aviation.

Chief Black cleared his throat. "On January 21, 2020, Taiwan declared independence from China without the support of Ri Xiong Di."

Several people booed, but Chase wasn't among them. Neither was Tristan.

He leaned across the seats between them with a whisper. "Ri Xiong Di translates to 'sun brothers.' It's supposed to imply divine right."

"I know. I went to elementary school," she returned. "Nice flat-hatting, Arrow." He leaned back with that annoyed yet engaged look that she actually enjoyed seeing on his face.

The chief continued. "On January 26, the U.S. stepped up to help Taiwan defend its freedom."

"The day of my grandmother's funeral," Chase said absently.

"What?" Tristan asked.

The video began, and no one could look away. Fighter jets flew in packs, the view switching between multiple onboard cameras. It felt like thousands of birds, but Chase knew from her history class that there were five hundred and seventy-nine fighter jets in that sky and eight hundred and twelve U.S. drones.

Chase's heart started to pound.

The distant horizon showed smoke above the tiny island of Taiwan, while from the south, a scarlet cloud appeared. The jets attempted maneuver after maneuver as the dogfight commenced. There was no sound, but Chase could hear the pilots like a nightmare looping through her thoughts. They were all calling Mayday. All asking what was happening.

All cursing prayers to an absent God.

In flashes that felt too closely edited, the tape proved what had happened in the sky that day: a complete loss. A mess of explosions and the swirl of crashing jets. The blue-green sea peppered with sinking, smoking heaps of American metal.

Chase's whole body hurt from gripping the armrests.

The screen went black, and her eyes found new focus on Kale's silhouette beneath the red glow of the emergency exit light. She hadn't seen him come in.

"You might be wondering why we're watching this tape," Kale said, walking toward the center of the room.

Someone sniffled. Chase was shocked to see Sylph off to the side, wiping tears. So the girl *did* feel things.

"We're watching this to remind you that although you are safe at the Star, no one is truly safe while we are at the mercy of Ri Xiong Di's control. Should they appear in our sky tomorrow, we would have to surrender. We would be absorbed into the New Eastern

Bloc's empire. The only reason it hasn't happened already is that they're still more focused on Europe, but…the hourglass is turned. We are all on a clock. This is why the military is experimenting with new defenses. New offenses."

"The Streakers," Baron threw in.

"Yes, and there are other attempts to fortify our borders. The Navy is developing new submarines while the Marines train for large-scale domestic defense. Everyone is preparing." He sat on the front of the stage before the screen, his hands folded in his lap. "Only three of you here fly Streakers right now, but you're all pilots. Someday soon, if the trials are successful, you'll all be flying Streakers. You'll all be facing red drones. What I want to ask you today is if you feel prepared."

No one answered.

Sylph's hand went up after a long moment. Her voice was wired. "Tell me why they didn't retreat. All those fighters just went after the red drones. It was suicide."

Kale checked the room. He found Chase. "Does anyone have an answer?"

Tristan spoke up. "The U.S. had never seen the drones before. The fleet snuck up from the Philippines, unveiling their superior speed, firepower, and maneuverability."

"Boola-boola," Baron tried to joke. Chase wanted to pummel him, but someone got there first. He yelped.

"Boola-boola?" Kale looked pained. "No pilot has ever been able to take down a red drone. Not one. None of our pilots survived that day. Those drones don't just aim for a jet. Their missiles lock on the *cockpit*, not the wings or engines."

"They're pilot-killing machines," Sylph said.

The room died once again.

"Nyx has seen the drones and lived to get away," Tanner said, turning in his seat to face her. His pride made her more uncomfortable than the general conversation. "Tell them."

Chase looked from Kale to the span of eyes in the crowd. "Wasps," she said. "I got too close to the d-line a few months back."

"What was it like?"

"Like nothing else mattered." Remembering them thrilled Chase, and not in a good way.

"Like we're already at war," Tristan added. Chase could tell by his tone that he'd seen them too. She fought the sudden urge to grab his sleeve like she'd done in the hallway before the debriefing.

"Cool," Baron said.

"Not cool," Tristan said at the same time Chase threw her pen at Baron. It connected with his stupid skull with a satisfying *thwick*.

Baron rubbed his head before turning a question at Kale. "But the drones can't overtake the Streakers, right?"

Kale didn't answer because there was no answer. No way to be sure. The U.S. had never captured a drone to chart its capabilities. Could the Streakers best one? They hoped and planned, but they sure as hell didn't know for sure.

Chase disappeared into her memory. She had been able to fly

away at Mach 4 the day she saw the drones, the fastest she'd ever flown, but she never bragged about it. That many drones *could* take down a Streaker, no matter how fast they could fly. If they all fired their missiles, there wouldn't be a direction to flee in.

That's what Pippin had said, and he was never wrong about these things.

"Cadets." Kale cleared his throat. "Pilots. It's important you know that a *cold war* only means our aggressions aren't public. But you should all bet your military-owned butts that things are always happening: in the sky, on the ground, at sea."

Chase could feel the heat of JAFA's blaze on her cheeks. Tristan stared at his boots. He didn't look like he was breathing.

"Where were you during the battle in Taiwan?" someone asked Kale.

"Still at the academy. It was my last semester." He didn't appear happy about the question.

"You know what though? Ri Xiong Di knows we're serious now," Baron said. "They got their fill a few months after Taiwan when Tourn got through with their drone base on the Philippines."

Chase crossed her arms to restrain her fists. Of course, an idiot like Baron would be a fan of her father's nuclear legacy.

"That bomb killed thousands of innocent Filipinos as well as destroying that fleet of red drones, Baron," Tanner yelled. No one hated Tourn like Tanner, which had always made Chase feel on the edge of disaster when they were together. "Tourn's nuke didn't stop anything. They had dozens of red drone fleets waiting."

Kale held up a hand. "Do not give General Tourn credit or blame for that bomb. He was operating under orders. That should be clear, despite the media's delight in blaming him."

Chief Black flicked on the lights. Chase was relieved this discussion wasn't going to devolve into a "let's bash Tourn" party. She appreciated that Kale had pointed out the hard truth about her father's past. Tourn had been a young hotshot pilot back in 2020. His higher-ups commanded him to fly over the Philippines and drop a bomb.

And he did it.

Everyone at the Star knew about following orders, and yet everyone hated Tourn. It didn't help that he had a reputation for being the absent lord of the Star—the one to hate for rules, restrictions, and leave time cuts. The one to blame.

Fault was a strong wind. She'd always felt it blowing in Tourn's direction, but she was starting to feel it on her own skin. Did her recklessness inadvertently cause JAFA's destruction? She glanced at Tristan. Did he blame her? As much as she didn't want to get friendly, she had to admit they had unfinished business.

"Wonder what it was like," Chase said, not realizing she was speaking aloud. "All those birds flying in. Outnumbered by the drones, a hundred to one."

"I imagine it was a nightmare. And then it was over." Kale clapped once and Chase jumped. "That fast."

All of Tourn's fellow pilots—his friends—had died in the sky over Taiwan that day. If he hadn't been on leave for his mother's funeral, he would have been up there with them. He would have been shot down. The five hundred and eightieth jet.

Then he never would have met Janice at a diner one night.

Chase swore her existence wavered like a match flame.

18

GRAYOUT

A Loss of Blood to the Head

The Streakers can travel twice the speed you know."

Chase almost tipped out of her chair. This was what she'd been waiting for since the moment the French Canadian engineer had appeared.

Dr. Adrien kept talking, but Chase was too busy thrusting her hand in the air, waiting to be called on. The elderly engineer didn't notice. She stood before a massive metal tube that looked like a gun scope with a grated vent at one end. The machine was so large that Chase could have walked through it.

The Streaker teams had been taken out of their usual classes for a special session. Chase couldn't help noticing that they were a dysfunctional group. Pippin scribbled, Riot ignored Streaker Team *Phoenix*, and Sylph shunned the whole room like she'd been elevated to a superior rank.

Chase waved her arm, leaning too far over the flip-top desk and dropping her notebook to the floor. The noise caught Adrien's attention, and Chase didn't hesitate. "*How* fast?"

"The speed is restricted to the pilot's ability to withstand intensely high G-force," Adrien said. Riot scrambled to pick up Chase's notebook, knocking heads with Tristan who had also leaned over to help. Tristan graciously handed Riot Chase's pen and—did Chase imagine it?—Riot *growled* at him.

That sealed it. Boys really were subpar humans.

Chase stole her things from Riot and turned her attention back to the lab-coated engineer.

"In short," Adrien continued through her strong French-Canadian accent, "how fast you can stand is how fast they will go." She walked to the larger end of the machine and opened a narrow door. Inside, Chase made out a pilot's chair and throttle.

"Up to this point, we have seen fit to keep a dampener on the Streakers' power so none of you accidentally go so fast that you lose consciousness. But it is time to 'open up' the engines, so to speak. And for that, we need to practice." She touched the huge metal machine. "This is the Star City Centrifuge, originally Russian-made. It will simulate high-g that you have hitherto only imagined. Speed equivalents to Mach 7, even 8."

"Wicked," Romeo said.

Chase couldn't keep down a smile. It *was* wicked. It was just about the coolest thing she'd ever heard.

"Akin to testing astronauts for takeoff, we need to gauge how well you handle prolonged G-force upward of, say, eight or nine. You have flown fast enough to feel more than that for brief moments, but today we will endeavor to keep you there for a significant duration." Adrien stopped by Tristan and put a hand on his shoulder. "You must keep your wits and fly."

Adrien flipped a switch, and a large view screen rolled down the wall. "You will have a monitor with a computer-generated landscape, and we will watch your progress here. Just pilots today. Tomorrow we will test RIOs."

"It looks dangerous," Sylph said.

Dr. Adrien waved her hand absently. "You might pass out. Or experience *grayout*. This is when the blood is restricted from the brain, creating a loss of colored sight followed by a complete loss of vision. Recovery is rapid in these situations, usually within minutes. Although, I *have* heard a few stories of brain aneurisms occurring."

Was Adrien teasing Sylph? The woman tightened her lips against a smirk, and Chase suddenly loved the old lady.

"You will control your blood flow with muscle tension in your extremities. It won't be easy, but unlike astronauts who can come in and out of consciousness under autopilot, we cannot have you blacking out up there."

"*Graying* out," Pippin corrected. Romeo and Tristan smirked, and Chase was a little surprised to see her RIO smile back at Tristan.

Adrien turned the centrifuge on. "I need a few moments to get it up to speed." It hummed to life slowly with increasing sound and vibration.

Romeo leaned over the aisle, staring a little too obviously at Sylph's chest. "I have a question for the U.S. Streaker jocks. Why two females? Shouldn't there be a girl and a boy to be more balanced?"

Chase put a hand over her laugh, readying for Sylph's response.

Sylph's eyebrow rose sharply. "Penises aside, *Romeo*, we competed for the Streaker project. Nyx and I are the best pilots at the academy. That's *why females*."

"You're not better than Arrow," Romeo countered. "Not faster anyway."

Before Sylph could bite back, Adrien asked for a volunteer. When Tristan was the first to stand, Sylph shot to her feet. "Like hell you will," she said to Tristan. She looked at Chase. "Nyx. This is your sort of thing. Snap to."

Adrien took Tristan's arm. "Mr. Router will do for starters. You'll all have your turn."

Sylph sat down hard enough to make her chair curse. The woman helped Tristan strap into the pilot's seat, peering through a small window at him once she shut the door. The centrifuge hummed loud enough to drown out the whole room. Adrien handed around the noise-canceling headphones that the ground crew wore. A projector lit up the large view screen on the wall, showing a digitalized sky with a woodsy horizon.

The simulation began.

Chase was mesmerized by the view from Tristan's cockpit. He turned fast and kept one wing a hint lower than the other. There was a state of ease in the way he flew, and she could sense her own brand of urgency…always wanting to go faster. She wondered if Tristan felt it like she did: an itch. A need.

Tristan was a fine pilot, and Chase watched Sylph realize it out of the corner of her eye. The girl looked bored at first, then skeptical, then stubbornly resigned.

Adrien notched nine-g before Tristan's flying began to show the strain. She gave advice through a small mic that must have propelled her voice into the roaring centrifuge. "Breath in short bursts," Chase thought she heard Adrien say. "Pull higher and throttle forward all the way."

Chase chewed her bottom lip. It was a rush to watch Tristan lift under the digital clouds and drive forward. It reminded her of their time together in the sky, and she wanted that again more than anything else in the world. His direction was tight and beautiful and *so fast*.

"That is Mach 5," Adrien said, powering down the centrifuge. "Nine times the weight of gravity."

Chase peeled her headphones off as Adrien opened the door. Tristan was slumped in his seat, his head hanging forward and his hair a mess. He was so deflated from his usual confident self that Chase felt an urge to help him. She didn't.

Romeo took Tristan's arm over his shoulder. Pippin got Tristan's other side, and the two RIOs lead Tristan to a seat on the floor against the wall.

Adrien was pleased. "If you have been in the air, you would have broken the manned airspeed record."

"Pippin," Sylph commanded. "Don't help him."

"Don't bark at my RIO, Sylph," Chase warned. Although it did feel slightly strange to watch Pippin pull Tristan's hair back from his neck and check his pulse. Pippin glanced at Tristan's pupils, and Tristan gave him a dazed grin.

"He's all right," Pippin said.

"Just tired," Tristan added.

Adrien hauled Sylph into the centrifuge next. Riot talked down about her the minute she was sealed inside, pointing out that she'd never broken Mach 3, let alone 5. He wasn't wrong; the centrifuge was barely revved up completely when she stopped flying and screamed to be released.

When Sylph got out, swearing and pushing the sweat into her hairline, she took Chase's arm. "Beat him." Her dark brown eyes were like staring down a missile. Chase suspected that something deeper was going on behind Sylph's rampant rivalry, but now wasn't the time to ask.

Chase nodded, but she didn't need Sylph's anger to propel her. She was already fueled by her own competitive streak. She strapped herself into the pilot's chair. The machine smelled like grease and metal.

Adrien leaned her head inside. "The best for last? You are the one who loves speed?" Chase liked the way Adrien said *speed*. Her accent hurried the word, made it taut and urgent.

She nodded ready.

Adrien shut the door with a rolling lock sound. Chase took in the metal circular coffin. It wasn't like piloting *Dragon*. The centrifuge was not slim and fitting like her cockpit, and the throttle and stick jabbed up through the floor beside her feet. But the view screen before her held a stretch of blue with a treed horizon…she could fly through that any day.

Chase dipped into it, taking off faster than the others. Her muscles went tight against the mounting pressure, and she leaned into it, breathing through her teeth. Her path was so fast that the woods blurred into an emerald scream.

Tristan had broken Mach 5. Chase was going to make it to six. He had to know she was just as tough and capable. That she would push herself until she passed out if she had to—flying was everything.

The pressure shrink-wrapped her skin to her bones, squeezed all the blood out of her fingers, her legs. The digital sky paled, a baby blue and then a hardly blue, while the trees lost all their green.

Chase heard Adrien's voice from far away. "Time to step down."

"More," Chase murmured. She pressed harder, and her thoughts about beating Tristan melted into her true motivation. *Dragon* would only be as fast as she could be, and she wouldn't let her bird down. She wouldn't let down Kale. Or the trials. Or her impossible-to-please father.

She'd prove she deserved to be here. To fly a Streaker.

The gray of her vision fuzzed at the edges, right before it washed completely white.

The Arctic wind blew, but Chase wasn't cold. She stood outside the Star on the runway, the ice world bright despite the dark. The dry

air sunk into her skin and made her feel more awake than she'd ever been.

Tristan appeared beside her, eyes on the horizon. He pointed. In the near distance, a snowstorm stirred up a deep purple before the whole sky yawned with fluorescent light. Tourn appeared where Tristan had been standing and shook his head.

"She's coming to," Romeo said, his accent stronger than usual. "Move back."

"You move back," Riot snapped. "She's my girlfriend."

"Of course she is, Riot," Pippin said, "just like she moonlights as a Ri Xiong Di spy."

"Not. Funny," Chase said. "Pippin?"

Her RIO's face appeared through the whitewash of her vision. "Did you G-LOC dream?" he asked. "Adrien said it could be vivid and bizarre, like tripping. You were laughing when you started to wake up. Kind of maniacally."

"It was creepy," Sylph said, looking down at Chase from what felt like a great height.

"I didn't dream," Chase lied. She tried to sit up, but hands held her shoulders. She realized her head was resting on folded legs, and she tilted back to see Tristan, upside down.

"You broke Mach 6." Tristan was steady, tuned in—and very close. His hair dangled over her face, and she resisted a catlike urge to bat at it.

"Let me up," she said.

"Not until you can see colors again." Adrien's voice floated down from a little ways away. She held out her hand. "What color is my ring?"

"Silver."

Tristan shook his head, his hair waving. "It's gold, Chase."

"Gold then. Let go." She tried to sit up, and his hands pushed back on her shoulders.

"Take ten good breaths," Adrien said.

Chase felt the way her stomach sank with each long exhale. She retreated to a deep place, remembering her dream. The storm opened like its violet sky full of crystal stars. And Tristan was there, standing next to her, his gaze sketched with sparks.

"Are you ready, Ms. Harcourt?" Adrien asked through her haze. "What color are Mr. Router's eyes?"

"Sapphire."

"With your eyes open please," Adrien said amid an explosion of snickers. Chase looked up fast enough to see Tristan's lips twist with amusement.

"Blue." She sat up, pushing everyone back. "They're goddamn blue." The world tipped this way and that as she fought to stay on her feet.

The view screen on the wall was blindingly orange, depicting fire. The smoking hole from her crashed jet. Chase went tight. Tighter than she'd been in the centrifuge. The digitalized wreckage mocked her—pointed out her huge error. She'd been willing to fly until she passed out, but she wasn't the only one who would take the brunt of stubbornness if this happened in the sky.

Sylph shook her head, while Romeo and Riot watched the floor.

Pippin gazed at the screen, the orange lighting up his cheeks. He gave a hopeless sort of shrug. "You killed us, Chase."

19

HOTAS

Hands-On Throttle and Stick

Chase was burning up and still a little sightless as she mumbled a bathroom excuse and fled the scene of her latest crime. She pushed into the locker room, and the bench wavered beneath her as she sat hard. *Crashed* was more like it.

Her breath came short and sharp as she relived the pressure of the centrifuge. How she'd wanted more, more. Wanted every pound of it until her body turned off like it had been unplugged. *Not good enough*, Tourn's voice barked through her thoughts, and not for the first time, she wondered whose spot she'd stolen in coming to the Star.

Maybe that cadet wouldn't have failed…

And *sapphire*? Christ. She wasn't going to live that one down anytime soon.

Her body felt about as hot as if she had been in a real fire. She yanked her shirt over her head. Her dog tags clinked, and she ran the metal links over the balled chain, holding on to the grating sound in the echo-tiled room. She didn't hear anyone come in.

"That's some scar."

Chase grabbed her shirt and held it over her bra. "What are you doing in here?"

"This is the boys' locker room." Tristan looked back at the entrance. "At least, there is a little man on the door."

Chase flashed hotter than ever. "My mistake." He wasn't turning away, and she didn't feel like bringing her shirt down so she could get it back on. She should have walked out, but she was too beat to even consider standing.

Tristan seemed to understand. He sat on the bench. "Can I ask you a question, Chase?"

She let her head fall forward, and sweat tingled as it slid down her neck. She didn't want his questions. "No."

He didn't accept that. "Why are you so hot and cold with me?"

She considered him for a moment. He was real right now, not overly pleasing or polite. Perhaps that's why she broke her standard evasive tactics. "Because you're two people. And I only like one of them."

"So you do like me, at least fifty percent of me." He was trying to make her smile. It was almost working. "I might have to tell Sylph on you."

"But then who would stop her from killing both of us the next time we hit the runway?"

"Come now," he said, his confidence peaking. "I haven't gotten up there with her yet, but I've seen enough tapes to know she can't keep up with us."

Chase was enjoying this a little too much. They hadn't been in the sky for a week now—the terror level was still too high—and the way Tristan said *us* made Chase flash to the way they'd flown together. Wing under wing and all that teasing.

"So." He pinched her arm softly. "Tell me about that scar."

She was in weird headspace. Warm and fuzzy and not herself. "I told Pippin it was from falling off my bike when I was a kid. I tell my hookups I got mugged."

"But those are lies?"

"Necessary alterations of the truth." It was a phrase she'd stolen from her dad's lexicon.

"You sound like a politician."

Chase ran her finger up the raised line that marred her from elbow to shoulder. The doctor who took the stitches out promised it would fade and settle with time. He was the real liar. The scar was as red and angry now as it had been five years ago.

The truth came slowly, dredged up from somewhere deep. She didn't want to give it voice, but Tristan already knew about her dad, so that made it so much easier. Too easy maybe.

"I had a run-in with some barbed wire," she said. "A long time ago."

"A long time ago? What're you, fifty-seven?"

"I was twelve." She folded her arms over her chest, a little more aware of what was under them than usual.

"Not too many twelve-year-olds have run-ins with barbed wire."

"Maybe in your family."

And there it was. Chase had brought Tourn into this. Would Tristan push to know more? He gave her a dark look that proved he was thinking about Lance Harold Tourn. Although she'd walked into this, she already regretted it. She reached for the first available distraction.

"Do you blame me for what happened to JAFA?"

He looked at her like she'd started to speak Chinese. "What?"

"If I hadn't gone after *Phoenix*, we wouldn't have been found out. JAFA would still exist."

He shook his head. "Adrien told me we were being watched all along. Our interaction might have sped things up, but we were already marked. It was a matter of time."

"Yeah, but if I hadn't gone after you—"

"*Stop.*" He hadn't yelled, but he might as well have. She could see him fighting with dark thoughts. She knew that battle intimately. Maybe he wanted to fight; it always helped her.

"Well, I feel guilty," she baited.

His face was red. "Like your dad feels guilty about the Philippines?"

She stood up. "Should he? He was doing his job. He *had to* do it!" Her words snagged on her conversation with Pippin. Apparently "had to" moments were genetic. She sat as suddenly as she had stood, but Tristan wasn't done.

He jingled her dog tags. "Why do you wear these all the time? I bet you sleep in them. At JAFA we only had to wear them in the air."

Chase elbowed his hand away. "We wear them because we're

a few heartbeats from enemy territory. Any day the drones could show up with a thousand missiles. I don't know about you, but I'd like for Kale to be able to ID my body when it's a blackened brick."

She'd gone too far.

Tristan fell into that damned place. Shock slid over him like cement. Sweat spotted his temples. He didn't seem like he was breathing. Maybe he saw JAFA burning. The explosions. The screams. Whatever it was, it had him by the soul and was twisting...

Chase shook his shoulder and tried his name. Nothing.

She wasn't good with boys, not in any real sense, but she knew what worked on Tanner and Riot. On all their predecessors. Chase turned Tristan's face and pressed her lips to his.

He pulled away instantly, stood, and pushed his forehead into a locker, making the metal wobble and bend. His breath was a mess, but he was moving. He was back. She called it a win.

Chase stood, swinging her shirt over her shoulder and trying to act cooler than she felt. In truth, she felt warm and crazy, like crying *and* kissing—which was an unsettling combo. It brought more feelings to her surface, and she let them out.

"I don't know how my dad feels about the Philippines. I never had the guts to ask." Tristan looked at her for too long. Pain seemed to puddle in both of them, between them. Then it lapsed into a sort of relief that was so strange that it made her want to lean on him.

He dug his hands into his pocket, but his sudden smile reached for her.

Voices skipped around the tiled room as Riot and Romeo entered.

"Nyx!" Riot took in Chase's shirtlessness.

"Relax. I was just getting some things straight."

Riot's face pinched with about six different emotions before he charged toward the back of the locker room. Romeo's eyes dove from her neck to her belly button. Chase winked and headed out, but not before seeing Tristan touch his lips with the back of his hand.

"I love this school," Romeo said. "Girls. Girls everywhere."

Chase stopped short of the door. The sound of smashing glass filled the tiled room, along with the howl of pain that couldn't be coming from anyone other than Riot.

The plastic pterodactyl was perched on the soap dish, judging her. Chase turned the faucet on hot. It scalded her knuckles and stole Riot's blood down the drain in a muddy-pink swirl.

"I could've used your help, Pip. It was nuts," Chase called through the bathroom door. "Riot kept yelling, and there was a piece of glass stuck in his middle finger. Romeo and Tristan had to hold him down so I could rip it out. He's getting stitches now." She dried her hands and stepped back into their room. "Sylph is going to murder me."

"You know I don't like the locker room," Pippin said. "Too much testosterone." He didn't look up from his notebook. "Only you could inspire a boy to punch a mirror, Chase."

"Yeah. That's hilarious."

"I'm not laughing." Pippin was in a weird mood, but what else was new?

Maybe it was time to talk about their feelings or whatever Pippin had tried to make her agree to a few days ago. She sat on the edge of his bunk. "Out with it. What's bugging you? It's the *Phoenix* team, isn't it? Everything has felt off since they got here."

"You're projecting."

"You're dodging," she snapped.

He shut his notebook and shoved it in the only drawer that locked. Chase heard it bolt when it closed. She reached deep for something to tell him, something that might make him open up. There was so much to choose from. Chase hoarded truth like it was jet fuel.

"I'm sorry I killed you in the simulation," she tried.

"You killed both of us," he corrected. "But it was just a game. That wouldn't happen in the air. I'd tell you before we hit the limit." Pippin was tying his bootlaces. The bow turned into a knot that fell apart as his fingers took a few wrong turns. Chase slipped to the floor and tied them for him. Pippin might have been able to speak four languages and draw the exact shape of every river in the world, but menial tasks sometimes stumped him. It was something she loved about him.

"Tristan knows about my father," she finally said.

He held his hands up, palms out. "I didn't say anything."

"He overheard me and Kale talking after the debriefing." Chase finished tying his boots, and he used her forearm to pull her up. They were standing close, and although Pippin had looked moody and sad for days, he now wore a smirk.

"Tristan won't say anything. That guy has got the warm squishies for you."

"No, he doesn't," she said. "He's trying to be my friend. It's…awkward."

"You didn't see him bust into the centrifuge when you blinked out. He got his head right on your chest to listen to your heart. I pointed out that the wrist has a pulse, but he seemed rather driven. Come to think of it, he might have been sneaking a feelsky." Pippin mimed grabbing a pair of boobs.

"Pippin!" She hit his arm hard enough to make his humor sour.

"Don't act surprised, Chase. Everyone gets into you at some point. You're a beautiful disaster, and apparently that's irresistible." He crossed the room and held the door open. "I'll never understand my sex's obsession with inaccessible love." A strong feeling backfired in his words, and he stared at the ground.

"Love is pointless, Pip."

"Should I go tell Riot how pointless his mangled hand is?"

"*Hey.*"

He scrubbed his wavy hair. "I'm sorry. But you kind of ask for it, you know?"

This was her chance to find out what was plaguing him. "What do you…" It took her so long to put the words together that he arched an eyebrow at her. "If you're so…" This wasn't working.

"We always ate together," she managed. "Until the Canadians arrived, and now you eat with them or in the room. Are you mad at me about something?"

Pippin's face was a blank wall. "My problems have nothing to do with you."

Chase couldn't stop herself from comparing this exchange to opening up to Tristan in the locker room—the way they'd traded their feelings until it felt, well, good. This felt terrible. The more Chase spoke, the more closed down Pippin became.

"I need more space than usual," he finally said. "You know how that is."

He left, and the slam of the door made her jump backward.

20

UP TO SPEED

What's at Stake

Chase headed to the chow hall alone. She swallowed hard, but the feelings wouldn't go down. Pippin was…upset about something. Did it have anything to do with the Canadians?

With Chase?

She caught herself searching the crowded cafeteria for Pippin. She watched for him in the food line, swathed in loud conversations and moving toward the buffet a few steps at a time.

Until Sylph stepped in front of her.

Instinct kicked in. Chase held her tray before her face.

"You've finally done it. You've broken my RIO. His hand at least." The blonde sighed and pushed down her shield.

"Are you going to kill me?" Chase watched Sylph's expression morph into an assassin's smirk. "Oh God, you really are going to kill me."

"I should," she said. "But I've been making a study of you, and I think you can't help it. You're drawn to people only to push them away. It's like a disease."

"Better step back, Sylph. I might cough on you."

"There was even a moment freshman year when we could have been friends, but you had to be so *bizarre*."

"You mean the forty-two seconds you were my roommate before you demanded to switch?"

"I don't remember it that way." Sylph plucked a few grapes off the fruit bar and popped them in her mouth. The chow line moved forward, and Chase elbowed Sylph out of the way. Sylph didn't seem bothered, though, and her calm was a lot more frightening that her usual fervor. "Nyx, I've decided you should use your unhealthy skill set on our new enemy."

"Excuse me?"

"You should slay Arrow. It's obvious he likes you."

"You want me to seduce him? On purpose?" Like Pippin, Sylph must have read into the way Tristan pulled her out of the centrifuge. "You've got the wrong idea, Sylph. Nyx was the Daughter of Chaos. Not the goddess of lust."

"Like you even have to try. Just do that thing you do. Lead him on…and then…" She lifted the corner of Chase's tray and let go so that it slapped down on the food-serving cart like a gunshot. Three people in line spun around until they saw it was Sylph—which made them turn back even faster.

"Why do you hate them so much?" Chase asked. "I've never seen you so motivated. Except when you were trying to beat me during the pilot ranking." Sylph had been merciless in those days. They hadn't known then that there was more than one Streaker, and Sylph wanted it so badly that she did everything outside of poison Chase. When Kale revealed that the top *two* pilots would be chosen, Sylph had backed off like a tiger receding into the jungle.

Something clicked. "Sylph, why don't I go ask Kale if they're going to cut one of us? Then you don't have to do this 'snake in the grass' thing."

"Maybe I like being a snake." Sylph's face was sly and leaning in. "So what do you think about seducing the Canadian?"

"I think you've finally started drinking your peroxide shampoo."

"I'm not the one getting summoned by the shrink. Kale asked me to pass this on." Sylph tucked a slip of paper in the front of Chase's uniform and stole her tray, hip-checking her out of the line. "Oh, and Kale said no ducking out if you want to fly the hop tomorrow."

"We're flying tomorrow?" Chase flooded with relief. "Thank God."

"You better thank Dr. Ritz if you want to fly. And bring her a cake. That woman has wanted to put you on the Down List since the moment you arrived."

"That's because I don't take her crap." Chase headed to the psychiatrist's office. Without flight in her veins, she was all wound up, and spinning her wheels against Crackers actually sounded like fun.

◉◉◉

Chase banged her way into Dr. Ritz's office without knocking. The psychiatrist sat at a small table with Tanner of all people. He looked shirtless for a hot minute, but that was only Chase's memories making a cruel play.

"Crackers. You wanted to see me?"

Dr. Ritz touched her forehead like it pained her. "Wait in the hall please."

Tanner picked up his bag. "I'm okay." He caught Chase's eye. "I'm done here." He shut the door right before she remembered his *love vampire* reference. She should have snapped her teeth at him.

Ritz stood by her desk. "Chase Harcourt, you get your way once again. Have a seat." This was always the tricky start to Crackers's system. There were only two spots in her office: a couch with a box of tissues on the armrest where the psychiatrist could sit beside her or the small table where Crackers could stare her down, eyeball to eyeball.

Chase chose the chair at the table where Tanner had been.

Ritz sat opposite her. "I've called you in because I spoke with Garret Powers in the infirmary earlier."

"Who?" Chase asked.

"Your boyfriend."

"Try again."

"Your *ex*-boyfriend then. The one who will bear scars from you for the rest of his life."

"Yikes." The woman had a gold star in melodrama. "You mean *Riot*. We were never dating. Just friends. With some benefits."

"There are no call signs here, Chase Harcourt. In this room, we use our birth names."

"Wrong again, Ritz. I wasn't born with this name." In her excitement to show up the shrink, the truth had slipped out.

The tiny woman sat up and rifled through Chase's file. Christ. Did she keep it on hand at all times? "Your last name was Tourn until you were twelve. Let's talk about that."

"Oh, *let's.*"

"I should remind you, Chase Harcourt, that you need my approval to keep your wings."

"Bully," Chase murmured. She relented with a breath big enough to let the truth out fast. "Janice thought it would be easier to get money from my dad if I had his last name. What she didn't factor in is that after their one-night mambo, he'd all but disappear." Chase laughed emptily. "When she finally tracked him down and learned who he was…let's just say she spat a few choice four-letter words."

Chase debated telling Ritz about the look on Janice's face when she had watched Tourn on TV, confirming to the whole world that he had dropped the nuclear bomb on the Philippines.

"Tell me about your father," Ritz said.

"Nothing to tell. I knew him for one summer when I was twelve, and I haven't seen him since. It was his decision to change my last name to my mother's, and it was the best parenting move he ever made."

"Because your father has a reputation." Ritz clicked her pen. "He wanted to help you avoid that."

"Crackers, *I* have a reputation. My father has a body count."

"Interesting." She lifted her fine wire glasses to the top of her head. "Let's talk about your reputation."

Chase's seat was still warm from Tanner's butt. "Tanner was complaining?"

"What is it you think he might be complaining about?"

"I used to like him. I changed my mind. He didn't take it so well." Chase crossed her legs. Uncrossed them. Folded them beneath her.

"And this has happened with several other boys. At least four I'm aware of."

"Don't forget the girl," Chase half-joked. "Curiosity and all." Ritz's frown bent severely, and Chase felt the demarcation line of dangerous territory. "Are you patterning my love life?"

"Do you see a pattern?" Ritz asked. Chase had admitted that much to Tristan, but like hell would she give Ritz the same clearance level. She played with the front point of her hair while the psychiatrist continued. "Have you felt any deep connection to the boys—the people you've become intimate with?"

Chase cringed. *Intimate* was the word adults used to make her feel guilty. "I say, 'kiss me.' They kiss me. It's that deep. And I only kiss, no matter what Riot says. I'm no skank." Crackers's face went canvas at the word. "I get a little skin to scatter heavy thoughts and—" She cut herself off.

"So it's about escape," Ritz said, and Chase hated how close she'd flown to the mark. "And you feel guilty about hurting these boys. That's good. That's the burden of caring."

Chase opened her mouth to say that she couldn't care less, but that's not what came out.

"I'm careless."

"With whom you date?"

Chase really didn't want to talk about this, but she was cornered now. "I don't date. I sidle up to someone. Wait to see if they like me. Then when I don't feel the same, I go my own way. That's normal teenage stuff."

The psychiatrist grimaced. "There is no *normal* when it comes to teenagers. That's what I've learned working here."

Chase rubbed her face and switched tactics. "You know what I need? Speed." Ritz's eyes got huge. "Not drugs, Crackers. I need to get up in the air. It...centers me. I haven't been skyward since the Canadians party-crashed."

"We should talk about this new addition to the academy. How do you feel about them?"

"I feel like they're here," Chase said. "And I feel bad they lost their academy. If that happened to me..."

Ritz seemed pleased. "The makeup of this school is very much like a family, and the introduction of this team changes things. Like when a parent remarries or has another child."

"Might want to choose a different metaphor," Chase said. "I don't have parents."

The psychiatrist squinted at Chase's file. "You do have parents. Your mother—"

"Oh no. Janice is a mother, but she's no parent. One of the

first times I came in here, you said, 'You give birth to become a mother, but you have to raise a person to become a parent.'" It had been one of the things that made Chase want to trust Dr. Ritz. Badmouthing Janice was the fastest way to Chase's heart.

"You listened to me?" Crackers looked entirely too touched.

"Well, it's true, isn't it? I don't have parents. I have the Star. Kale. *Dragon*." *Pippin*. For whatever reason, her RIO's name stuck in her throat.

"Have you thought about what the Star will be like after the trials?" Ritz asked. Chase stared as the doctor continued. "If the Streaker project fails, the jets will be scrapped and you will fly the older models."

Chase closed her eyes. The older fighters sucked. "The Streakers aren't going to fail." They had to pass. They had as much to prove as Chase did. It was one of the reasons she loved her prototype jet so much.

Ritz continued. "If they pass, there will be dozens of Streaker pilots. You'll be one of many. Of a fleet. Have you thought about that?"

Chase scowled big-time, turning over a new question. Would Kale still care about her when there were dozens of Streaker pilots? Would he still find her antics clever? Not likely.

"Let's switch gears." Ritz produced a piece of paper and drew a shape. "This is the heart's circle."

"Is it made by leprechauns?" Chase asked. Ritz gave her a cool eye and pointed to the drawing. It reminded Chase of an engine—a gaping hole that stole wind and spat scorching vapor in its wake. "I stopped putting stock in love when I was a kid, Ritz."

"Think of it as a trust circle then. Ask yourself: 'Who is in my circle? Who is close and important to me? Who do I trust with my secrets?' Write these people in, and I promise you'll realize that those you don't seem connected to are already central in your life."

Chase surprised herself by being angry. No. Furious. "That is the craziest thing you've ever said, Crackers! You think I should write down some names and people will magically matter to me? I do know *how* to care, you know. I care about flying. About the trials. If I don't win, they'll scrap *Dragon*, so believe me, I *care*."

Dr. Ritz was quiet for a long moment. "Your flying is not a matter of winning or losing. I keep having this conversation with Leah Grenadine—you teenagers need to put everything in terms of competition. These trials are about improving national security, Chase Harcourt. They're for the future of the Air Force."

Chase rubbed her neck. "Never pegged you as a patriot, Crackers." The woman gave Chase a sharp look. "I mean, Doctor."

"Keeping your eye on the *real* ball might be what you need. Especially if you can't see what's festering at your core."

Chase winced. That sounded graphic. "Right. I'll keep doing what I always do. Talk about a freakin' circle." She didn't wait to be dismissed. She headed toward the Green, taking a few minutes in one of the glass tunnels that connected all the buildings at the Star.

High above, the yellow-green northern lights writhed against a black sky. Chase blew hot breath on the glass and drew a circle in the fog. Then she wrote *Pippin* in its center.

It didn't work.

It didn't make her realize that she trusted him. That he was "central in her life." It only reminded her of his distant-blank expression—and his recent demand for space.

Chase smeared the circle and name away a little too forcefully, making the glass wobble in protest. If she were being honest with herself, these days Pippin felt more like a stranger than her best friend.

21

PLAYMATES

Friends for the Mission

Chase strode into the hangar with her helmet under her arm, all but jumping to get into the air. The rest of the Streaker teams were standing before the brigadier general, and she fell in line with nothing more than an annoyed look from Sylph.

Kale touched *Phoenix*'s wing while he spoke. "The original plan was to have the American Streaker teams dogfight with *Phoenix*. The Canadian pilots had the advantage of having studied Harcourt and Grenadine's flying patterns. Should the Streakers pass the military trials, it will only be a matter of time before the New Eastern Bloc either steals or duplicates the technology. We need to understand how the jets perform against similar machines."

He looked from Tristan to Chase. "But since you have all had a taste of each other's styles, we've seen fit to change the trials. You'll be facing a different sort of combative test. Not even I know what it will entail"—he shot a look at Chase—"so don't pester me."

Kale continued. "One element of the trials will be based on your maneuverability at high speeds. This might be the most important factor in determining whether or not the Streakers will be accepted as a large-scale military investment, particularly because we still don't know the redlining speed of the drones."

Chase raised her hand. "Permission to speak, General?"

"If you have to, Harcourt."

"I do." She glanced at Sylph. "Are you taking one of the Streakers out of the trials?"

Kale narrowed his eyes. "Who said that?"

Pippin was looking around like he wasn't interested. Like he hadn't been the person to tell her exactly that. It made Chase redden from the neck to the cheeks. "No one. It just felt like that's the way things were headed."

"You're all factored into the trials," the brigadier general said. "All three teams."

Sylph's relief showed in the way her shoulders released. Tristan was at the far end, his hair tied back tight and his eyebrows sunk into a *v*. He looked distinctly uneasy.

Kale noticed Chase's stare and snapped his fingers in her face. Romeo and Pippin laughed together, while Sylph looked pleased. Riot examined his bandaged hand.

Tristan didn't notice. He really *was* out of it.

"What's the hop today, General?" Sylph asked.

"You three are going to…" Kale sighed. "The easiest way to explain this is that you'll be racing. But it's not a competition."

"*Buuullshiiiit*," Pippin sang. Everyone laughed.

Kale's eyes couldn't hide their delight. "It's a bit of a competition,

Breaking Sky

but we're collecting speed records, not ranking you. Stay safe but also let loose." A whoop came from several of them, including Chase. It was exactly what she needed: to get in the air and open up. "The three of you will be linked via shortwave radio. It won't connect you past a few dozen miles, so stay close. It should be clear from hacking."

"*Espérons que,*" Romeo muttered. Pippin muttered something back in French. Apparently her RIO had found his nerd brother in Romeo. It stung a little. She wasn't used to seeing him joke with anyone other than her.

"One more thing," Kale said over the chatter. "Stay out of the gray zone. If you begin to lose your colors, throttle back immediately." He looked at Chase again. "The satellite restrictions needed to fend off Ri Xiong Di's overrides also mean that we cannot control the jets remotely. Should a team lose consciousness…" He didn't have to say it. They all knew the "crash and burn" gist. "Is that understood?"

Chase nodded.

"Trust each other up there. Work together. *Help* each other. That's an order. Dismissed."

Everyone except Tristan and Chase climbed the ramp stairs into their cockpits. Tristan was stiff. He took a little too long getting his helmet on, and Chase secured the strap for him.

"You ready?"

He didn't respond. His eyes were glassy and downcast.

"Don't make me kiss you again," she muttered.

He looked at her, his expression beyond serious. "Don't play with me, Chase."

"I was *trying* to help you." She avoided his apology by slamming her helmet over her ears. "Don't care. Just fly."

Chase pushed past him, her chest strangely hot. Tristan headed to *Phoenix,* and Kale touched her shoulder. He had been watching them talk.

"Did you notice Powers, Harcourt?"

"Riot?" She couldn't stop herself. "What? That he's a child?"

"He needed a few stitches. You wouldn't have anything to do with that, would you?"

"Oh yeah. I hypnotized him and made him punch a mirror."

"I don't doubt it," he said too knowingly. Had he been talking to Ritz? Christ. Chase panicked, looking everywhere but at the brigadier general. "Harcourt, I do try to keep my head above the teenage gossip of the academy, but there are certain lines we should observe." He cleared his throat. Chase rushed with embarrassment, feeling like she was about to get the Star's version of a sex talk. "There are some concerns…"

"Spit it out." Chase pulled too hard on her leather gloves and gave herself finger wedgies.

"I'd rather you not get *friendly* with Router."

If she'd thought she was red before, she was scarlet now, and Kale's neck flushed to match. "Right." She hurried to her cockpit.

"What was that about?" Pippin asked as she swung into her seat. She fastened her harness. "A dose of mortification."

"What?"

"Like you care," she muttered. She switched the mic connect between their helmets and revved the engines. *Dragon* was warm and ready. It was exactly what she had been missing this past week. It would help her get past everything.

Pegasus headed onto the runway, followed by *Phoenix*. Chase left the hangar last, watching Sylph shoot into the air, her whole being glittering with impending lightness.

"Ready for the speed of heat, Pippin baby?" A little ire slipped in with her zeal.

"Always, Nyxy muffin," he deadpanned while messing with his controls. Someone chuckled over the radio, and Chase bristled.

"What's so funny?" she demanded.

"Nothing, honey badger," Tristan said. Romeo laughed as *Phoenix* swept off the runway. Maybe Tristan was trying to tease her out from under his cold snap a few minutes earlier, but it wasn't working. Especially after Kale's awkward warning.

"Nyx. Quit flirting," Sylph cut in from roughly two thousand feet. "Time to fly."

Chase gritted her teeth. *Dragon's* throttle hummed in a new, exciting way. She closed her eyes and tried to mold her thoughts around the vibrations. She needed to sink into a place where Crackers wasn't after her wings. Where Riot hadn't confirmed Tanner's colorful title for her.

She opened her eyes and set her sights on *Phoenix*.

Her hands tightened on the stick and throttle until each knuckle strained. *No worries, Kale.* There was no way she was getting *friendly* with Tristan. Chase was going to knock him out of the sky. The poor boy—he had no idea.

①④①

A half hour later, *Dragon* and *Pegasus* flew wing to wing before a stretch of Canadian wilderness. The pines undulated as the land phased into low mountains. Silvery lakes spotted the woods.

Phoenix was nowhere in sight, having lagged back not long after takeoff. Chase might have thought something was wrong, but before she could worry, Arrow met them at the coordinates, announcing his arrival over the radio.

"My country," he said.

"Think they get Wi-Fi out here?" Pippin asked, and Chase snorted.

"Let's get this over with," Sylph said. "They want to see which one of us is the slowest. As if we don't already know." Chase felt for Sylph. She *was* an amazing pilot, but speed was not her strong suit, and the Streakers were becoming increasingly about just that. "Who's going to count off?"

"Let Pippin do it," Romeo said. "We've seen his file. You guys know his IQ is like eighty points higher than the rest of us put together?"

"We know," Sylph and Riot droned together.

"If anyone's qualified to count from ten, it's him," Romeo added.

"In what language?" Pippin's voice cracked, and the radio went full volume with laughter. Romeo added a few words in French, and Pippin quipped back.

"All right already," Chase said. "Pippin, call it."

Pippin counted down, and Chase glanced at *Phoenix*. Tristan's face was lost behind his visor and mask, but he was looking her way, and she could almost feel the heat behind his eyes.

She had to beat him.

Chase centered her breath and locked her vision straight ahead. A thousand miles due northeast had been cleared of all military and commercial flights. Enough space for a serious drag race. And the new throttle was so sensitive...

Pippin called three, two, one—and Chase shot forward. The press of gravity restrained her for the briefest of flashes before she broke forward, hitting Mach 1...2...3. Sylph fell behind. Her RIO's breath came loudly through his teeth. Tristan stayed too close, his nose under her left wing for a few hundred miles that passed like heartbeats.

"Hey, you have to warn me before you hit the gas like that," Pippin said. "I need to get ready."

"Then be ready," she snapped. There were so many elements out of her control—Tourn, the trials, Ri Xiong Di, and her best friend's increasing distance. But what she could do was fly, beat Tristan, and prove she was not only good enough to fly a Streaker, but also the best pilot among the three of them.

She hit Mach 4, feeling like she was about to turn into a solid strip of silver light. The pressure made her tremble while the land below turned a green bleeding color. Fear trickled through her, and her body agreed. The monochrome crept in.

"I'm feeling pretty gray, Nyx. Talk to me," Pippin said.

"Oh, now you want to talk." She hit the throttle even harder.

"Nyx!" Pippin shouted. "This is too much!"

"So tighten up," she yelled. Tristan could go faster than this—he'd proven it in the simulators. She set herself tighter. Pippin would just have to come back when it was all over.

"Stand down, *Dragon*," Arrow said. "Your RIO is calling Mayday."

"Shove off, Arrow." Chase flicked off the shortwave. "Don't make me lose this, Pip."

"*I'm* losing it!" Pippin yelled. "Chase, please! *Please!*"

Phoenix dropped away at that moment, falling back so swiftly that he vanished.

She'd won.

Chase backed off the throttle, realizing how hollow her vision had become. How swilled and tilted her mind felt. She sucked oxygen, hung her head, and swore in a long, slow string.

"I gather you're mad at me," Pippin said.

Chase turned them back toward the Star. "Mad? Try disillusioned," she said. "That's one of those fancy words you like."

"You're a piece of work, you know that?"

"I do." She hit the throttle without warning, making him grunt.

22

RED FLAG

Mock Air War

The flight home was ugly-silent. Kale met them in the hangar to download the footage from their onboard cameras, and Chase came down from her cockpit last. Maybe she should have been walking tall, but the victory didn't feel right.

She was still too riled to make eye contact or to even try to talk to Pippin, but then, he wasn't hanging around. He took off toward the locker rooms in a hurry. Without Pippin to be angry with, embarrassment knifed its way in. Making her feel pinned down.

"Nyx won," Tristan said to Kale.

"Like hell," Romeo chimed in. "She messed up!" But Tristan put a hand on his shoulder. They left arguing.

"What was that about?" Kale asked Chase.

She shrugged and walked off after Sylph.

"Bravo Zulu," Sylph said to her, more command than compliment.

Chase watched team *Phoenix* disappear around the side of a helo. "What was Romeo complaining about? I didn't mess up."

"Arrow let you win." Riot's voice was sharp. "We know he can stand to go faster than Mach 4. The simulators proved that."

Chase got so angry so fast that it was a wonder she didn't punch everyone. "Why in the world would he let me win?"

"Don't make me spell it out, Nyx." Sylph scoffed. "Arrow let you win because he wants to…" She made wet kissing sounds. Chase sprinted at her, and Sylph laughed her way out of the hangar, outrunning everyone on her stork legs.

① ④ ①

Chase couldn't cool off. She headed to the rec room to play pool, but the only person who wasn't watching the main event was Sylph. Ugh. The girl couldn't keep from scratching if her wings depended on it.

Sylph whacked at the cue ball, sending it spinning against the sides pointlessly before it sunk in the side pocket. "This isn't my game."

"No shit." Chase's anger was barely in check. Her heartbeat had never really come down after her spin out in the sky, and she closed her hand on her stick over and over like she was trying to pump her pulse into a casual rhythm.

All matters were made worse by the distraction of Romeo and Tristan facing off at the flight simulator game in the back, a sizable crowd surrounding them. Chase watched Tristan's bird dip and double cross Romeo's, flipping him out of the sky to an assault of cheers. Fistfuls of money were slapped around. Pippin had a scratchpad—organizing bets, no doubt.

"Arrow didn't let me win." Chase leaned over the table and took a swift shot, knocking the red ball into the side pocket and sending the cue spinning off in the opposite direction. "He didn't."

"All evidence to the contrary," Sylph snorted.

"If he let me win, then I hate him. And if I hate him, then I have to take him out."

Sylph smiled thinly. "I've never heard you go mobster before. It suits you."

One of the simulated jets crashed, and the crowd booed.

Chase took a shot and missed everything she was aiming for. Pool wasn't her game either. It was Pippin's. "Well, I'm not going to seduce him on purpose, so you can let that one go."

Sylph jumped up on the edge of the green felt table and crossed her long legs. She glanced at the crowd, as distracted by them as Chase was. "Just ask him if he let you win," she said. "Here's your chance."

The simulator game ended with a roar of cheers and groans. Romeo jogged over, a grin splayed across his caveman cuteness. He had Pippin in a headlock, and Chase's RIO was practically twisted upside down. "I won," Romeo said. "Let Arrow have the credit for the jet, but I can beat anyone at a computer game."

"Your RIO *beat you?*" Chase asked Tristan, but he ignored her. He was talking with an ebony-skinned sophomore, the girl who, according to Riot, had legs that "didn't quit." Chase felt her anger rise up as he turned his back.

The rec room was hotter than it had ever been. People were everywhere, calling out to Arrow and Romeo, and endlessly laughing. Chase chucked her cue stick across the green felt table, whacking Sylph in the butt.

"Arrow," she yelled. Tristan held up a finger at her, telling her to wait until he was done talking.

A finger.

She grabbed his hand and twisted it, tucking his arm behind his back. Then she leaned into his sweaty hair and asked, "Did you let me win?"

"Yes."

Chase was numbed by his answer. When he swung around and broke her hold, she collided with the edge of the pool table. He stepped way back, revealing a new quiet that proved the whole room had tuned in to their conversation.

"Why?" Chase wanted her question to sound hard, but it wavered. It felt fragile and damning, and an anger spasm filled her chest. She glanced at Pippin and found him looking distinctly mortified. Good.

Sylph stepped in between them, catching Tristan by the shoulder of his uniform. "*Hey,*" she commanded. "Take it to the mat."

"I don't want to spar with her," Tristan said.

"At the Star, we don't let fights turn into feuds. You and Nyx have to work this out. *Now.*"

A few minutes later, a serious crowd—what felt like the whole academy—surrounded the boxing ring. Sylph ducked under the rope, tightening Chase's gloves. "I don't know what's going on between you two," the blonde said, "but I love it."

Chase squeezed her fists, feeling the worn-through spots on the padding. "Advice?"

"Yeah," she said. "He's going to cream you. Don't let him."

"That's your advice?"

"When we spar, you let me hit you like you'll be able to shake anything off. A good slug from Mr. Chivalry will knock you out. Stay light. Dodge."

Pippin stepped close. "Chase. I'm going on the record as saying this is suicide."

"Noted." Chase stared into his boyishly cute face. "You're next."

His laugh was short and dismissive. "Like I'd get in the ring."

"I forgot. You would never fight with me." Tears burned at the edge of her eyes, and he could see them.

Pippin chewed his bottom lip and shrugged. "It's not worth it." She tried to turn her back, but he grabbed her arm. "Tell me why *this* is worth it. Why prove he can beat the bones out of you?"

"Because I can take it," she snapped. "And he should know that." Tristan should know she wasn't some weakling who would pout if she lost. She could take whatever he could dish out, *including* being beaten by him—if that had to be the case.

Pippin tried to catch her arm again, but she pulled away. He ducked out of the ring.

Chase watched Tristan from across the mat while Sylph worked her shoulders like a trainer. Tristan's beautiful sophomore stood behind him on the other side of the rope, and Chase just about threw up when the girl finger-combed his hair and spoke into his neck. Tristan nodded, rolling up his sleeves to show off notable arms.

Chase hoisted a sigh. She'd spent too much energy trying to ignore his body, his blue-eyed stare. The way his sharp cheekbones juxtaposed an entrancing mouth. His elements added up into one striking truth: the boy was magnetic.

"Wake up, Nyx." Sylph gave her a quick slap. "You're staring Arrow down, and not in the 'I'm going to kill you' way."

"He's hot. I'm not imagining that, am I?"

Sylph grimaced. "He is. It's an unfortunate reality. Long hair on a boy has about a ninety-eight point two percent chance of being ugly. But he's somehow weaseled himself into the remainder."

"Great. At least I'm not crazy."

"We're not ugly either. Keep that in mind." Only Sylph could pull off blatant immodesty. "I don't like to admit that you rock this sort of badass girl look. But. You do."

"Did you just give me a compliment?"

"You get one for the year. Hold on to it." Her brown eyes narrowed on Chase, and she leaned in close. "I can't believe *he let you win*. That's really got to burn."

Chase smacked her gloves together. "I'm already keyed up, Sylph. Let me take him."

Sylph ducked out of the ring, hitting the tiny bell on the wall as she passed. Tristan stopped talking to his fan club long enough to give her a heavy look. It swung between apology and pity. Was *that* why he'd let Chase win? He felt sorry for her?

"Rules?" he asked.

"None. Say 'uncle' when you can't take any more."

"Done."

Chase found out fast that he wasn't afraid to hit her. His first punch grazed her shoulder. Threw her into a spin. She came back and connected with his jaw, happy to hear a grunt. Pushing forward, she aimed for his guts. His nose. She went after all his soft spots until she was winded, which seemed to be exactly what he was waiting for.

He popped her in the face. She fell, and he pinned her chest to the mat, his body against her back. The room was a mutiny of voices.

"We don't have to be enemies, Chase." His breath was in her ear. Raspy and tight—the way boys gasped when kissing went beyond lips on lips. She closed her eyes and focused on the fight, but something deep responded to his closeness and the very personal press of his weight. This wasn't the time...not in the slightest.

"You let me win," she insisted, more to keep herself angry than anything else.

"You could have crashed. You ignored your RIO. You wouldn't have stopped until both of you were knocked out, as good as dead." She tried to twist free, but Tristan pulled her arms tighter, pushed her harder into the mat. "Didn't you hear him pleading with you to stop?"

Chase threw Tristan off, more angered by the truth than he could ever have imagined. She actually thought she saw red. At the very least, she could taste it.

"Guts have costs," she heard herself say. They were Tourn's words, his barked mantra from the summer she'd spent at his base, incessantly running drills. Endlessly pushing herself to the limit for his attention.

She jabbed, but Tristan slipped past her glove, driving an arm down on her elbow and landing a right hook to her stomach. Cheers rose as the whole ring spun.

"Listen to me," Tristan began. They weren't against the mat anymore. The nearest people in the crowd, the ones really listening, could definitely hear. "Whatever your faulty sense of accomplishment, guts shouldn't cost your RIO his life."

Chase looked at Pippin and saw that he'd heard. He closed his eyes slowly and winced.

Tristan hit her when she wasn't looking. Not hard, but right in the face. She closed her eyes and shook her head. He leaned in and held on to her with his tight arms. "And you know what? You're a bad pilot when you're mad, Chase."

He stepped back, and she gasped. Everything else was up for question. Her character, her morals. Her intelligence. Not her flying. Never her flying.

It was all she had.

"You asshole."

"We're done here," Tristan said. He was about to say "uncle." To let her win *again*.

She lunged. Stepped right into Tristan's hammer of a punch.

And dropped like a broken-winged bird.

23

HAWK CIRCLE

Looking to Land

The alarm sounded every hour.

"Chase." Pippin shook her awake on the top bunk. It was only around two, and it felt like they had been doing this drill forever. The room tilted as she sat up. He handed her a glass of water, and she took a few sips. "Arrow should be doing this. He's the one who gave you a concussion."

"I could've stayed in the infirmary."

"And have Kale all over us for being so reckless? I'll pass, thank you." He took the glass and touched the side of her head, feeling the knot from Tristan's grand finale of a punch. "Swelling's going down." He collapsed on his bed.

"I don't like that you're taking care of me. I'm still not happy with you."

He ignored her. "See you in an hour."

Chase fell asleep against her will, like the world had swung a black cape around itself and disappeared. When the buzzer sounded next, she watched Pippin shuffle to his desk to slap it off.

"Good. You're up," he said.

She was already gritting her teeth, ready to have it out once and for all. "You don't even want to know why I'm mad."

He sat at his desk. "I don't. But what I would like to know is why all of a sudden you want to have a feelings powwow. That's not our style, Chase."

"You're hanging out with other people. Romeo and Arrow. And you're avoiding me—"

"I'm avoiding you because you keep pushing. I told you I want space." He sighed. "Keep in mind, I *tried* to talk to you awhile back and you blew me off."

"So now you're blowing me off?"

"Now I'm acting the way we always are together, which seemed to make you plenty happy two weeks ago, I might add."

Maybe Pippin was right. Hadn't they always been this way? Sarcastic jokes. Sharp and short conversations. But then if that were the case, why had she duped herself into believing they were best friends? Because he was her roommate? Her RIO?

A wave of loneliness crested over her, and she punched her pillow. Her head throbbed. "So maybe now I want to know about you." She switched tactics. "Are you okay?"

"Me? I'm not the one with mild head trauma."

"I mean in general. You're evasiveness is…" She hoped he'd fill in the rest.

"Am I okay?" He rubbed his face. "*Okay* is one of the more inexact words in the English language. I will agree to being *okay*."

The silence that filled the room was tight. She couldn't find a way through it.

"Is it still my turn?" he said. Anger and exhaustion seemed to rise together in his tone like twined snakes, and his face was red even through the dark. "All right, I've got a good question. Is Tristan the next one?"

"The next what?"

"The next guy you're going to mess with before you pull up faster than a Streaker out of a canyon." Before she could answer, he stumbled to his bed, and she lost sight of him. His voice drifted up. "Poor Riot. He's still a mess, and you're already on to someone new."

"I'm not after Tristan. I want to beat him in the trials—to use him to show the government board what the Streakers can do. Tristan understands this."

"You don't ever call me Henry."

"What?"

"You call him Tristan, but you always call me Pippin. Never my real name."

"I didn't know you wanted me to," she wondered aloud. Why *did* she call Tristan by his first name? She even thought of him that way. "But I sparred with Tristan. He gave me a concussion. Does that sound like a crush to you?"

"Yes."

"He's just another Streaker pilot. Like Sylph."

"*Phoenix* is not like *Pegasus*. They were trained to bring us down,

Chase," Pippin said. "Arrow has all kinds of know-how on evasive maneuvers we haven't learned yet. When we get up there with him for the big show, he's going to destroy us. Keep that in the forefront of your thoughts. Not the fact that he's manly gorgeous."

"*Manly gorgeous*?" Chase laughed. "Pip, this is no time to turn super gay."

"Yes. It's no time to be myself. How you've nailed it, Nyx."

Silence.

She leaned over the bunk, the lump on her head growing heavier as she tried to look down on him. "Hey…"

"I don't want to explain it to you, Chase. Don't. Ask."

"I don't need an explanation. I know you're…"

"Just stop!" He stood, and they almost knocked heads. Chase swung upright to face him. He looked like he was about to cry, but his eyes stayed dry. "Let me make this clear to you." He pointed at his chest with both hands. "This is my life." He pointed at her. "That's yours. I vow not to go snooping around in your sordid love affairs, and in return, you leave my sexuality *alone*."

The quiet that snuck around them was chilled. Chase shivered. "I…I'm sorry."

"I know." Pippin ducked back into his bunk. "Go to sleep," he grumbled with the kind of finality she wasn't going to push against.

Chase couldn't move. This wasn't exactly a surprise. Pippin had never appeared interested in guys, but he'd certainly been uninterested in girls. Chase had been hanging back on the subject until he was ready to talk. She'd even imagined it a few times. Pippin would sit her down and say, "So…I'm gay." And then she'd say, "Of course you are," and it would all be smoothed over. Accepted.

She'd never imagined it coming out in the middle of the night like a slap. Pippin was smart enough to fly circles around her; he'd never tell her something this important before he was ready, and yet that was exactly what had seemed to have happened. She had pushed him. Chase felt cruel all of a sudden, even guiltier than when she'd ignored his pleading during the race.

Tristan had been right to knock the pride out of her.

When the alarm sounded again, she hopped down from the bunk on shaky legs and turned it off. Pippin was snoring. The lump on the side of her skull stung when she touched it, but not as bad as the throb of remembering that she deserved it.

"Careless," she whispered.

Tristan had told her she was a bad pilot when she was mad, but it was worse than that. Chase was a bad pilot when she was emotional—she couldn't do anything when her feelings took over. How long would it be before she crashed *Dragon* because she was upset with Pippin or annoyed with Arrow? Tomorrow? During the trials?

She had to go back to how she flew before *Phoenix* showed up. To being cold and clean and clear.

Without care.

Tristan wasn't hard to find. He was hard to find alone. Cadets trailed him between classes and at the chow hall. He was constantly being fangirled the way Chase was used to getting attention for being Nyx.

Although with Arrow around, Nyx was pretty passé.

It didn't make her jealous so much as curious as to why her peers' allegiances had gone Canadian. Then again, Tristan knew their names. He asked them where they were from and quizzed them on what they wanted out of their careers. He engaged. Eh, that seemed like so much work…

In the end, Chase found him in the hangar during free hour, talking to *Phoenix* the way she sometimes talked to *Dragon*.

"Is *Phoenix* a girl or boy?" she asked.

He turned around and eyed her cautiously. "Boy. Yours?"

"*Dragon* is a dragon," Chase said. She climbed to the top platform of the ramp stairs so she didn't have to stay close to him. She put her back to *Phoenix*'s cockpit, her eyes taking in *Dragon*. Her baby's silver skin was bent and hammered, unlike the other two Streakers, the mirror sheen lost in a patchwork of mends and scratches. A running tally of Chase's slip-ups. Her reflection in the metal was a blob of uniform and a stand-up stretch of messy brown hair.

Tristan looked up at her. "Here for a rematch?"

Chase leaned over the rail, looking down at him. She'd come to apologize for the fight. To smooth things over so there were no hard feelings—no any kind of feelings—between them. It was harder to find the words than she'd imagined.

"What are you doing here?" she asked.

Breaking Sky

He twisted a mechanism in the engine bay. "One of my stability lights has been going on and off. I'm checking to see if it's the censor or an actual problem."

"Who taught you how to do that? They never let me anywhere near the engine."

"Adrien." He wiped his greasy hands on a rag. "She wasn't supposed to, but I paid close attention. She's a bit odd in all those classic genius ways. You know. You have Pippin." He smiled, and it knocked into her. She looked away. "Plus, if I'm going to fly a bird, I'd like to know how she stays in the air."

"Adrien created the Streakers, didn't she?" Chase had been mulling that thought since the elderly engineer had arrived. "I'd assumed they were all-American."

"Does it change your love of *Dragon* to know she's a foreigner?"

He was probably teasing, but Chase answered flatly.

"No," she said. "But it puts this whole project into new perspective. Canada reached out to America despite the danger of attracting Ri Xiong Di's attention. It's a tangle of deception, and now there are two countries on the line."

"Think of it this way." He looked up at her from the bottom of the ramp stairs, leaning on the rail. "Canada had a strong gun, so we looked for a strong arm to handle it. Weaponry is nothing without manpower. Besides, we've been trying to help America since Taiwan. Although, the Star cadets have told me it doesn't feel that way from the U.S. side."

"Americans are very good at thinking we're on our own. We

tend to parade that truth through the streets. Ri Xiong Di played to our weakness by isolating us."

Tristan climbed the ramp stairs and sat next to her. She scooted to the far side and gripped the rail.

"I came here to apologize," she said without looking at him. "You were trying to help me during the race, but I...I didn't see it. I'll be focused from here on out."

He crossed his arms over his chest. "Should I be recording this? Seems like Nyx admitting she was wrong is a big deal."

Chase fought a smirk. "You're thinking of Sylph. I'm wrong all the time. I'm just usually too fast for people to notice." She meant in the sky, but the sentence found a different meaning. Chase was too fast on the ground. Too fast with people. But then, slowing down left you vulnerable. Like now.

What was happening? Every time she talked to this guy, she spilled feelings. "I have to go," she said, but he grabbed her arm.

"You don't have to go."

"You have no clue what I have to do."

"Well, I don't accept your apology until you tell me what you meant by 'guts have costs.'"

She pulled her arm back and looked at him from the side. "I don't need you to accept my apology." But she did. She could feel it all over. She'd been an idiot—a bad pilot. And that was the only thing she could not afford to be at the Star.

He raised his eyebrows at her like he knew these things, waiting for her to speak.

Breaking Sky

"That saying…*guts have costs*…that's something my dad told me the day I got this." She held out the scar on the back of her arm. "I was trying to run the recruits' landmine obstacle course on his base. I didn't make it."

"Then what happened?"

She almost snapped "That's none of your business" out of habit. But she kind of wanted to unload. Tristan had brought this sort of purging into her life with his innocent questions and "no judgment" looks. If only she could find a way to talk to Pippin the way she'd opened up with Tristan…

Her eyes moved to Tristan's slowly. Carefully. "I nearly bled out. I had to get a transfusion, and by the time I woke up, I was a few thousand miles away. Back in my mom's apartment." Chase remembered being groggy and bandaged, her nose already drying out from the stale smoke in the air. "The next time I talked to him was…"

"A few weeks ago?"

"That obvious?" She took a deep breath. "He never wanted me there to begin with. I have no clue why he invited me." Chase lined up all the events that had brought Tourn into her life. And then she found herself reliving them. *Aloud*. "Sixteen years after the Philippines bombing, a jackass journalist paid for the name of the pilot who dropped the bomb. I didn't know who my dad was until I saw him on TV making *that speech*." She glanced at Tristan. He nodded slowly, proving he knew what she was talking about.

215

"I'm proud to have served my country so profoundly," Tourn had said, seeming the best sort of steely-eyed. Maybe Chase should have thought that he was a monster like everyone else, but she already had one of those beside her, puffing like an industry smokestack.

"Janice fell off the couch when she saw him. Burned a hole in the rug with her cigarette."

"Janice?"

"My mom. She told me to write to him. She wanted money, and she could see all the shiny stars on his uniform." Chase shrugged. "I told him I wanted to be a pilot, so he hijacked my dream. Drilled me all summer like he was going to help me get into the military, and then he returned me when I failed."

She took a deep breath that filled places she hadn't known were empty. "So that's my insignificant tragedy. I didn't want to risk Pippin's life yesterday. I just sometimes have...blind spots." She folded her arms over her chest. "I know how to be better."

But first she had to stop talking. Why was it so hard? She reached for the side of her head at the same time that Tristan did. Their fingers met over the knot on her skull. It wasn't electric to touch Tristan. Not in the slightest. It was worse—it was welcome. She fought the urge to lean into his shoulder and rest.

"I'm sorry about knocking you out," he said. "I tried not to mangle your face."

"It's too bad. You would have scored points with Sylph for uglying me up."

"Sylph scares the crap out of me. Frightens Romeo too, although he's still interested. Nothing more terrifying-slash-tantalizing than an Amazonian blonde."

"Sylph would be delighted to hear that. Riot calls her Jet Fighter Barbie."

"That's kind of perfect. What about you?"

She rubbed the toes of her boots together. "Riot calls me more unpleasant names."

He tried to cover, which was kind of sweet. "But there's nothing plastic about you. Nothing predictable. Makes you a fearsome pilot. You do realize you're like a living legend to some of these people."

Oh, so they were going to exchange flirty compliments now. Chase bit back her smile and felt a door open in that moment, something between them that had its own breeze. "Because I'm so legendary, tell me what happened before we raced. When you fell behind." Tristan looked away, but she kept going. "You're not flying like yourself. I might not have watched tapes of your style, but I've seen enough to know you have a natural tilt to your wings."

"It wastes fuel," he said automatically.

"It's you. Don't fight how you fly."

"Is that a piece of your wisdom?"

"That's the whole cake, Tristan," she said. He held off a laugh, and she wanted to ask why. "Is it nerves? Are you remembering JAFA up there?"

"Yes…but I'm getting a hold on it. It won't throw me off again. I think."

"You should chase a ghost. That's what I do," she said. "Although, I shouldn't call him a ghost because he isn't dead. Not yet." The ease with which her father came up shocked her into continuing. "Kale says I fly like Tourn." She shook her head. "Christ, I have no idea why I tell you things. I swear I leak truth around you."

"I'm a third party. It's easier to talk to people who are on the outside."

"Maybe." She looked down *Phoenix*'s narrow engine bay. It reminded her of Crackers's heart circle or trust circle or whatever the woman had called it. Chase still wondered how they could be interchangeable. Love was one thing—a fluffy Easter bunny sort of thing—but trust was real and rare, and she believed in it. Did she trust Tristan? Could she? She barely knew him.

The question reminded her that she had one more confession. "I also wanted to apologize for kissing you in the locker room the other day. I wasn't making a play."

He finger-combed his hair back, and the shorter pieces broke free, brushing his cheeks. "I get that you wanted to surprise me. And you did that much."

"I don't want you to get the wrong idea. Especially with everyone saying that we're…that I'm going after you." God, this was a terrible topic.

"Who is *everyone* exactly?"

"Riot," she started. "Sylph and Pippin. Kale…all the cadets who saw us spar."

"That really is everyone."

"You're the one who rolled on top of me for like ten minutes." Her ears warmed as she remembered what it had been like to be under him, his breath wild on her neck. She held her hands over her cheeks, trying to block his view of her flush. A little late, she got the impression he was reading her body language negatively.

"I'm under no illusions, Chase. I suspect that's why you don't like me."

She stared at his eyes. Flame blue and so steady. "I never said I didn't like you."

"Is this what you do to someone you like?" He pulled up his shirt and showed off his stomach. Beyond being ripped, it was covered with purple bruises.

"Whoa. Sorry."

He dropped his shirt but held her eyes. "Do you know what helped me get my nerves in check in the air the other day?" he asked in a low voice. "Chasing you."

"I am aptly named."

He grinned. "How often do you get to use that joke?"

"Not enough." She took her dog tags off and wrapped the chain around her wrist. "I'm glad I could help you up there." It was no use; no matter where she looked, the air was growing heavier. She could feel his eyes endlessly pulling at her. She forced a laugh. "With this much tension, we really will put on a good show for the government board. Don't you think?"

"What I think?" He took her dog tags and ran his fingers over the imprint of her name. "I think about what will happen after the trials if Ri Xiong Di doesn't back down. It's all I can think about. What about you?"

"I don't," she lied instinctively. She stole her dog tags and jumped down the stairs. It had felt good to open up to him until this moment. If he was going to start talking about the Second Cold War, she was done.

"See you later, Arrow." She felt herself flee inside even as she jogged out of the hangar. Guns, missiles, dogfights. Bombs.

Death.

That's what would happen if they couldn't find a way to make Ri Xiong Di back down. That's what was on the other side of the trials. The sheer fact that this was not a game.

24

BOOLA-BOOLA

The Call for Bringing Down a Drone

The sky was an old friend. Chase spiraled through a thick cloud and into the wisp-blue of high altitude. The week hadn't been kind. Not after a mild concussion and a fight that lingered in every word she shared with her RIO. "Ready for a little heat, Pippin?" she asked.

"Yes," he said. No snappy words. No joke.

She punched the throttle, imagining *Dragon's* fiery wake. Whenever she thought about her midnight smackdown with Pippin, she felt some sort of spiky creature reposition itself in her chest. She was dying to let it out, but Pippin's stringent lack of eye contact proved that to be impossible.

So she focused on flying. The trials were in less than two months—she had to *focus*.

"How's the weight?" Pippin asked through the amped volume of their helmet mics.

"The weight?"

"The missiles, Nyx."

Chase wobbled left and right, testing out the latest wrench thrown into the Streaker pilots' training: deactivated missiles snuggled beneath her wings. "The drag is mild, but I still can't imagine firing them."

"You've got to learn how to aim first."

As if on cue, *Phoenix* shot up from behind. *Dragon*'s warning alarm blared through the cockpit. Chase punched it off and flipped on the shortwave radio. "We got it, Arrow! You know how to get us under missile lock. Give me a chance to work this out!"

"I thought Nyx was supposed to be the fun one," Romeo responded. "She's complaining like Sylph these days."

"I am on the same frequency, you punk," Sylph growled over the channel. *Pegasus* pulled up from a thick cloud and chased *Phoenix* across the horizon.

Sylph had about as much luck as Chase in getting *Phoenix* between the crosshairs. Tristan was as fast as ever and executed evasive maneuvers she hadn't even heard of. What made matters worse—he knew how to engage missile lock while he seemed to be trying to escape. He got Chase twice by hitting the brakes and pulling an inverted loop to maneuver behind her.

Chase swore under her breath in a long string, but she also kind of loved it. Speed and a solid challenge were exactly what she needed to get her head back into trial preparation.

Pegasus reappeared without *Phoenix*. Sylph attempted to get a lock on Chase, but she pulled one of Tristan's moves—inverting them long enough for Pippin to complain.

"Warn me next time," he said. "All the blood is in my face."

"What say we take out Sylph?" Chase asked, hoping a common enemy might bring them closer together. Pippin didn't respond, but Sylph did.

"We're taking turns, Nyx," Sylph ordered over the radio. "Swapping defense and offense. Those are the rules you agreed to."

"There won't be any rules when we're up against red drones," Chase pointed out.

"Indeed," Pippin said, and that tiny moment of accord blunted her thorny feelings inside.

Experimenting with more of Tristan's moves, Chase went after *Pegasus*. By the time she'd achieved missile lock on Sylph four times, she was feeling much better. Chase fielded Sylph's protest and agreed to let *Pegasus* attack in the next round.

Chase counted down. "One, two—"

"Three," Tristan's voice cut in.

Phoenix flashed by so fast that Chase took seconds to recover before blazing after him. Sylph vanished from her thoughts as she sped after Tristan. She caught him at Mach 3, streaking over the green glisten of the Great Salt Lake. His low laugh filled the shortwave.

The two jets spiraled together until Chase went light-headed. When they reached the thinnest layer of atmosphere, *Phoenix* and *Dragon* dove in tandem. Tristan broke left, and she swept under him, their metal bodies grazing. Chase couldn't help wondering what it might feel like to get that close to Tristan without jets. Skin to skin.

Her body thrummed, so much so that she missed the first emergency beacon lighting up her controls. "What's the problem, Pippin?"

"Emergency code from the Star. They're paging in a satellite link."

Chase held her finger over the switch. "But it could be a code virus trying to get control of the flight software."

"Is it coming from the Star?" Tristan asked.

"Yes," Pippin said. "Unless Ri Xiong Di has figured out how to reroute the signal."

"But if it's home base, and they're bothering to reach out, this has got to be important." Chase didn't wait to deliberate. She flicked the link on, holding her breath and waiting for *Dragon*'s controls to be overridden.

Waiting.

Kale's voice came instead. "*Phoenix* and *Dragon*, get to *Pegasus*!" He yelled so loudly that Chase's ears hurt. "Get to *Pegasus*!"

"Where is she, Pip?"

"Balls of fire." Pippin filled in the coordinates that came over the line. "Sylph's too far west. Past the coast. She's over the demarcation line."

☽ ④ ☾

Chase and Tristan flew like a pair of bullets. They reached Mach 4, the world going blurry beneath them long before the silver flash of *Pegasus* appeared high in the sky.

Breaking Sky

A maroon dot caught Chase's eye. It was too close to Sylph. Too close at every turn.

"Is that a—"

"Red drone." Pippin's voice cracked. Chase's speed faltered as her arms shook, pulling back on the throttle.

"What's she doing out here?" Pippin asked. "And how'd she pick up that tailer?"

"You mean, why hasn't she lost it yet?" Romeo yelled in. "We're supposed to be way faster than them."

"Shut up," Tristan snapped. "What are we doing, Nyx?" She tightened when he said her call sign, her whole body tuning in. He was deferring to her, asking for her lead, which was kind of shocking.

"Sylph's too slow. She won't be able to break away, and she won't bring the drone over land."

"She can't," Pippin said. "We don't want that thing anywhere near civilians."

"It'd be nice if these freakin' missiles under our wings were more than ornamental," Romeo said. "If that thing scans one of the Streakers…"

"Oh God!" It was Riot, close enough to pipe through the short-wave feed. "Help us!"

"Sylph!" Chase cried out. "Say your state!"

"Low fuel." Sylph gasped. "This thing has locked on me over and over. I keep shaking him, but I can't outstrip him. I can't even focus! Why is it so fast?!"

"Nyx." Tristan's voice was cool as glass. "What's the plan?"

"Lead her home, Arrow. I'll lose the drone."

225

"I'm faster," he argued.

Chase was a crazed mixture of fear and confidence. "You're the offensive pilot, which would be great if we were armed. I've been trained for defense, remember?"

"We've got this," Pippin said. "Chase can do it." They were close enough now to see Sylph's Streaker clearly, jerking toward the sun and back down.

The drone was cruelly beautiful, sleek with folded back wings and a narrow nose. Being unmanned, it didn't need a cockpit, and the effect was a seamless maroon body—and large missiles. Up close, Chase finally understood why the drones were bloodred. Military machines were always camouflaged. Even the Streakers were silver-blue in order to blend into the sky. But not these drones. They were meant to be seen. To be feared.

Mission accomplished.

Phoenix broke right, swinging in to meet Sylph just as her frantic voice came over the radio. "Get this bogey off me!"

"Follow *Phoenix*," Chase told Sylph. "He's going to take you the long way home so they don't track us."

"What about you? That drone is *fast*, Nyx! Faster than we knew."

"Go!"

Phoenix spun behind *Pegasus*, washing the drone off course with a burst of speed. Chase drove herself into the drone's path, letting it grab her heat signal as the other Streakers escaped.

The twin cannon of their sonic **booms** resounded through her chest.

"We don't have enough fuel to outrun it for long." Pippin was so calm. Her rock.

"Okay then. We outfly it right now."

Chase sent them past Mach 3...4. Sweat appeared all over her body, and she would have been shaking if gravity weren't cementing her muscles. The pressure took each breath and drove it back down her throat.

And still, the drone was only a few hundred feet behind.

She had to stop it from coming any closer to the western seaboard with those massive missiles. And she could not let it return to Ri Xiong Di after having scanned the Streakers. Her only choice was to make it redline. Make it go so fast it broke itself apart.

"Nyx! I can't...I'm graying out!" Pippin cried.

Chase heard him this time, but she couldn't back down.

"I'm sorry." She shot them faster. Tears bled from the corners of her eyes. "I'm sorry!"

Mach 5 came with a stripping of color. She touched the speed, clung to it. Her whole world turned a white-gray blur. There was a chance—a good one—that this wouldn't work. That the drone could go as fast as the Streakers. She throttled even farther forward.

Chase had no idea where they were. All she saw was ocean. She pulled low without letting up on the throttle. Alarms screeched through the cockpit, announcing the drone's missile lock. Chase shot up just as a missile passed beneath *Dragon's* belly.

"Pippin!" she yelled. "Check six!"

She prayed that he hadn't passed out. The pause was too long, but her RIO's voice returned unevenly. "It's wobbling. It might. Somersault. Maybe."

Maybe wasn't good enough. Chase went *faster*. A large marker buoy—a metal tower—bobbed on the horizon, and she went straight for it, only pulling above it at the last second. It paid off. An explosion of orange fire behind her announced that the drone hadn't cleared the buoy.

"Boola-boola," Chase whispered.

Darkness enveloped her vision, shrinking in. She sucked oxygen, but it didn't help. "Pippin?" She pulled on the stick to get them some more altitude. To buy some time for her to get her vision back, but it was too late. "Pip?"

Chase slammed at the controls as the crystal sky and the blue earth swirled, and she fell into a hollow.

Black.

Space.

CHARLIE

25

DEADSTICK

Downed

Chase woke on stone or ice. It felt like both. She recognized the dense cold air of the hangar with so much relief that she almost cried out.

"She's all right," Kale proclaimed. He put an arm around her shoulders and sat her up. "You're all right," he murmured just for her, and the strain in his voice made her hold on to him.

"Pippin?" she asked.

"He's fine. You both went full G-LOC, but your RIO was lucky enough to engage the autopilot before he lost consciousness. He came out of it a few minutes ago. They're walking him down to the infirmary."

She vaguely remembered trying to punch the controls—to do what Pippin had managed—but it felt like her brain wasn't plugged in to her body. She blinked at the hangar, and the scene blinked back like a black-and-white film. "I'm still seeing gray."

"Oxygen starved. You may faint again if you stand." Kale threw commands to the ground crew staring down at her, finishing with, "And someone get a stretcher!"

"No stretcher." She tried to stand, and Kale pressed her to his chest. He smelled like coffee, and he felt different this close. Safe—and yet a firm reminder of what had almost happened. Chase squeezed her eyes and saw the drone's missile breeze by. She twitched with the remains of her much-depleted adrenaline. Where was her jet?

"*Dragon*?"

"She's going to need some fixing. Skidded out on the landing— autopilot was never designed to set down. I'll get Adrien on it." He swore. "It could have been so much worse, but we'll worry about that later. You're a hero for the moment, Harcourt." Kale's words fell on her like a blanket, and she ached to close her eyes and tuck into it. "Get a stretcher," he called again. "I can't carry her, not with my back."

"No stretcher." Chase tried to stand, but her vision popped with black spots. She loathed the idea of being wheeled through the academy like an invalid. "I'll make it," she said, wavering on her feet.

"I'll take her."

Before Chase could sort out the voice, someone swooped her up. Her head tipped against a neck. She smelled salty sweat and stared into a tangle of black hair. "Tristan," she murmured. His name sunk through her and warmed everything.

Tristan shifted her weight, walking so fast that the motion rocked her into a half-conscious daze. They were on the Green when she came to again. She would have known the stillness of the leaves and the rhythmic knock of the brick path underfoot anywhere.

"What was Sylph doing over the line?" Tristan asked Kale.

Good freakin' question, Chase thought.

"Even if I knew, you know we can't discuss it," Kale said.

"Of course." Tristan's tone edged. "Any guess how Chase destroyed that drone?"

Kale spoke in a hurry. "General Tourn already requested her flight footage. He'll call a meeting after he reviews it, but I think it's certain this will have serious repercussions."

Not him. Her mind cartwheeled over her father. His curse of a name. His too-large forearms and clipped gray hair. She held Tristan tighter, and he lifted her a little higher, closer.

"But it's the first drone anyone's managed to knock out of the sky," Tristan argued. "It has to mean something good."

"Does it?"

The silence that followed Kale's question held too many answers. If Ri Xiong Di knew that the U.S. had airpower capable of taking down a drone, they might attack in a hurry. Chase's breath cut out. Maybe tomorrow. Maybe before this night was done with its darkness…

"Will this affect the trials?" Tristan asked.

"They won't look kindly on her passing out like that."

"But her RIO hit the autopilot in time."

"What if she hadn't brought down that drone before she needed the autopilot? Or there had been a second drone waiting? *Dragon* would have been a sitting duck. We can't afford to lose multibillion-dollar jets that easily."

"She's the only one of us who could have outmaneuvered that drone. You have to tell them that. That thing was *fast*."

"I know." Kale took a very loud, deep breath. "But no one wants kamikaze pilots."

Chase lost her grip on Tristan as Kale's words fell all over her like dead weight.

Tristan only held her more firmly. "Nyx could have lost that drone, but she stayed in front of it. I know what she's like in the air. She made sure it didn't bring its intel back to Ri Xiong Di." His hold on her tightened as his words grew tenser. "Come on, Brigadier General. If your military can't—"

"Cadet. Let me remind you that you are under my command while you train here."

Silence knifed its way in. Chase's brain had woken fully from the heated exchange. Why was Kale dismissing Tristan's concern? Why did Tristan seem like he wanted to deck the brigadier general? For once, Kale's hardness felt overly stubborn—and Tristan…the way he kept defending Chase made her want to tangle up with him. Hands, arms, and lips.

When Kale spoke again, his voice had softened, sounding more like himself. "We need to start thinking as allies, Router."

"Yes, Brigadier General."

Chase heard it all too slowly to respond. She locked her fingers around Tristan's neck and peered at a few brown freckles on sand-hued skin.

So she'd gotten her colors back.

When they reached the infirmary, a commotion eclipsed the warmth of being close to Tristan. Voices shouted all over the place. She heard Pippin yelling at Sylph about the drone and Riot telling everyone to chill out. Chase tried to stir, but her mind still felt behind, and she felt too beat for flyboy drama. She groaned, and Tristan seemed to understand. He didn't leave her in the midst of the arguing. He took her to one of the beds in the back, through the sea of curtains, where it was much quieter.

"Let go, Chase," he said, unwinding her arms from his neck. She settled into a mound of pillows. Now that she was inert, she felt more awake.

Or maybe it was because she was alone with him.

"What, no kiss?" she mumbled.

Tristan leaned in and pinched her ear. "Maybe next time."

But then he did kiss her. A brush of lips so fast that by the time she'd woken up her mouth, he was pulling away. She grabbed the front of his flight suit and hauled him closer.

He was more than ready. One hand took the back of her neck and the other braced his body over hers. His face tilted in, and she felt fire and wind and *so much speed* in every brush and push of his skin.

A minute passed. Maybe an hour. Someone cleared his or her throat, and Tristan pulled away sharply. A twentysomething medic stood at the edge of the room, her eyebrows raised.

Tristan turned to leave so fast that he headed straight into the curtain. He swung his arms to get free of the draped cloth, swearing in the strongest Canadian accent she'd yet heard from him. When he finally emerged, his sweat-battered hair was a complete mess, and he spun in a circle before heading for the door.

"Feeling better?" the medic asked sarcastically as she watched Tristan's hasty exit. She began to take Chase's blood pressure. "I miss being a cadet," the woman grumbled. "Haven't gotten any in ages."

Chase ignored the medic and held a hand over the radiating blush on her face.

So. Tristan kissed like he flew. Christ, the boy was amazing.

☽ ☽ ☽

Chase snuck out of the infirmary at what Kale would call an ungodly hour, sick of being treated like she had been hurt. Her loss of consciousness had been more significant than Pippin's because her mask had unsnapped during her mad dash to engage autopilot.

Thank God her RIO had managed it. If he hadn't…

She couldn't even think about it.

Chase's body had been starved of oxygen for several minutes—or so her sex-deprived medic had informed her. No permanent damage, just a crushing headache. The throbbing pain couldn't hold Chase down, though. She needed to find Sylph.

They had unfinished business concerning the demarcation line.

Chase went to the room Riot and Sylph shared. She knocked for a solid minute before a sleep-washed Riot answered the door. "I need Sylph," she said.

"She's not here," Riot said through a yawn.

"Why were you guys over the d-line? You shouldn't have been closer than a hundred miles from it."

He ignored her question. "Try the hangar. She goes to *Pegasus* when she can't sleep." He shut the door on Chase, almost snipping her face. His bandaged hand was the last thing she saw.

Chase headed to the hangar. The chilled air of the concrete building took hold faster than usual, along with a flash of red through Chase's thoughts. That drone had been so terrible, and yet beautiful—a sleek death machine.

It should have killed them.

Dragon sat where she always did, but her landing gear had been disassembled. Again. Sylph's bird was parked next to hers, pristine and girly like always. Even after its run-in with the drone, the jet appeared unscathed. Chase heard a strange shuffling as she took in *Pegasus*. She stepped around the wings and braked hard. Boards out.

Sylph was pressed against the jet's side, her arms and lips locked on a young airman with a familiar hawkish face. He had his hands up the back of her shirt, and Sylph's too-long legs were wrapped around his waist.

"Whoa." Chase's heartbeat shot off the charts. The way they devoured each other made Chase's make-out sessions seem like kids at play. "*Whoa*," she said even louder. They stopped kissing and scrambled to detangle themselves. The airman buckled his belt while Sylph smoothed her hair, calmly eyeing Chase.

The guy's face, however, was turning reddish purple. Embarrassment smeared with fear.

"You!" Chase heard herself saying. "You work up in the tower." She checked the front of his uniform: MASTERS. He had been the staff sergeant who lipped her after she'd first spotted *Phoenix*. "Am I hallucinating?" Chase blinked hard. "I must be."

Masters looked like he was going to bark a command, but Sylph whispered in his ear. He nodded, gave her another scorching kiss, and left. Sylph approached, casually braiding her hair back.

"What was *that*?" Chase asked.

"Get over it," Sylph said. "This has nothing to do with you, and you're not going to say anything to anyone."

"I'm not sure I'd know what to say," Chase said honestly.

Sylph hooked arms with Chase and led her through the hangar, more purposeful than friendly. "Liam and I are in love, Nyx, and I'm eighteen, so it's legal."

"Legal nothing. Kale will crap a mongoose when—"

"He *can't* know." Chase thought Sylph was going to get fiery with her, but Sylph's mood went the other way. She seemed…scared. The effect took years off Sylph's ordinarily hardened persona. "The trials and that drone—if Kale finds out, he'll put me on the Down List. Liam's the most important thing to me." Sylph looked at *Pegasus*. "But I don't want to lose my wings."

Liam? It was weird to think the hawk-eyed staff sergeant had a first name. Then again, Chase had just seen his tongue in action. She eyed Sylph. The girl was much less daunting at this angle, not to mention she almost glowed when she said *Liam*. "I won't say anything, Sylph. But you have to tell me what in hell happened yesterday."

"Blackmail. That's how you want to play this."

"No. I want you to tell me what happened. I think I deserve that much."

"You saved my life." Only Sylph could say that without gratitude. "So I *will* tell you. But after all the crap you've pulled over the years, you better not judge." Her eyebrows scrunched. "You and Arrow blasted off together faster than I've ever been willing to go, and I didn't want to be third best anymore. I was…it was just supposed to be a hop across the d-line and back again. That quick. I wanted to be the first to cross it." Her smile was downright heartbreaking. "And I was. I'll always have that over you. Even if they take my wings for it."

Maybe it was because Sylph was being so un-Sylph-like, but the truth rose up from Chase's chest and burned its way out of her. "They're going to take my wings, not yours. I heard Kale telling Tristan. I'm unsafe."

Sylph's expression prickled back to normal, full cactus. "Of course you're unsafe. You're unpredictable. The drones are on a grid flight plan—software—and when I head up there, I fly by their rules. I don't know how not to. Don't think I haven't tried. But then you streak in and attack like a wild animal. Those computer-brained machines will never outfly you."

Chase shook her head. "It doesn't matter what I can do.

Kale...Kale said the government board won't like how I handled that drone."

"Nyx. Are you opening up to me?"

"Could you just be a human for once? They might take my wings. Before the trials even. *Tomorrow.*"

Kamikaze pilot.

"*That's* what you're worried about, Nyx? I swear you're never aware of what's at stake. After the trials, if the board approves the Streakers, you and me and that Cutesy-Pants-Canadian are going up against Ri Xiong Di. Think about it. They're never going to back down without a demonstration of what the birds can do against the drones."

Sylph stepped a little closer. "Yesterday was my awakening. I won't mess up again. From the first time I got up in the air in *Pegasus*, I've imagined flying against the drones. I'm ready."

Chase stared blankly. "I've never imagined flying against drones."

"That might be your real problem. This isn't a game. Never has been. Once you get your head around that"—Sylph sighed—"you might be a good pilot after all."

Chase felt frozen to the concrete. Everything was linked to her flying. Her attitude, her relationships. Her fear of her dad and desperation to prove she belonged. Her mounting curiosity in Tristan and her ache to be closer to her RIO. All connected. Inexorably.

And suddenly the trials were simply a speed bump. The real test would be facing a drone fleet. Would it happen in ten weeks? Six months?

The only sure answer was *soon*.

"Nyx." Sylph put her hand awkwardly on Chase's shoulder. "Don't look so destroyed. We have two months before the trials. I'll help you face your fear before then."

"Help or drill me into submission?"

"The difference being?" She risked a rare smirk. "You really won't say anything about me and Liam? He's my future." The tall blonde looked around the hangar before letting her deep brown eyes settle on Chase. "Everything else could fall apart so easily."

"I won't say anything."

Sylph left.

The word *future* hung in the densely cold air. *Dragon* had felt like her life for years, but Sylph was right. Chase's world was so much larger than one jet—and yet it was still only one bombing from turning to screams and ash.

26

BEHIND THE POWER CURVE

Letdown

Chase headed to her room. Even though she sat on the edge of Pippin's bunk softly and touched his shoulder gently, he jerked and pulled away when he woke.

"We need to be okay." She rolled her eyes at her word choice considering Pippin's dismissive definition of *okay*. "We need to be better. I need you. To fly."

"To fly?" Pippin sat up. She half expected him to launch into one of his defensive maneuvers, but he didn't. "How do you propose we achieve this 'better' state?"

"I don't know. I only know that Tourn could show up tomorrow and take my wings." She felt tears, but she held them in lockdown. "Things are heating up with Ri Xiong Di. That drone was..." Pippin nodded, and she could see in his eyes that that drone had scared him as much as it had terrified her. "There's more. Kale called me a kamikaze pilot."

"Shit."

"Yeah." She pushed forward. "I know you don't think I care

about anyone, but I do. And I know you're going through something. I am too." She took a deep breath, wanting to tell Pippin about the talks she'd shared with Tristan. And that mad heat of a kiss. "Tristan…"

"Wait." Pippin looked like he might be sick. "Did Tristan tell you about the hangar?"

"What?"

Pippin's shoulders let down a little. "Nothing. Never mind."

"You're really hard to talk to, you know that?" She shook her head and forced herself to cool down. "When I'm with Tristan I have to do my damnedest not to tell him my life story, but you? You're a wall, Pippin."

"Look who's talking."

"Fine. I'm terrible at this! So answer me one thing. What would you do if you were me and you were trying to patch things up? And don't say *space*."

He leaned back on his pillow. "I'd fly *Dragon*. That's what I'd do if I were you. All of a sudden you're picking fights, messing up hops… Your head's not in the game right now."

"This isn't a game," she muttered.

"I know that. I've always known that. Do you?" His temper rose with each word. "I've seen the way you and Tristan look at each other. The way you're scheming with Sylph all of a sudden." He checked himself, and she could tell how much energy it took by the strain on his face. "You've always been the best at acting like no one else matters because the Second Cold War, the military, the

Star, et cetera, and so forth—they're all more important. I've hated you for that in the past, but right now I wish you'd quit needling me and just fly."

"Hated me?" Her voice was small.

All of his anger was gone. That fast. "You know that's not what I mean."

She didn't. She didn't know what he meant at all these days. "So now we've gone from me not understanding you, to you avoiding me, to you being a stranger, to you hating me. Man, I'm glad *Phoenix* came to town." She got up and left.

"Nyx!" he yelled after her. It was the wrong thing to say, and he knew it.

It wasn't her name.

Chase fled to the Green. Dawn was being simulated by the gradual increase of the sunlamps over the grass, while high above, the black sky was as bleak and dark as the Arctic in November. She sat beneath her favorite tree and remembered climbing it with Pippin freshman year. The day she first became Nyx.

Chase had lugged up Kale's book on Greek mythology, certain her call sign was hiding in its pages. Pippin had come with her, balancing on a thick branch while reading the Orpheus poems, his headphones snuggled around his neck.

"Here's one about the goddess Nyx, Daughter of Chaos. She's a shadowy figure who only shows up when things are going real bad," he had said. "Sounds like your brand of mischief. Listen: 'Dissolving anxious care, the friend of Mirth, with darkling coursers riding round the earth. Goddess of phantoms and of shadowy play, whose drowsy pow'r divides the nat'ral day.'"

"Perfect," Chase had said, reaching so high on the top branch that she could feel the radiating heat of the sunlamps. "I'll be 'Darkling Courser.'"

"Or you could be 'Nyx.' Which is shorter and not so highfa-lutin pretentious."

"Nyx." She had tried it out a few times. "It's better than Chase. I hope people call me that instead."

"*In addition to*," Pippin had corrected. "*Instead* implies you're being replaced by this new persona."

Chase had laughed. "Can you replace yourself? That sounds awesome."

"But then how will I know who I'm dealing with?" Pippin had asked. "Will the two Chases wear different hats?"

She had climbed even higher until she had heard the whining crack of a branch about to break. "I'll tell you what they both love. They both love to fly." Chase had let go and held her arms out. When Pippin had grabbed for her, the book fell, breaking its spine on an upraised root.

Its pages had scattered.

Chase came back from the memory. Her chest was heavier than ever as she remembered how pale Pippin had turned when he thought she was going to fall. She still sharply recalled how strange it felt to have someone scared for her.

She wanted to say that he no longer cared, but that wasn't true.

Something deeper was happening with Pippin. She thought over the last conversation until she snagged on the way he'd acted when she brought up Tristan.

She stood up fast, realization knocking into her like a headwind.

Did her RIO have a crush on Arrow?

It made so much sense. Pippin was always with Romeo and Arrow these days, and he'd already been busted trying to hide that fact from Chase—telling her to leave him alone.

She pressed her fingers to her lips and remembered the kiss only hours earlier that had sent her soaring. Was she developing feelings for the same person her RIO was crushing on? Chase might not have been the girliest of girls, but she knew that that spelled crisis.

Oh hell.

⚙ ⚙ ⚙

Chase finally fell asleep in the rec room and woke up late for the debriefing of the drone event. When she opened the door, many eyes met hers. Adrien, Sylph, Riot, Tristan, and Romeo were seated along with several higher-ups in their crisp-shouldered uniforms. Kale stood at the head of the table.

"What is this interruption?" Tourn's voice came through the speaker in the center of the table, but his image faced away. Chase breathed easier knowing he wasn't there in person. Her relief was short-lived. "Brigadier General?"

"The last cadet has arrived," Kale said, motioning for Chase to come in.

"Who?"

"Cadet Harcourt."

"Why wasn't she here with the others?" Tourn barked.

"She's been in the infirmary. It was quite an ordeal, General." Kale was talking back to Tourn, and Chase's heart started to hammer at her chest.

"Brigadier General," Tourn continued. "I am seriously beginning to doubt your ability to produce diligent airmen." Chase knew the bleeding contempt in her father's voice. She saw the flush of Kale's neck. The tightening of his mouth. She felt sick for him. Tourn's insults continued like a storm. "You let your cadets have entirely too much freedom. They will continue to be ill-prepared when they get to the academy in Colorado Springs if you don't—"

"General Tourn, permission to speak?" Chase interrupted.

The pause was too long, and the whole room stared at her like she'd grown antlers. Even Kale.

"No, cadet," Tourn said finally. "Take a seat and act like you belong."

Her face went scarlet.

Chase dragged her chair across the floor, hoping the noise covered the painful pound in her chest. *Asshole*, she couldn't help but think. *Asshole*. The word helped a little. She glared at the wood surface, avoiding Tristan's gaze and Sylph's what-are-you-up-to gawk.

"As I was saying, we've had word from the intelligence office. Ri

Xiong Di's forces have tripled their sky patrols along the demarcation line. It's our understanding that they are aware that they lost a drone but perhaps are not sure how. That is the best-case scenario."

Tourn continued after an ugly pause. "Worst-case scenario is that Cadet Harcourt did not act fast enough, and the drone was able to scan the Streaker and wire the logistics back. We must assume the worst-case scenario."

He gave one of his grunts that made Chase flash back to his tiny quarters that summer when she was twelve. She had sat opposite him on a hard kitchen chair for over an hour. Eye to eye with the man she had built up in her mind—only to find he knew less about being a father than she knew about having one.

"We need to act. The trials for the Streakers will take place in three days instead of two months from now. On Monday."

The room rustled with objections.

"That is impossible," Dr. Adrien said. "We need two months. Three days will not be enough time to test the tandem ejection module, let alone the enhanced inverted capabilities."

"You'll have to make it work, Doctor," Tourn said. "Also, the trials will not be public knowledge. There will be no fanfare or involvement from the academy. Let's not forget we are playing a game we are not likely to win, but if the cadets can convince the board to expand the Streaker project, we might have a chance to launch a fleet by spring. And for that, we need the government's money. Get it done. I will be there on Sunday to help Brigadier General Kale prepare."

His image broke as he hung up, and Chase's chest swelled so fast that she thought her rib cage might split. Two days until Tourn. *Three* until the trials.

Adrien shook her head. "It will not be enough time. We have not even been able to test the double parachute. I feel very strongly that the pilot and RIO should not be separated in the event of a crash. At average Streaker speed, if they eject separately, they could collide and kill each other."

"Let's not do that," Pippin said. The teams exchanged desperate looks. Romeo started to rant in French to Pippin, who nodded fervently. No matter her fight with Pippin, her RIO talked with Streaker Team *Phoenix* easily. Chase tried not to burn as she looked at them, but with her father's damning words hanging in the air, everything was making her smoke.

Kale stared at the corner of the room. "We'll have to push up the parachute test. Make it happen tomorrow."

Adrien argued back, but Chase lost track of the conversation when she saw Tristan's eyes on hers, along with a shot of pity. Nothing pissed her off faster than pity.

Cadet Harcourt did not act fast enough.

Act like you belong…

Chase dug her nails into her palms. She'd broken the manned airspeed record—killed the first red drone—and still she'd failed her father. She stood up so quickly that her chair smacked backward against the tile floor.

Everyone turned to her, and she was glad. The last time she

had been in this room, Tourn had brought her to tears. Not this time. "Come on," she barked at her fellow flyboys. "We have to prepare."

27

MERGED PLOT

Direct Contact

The Streaker teams followed Chase to the room she shared with Pippin. Chase realized her mistake in bringing them there when she saw everyone try to squish into the small space. Romeo flung himself on Pippin's bunk. Riot sat on the desktop while Sylph took over the chair. Tristan was left standing in the center of the room, right in Chase's pacing path. She moved him bodily to the corner, ignoring the way that getting her hands on him made her concentration fog.

If Pippin had a crush on Tristan, that made the boy off-limits.

Didn't it?

She glanced at her RIO and found him scrambling to get his things out of the way. He stepped close and whispered, "Do they have to be in here?"

"The academy doesn't know about the trials," she reminded him. "We can't talk in public."

"Yeah, but still." He shoved three journals into his sock drawer. "This is beyond claustrophobic." Pippin perched next to Romeo on the edge of his bed, glancing at Tristan's back just a foot away. Chase couldn't stop herself from watching the two of them. What had happened that Pippin was so terrified of her finding out about?

"Nyx." Sylph threw a rolled-up sock at Chase. "Start the meeting."

Chase blinked and tried to refocus on what had just happened. Tourn. Trials...

Did Tristan tell you about the hangar?

Romeo tapped his wristwatch through the awkward pause. "I've set a countdown. Sixty-one hours and twelve minutes until the trials."

"How incredibly helpful," Sylph said flatly. "Now we won't forget."

Chase popped her knuckles. "All right. So we have three days. *Three*. And we have to have a plan."

"A plan for what?" Riot asked, picking at his bandaged hand. "We're pawns."

She threw a pleading look at Sylph. Plans were the blonde's forte.

Sylph sat taller. "Nyx is right."

"Never thought I'd hear that," Riot said. Pippin snorted, and Chase threw a dark look at her RIO. He could mouth off at her when they were alone, but not in front of everyone else.

Sylph continued. "They're not giving the U.S. teams enough time to work on our offensive maneuvers and weapons training, so we need to discuss how we're not going to look like idiots up there."

"Keep in mind I still don't know as much as you do about defense," Tristan said. "We're all ill-prepared."

A dead sort of silence filled the room, and Romeo reclined on Pippin's pillow, staring up at his family snapshots. Solid minutes ticked by, only broken by Romeo pointing to one of the pictures. "Is that your mother, Henry? She's kind of *hot*."

Pippin's face flushed so darkly that Chase barely recognized him. In fact, Pippin seemed more uncomfortable than she'd ever seen, which made her own skin feel too tight. He looked like he was about to blow.

Sylph interrupted her thoughts. "I haven't been this on edge since my aptitude tests for my Star application." She flung her braid behind her shoulder and faced Tristan, hard. "Do you have any ideas, Arrow?"

"Who, *me*?" Tristan asked coolly. "You're inviting the Canadians into the conversation now? Keep this up and we'll start feeling welcome, Sylph."

"We're in this together. Chase is right to get us talking strategy as a team."

Tristan's eyes darted toward Chase's briefly, almost flirtingly. Her cheeks warmed like traitors, and she buried a flash of their kiss as deep as humanly possible. It wasn't easy, but whatever had happened in the infirmary had no place in the oncoming storm.

And then there was Pippin.

"The trials will be as expected," Romeo said. "What we need to worry about is being punched out of a cargo plane tomorrow. We're going to test the already sketchy ejection system, and let me remind you that Adrien is not exactly confident about it."

"They won't send us up without some assurance that it'll work," Chase said.

Tristan and Romeo exchanged glances. "Adrien won't risk our lives, but…"

"But?" Riot leaned in. "*But* is not the word I want to hear in that sentence."

"But she's being pressured by General Dickhead Tourn," Romeo said. "He's the one that'll get us killed. Not like he's concerned with human life."

Chase stared down. She didn't want to know if Tristan or Pippin was looking at her. They should be; it was her fault. She'd long since suspected that her involvement in the Streaker project kept Tourn invested. Kale had even told her that her dad kept tabs on her flying. For the first time, she wondered if that was proof he really did give a damn.

"General Dickhead is his official title," she said because the group was too quiet.

Sylph crossed her legs, and Romeo stared at them. "So how are we going to dazzle the government board?"

Pippin made a dismissive sound, and Chase glared his way before talking over his objection. "Sylph's right."

Riot's eyes got a little big. "Now they both agree with each other. Anyone else feel like we're entering dangerous territory?"

"I do," Pippin said. "I don't trust them working together."

"*Pippin.*" Chase's eyes were on his fast and hard. "We have to trust each other."

"Even if some of us are harboring secrets?" His words jabbed.

The room went extra quiet.

"Don't," Chase managed. Pippin looked away, his face blotching red.

"Okay. That was awkward." Sylph cleared her throat. "Listen. I say we set up drills that show off all our strengths. We *make* each other look good. What do the Canadians think?"

Tristan took the edge of the bunk in one tight fist. "I think I'm still not over the fact that we're *friends*, especially after your stunt yesterday that almost cost Chase and Henry their lives." Tristan left the room so fast. Romeo followed his pilot.

"What is wrong with them?" Sylph asked. "Nyx pulls a thousand stunts, and I do *one* and look at everyone freak out at me."

Pippin's expression was still too dark. "Nyx gets special allowances because of her daddy."

Chase's heart flew into action. "Pippin!"

He wouldn't look at her. "Papa Kale lets her get away with everything," he added as a lame cover-up.

Sylph looked pleased. "This is true."

But Pippin had meant Tourn. He'd lashed out at Chase in her most vulnerable spot.

"Fuck you, *Henry*," she said, her voice low and mean.

"Whoa. Guys." Riot whistled. "Let's chill."

Sylph stood between them. "I've never seen you two go at it before. Now's not the time. Make up." She grabbed Pippin by the back of his shirt and hauled him to his feet like she was going to force them to hug. He yanked away from her, threw a crumpled piece of paper on his bed, and left.

The door slammed, and the moment ticked between them like a countdown.

Sylph's eyes were huge. "Nyx. You can't fly if you can't talk to each other."

"I realize that."

"So go make up with him."

Chase rubbed her face. "I'm trying. He doesn't want to make up."

"But aren't you two like mirrored souls or something?" Riot asked.

"Don't you have trouble with mirrors, Riot?" Chase snapped back.

"*Hey*." Sylph smacked Chase on the cheek and not lightly.

"Leave," Chase said, rubbing her smarting face. "I have to think."

Sylph and Riot left, and Chase sat on Pippin's bed. Sylph was right. There was no way they could survive the trials if they couldn't be in the same room, let alone the same cockpit. She picked up the piece of paper and smoothed it out. It was the picture of Pippin's mother.

"Mirrored souls," she muttered. She remembered the spiderweb smash across the glass in the boys' locker room after Riot took his fist to it. The shards crunching on the tile underfoot, glittery and knifelike…

Chase collapsed on the bed. If they were mirrored souls, one of them was broken. But which one? Or were they a complementing pair of cracks?

Maybe they always had been.

Chase didn't last long on her own. Her thoughts ran heavy and sluggish, and she soon found herself racing for the rec room, hoping to run into Tristan. Pippin's crush be damned; she needed to talk with the one person at the Star who wasn't currently driving her mad.

A Ping-Pong tournament was the main event. Cadets surrounded the game, hollering at the two fairly advanced players. Chase envied their laid-back enjoyment. They had no idea that over the next few days the whole Star was going to be secretly overrun with officers and government officials.

She found Tristan on the far side of the room, flying the jet simulator game. Wonder of all, he was alone.

The flight simulator consoles were wedged into the darkest corner of the rec room, complete with oversized pilot chairs and a massive view screen. Chase stood behind him, enjoying the zip of his flying. It made little sense, but just being near him made this whole crazed situation a little straighter in her thoughts.

"I can feel you watching me," he said after a minute.

She sat in the adjacent chair and picked up a controller. She talked fast and messy. "So. Giving Sylph a taste of what she deals out? That's gutsy. She won't put up with it for long. This is her academy."

Chase logged on to the simulator to avoid the sudden awkwardness, and her fake jet dipped through a ruined city. She steered toward the coastline, firing a missile at a large dock. It plopped into the ocean, and she swore. "Would you please show me why I can't figure this out?"

"You're flying too fast to aim straight on," Tristan said. She dropped a second line of missiles, all of them creating rings along the computer-generated ocean. "Unless of course you're aiming for submarines." He reached for her controller, and she could feel his attention like heat coming off an engine.

"I'm figuring it out," she said coolly, pulling her hands farther away.

"Let me help you."

"Are you supposed to?" She locked her eyes on the screen and flew her fake jet even farther over the ocean. "Aren't we supposed to be opponents?"

"A little bird told me that we'll have new offenses to face during the trials."

"Is that bird white-haired and lab-coated?"

"She is." He touched Chase's arm and she crashed. "You're all right, aren't you?" The tenseness of his voice directed her toward his meaning.

"The drone?" she asked. He nodded. "I'm fine. We're all *fine*." She ground her teeth on the word, trying not to remember Pippin's cruel snap.

A glimmer of his anger from earlier returned. "Sylph should have lost her wings."

"If that were true, then you should have lost your wings for leading me back to JAFA all those weeks ago. And I should have lost my wings about sixty times." She stared at the spot where his hand held her elbow and remembered the way their jets had glided across each other when they passed too close. Her skin tingled, and she wanted his palm against hers, fingers laced, in a uniquely brilliant way.

It made her heart rev like an engine…and then wonder what she was doing. Was she getting back at Pippin by getting close to his crush? No. In fact, however much she wanted to give her RIO a taste of her fist right now, she did not want to sweep in and steal his crush.

Tristan returned to his controller, firing a string of missiles to take out a structure similar to the Golden Gate Bridge.

"See, that! How did you do that?" she asked.

"Here." He moved to the edge of his seat. She slid next to him, her hip and leg against his while the light from the simulator danced over his eyes. He handed Chase his controller and pointed to a trio of battleships. "Swing back around and try to hit the middle one."

Chase did, and he folded his hand over hers on the controls. "You have to aim before you get there. The missile has a trajectory like a jet." Tristan's finger twitched over hers, and she fired, hitting the middle ship. It tipped and burned, sinking fast. "There you go."

She swung the jet back around and shot at the first battleship. It hit straight on, and Chase couldn't help letting out a whoop. The fake boat split and sank like the *Titanic*, butt up. When she turned, she found Tristan too close.

He bumped her leg with his. "We work well together." His smile held a fair amount of swagger, like he loved how much tension bounced between them. She eyed his lips. *All* she could think about was that kiss, and she couldn't help wondering if he was thinking about it too.

"Should we talk about what happened in the infirmary?" Apparently, he was.

"Do you want to?"

Now *he* was looking at *her* lips. His smile started to lean in and she looked away.

"Pippin," she said. Her emotions corkscrewed through her chest from his name. "He…pointed out that I've been distracted. I need to focus on flying."

"All right, I have to ask. What's up with your RIO? Is he always this bipolar?" Tristan said. "Romeo is worried about him. We can never tell if he's going to hang with us or act like we don't exist."

"I have to admit that I'm glad I'm not the only one he does that to." She paused and chewed her thumbnail. "Have you and Pippin had a moment or something? In the hangar?"

Tristan blushed through the cheekbones, and she wasn't imagining it. "What? You can tell me," she said. "I'm cool about whatever." Her voice cracked ironically.

"I'd rather not say. It was embarrassing for everyone involved."

"Okay…" Whoa, what in the world had gone down? Did Pippin come out to Tristan? Tell him about his feelings? "What…how…"

Tristan saw her spinning out. "Hey, look, it was crazy when you guys got back—after the drone. He woke up on the concrete and thought you were dead. It took Romeo five minutes to get him to stop screaming. Pippin loves you, Chase, but I think he's melting down inside. I admit…I was pretty upset too."

Chase gave his speech a solid minute. Picturing Pippin like that—*losing it*—made her feel like running after her RIO that second. But what would she say?

"We're all melting down." She looked at Tristan. "Is there anything else going on?"

Tristan didn't catch her nudging. Or he caught it and went another way. His eyes drifted over her neck. "You tell me. What about our moment?"

Chase's mouth went dry. Tristan was. So. Close. And it sounded like he thought about that kiss as much as she was *trying* not to think about it. Another reason not to burst out. "Kale," she said like she was coming up from underwater. "He doesn't want us to get friendly."

Tristan sat back, frowning. He felt bigger than he had a few moments ago, like a sudden aggravation had puffed his shoulders. "You always do what Kale tells you?"

"Wow. You really don't like him," Chase said, factoring in the tense conversation she'd overheard. "Why? Kale's a seriously decent commanding officer. Haven't you seen how relaxed he runs this place? How many freedoms he gives us?"

Tristan didn't answer. His eyes trailed some faraway spot.

"Kale has saved my butt so many times. You wouldn't believe what he's done for me." Her mind skimmed the day she'd met the brigadier general. The way he'd given Janice murder eyes. "He's the only reason I agreed to come here," she admitted.

"I understand you have a relationship with him, but that does not extend to me." Tristan paused. "And he already told me to stay away from you."

"He did *what*?"

"I went to him last week. I asked him about what happened with JAFA, hoping that if we had an open conversation about it, I wouldn't be so uneven in the sky. I took a big risk and told him about my freezing up in the air, and I even admitted you've been helping me. That's when he told me to keep my distance from you."

"I'll kill him."

"Why? Isn't that the exact thing he said to you?" The simulator light played on his cheeks, brightly coloring Tristan's sudden sadness. "So many people died," he said. "My teachers and friends. I don't even know who made it. Who didn't."

Chase touched his chest. He looked like he was about to turn to stone, and she wanted to keep him with her. She sat closer. He reached for her face but pinched her ear instead, like he'd done in the infirmary.

"Why do you do that?" she asked.

"Seems like a safe place to touch you when I…feel like I have to."

She knew that feeling. It was the one keeping her hand tight on his chest. He had a way of making her lean in. Encouraging her to talk *and* listen. It made her feel the rush of what she wanted to do with him like it was brand new. Like she'd never kissed anyone before.

"Harcourt."

Kale appeared over the back of the simulator chair, making her jump even closer to Tristan. The brigadier general's eyes narrowed. "Take a walk with me. Now."

28

FUR BALL

Cross-Eyed in the Fray

Kale marched her to his office without a word. Despite the ominous nature of their meeting, Chase filled with a sense of familiarity in the small, warmly lit room: the coffee scent that almost seemed painted into the furniture; the overgrown, weepy-armed plants; and the line of old muskets on the wall that she always wanted to throw against her shoulder and take aim.

Kale surprised her by sitting in the squishy leather chair—her chair—and picking a mug off his desk. "Have a seat," he said.

The only other chair was behind his desk. After a pause, she sat in it, marveling at the new angle of the office. The Stars and Stripes on the opposite wall had never seemed more prominent. Chase aligned her thoughts on how she'd defend her friendship—it was a friendship, wasn't it?—with Tristan, but her order left her as soon as Kale spoke.

"I hear you're fighting with your RIO."

"What? How…" She grabbed the top of her legs and squeezed. "Who told you?"

Kale rubbed his eyes. "Doesn't matter."

"Damn it, Sylph!" Chase's hands turned to fists and pounded. "I'm going to ki—"

"You're going to do as you're told and be thankful you have someone like Grenadine watching your back."

"Yeah. *Thankful*," Chase grumbled.

"I'll ask you two questions, Harcourt. The first—do we need to have a joint meeting with Doctor Ritz?"

"No," Chase said. "I can deal with Pippin." Her words came out a little harsh. A little mobsterish, and they seemed to hang in the air and brag her overconfidence. How could she make up with Pippin? Every time she tried, she only made things worse…

"Your second question, General?"

"What's wrong?"

Chase stared at Kale. He was lying back, revealing neck whiskers that were even grayer than his wavy hair. She'd been angry at Kale on her way to his office, but all that evaporated when she saw how tired and beaten he looked. "Can I say 'everything'?" she asked.

"You can, but you'll have to follow up with specifics."

"How do I do that?" Chase felt slightly explosive. "Why does everyone assume I'll just spill my guts so easily?" It might work when she was under the spell of Tristan's challenges and too-blue eyes, but with everyone else—Pippin *and* Kale—she was still closed-down Chase. Nyx. Tagline: Off-limits.

Through Chase's lip-biting silence, Kale sipped his mug. Finally, he deposited it on the edge of the desk. "It's been a day, hasn't it?"

Breaking Sky

Chase peered into the mug, ready to find the hard stuff. "Is that...are you drinking milk?"

"Whole milk. That's how you know I'm on the edge." He rubbed his hands over his face. "Your father digs right into me."

"We have that in common." She sniffed the mug, but it really was milk. "General?" She dug for the words and felt red and raw. "He won't take your command away. I mean, he can't just up and fire you. Can he?"

"He could. It was a bit of a joke that I got this post in the first place. I wasn't star material before I got the Star, so to speak. But your father insisted. He wanted me here, and everyone takes his postings very seriously."

"Mind if we call him Tourn? When you say 'your father,' it makes me feel like turning around to see if you're talking to someone else."

Kale nodded slowly. He understood. He always seemed to understand, and she held on to that feeling. Chase shuffled some pages on his desk. "I've heard stories about what the Star was like before you came here. Hundreds of rules. Inspections and dress codes. No fun."

"When I came here, I found an academy of promising cadets who were too young for military restrictions. They were warring with each other. Flyboys versus the ground crew. Seniors preying on freshmen. Nasty attitudes and backstabbing. I made some unpopular changes. Instituted more relaxed policies. Heck, I even let you kids swear."

"I love it here." Chase found tears rather close. "They won't get rid of you, General. Not after the Streakers are approved. You're...cool."

He smiled briefly. "The government's representatives will be scrutinizing more than your flying when they're here. The Star used to produce valuable cadets for the U.S. Air Force Academy by being hard on them. Curbing their youth. Tourn wasn't wrong about my cadets. 'They enjoy too much freedom,' I've been told. Academy life in Colorado comes as a shock."

"But we don't need to beat kids into military service. We need those who are willing and ready and able." Chase sounded like her father, but she didn't care. "Tourn understands that. He'd rather have five good men than fifteen conscripted ones. That's one of his mottos."

Kale sat forward and put his elbows on his knees. "I don't know what's made you talk about your—about Tourn so civil-like, but it's good. It'll help when he shows up on Sunday."

"He's not going to make me fall apart," she said, more for herself than Kale. "I'll be ready." She held back from adding, *Although I have no idea how.*

"We both will."

Snowflakes swirled outside Kale's small window. The black backdrop made each white crystal stand out. "General Kale?" she started. When Chase and Tristan talked about Tourn, the words just seemed to fall out, but it wasn't like that with Kale. These words weren't connected. She had to line them up, slow and painful.

"I've actually been thinking. About Tourn. A lot."

"A dangerous pastime."

"Seriously. He...he seems so hated. I mean, even the Canadian officers bristle when he shows up on screen. So why does he have so many stars? He's been plastered with promotions ever since the world found out what he did to the Philippines."

"First of all, the only thing he did was follow orders." Kale leaned back. "Secondly, Tourn has a knack for organizing bases and planning operations. The men and women under his command do their best because they're never left wanting. I've seen it time and again. You know I don't praise him for the fun of it, but he knows what people need, and he gets it for them."

"Except me." Now she couldn't stop herself. "He couldn't figure out what I needed."

"Didn't he make sure you made it to the academy?"

"You could say that. He definitely faked my application." Chase's hands searched for her knees. For the edge of the desk. For something to hold on to. Nothing stilled them until she clasped her wrists and squeezed.

"Go on," Kale said, not unkindly, but with an edge sharp enough to suggest that what she was admitting to was as big of a secret as she always thought it would be.

Kale's office turned too quiet as the truth unfurled like a wet and clinging flag. "You showed up at my apartment all those years ago with a plane ticket, and I thought escaping Janice sounded like the best thing in the world. I...never meant to deceive you." She sighed. "When the government board gets here, they're going to go through every word of my file. Something won't add up. I'm sure of it."

A new idea burned like a splash of jet fuel. "Tourn could get in trouble."

"Harcourt, listen carefully," Kale said. She focused on the wave of his hair and the way he looked at her like she mattered. "First, the government would never touch Tourn. They need him to shoulder too much guilt."

Chase breathed a tad easier. Had she actually been worried for Tourn? No way. Never.

"And"—Kale leaned back in his chair—"I know about your paperwork, or I should say, I expected as much. New cadets are thrilled when they get their invitation to the academy, seeing as how they've been working on their application for years. I've heard stories of celebration parties where the whole town is invited." He paused. "Do you remember what you said when I showed you the acceptance letter?"

She shook her head.

"You leaned in so your mother couldn't hear and asked, 'Will *he* be there?'"

Chase looked down at her hands while Kale continued. "After that, I didn't think I could convince you to attend, but you surprised me. Reversed your attitude and energy in one conversation."

Chase swallowed. Kale was still on her side, and now she felt a bit sheepish about doubting him. "What *will* happen if the government board figures it out?"

"I've gone over your files, and it all appears in line. We'll move forward as though it's going to be okay." He sat forward. "I'm glad you admitted the truth. That shows real maturity."

Chase stood, as shaky as if she had cried, and yet also a good deal lighter. "I couldn't tell you before. I was too afraid you'd kick me out."

"What's different now?"

"Tourn is coming." And opening up to Tristan was unwinding things inside of her and proving that it was never honesty she was afraid of. It was the rejection that came with it.

"Remember, Harcourt, Tourn hasn't had a hand in your success here. He might have gotten you in, but *you* earned your wings. You became the best pilot in your class, and you won the opportunity to become one of the first Streaker jocks. And you're going to prove that in three days." He paused. "What will you do about Donnet?"

Her head grew heavier, that fast. "I don't know."

"I think you should take a page out of this book. Talk to him. Openly and alone."

Chase held back from pointing out that she'd already tried that. "He's avoiding me pretty stealthily."

"Not tomorrow. Tomorrow he'll be strapped to you and falling a good thirteen thousand feet. Apply your usual fervor and you'll get him between the crosshairs." She half-smiled, always enjoying when Kale tried to speak jock pilot. He stood up. "And though I'm so very *cool*, you should be in your barracks. It's late."

Chase felt surprisingly...good. She had Tristan to thank for that, which reminded her. "Wait. I need something. The casualty report on the JAFA bombing."

Kale was shaking his head before she'd finished. "That's classified, and you shouldn't even be talking about it. Router needs to let this go." He looked at her sideways. "Did he put you up to this?"

"I know I'm not supposed to be *friendly* with him or whatever, but we're wingmen." She felt strangely proud of herself all of a sudden.

Kale scrubbed his hands through his hair. It reminded her of the time Tristan had done that in the locker room, how it wasn't an attractive look but one that bled anxiety. "You aren't going to say you're in love with him, are you?"

Chase couldn't tell if he was joking or crazy. "No, General. He and I...we're just similar. We understand each other in the air. I trust him."

As soon as she said it, she knew it was true. It made her stand taller, although Kale only laughed like his terrible day had just received a punch in the nose. "That's so much worse." He got up and held the door open. "The intel you're after is above my pay grade, Harcourt. Even if I wanted to, I couldn't."

She readied objections but didn't have the chance. He pushed her out the door. Shut it.

Chase stood in the dead hall. It was past curfew. The timed lights clicked off in sequence down the administrative offices hallway, and Chase made her way to her room by the red glow of the emergency signs.

29

PUNCHING OUT

When Flying Is Falling

The back of the cargo plane opened, revealing flat land patched with varying greens. Farmlands in a Midwestern state Chase didn't recognize. She glanced back at Pippin, but he was looking at whatever wasn't her—and had been since yesterday.

Chase was weary from a midnight exercise fest. When she'd gone back to her room after talking to Kale, Pippin wasn't even there. And as soon as she'd tried to lie down, her thoughts about the trials left her sleepless. She went to the weight room and took a treadmill at its highest speed. Her heart rate shot up while her body lapsed into training mode. Muscle and motion. Strain and sweat.

She had pushed the track elevation to its steepest setting, feeling the burn in her calves. She had made herself think about Tourn's impending arrival instead of Pippin. It was a surprisingly easier subject. What would Tourn be like after five years? Would he try to talk to her? No. She knew that answer in her pulse. Tourn was all business. Cold and mechanical. A cog in the military machine. Careless.

She'd crashed. Literally. Tripped and shot backward off the treadmill, hitting the floor with a thud. The proof was a livid bruise on her knee this morning. She'd wanted to show Pippin, but he'd shown up late with Romeo, chatting in French.

But he couldn't escape her now. They were strapped into a metal pod Adrien had built during the night. It looked like a Streaker cockpit, except for the fact that there was no jet around it. Just two seats in a metal-skinned frame.

A rush-swirl of crazed air filled the C-130 Hercules. The plane probably hadn't seen atmosphere in a few decades, and yet she was about to parachute out its backside. The gusts tugged at her breath, and although Chase enjoyed the push of high winds during flight, she preferred a canopy. A glass shield.

Not this time.

Adrien fussed over the straps on Chase's harness. The engineer was red-eyed and huffing, more exhausted than Chase.

"This will work, right?" she yelled.

"You will survive," Adrien yelled over the engines. "We have two backup parachutes. You'll be jettisoned from the frame in your chairs and connected to each other under one double parachute. Questions?"

Chase shook her head. She'd watched the other two Streaker teams drop out of that door first; she was fairly certain it would work a third time.

"I got one. Why aren't we using dummies for this?" Pippin yelled.

"To test you as much as the ejection mechanism. So you'll know what to expect and how to react if you have to punch out. Especially in the likely chance of a water crash."

"*Likely?*" Pippin cried.

"We've skydived before, Pip," Chase said, holding on to the *X* of the harness over her chest. "We'll be fine." Her courage might not mean anything to Pippin right now, but she gave it to him anyway.

Adrien and a handful of airmen rolled the whole pod toward the doorway and stopped at the lip of the drop. She glanced back at Pippin and saw that he was also not enjoying the torturous sensation of being half out the door.

"Okay," Chase yelled over the racket, looking into the wisp of clouds. The air combed at her skin and hair, and she fought to breathe. "Okay, do it!"

The pod clanked as it dropped from the Hercules. The height of the fall was overshadowed by the click of things happening in the metal frame. They fell and fell and fell until Chase began to hyperventilate. Pippin shouted the all clear, and she yanked the ejection lever. They shot out of the metal frame, their chairs connected in a churning plunge before their parachute snapped open, caught the wind, and jerked them to a slow drop.

"Pippin? You all right?"

His answer was a string of curses.

"I'd say it works." She watched the metal frame pop its own parachute far below. She felt the seat beneath her and the parachute above, ballooning and wafting. The ground became clearer, more detailed. A tiny house stood at the corner of one lot and a dirt road ran down the center of another. Cows spotted the field.

She twisted around and found Pippin looking pale. "You all right?"

"Glorious." His voice was punchy.

"We'll touch down and get picked up. No problem." She tucked her bottom lip between her teeth for a moment, remembering Kale's insistence that she talk to her RIO. Now.

She dragged the words out, kicking and screaming. "I don't know what to say to you, Pippin. You keep looking at me like there's something I can do to fix this, but I have no clue. I'm really bad at this," she admitted.

"You are," he said.

Something dawned. "But so are you."

Pippin didn't answer. Chase was so used to the roar of a Streaker engine drowning out the world that the wind sounded like a seashell held to her ear. She heard its whisper and pull, the resonance of silence. "Do you have a thing for Tristan? Is that what this is all about?"

Pippin laughed in a sad way. "Of course you'd think I'm after your boy."

"Hey, he's not *my* boy. I'm…I'm just trying to get through the trials."

"You're suffering a personality change," he said. "Wanting to talk. Planning with Sylph."

"What about *your* personality?" She kept twisting to get a better look at him. "You're acting like being gay is a bombshell that should blow the top off my skull. News flash, Pip. I know. I've known for years."

Now he looked like he'd been hit by an explosive. His eyebrows were high, and his mouth was in a small *O*. "How do you know?"

"Intuition. Or something. And I never said anything because I could tell you didn't want to make a big deal out of it. I thought you'd talk when you were ready." She waited, but he was still too quiet. "I don't think anyone else knows. Keep it to yourself for as long as you want."

"*Of course* everyone knows, Chase. People tend to pay attention to that sort of thing. And everyone can tell I have a crush on him. It makes me nauseated."

"Well, I can't tell. Who are you talking about?"

"You can't tell because you live in the Nyx Show." His tone was more hurt than mean, but she still stung from it.

"*Hey*. I'm trying here."

"Don't get upset. Remember, I'm not allowed to ask about your dad. Or your childhood. Or your mom. Or why you act like you have to prove you're the most unique, untouchable pilot at the Star every single hop." The breeze picked up and blew them off course a little.

"You respect my privacy and I respect yours." It had seemed so natural up until this moment. "That's what best friends do."

"That's what walled-off people do. I swear *that's* the only real thing you and I have in common," he said.

"So what are you afraid of? Be gay. This isn't some

turn-of-the-century homophobic military. Kale wouldn't even care." She tried to face him, but her harness was too tight—she was breathing too hard.

"I'm not afraid. Or ashamed," Pippin said. "I'm just not ready, and I was *fine*, dealing with it in my own way, until he showed up with his flirting and touching me all the time."

Now that couldn't be Tristan. He hadn't flirted with Pippin. She was certain of that—which left only one other new person at the Star. "You have a crush on *Romeo*? But he's so…"

"Straight?"

"I was going to say boob-happy, but yeah." She tried to add it all up. "Well. Shit. Pippin, that's the real problem."

"Indeed."

"Why didn't you just say so?"

"Because I'm embarrassed. I'm *smarter* than this." They were quiet long enough for Chase to listen to the wind again. When Pippin spoke again, he sounded soft and yet sure of himself. "He's from Quebec City. He speaks French without an English accent even though it's not his first language. Do you know how rare that is?" He continued in a rush. "He's a thoughtless flirt, but he's a decent guy underneath, I swear. We've been spending a lot of time together. I know you think he's an idiot."

They were slowing down, the parachute breaking their fall.

"He's a lot sweeter in French." Pippin blew out a breath that was so much more than a sigh. "And while we're airing things out,

Tristan Router is in love with you. Bravo Zulu. You're going to need a bigger basket for all those stolen hearts."

Chase held her hand over the edge. The ground never seemed so distant as when she reached for it. "How can you tell...that?"

"You guys are like magnets whenever you come into the same room. You fly like you're making out, which is really awkward for Romeo and me. Thanks for that. And when I thought you were brain-dead on the hangar floor after the drone incident, Tristan held on to me. Like he was as scared as I was, which was pretty damn scared."

All of a sudden, love wasn't so pointless. It was sharp when she pictured Tristan and Pippin...when she imagined frightening them. *Sharp.* It made her want to withdraw to her protected, unemotional place, but now she had no clue how to get there.

She was stranded in caring. Christ.

A few seconds later, they landed hard in a muddy patch of field. Chase unstrapped, offering Pippin a hand up. "You're my best friend," she said. "With everything that's about to happen, I need you on my team."

He looked at her hand. "I'm always on your team. Whether I like it or not."

"Let me help you."

He took her hand to get up, but his words were beaten down. "Help me do what? Fall out of love with a straight boy? How does one do that exactly?"

"According to you, moving on from people *is* my forte."

They picked their way through the mud before Pippin spoke. "True. But, Chase, you don't even care about them in the first place." His words burned while his shoulder bumped hers in a forced friendly way.

She wanted to point out that he was *wrong*. She cared. She cared about everything so much that she often felt exposed. Falling. Grasping at the sky. That's why she needed the speed. It made the very air something she could hold on to.

"I'm sorry," he added, and she couldn't tell if he meant for everything or this latest insult.

"Sure." She swallowed it regardless. "I'm sorry too."

30

WAYPOINT

The Heart of a Compass

"Except I'm not sorry," Chase told Tristan as they walked through the Green.

After a burst of a helo ride, followed by a trip home in the Hercules, Chase found herself back at the Star, no longer fighting with Pippin, and yet feeling more irked by him than ever. She'd pulled Tristan aside and hauled him into a confession of their situation that pretty much covered every word—except for Pippin's thoughts on Tristan's feelings for her.

"Should I be sorry? I mean, I'm kind of *mad*." She popped her knuckles. She'd been hoping that telling Tristan would make her cool down, but it was having the opposite effect. "I *am* mad. Ever since he's felt persecuted, he's been…cruel. And now I don't want to point that out because we're finally talking to each other."

"Well, first of all," Tristan said. "Romeo is about as hetero as they come."

"Pippin knows that. He's just got a crush. A *big* crush. And he's caught up in the futility of his feelings." She eyed Tristan, wondering if he felt the same way. She kept her hands in her pockets and ignored him when he pinched her ear. If Pippin was right and Tristan was in love with her, she wasn't going to mess with him. Hurt him.

They would be friends. Just friends.

Chase roughed up her hair only to smooth it back down. "Want to see something?"

He smiled, and even that was flirty. Tristan was standing too close, but in that moment, Chase realized that any distance with him felt close.

Chase led Tristan to the chapel, a place she never went. She dragged the thick oak doors open and watched his face go bold with wonder. The chapel could do that to a person. Strike them with secret greatness and remind them of the Grander Everything. She pointed at the steel and stained glass.

"It's a replica of the Cadet Chapel at the U.S. Air Force Academy in Colorado. It's supposed to make us feel connected to our life after this. The *real* academy. Where we become airmen."

Tristan walked down the center aisle. The door clamped shut behind them, and they were alone. "It's weird," he admitted, "but beautiful."

The skin of the walls reminded Chase of a jet, while the patchwork of colored panes lit up like a scene from a sci-fi movie. She sat in a pew and rested her elbows on her knees, her head in her palms. "Lots of cadets love this place."

"But not you," he said from a few feet away.

Breaking Sky

"Not me," she agreed. "I saw the real thing once. My father got me up at zero dark thirty, tossed me into a fighter without explanation, and flew us out to Colorado. It was my first time in a jet."

She closed her eyes and remembered the sort of awe-fear of speeding toward a sliver of sunrise. They had brushed by white-peaked mountains and set down on a patch of grass before a building shaped like a dozen upended fighter jets. Silver steel spires had caught the gold of the sun.

"That sounds like a good memory." Tristan sat backward in the pew in front of her.

"There are a few," she admitted. "If my time with Tourn had been all bad, I would have called it a nightmare. But there were a few sunrises. Maybe what I should really hate him for is giving me hope." She looked up and felt the breeze of relief that she now associated with talking to him. "You know, I've never told anyone that."

"Not even your RIO?"

She let silence be her answer and then wondered how many times she'd shut down when Pippin reached out. She always held back, pushed him away, but then he did too.

Chase laughed hollowly. "I think Pippin and I have been so wound up in being inseparable that we never bothered to get to know one another. It's weird." She got up and paced the aisle. It made so much sense. Pippin didn't really know why she pulled away—he didn't know the nasty details about Tourn. About Janice. And Chase didn't know about Pippin's family. About why he was at the Star, if he so clearly didn't want to be in the military.

285

Could it really only be about money for his family?

"I don't know how to talk to him. Not about important things," she admitted. "I tried questioning him a few days back, and he made it out to be the Spanish Inquisition."

Tristan was watching her storm back and forth with a crooked eyebrow. "Do you trust me?" he asked.

"That's not a question." She tried to hide the flash of a smile. "That's missile lock."

"Then pretend I have you in my sights," he said. "Important topics have to be worked up to. For example, tell me something small, but something you wouldn't tell anyone, least of all me."

"How will that work?"

"It'll help you relax. Or distract you at least. Think of it as a dare if you want."

"I love dares."

"I know. That's the one thing everyone seems to know about you."

Chase sat on the pew before him. "I'll try, but no promises." She closed her eyes and imagined her life as a sky and her body as a solitary jet speeding through the blue. It had never felt like anything could touch her. Or keep up. And after the heartbreak of failing so hard at pleasing Tourn, she'd embraced evasiveness as her true nature, but it wasn't. Not really. She selected a leaf—a small one—out of her sky.

"Your hair," she said.

"My hair?"

"Ilikeit.SometimesIwanttotouchit." Chase snuck a look and found his smile.

"It reminds my mom of her brother," Tristan explained. "He died before I was born. I'm named after him."

"And here I was thinking you were named for that ancient love triangle." She paused. "Pippin told me about Tristan and Iseult. Inescapable, cursed love. Stolen hearts. Depressing stuff. Pippin seemed to think it was unrelentingly romantic. He's that way about most fictional relationships."

"I've never read it." Tristan's expression was cool, sure of itself, and unyielding. She already liked it ten times better than his polite look. "I don't believe that fate can be malicious. Bad things happen, sure, but they're not deliberately aimed at certain people. That's just the great love story lie."

He made her laugh, and Chase felt surprisingly light. Happy almost. "Tell me something from your sky." She wondered if he'd ask what she meant. He didn't.

"In the name of even trade, I will say: your hair."

"What about it?"

"How does it stand up like that? You must put a pound of stuff in it to make it so gravity defying."

"Nope. Nothing. It's all in the cowlicks. I couldn't get it to lay flat even if I wanted it to. Touch it if you don't believe me." She leaned way over the back of the pew, making the wood creak.

He poked her hair, which quickly turned into a lingering moment by her temple, before tracing her cheek and jaw. When he got too close to her mouth, she snapped her teeth playfully. "Very friendly," he said. "You better sit back or you're going to fall."

Too late, she thought wildly.

Chase swung her body over the pew and sat beside him. Their proximity was a creature. She felt it, wanted to touch it, but at the same time, it frightened her. What if she hurt Tristan like Tanner? She'd never forgive herself.

She grabbed another leaf from her sky. Held it out fast so she wouldn't be able to change her mind. "Pippin lectured me about stealing hearts today." She had to look down to keep talking. She wanted to tell him that Pippin thought she'd stolen Tristan's heart, but instead she muttered, "He says I keep them in a basket."

"You don't look like the Red Riding Hood type to me," Tristan said. "And ignore Pippin. That's just the other love story myth. Hearts don't get stolen. They're given away."

He took her hand and played with her fingers, opening and closing them. Chase marveled at how such a simple move could make her feel like she was already stranded in the myth.

When he looked at her this close, she could read the pressure of the trials in the tightness of his skin. In the hard set of his eyes. "Feels like the whole weight of the Second Cold War is on our shoulders. My commander wrote me a note about 'righting the world order.'"

She leaned back, sliding her hand out of Tristan's. "The shrink told me that if the Streaker project fails, the cold war will drag on. People will suffer. She said it like it's my fault if it fails."

"It's not our fault," he said. She looked up to hold back some sudden tears, tracing the lines of stained glass as they outlined endless triangles.

"I'm terrified," she admitted.

"Me too." Tristan pulled her to her feet.

She rubbed at her eyes. Forced a laugh. "Oh, I see what you did. You got me talking about hair so we could hash out the pressure of the trials. Nicely done. You deserve a medal in this kind of thing."

He shook his head. "Nope. I failed. I was trying to get you to talk about something small so I could work up the courage to kiss you again."

His eyes were as clear as the colored panes, his hands on her hips. Tristan's hold was like his flying, tilted in, unabashed. Chase touched his wrists and slid her hands to his shoulders. Not for the first time, Chase felt something fly open between them like a door. It revealed a wide abysslike sky that she could fall into and never be seen from again.

He was so close that his breath tugged.

Chase pulled back from the edge. "Let's not ruin this."

"Ruin?"

"You saw what I did to Riot."

"Riot did that to Riot."

"What about Tanner?" She watched Tristan catch on, realize she was pushing him away. He gave her a few inches. "I have this track record. I like someone until I don't. Until I'm sick of them. I'd say you and I are at optimum liking range on my part. Everything else is downhill."

"I don't believe you."

"Can't fight the pattern." She walked toward the door, shelving her feelings for Tristan with her past hookups. He stuck out like a novel among magazines—but she couldn't take it back. "Having a crush on you is the best thing to look forward to right now." Yes, that made sense. "I'd like to keep it."

"A crush? That's what you think this is?" He crossed the space between them and put a hand on the door. "This might sound crazy, but hear me out. Have you ever been in love?"

She wanted to know what Tristan looked like when he talked about love, but she couldn't risk checking. Instead she studied the spread of his fingers across the oak. He had nice boy hands. Chase wanted them testing all her curves—but even as she felt herself crest toward him, she brought herself back down. She was going to play it safe this time.

"Love is…" She searched for her own answer to this never-ending problem. "Love doesn't really work. Not for me."

"I understand why you're holding back. A week ago, I was ready to glue my hands in my pockets just so I wouldn't be tempted to touch you."

"And now you think it's a good idea?"

"Feels like the only idea." He put his forehead against hers. "I was wasting a serious amount of energy keeping my distance. You don't feel that way?"

She did—or had. It was confusing. Somehow things had gone too far.

"I'm sorry." She leaned in without meaning to, her face so close to his that she jerked when she pulled back. "This is too complicated."

He opened the door for her. "You're going to have a hard time convincing me to give up, Chase. Especially when you look at me like you just did."

They left together. Chase kept waiting for them to part ways, but Tristan followed her to the rec room. He really wasn't going to give up, and he'd even snared her into another minor conversation—this one about how much weight she could bench—when everything changed.

All of the screens in the rec room were blaring red. A few dozen cadets were standing there, silent. Gaping.

Horrified.

The brilliant red of the New Eastern Bloc's flag took up the whole screen, the parade of stars standing almost three-dimensional against the vivid color. A voice blared. The language felt fast and angry. A threat. Chase thought it might be Chinese, but then it switched, turning to Russian before it lapsed into Hindi.

Ri Xiong Di was making a move.

The brigadier general rounded up the Streaker teams in his office. "Get comfortable," he said, but there weren't enough seats.

They lined up along the wall while Sylph dominated Chase's leather chair.

The television showed the red flag while the threat looped at them. Chase's heart banged while she waited for someone to speak. Translate. Make sense of the endless words. She looked to Pippin; he could understand at least one of those languages—but he was paler than he had been when they were falling through the clouds.

She scratched at her shoulder nervously, needing to hold on to something. Tristan's hand was there within a beat and locked fingers with hers. It grounded her even as she lost herself to imagined flashes of atomic bombs. Mushroom clouds spotting the western seaboard. She stepped back against Tristan's chest, and his free arm wrapped around her waist.

Kale muted the television. "Ri Xiong Di is showing off," he said. "They've hacked every station, every secure link. Even the Internet is locked red. They've been playing this nonstop for half an hour."

"What does it mean?" Sylph asked. "It's clearly a warning."

"A threat," Pippin said, his voice cracking.

"It's a reiteration of everything we've been warned of in the past. Not to band together with other countries. Not to make a show of military advancements. General Tourn was more than likely correct that they're now aware that the Streakers are impervious to their advanced hacking abilities and that we were finally able to bring down one of their drones.

"Our older jets are at Alert 15, but they're too likely to be wirelessly overridden. Ri Xiong Di would delight in turning our own birds against us for the show alone."

Riot stood forward. "Screw the trials. Let's launch the Streakers at them now."

Kale held up a hand. "It's never that simple. The trials will be two days from now, and they're more important than ever. I know it doesn't seem this way, but we're lucky. They've sent us a warning, but they haven't acted. We have to hope they don't act before we're ready."

Pippin stood up from where he'd sat on the floor. "Of course they'll act before we're ready. That's what they do. Intercept. Prevent. Thwart. They've been knocking our knees out every step of the way for decades. That's how they stay on top."

Kale nodded as though he was only half-listening. The muted threat continued behind him, the red flag almost vibrating with brightness. "Things are coming to a head. I…there are things the government would like to keep from you, but I don't agree. Maybe it'll cost me my job, but we know Ri Xiong Di wants a Streaker more than anything. The spy network is abuzz about it. Every time you go up, you need to worry about that. We're going to keep you as far from their territory as possible, but still, be aware that you're—for lack of a better phrase—being hunted."

The room crashed into silence.

"Those dummy missiles you've been flying with…they're being swapped out for active ones as we speak. You're flying hot from now on."

Chase pushed against Tristan a little more. She had imagined flying hot, but now that it was happening, she couldn't believe it. Active missiles under her wings? *Active?*

The only sound was Riot breathing too hard while Sylph rubbed his back in tight circles. Kale flipped off the television. The room dimmed without the blaring red.

"Inconsiderate a-holes," Sylph muttered. "The least they could do is subtitle that shit for us."

Romeo forced a snicker, but Chase couldn't feel the humor. Terror was on the horizon, and it was more than losing *Dragon* or facing Tourn. It was the pursuit of world war. She could feel it like a trailing missile, already fired.

Heat-seeking.

Inevitable.

31

PUCKER FACTOR

What to Be Scared Of

The next morning, the Streaker teams were scheduled for full physicals to clear them for the trials. Chase dragged herself through breakfast, her stomach remaining empty.

She'd also dodged Pippin, not wanting to hash out what was still bothering her when they had supposedly made up. She had to pretend like everything was all right. They had to get through the trials, and then? Find a way to face Ri Xiong Di.

"You all right?" Tristan asked when they met at the door to the infirmary.

"Not looking forward to being poked and prodded," she said. "And I'm a little…you know?"

"Yeah." He placed a hand on her shoulder, but his fingers tickled the back of her neck. She grabbed his thumb and flipped it behind his back, but that only brought her chest against him, his other hand reaching behind for her waist.

Pippin turned the corner to witness, and he gave Chase a look that made her feel like she'd done wrong. He was getting too good at judging.

"I need a word with my RIO," she told Tristan.

"Course." He cast a quick glance at Pippin and turned into the infirmary.

Pippin leaned against the wall. "Looks like things are going well with Cadet All-Shoulders and Flowing Mane."

"No," she said. "I turned him down last night. You'd have been proud."

Pippin laughed. "You thought I'd be proud that you've been making out with people you barely tolerate for years, and the one time you have real feelings, you manage to abandon them? No, Chase. I'm not proud of you."

"I already know what you think of my love life." She crossed her arms tight. "But you know what, yours doesn't shine that much brighter, does it?" She waited, but like his affectionate quirk, his comebacks were MIA. "I want to help you, but first, quit lashing out at me, will you?"

"Help?" One of Pippin's hands flew to his chest, his fingers drumming an about-to-lose-my-temper beat. "How is it that you're planning to help again?"

Sylph and Riot turned the corner, catching Pippin's glare and the tail end of their heated words.

"Get along now," Riot said. "We've got to save the world tomorrow."

Sylph hauled him into the infirmary before he could say anything else.

Through the awkwardness that followed, Chase looked over Pippin. He'd been an acne victim when he arrived at the Star, but his face was now clear except for the temples. She was surprised to realize he was combing his hair a little differently. Maybe taking more time with his shaving too. She was even more surprised to find tears in the corners of her eyes.

"You should try truth, Pippin. You think people know about you, but that's different than being out. Being open." The idea seemed even better when she said it. "Being honest worked with Tristan. I've been talking to him about Tourn, and it makes me trust him—"

"You've been talking to Tristan about your father?" Pippin sprang from no emotion to radiating. "That's perfect. Tell him everything. Even though I've been here from day one, supporting you, keeping your secret. Like one of your lovesick tailers."

"You know you're not like that."

"Then don't treat me like one!" Pippin slammed into the infirmary.

Before Chase could get herself together, Romeo sauntered around the corner. "Pretty lady at twelve o'clock," he declared. "Want to find a quiet place and get busy?"

Chase caught him by the arm and shoved him against the wall. "You always have to talk like that? To everyone? Don't you ever worry about leading someone on?"

"It's my natural state of irresistible." He looked at the way she was holding on to him. "Are we going to kiss? Because I will get decked by my pilot. Not that it wouldn't be worth it."

She let go. "If one of us had a crush on you, would you want to know?"

Romeo looked delighted. "Of course."

"And it'd change your behavior? Make you act like a human around that…person?"

He held up his palm like he was taking an oath. "I'd be the perfect gentleman. *Je jure.*" He dropped his hand. "So are we going to make out? No? Were you talking about Sylph? It's Sylph, isn't it? Come on. Tell me quick."

Chase left him spinning out in the hall.

☉ ☉ ☉

The cadets sat around a too-white bed next to a curtained-off section. The doctor was seeing them one at a time behind the white sheet, which meant entirely too much waiting.

It was painfully quiet. Chase thought it had to do with the fact that the threat from Ri Xiong Di had spread through the Star, and everyone was incapable of talking about anything else. She tried to convince herself it wasn't because the Streaker teams knew she was still fighting with Pippin.

Tristan sat on the bed with his back to Chase, and she turned, pleased when he leaned his shoulder into hers. Sylph lounged across the foot of the mattress. Riot was being seen first, and they heard him yelp from behind a curtain.

"Nut-sack inspection," Romeo joked. No one laughed. He checked his watch. "Twenty-three hours. Less than a day."

"If you do that again," Sylph said evenly, "I'm going to break your arm."

Romeo raised his eyebrows but said nothing. Pippin shuffled his feet against the floor from his chair at the far end of the room. *Pretending*, Chase thought. He was always pretending to be someone he wasn't—or holding back, which amounted to the same thing. It made her ache for her RIO. She knew what it was like to have a secret hovering over every moment of every day. Wouldn't it be better if he came out?

Would it be better if Chase told everyone about her dad?

Romeo pushed closer to her, interrupting her thoughts. "I can't wait, Nyxy. Tell me. Who is it?"

Chase glared. "Shut up, Romeo."

"What're you talking about?" Sylph demanded.

"Chase says one of you has a crush on me." He looked from Chase to Sylph. "Either way, I think I win."

Pippin's face was scarlet. His hand tapped a thunderous beat on his leg.

"That's not what I was saying," Chase tried. "I was only thinking that we should, you know, be open with each other. Learn to trust each other."

Sylph squinted fiercely. "About what exactly?" She was obviously thinking of Liam, her airman boyfriend. Chase had the distinct feeling she was about to get slugged by more than one person in the room.

Tristan turned on the bed, a warning look in his eyes. "What are you doing, Chase?"

"Yeah, Nyx," Pippin said, his voice too smooth. "What are you doing?"

299

"I—" Chase broke off as a staff sergeant barreled into the room. He thrust a piece of paper in her hand and left. She opened the folded note and read the message twice.

Bad news.

"What is that?" Sylph snapped. "You look like you just read that you're on the Down List. *Are* you on the Down List?" She glanced at Pippin. "This is because you two can't stop snapping at each other."

"No, it's from Kale," Chase said. "About General Tourn." She should have lied, but she was too stunned. "He's arrived on base."

"So?" Sylph fished. "That doesn't change anything. Why would Kale tell you that?"

Chase's heartbeat took off without her. She looked around dazedly.

"Why would you need to know about General Dickhead?" Romeo asked.

Riot pulled the curtain back, rubbing a spot on his arm where he had gotten a shot. "Pippin, you're up." He paused to take in the weird quiet in the room. "What's happening?"

"Nyx got a note from Kale about General Tourn," Sylph said.

"It's nothing," Chase tried, but she saw Pippin sit forward.

"Tell the truth," Pippin said, his voice cold. "Be open so we can all trust you. Like *you* suggested."

"Henry," Tristan warned.

"Tell me what's happening," Sylph commanded.

"Fine." Chase stared at Pippin, and the truth scraped as it left her throat. "Kale wanted me to know because Tourn is my father."

The silence was like flying into a cloud. All white. No sign of the world for a solid minute.

"You told me you were an orphan," Riot said finally.

"Wait. *Tourn?*" Sylph asked. "The murderer of the Philippines? He's like a hundred years old."

"He's in his fifties," Chase said, finding it bizarre that the first thing they'd be discussing was Tourn's age. Weren't they appalled? Angry with her?

Romeo swore in French, while Pippin looked disappointed. He left for his physical without another word. Chase made a quiet, strangled sound at his back. Pippin didn't know what the rest of the note said. She had to tell him.

In the meantime, Sylph launched an interrogation. Chase answered truthfully, all the while feeling like she was being emptied with each confession. No, she didn't know Tourn well. No, she didn't like him. No, she didn't know how he felt about having dropped the nuke.

Tristan's hand slid across the white sheet and held on to hers. He had to stop doing that. She was starting to like it too much.

"Well," Sylph concluded after her questions ran dry. "Sucks to be you."

①④①

Kale's note was a brick in her pocket. Chase could think of little else. Not only was her father there—at the Star—but he'd requested to meet her in the hangar. ASAP. She went through her physical absently, barely even jerking when the medic stabbed her in the arm to take blood.

When she stepped into the blaring fluorescent light in the hallway, Tristan was leaning against the wall with Romeo. Waiting for her. "Where's Pippin?" she asked.

"He took off," Romeo said. "He seemed pretty hostile."

"But…" Her voice ran out of fuel. "Romeo, do you think you could find him and tell him I have to meet my dad in the hangar?"

"Do you want me to tell him to meet you?"

Yes.

"No." She couldn't keep the hurt out of her tone. "He's probably too busy being pissed at the world. I just…want him to know." Chase began the long walk, making excuses when Tristan tried to follow her. She had to do this alone—well, Pippin was the only one she wanted with her, and he was gone.

Truth was, even if they'd been fighting for a year, she'd still want Pippin there above everyone else. She didn't have to tell him why her father haunted her for Pippin to know that he did. He knew. That's what was so strange about them. They knew the deepest things about each other without ever having the details. They just knew.

Chase met her father beneath *Dragon*. Tourn had his hand on her wing, and it just about made her growl. Her pulse, which had grown erratic in the buildup to seeing him, began to chill. He was the same as five years ago. The same as the view screen images in the conference room. Clipped gray hair and overly round forearms. A uniform pressed so sharply that it felt like a plastic mold he had been poured into.

For a long moment, she watched him examine the engine bay and fiddle with the landing gear. She recognized a pattern to his searching; he was performing preflight checks. It made her remember that he was a pilot. *The* pilot.

He turned around, and she clipped her hand to her forehead, strictly out of habit.

Tourn saluted back. "At ease." He took too long to speak. Long enough for Chase to remember she wasn't the only one who had no idea what to do with their biological relationship.

"General Tourn?" she finally said. "You requested my presence."

"Surprised you, didn't it?"

She didn't answer. Was he *trying* to surprise her? If so, why?

"It's been a long time," he added. Boy, this was going nowhere fast. Tourn felt it too. He started talking. At her. "When I first saw the specs for these birds, I thought it was a joke. HOTAS control? Manual navigation from a backseat RIO? Ridiculous."

Chase wasn't amused. She knew the Streakers were an odd mix of old-school design and killer engines, but that was why she loved them. Tourn appeared to appreciate them despite these qualities. The term *essential differences*, one of Kale's favorites, sprang to mind.

"Then I saw these birds in the air. Unbelievable." He looked like he was waiting for her to say something. She didn't. He touched the missiles beneath *Dragon's* wings. "I flew with these type of sidewinders once. Aim left of center, no matter what the target reader says."

"Excuse me?" Was he really giving her tactical advice?

"I've been watching your tapes, cadet. You've got a gutsy streak. It works for you, but you need to remember to listen to your wingmen. You surprise the enemy—that's good. Surprise your wingmen, and you might cost them their lives. Understood?"

"Yes, General Tourn." So this was just a standard maverick pep talk. Great.

"You're ready," he added with a grunt.

Ready? Chase choked on that word the second it came out of his mouth. A jet fired up somewhere nearby, and the whole hangar turned into a mess of sound for long minutes. When it had left through the great rolling doors, Chase and her father still faced each other. She didn't see herself in his watery blue gaze or the harshness of his features. She didn't feel any resemblance to his calculating heart.

They were the real strangers.

"So you think you know so much about me because you know my flying?" It was exactly the kind of petulant thing she didn't want to say. It would lead down a negative road. Remind her that she wasn't a person to him. She was a pilot. A cadet. A cog he'd put into the machine.

Chase was supposed to be at ease, but her whole body was so tense that if she had fallen over, she would have smashed like a pane of glass. She felt like that was going to happen at any minute. At the next word maybe.

But it didn't.

The sound of feet beating the concrete found them, the hammer of full-out sprinting.

Pippin burst onto the scene with his hair messed up and his uniform askew. He slid to a stop, making his boots screech. The near-panic look on his face faded as he locked eyes with Chase. "I'm sorry I'm late," he said to her, a bouquet of forgive-me-nows in his expression.

"What are you doing here, cadet?" Tourn snapped.

Pippin looked at the general with a casualness that only a boy with an astounding IQ and a vital position in the military could get away with.

"Team Nyx," he said with a shrug.

32

QUICK FIX

A Stopgap Measure

You railroaded him!" Chase couldn't keep from smiling as she and Pippin walked the Green. "He had no idea how to come back from that."

"There are a few perks to being a hot commodity in the military." Pippin broke into a smile too. An easiness existed between them that had been absent since before JAFA. She didn't know why it was there, but she wanted it too bad to question it.

"I almost lost it on him right before you got there." She rubbed the lingering hangar cold out of her arms. "It was a close one. If I had blown my top at him, really told him what I think, I'd be on a plane back to Michigan right now."

"I should have been there earlier. I didn't know he had summoned you until Romeo found me. You knew I'd come, didn't you?" She nodded, but it felt meager. Must have looked it too. "I don't care what we're arguing about. You don't ever have to deal with that blockhead on your own, Chase. Promise. Didn't I tell you that the night I found out who he is?"

"You did." She took a deep breath. "We've just been so unbalanced lately."

Pippin rubbed his temples. Hard. For a second Chase worried it was all going downhill again. "I'm going to say it fast, so stay with me. I've been Voldemort. You've been Darth Vader."

"Why do I have to be Vader? Voldemort is so much more badass."

"You can't be serious. Fine. How about I'm Saruman and you're Sauron?"

"You've always been too much Tolkien for me." She paused. "How about Dr. Frankenstein and Mr. Hyde? One of them is morally insensitive"—she motioned to herself—"and the other is a rage with primal urges."

"I'm not *raging*, but nice one." He stopped walking to face her. "Dark guises aside, I'd like it if we found some unevil things to say to one another, especially before tomorrow morning."

"Agreed," she said. Did this mean she had to go first? She didn't care; she had to confess before something else got in their way. "I wasn't trying to out you to Romeo. I just wanted to talk to him. He's kind of ridiculous, you know."

"I know," Pippin said. "Now I'll admit I wasn't trying to be a complete dick to you about Tourn. Scratch that. I was trying to be a dick because I was...*am*...really frustrated. Watching you and Tristan has been hard."

"Watching us? Why?"

"The way he looks at you like you..." Pippin was rallying something snarky. She saw it forming on his lips, and then it was gone and the truth fell out. "It's everything I want from Romeo. You know, a serious interest. *The* spark."

They kept walking, heading for their barracks.

"I'm trying not to feel bad for myself. It's extraordinarily hard."

They reached their room, and she sat down hard on the bunk, kicking out of her boots. "Pippin, I think you're right. Things with Tristan are…different?"

"You don't sound so sure."

"I'm not. You know this stuff isn't coded for me."

"Then allow me to translate." Pippin sat beside her on his bunk. They weren't the sort to put their arms around each other, but his proximity did something along those lines. "Go for it."

"What?"

"Go. For. It. You have nothing to lose with Tristan."

"I could hurt him, Pip. I have a feeling that Tristan's jilted heart will make Riot's look like rumble strips."

He shook his head. "I don't know about you, but I'm sick of playing it safe. It's getting me nowhere."

Chase smirked. "Does that make me sick of playing it reckless?"

He looked at her from the side. "Maybe it does."

"So what now?" she asked. "What can we do before tomorrow?" The trials reared up in her thoughts, making her nerves run a few spastic jumping jacks.

"I suggest you find Tristan and make the best of the countdown to doomsday. I have a date with Romeo. I'm teaching him how to play pool. Well, he doesn't know it's a date, but that works for me." He looked at Chase from the side. "I like being near him. It's pure energy. Even when all I want to do is strangle him for all his blind flirting."

"That's love, isn't it?" she asked, remembering how desperate she had been to spar with Tristan. Pippin nodded.

For the first time in her life, love made so much stupid sense.

She pressed her head to his chest and wrapped her arms around him. Pippin wasn't into hugs, but she held on until his arms fell loosely around her. "I realized something when I was about to take Tourn's head off," she said. "He's the real stranger. I don't know why he does anything he does. But you—I can always see what's going on underneath, even if I have no clue what's happening on the surface."

"Maybe we should work on the details," he said. "All the… inconsequential stuff."

"We've got a whole career together ahead of us. Suppose we should be open." She took a deep breath. "For example, I know you don't want to be here, but I don't know why."

"My family needs the money," he said.

"That's not really an answer though, is it?"

He ruffed up his hair. "When I was nine, I told my mom about—well, me. She's such a loving person that I thought she would make me feel better about being different."

"And she didn't?"

"She did not. And neither did my brothers when they found out. The teasing was…" Pippin's eyes were dark, his expression heavy, and she held him a little tighter. "It's not that I don't want to be here, Chase. I've never felt welcome anywhere. Not for who I really am."

"So the gay genius RIO and the hated general's daughter. We're quite the pair."

"Indeed."

◌◌◌

In the hangar, the Streakers stood together, wing to wing. *Pegasus* first, polished and beautiful. *Dragon* next, with brand-new wheels and more than a few dents and scratches. Tristan ran his hand over the metal skin, like Chase had done so many times with her bird.

"*Phoenix* reminds me of you," she said, surprising him. "Cocky. Intense. A little sexy."

Tristan turned around, his smile ready. "Sexy?"

She nodded, not bothering to hide a blush that seemed to start at her knees and spread ever upward. She stepped under *Dragon*, touching her jet's smooth skin. The pearly silver was her favorite kind of beautiful.

He stood close to her back. "If the Streakers don't pass, tomorrow might be the last time we fly together. I hate that thought." Chase did too. Instantly. She rested against *Dragon*, and he took it as an invitation. He palmed the jet's side with both hands, Chase between his arms. Her body lit up as he leaned in.

Then he paused.

"I'm waiting for you to say that this isn't a good idea." His eyes were their most fiery, and his hair was in need of some messing up. The kiss in the infirmary came back to her, wild and so much wanting. She took a breath and chose a small truth.

"You make me feel like I have six hands," she said.

"I make you feel like a mutant?"

"No. I mean, you make me feel like every part of me is reaching for you."

He made a sound like she'd just kissed him and punched him at the same time. "Chase, I—"

She put her hand over his mouth and led him up the ramp stairs to *Phoenix*'s cockpit. "In," she said.

He gave her a questioning smirk but sank into his pilot chair. His hands rested on the throttle and stick as though he might twist up into the sky at any moment. As she looked down at him, she felt scars on the inside, contrails that crisscrossed her mind without fading. She could tell Pippin that she wanted to love Tristan. She could even admit it to herself, but how could she get from the feeling to his lips?

She took the mach approach, climbing on top of him and strad-dling his lap.

He became very still. "What's going on, Chase?"

"I think…yeah. I'm just having a nervous breakdown."

"Is that all?"

She traced his collarbones to the hollow at the bottom of his throat. "Distract me?"

"Gladly." He touched a button on the side of his chair, and the seat reclined, bringing her farther onto his chest.

She surprised herself with a laugh. "Hey, I didn't know the chairs could do that."

"I'm still growing. An inch and a half this semester alone."

"Really?" She wasn't listening. She was too busy staring at his mouth.

"Why the breakdown, Chase? Did Tourn say something to you?"

She surprised herself with her answer. "No. Everything is okay. I mean, we have the trials, but I talked to Pippin, and I'm just…we're going to be okay. We'll pass the trials tomorrow, and then…" She messed with her hair. "Then we take Ri Xiong Di. No problem."

"Yeah, no problem." His doubt was playful. "So maybe I should kiss you—to pass that optimum interest in me or whatever you were worried about."

"I don't think it's going to work this time." Chase's chest rattled like a wild thing was beating against the cage of her ribs. "Besides, there are so many more important things right now. Not the least of which being the fact that we're going to be *hunted* in the sky tomorrow."

"They won't bring us anywhere near the d-line," he said. "We'll be all right."

"That's a good lie." She forced a laugh and leaned her face to his. "Say it again?"

"We'll be all right."

She kissed him.

313

His lips tugged hers in a way that made her pull him closer. Closer. She couldn't tell if he was a better kisser than everyone else she'd tried or if she was just better with him.

Maybe both.

Chase hit the canopy release with her elbow, and the dome folded over them. She felt like she was thinking clearly, and at the same time, wasn't thinking at all. Her fingers sunk into his hair while his hands slipped from her face to her waist.

A dizzy, weightless sensation emerged as she felt that wide open everything that existed between them. And before she could decide what to do, she was already off that impossibly high ledge—and he went with her.

Chase kissed him hard and fast, and she felt like she was falling, falling, falling without ever coming near the ground.

33

PREFLIGHT

Preparing for the Big Show

*P*hoenix's cockpit filled with a knocking sound. An urgent pound. Chase lifted her head off Tristan's shoulder. She'd exhausted herself in kissing and late-night talking and then slept like the dead. Her body was twisted and knotted from the way she had curled up on him all night, and yet it might have been the best sleep she'd ever had.

The dome of the cockpit was incriminatingly fogged, although they'd done nothing more than kiss. She'd completely let go, and she was a little startled to find that when she stopped trying to escape feeling, she didn't need skin or the drug of touching. She just needed him.

But it was morning now, and they'd overslept.

"Tristan, get up."

"Can't," he said. "You're on top of me." He lifted his head and looked at her. Chase was ready for that guilty distraction she felt after hooking up, but it didn't come. Instead, she kissed him all over again and found his mouth warm and wanting.

"Hey there," he said when she pulled away. "Good morning to you."

The knock came again, and Chase jumped. "Someone knows we're in here."

"I can hear you, dumbasses." Sylph's voice shot through the thick glass. "Open up."

Chase struggled to fix her uniform while Tristan hit the release. The cockpit opened, and Sylph glared down from the top of the ramp stairs.

"Let me guess. It's not what it looks like."

Tristan glanced at Chase in a way that made her heart dive.

"It pretty much is," Chase said.

Sylph grabbed her arm and pulled her out of the cockpit. "Everyone is heading down here in twenty minutes. I've already seen the government board members." The tall blonde shuddered. "You two need to get your butts in your zoom bags."

Tristan and Chase split directions at a sprint before they said good-bye.

Chase was halfway to the Green when she ran into Pippin. He had her G-suit and helmet. She began to dress behind an old drone covered by a tarp while Pippin played lookout.

"I think your night went better than mine," he said. "But tell me you didn't sleep in the cockpit. Just thinking about that makes me feel smooshed."

Chase stuck her head out from behind the tarp. "It was so smooshed and so worth it."

Pippin gave her a quirk of a smile. "You're in love, so I'll allow that one."

"How gracious." She finished zipping up, tucked her helmet under her arm, and stepped out. They started walking back toward the Streakers, where they were supposed to meet everyone. "Sylph said she already saw the board."

"I did too. A whole series of deep frowners, and your father is their king."

"What else is new?"

"I told Romeo I'm gay."

"You did?" She found herself choosing her words as if they were steps on uneven ground. "And it went...okay?"

"He immediately began to select boys for me from the crowd in the rec room." He gave her an exhausted but amused look. "So, yes. It went *okay*."

"That really is an inexact word."

"Multipurpose." He rubbed the back of his neck. "But I feel like I've turned a corner, you know? Maybe I'll reinvent myself in the public eye. The Air Force is big enough for one super gay RIO, you think?"

"I highly suspect you're not the only one."

"Maybe I'll start a club."

Chase and Pippin locked eyes. It was too funny. Too surreal. They burst out laughing.

They turned the corner around a C-130 Hercules and found everyone waiting.

Cori McCarthy

①④①

A fistful of moments later, the Streaker teams stood at attention before a host: the government board, Adrien, Lance Howard Tourn, Brigadier General Kale, and a dozen higher-ups from both the American and Royal Canadian air forces—and just for giggles apparently, Dr. Ritz.

Chase gave Crackers a wink when she caught the woman looking her way. Ritz's expression bugged out, and Chase had trouble holding down a snicker. Man, she'd love to let the psychiatrist know about the latest turn in her love life. A memory of the previous night poured all over her until she felt liquid hot inside, and she was unable to stop herself from glancing at Tristan. The boy got better looking every time she saw him.

Chase pulled back to reality against her will, forcing herself to assess the people who were deciding the fate of the Streakers. The government board was made up of four women and three men—all wearing tight, appraising expressions. Lance Howard Tourn seemed to hover over them like a smoke cloud as they conferred with the leader of the group, a man with coffee-colored skin named Mr. Archmen.

"He's so important, he's plural," Pippin whispered after the introductions. Chase hid her smile in the tightness of her mouth.

Tourn didn't seem to see Chase or anyone else as he began to lecture, keeping his eyes on the Streakers as though they were his real audience. His growl of a voice wasn't as deep in person as it had been over the conference room video line, but his choice of words was familiarly cold. He spoke of the importance of rebuilding the Air Force and of each and every piece of airpower. He said that the U.S. was a nation founded on these sorts of days. The sorts of days that changed everything.

Tourn concluded by bringing up the afternoon when the U.S. lost five hundred and seventy-nine fighter jets in the skies over Taiwan. She wondered if he'd get choked up while remembering all his friends who had died. He didn't. But he added that this day's success would make up for that tragedy.

"So no pressure, guys," Tristan whispered down the line of cadets. Chase slipped on a smirk while Romeo whispered something in French. Sylph hissed a hush sound that made Kale look over all of them with a parental eye.

Mr. Archmen stepped forward next. He examined the line of cadets long enough for Chase to notice that he took an extra few seconds on her, searching her face for the Tourn family resemblance, no doubt. He turned away disappointed, and Chase was happy for the first time in her life that she was practically a carbon copy of Janice.

Archmen presented interactive tablets to the representatives, Kale, and Tourn, including a syllabus of the trials split into three subjects: speed, maneuverability, and combat. Chase tried to focus on the rundown, but Archmen was purposefully vague. What kind of combat? Did they expect her to dogfight with Tristan or Sylph? Fire simulated weapons at each other?

No.

Their weapons *weren't* fake. Kale had told them only two days ago they would be flying hot. Whatever playfulness she'd gleaned from being with Tristan and joking with Pippin was beginning to leave her. Why wouldn't they tell the teams what the trials entailed?

Chase listened through the rising pound of her anxiety, her eyes dragging back to the spot where her father watched her. His clipped hair was thinning and his eyes were a fading color, but the scar along her arm still burned.

"All right. Let's get to it," Kale said, interrupting the last of Archmen's words. The Streaker teams saluted, and Kale took Chase's elbow and whispered, "Aim high. Fly, fight, win."

She nodded, a tight feeling in her throat that was some amalgamation of pride and fear. The representatives followed Kale to the tower to watch the takeoffs and monitor the onboard cameras. The Streaker teams looked at one another, and Romeo's wristwatch alarm sounded.

Sylph grabbed him, ripped off the watch, and stomped it into a pile of parts on the floor. When she looked up, a few blond hairs had broken loose from her braid. "I feel better."

They shook hands and wished one another good luck. Chase saved Tristan's hand for last, but he didn't take it. He pinched her ear instead.

She couldn't stop herself from giving him a hug. "Fly fast," she whispered into his neck.

"I'll try to beat you. Always works." He sounded confident, but his arms tightened around her. The fact that this might be their last flight as wingmen made it impossible to let go.

The teams separated to perform preflight checks.

Sylph hung back. "Be careful, Nyx."

"You be careful," Chase replied. "I can fly these challenges with my eyes closed."

"I was talking about that boy." Sylph arched an eyebrow. "I'd keep both eyes open with him. Wouldn't want to end up a mere mortal after all your faithful years of myth building, Goddess of Chaos."

"That's Daughter of Chaos, Sylph."

Sylph glanced behind Chase. "Isn't that the truth."

It wasn't until Sylph had stepped around to the other side of *Pegasus* that Chase heard the throat-clearing grunt. Tourn was standing right behind her.

"When the time comes, don't flinch," he said. It was a weird moment, and she thought he might say more. Something important. Nope. "Get to it, pilot."

Chase felt herself against a wall again, but this one wasn't of her own making. This was the barrier her father had constructed to keep her out. To make sure their relationship would always be on his terms. Chase had no idea what came over her, but it came on strong. "Kale told me you know how to help everyone under your command. You get everyone what he or she needs. That's your superpower."

"I'm a man. Not a superhero."

She fought for more words, but they weren't as certain as the first ones. "Even so, you couldn't figure out what I needed. And it was so obvious."

"I got you into the Star, didn't I?" His tone leaked annoyance. "Isn't that what you wanted? Didn't you tell me that fifty times?"

"*Want* and *need* are different. And you shouldn't have faked my aptitude tests. If anyone found out, I'd—"

"Faked?" He grunted. "You took those tests the summer you were with me. Don't you remember?" Chase was stunned. She did remember working constantly. Studying and reciting information. Running drills and learning how to use the flight simulator.

Tourn hadn't fabricated her application?

Chase was struck rigid. The whole time she'd been here, she'd thought she'd stolen someone's spot. "But you…faked…"

"I did no such thing."

The truth stung more than the lie she'd always believed. Without it, she had to accept that she deserved to be at the Star. That she was as smart as her peers. As driven and dedicated. No way. She was tantamount to a screwup, wasn't she?

Her breath became uselessly fast. God, Tourn was so good at taking out her knees.

Chase touched the back of her arm. The long scar was raised even through the layers of her flight suit. She tasted the mud of the land-mine obstacle course. "You…you left me beneath that wire for hours."

"I wanted you to get yourself out." He looked away first, and it surprised her.

"Christ," they said at the same time.

"Understand, cadet, that I am no father figure. It's not part of my mechanism. But I accept that, and I've made sure you were looked after at the academy."

"Looked after?" Chase switched on, revving so fast that her chest felt tight. "Kale. You told him to treat me special, didn't you?"

"I told him you were my offspring. That's all I had to say."

Chase was stunned, her shock bordering on panic. "Am I Kale's *assignment?*"

"Don't be such a woman," he commanded. "He acts outside of my orders repeatedly, especially when it comes to you. I even heard he personally invited you to the Star."

Chase fell into the memory. Kale in her apartment, with those shoulders that could hold up anything. Fourteen-year-old Chase had thought Kale was there to tell her that her father was dead, but then he sat down with Janice and showed them the acceptance letter. Kale had said that Chase's tests showed she had real promise to be a pilot, and when Janice laughed, he'd shot the woman a look that should have killed her.

"So you gave me Kale."

"I gave you a life here. Don't blow it." Tourn stalked off, and Chase was so disoriented that she couldn't make it through her preflight routine.

"It's cool. I took care of checks," Pippin said, coming around the right wing. "Hey. You don't look so great."

"I'll be fine," she lied. She climbed the roll-away stairs, ducked into the cockpit, and fastened her harness.

323

"What did he say to you?"

"I…I don't know."

"But you survived, Chase," her RIO said through the link in their helmets. "Now we have to fly. Harness up those feelings and whatnot."

Chase couldn't stop herself from watching Tourn walk through the hangar to rejoin the government board. The other higher-ups didn't talk to him. Didn't look at him. It had been that way at his own base, everyone giving her father a wide berth. "They hate him."

"What?"

"They look at him and they see dead Filipinos. They see all those media images of the radiation poisoning." She felt sick. "It doesn't matter that he was ordered to do it."

"So?"

Things began to line up. Tourn lived as an outcast, seldom leaving his base. Never answering the criticisms on the bombing of the Philippines, which the media dug up whenever ratings were low. It was a wonder he even had that one-night stand eighteen years ago. And when he had finally met the product of that encounter, he'd been so obviously unhappy with her.

"Did he reject me because I'm too much like him?"

Pippin was quiet. She felt a change in his breathing through the amplified sound in their helmets. "Chase. Listen to me. You're both pilots. That's where the similarity ends."

"I always thought I couldn't cut it, but maybe he didn't

want a clone." Chase had shown up at his base, ready to enlist. A ridiculous twelve-year-old who bragged she could do fifty push-ups. The way he'd looked at her...so startled. Taken aback even.

"Think of it this way, Chase. If there's any kind of decent in that man, he would have kept you far away from him. Protected you from his reputation."

"You mean like change my last name to Harcourt instead of Tourn?"

"Your last name was Tourn? Chase Tourn? That sounds like a comic book hero."

"He paid Janice to change it—a week after he sent me back. My stitches were still bleeding," she said.

"Your stitches? I don't know what you're talking about, Chase." Pippin's voice was all nerves. "We shouldn't fly right now. You're really upset."

"We have to." She fired the engines and felt the roar envelop her. *Phoenix* and *Pegasus* were already on the runway. "Can we check in with Arrow...and Sylph?" she added, hoping to camouflage the fact that she just wanted to hear Tristan's voice.

"There's no shortwave radio connection allowed," Pippin said. "We're on our own up there. Archmen covered that in the rundown, remember?"

She directed *Dragon* out of the hangar and watched *Phoenix* screech into the sky. Tristan held his hand up. A cocky wave that brought her back to her wings ablaze and the blue silver of *Dragon*.

325

"I can do this," she told herself. "I have to." She took a deep breath. Then another. "Ready, Pippin baby?"

"Always, Nyxy muffin." Pippin's tone didn't have its usual zip. Perhaps he knew better.

34

REDLINE

Breakneck Speed

Chase pulled it together enough to win the speed test by the length of the Green, hitting Mach 5. Tristan held on to Mach 4, while Sylph made herself comfortable at three.

Chase's body thrummed with adrenaline by the time she reached the coordinates for the maneuverability test. Hundreds of old fighter jets hung in the air, creating a cloud of bogeys that reminded her of the swarm of drones she'd seen a few months back.

"Look at that, Pip."

"They're set up like a maze. You've got to maneuver through them like an obstacle course."

A sour taste filled her mouth. Obstacle courses weren't her thing. And if she made a false move, she'd smash into a jet with a poor pilot inside like a sitting duck. She settled herself between *Phoenix* and *Pegasus* on an imaginary line and waited for the go-ahead while her hands grasped the throttle and stick uneasily.

When the signal came, she took off with her heartbeats striking noticeably in her chest. Sylph sprung ahead, showing off her impressive maneuverability. She even looked like she was going to win for half of it, but Tristan picked up a rhythm and ended up beating her by a Streaker wing.

Pippin and Chase had a good view of Sylph's swearing, slamming anger in her cockpit a few hundred yards away. "She's going to make Riot's ears bleed," Pippin said.

Chase eyed *Phoenix* off and on, feeling flashes of the previous night's engagements. She held on to the image of him kissing her, making her laugh. And then the conversation that stretched on and on until they were punchy with exhaustion. The memory almost managed to push away her stinging thoughts about Tourn.

And her thumping anxiety over the final test.

"What now?" she asked Pippin.

"We wait to find out what this combat is all about."

They didn't have to wait long. The fighter jets started to weave. *All of them. Dragon's* missile lock alarm went off, making Chase seize in her chair.

"Every single one of those birds is engaging!" Pippin yelled.

Chase watched the cloud of jets come to life and turn at her. "Holy shit, they're trying to lock on us!"

The Streakers split up, and the fighters chased. They weren't fast enough to keep up, but there were enough of them to get in the way and completely muck up her escape. Plus, she knew deep down that she wasn't supposed to escape. This was the combat portion of the test.

A dogfight to end all dogfights.

Chase pulled Tristan's maneuver, the back loop, and missile locked on an F-18 Hornet. The jet bugged out as soon as it had been tagged. "Well, there's the secret. We have to tag every single one of these suckers. Here we go."

Pippin didn't answer; he was too busy keeping their tail clear.

Chase glanced over and saw that *Phoenix* and *Pegasus* had caught on too, and the long pursuit began. It seemed to take many hours, although it probably wasn't more than two. Chase's eyes went blurry from exhaustion. Her ears stung from hearing the warning alarms when the jets flew too close, but in the end, the Streakers proved they could outfly and outmaneuver every single jet up there.

Dragon felt like a hummingbird among crows, darting circles, in and out before the jet in question saw her. Her body lined with sweat, and her hands were shaking by the time there were only three jets left in the sky. Three Streakers.

"Are we done?" Chase asked Pippin.

"Nope. We're supposed to get flagged when it's over."

"Then what are we waiting…" Chase's voice died out. She saw *Phoenix* move into a striking position behind *Pegasus*. "No way," she said. "This is a 'last jet in the sky wins' kind of thing, isn't it?"

"That sounds about as original as the military can muster. So, sure."

Chase watched Tristan gain missile lock on Sylph, who then left the scene with an angry burst of speed. Now it was just the two of them. "This should be interesting," she said. "He won't let me win this time."

329

"Does anyone else feel awkward?" Pippin asked. "I feel awkward."

Chase threw herself into the throttle and felt the magnetic surge of *Phoenix* blasting after her. They flew for heartbeats, for minutes. Forever. She swung around when they were way over Canada, engaging him full-on, a strong smile spreading over her face.

"Nyx!" Pippin yelled, snapping her concentration. "Do you see that? Look at the screen."

Chase glanced down and saw a blip coming at them. Fast.

Faster than fast.

She peered at the horizon until she saw something small.

Something bloodred.

Chase lost Tristan in a sunburst. "Red drone! It's fake, isn't it?" She was already running evasive maneuvers, but her mind was a blaze of denial. "It's for the combat test, right?"

"Looks real to me!" Pippin yelled.

She flew zigzagging getaway patterns, but the drone was faster. "Where did it come from?"

"It must have caught wind of our maneuvers. We were in the sky too long after what happened last week." Pippin was frantic, punching at his controls.

"Can't you get the tower on the radio?"

"No joy. Can that drone jam our signal?"

Kale's warning from a few days ago lit up her spine.

"*Hunted*," she murmured. "So I guess it's good we've got real missiles now, huh?"

"*Good* isn't the word I'd use."

Phoenix was flying tight beside her. She checked the desire to look over at his cockpit. She had to go faster. They had to split up. The drone would only be able to follow one of them.

Tristan must have understood. He broke right. She went left.

"I guess we win," Pippin said as the drone swung after them. "Or lose."

Chase dropped her altitude and speed until the drone was right on her butt, then rocketed *Dragon* out over a gorgeous patch of wilderness, complete with emerald fields and a huge bottle-blue lake.

"There's no one here," she said, gasping between each word. "No people down there. We should do it here." She flipped up the switch cover of the missile control and put a stiff finger on the trigger. "That drone can't go back to Ri Xiong Di, and it *can't* follow us to the Star, right?"

Pippin's response came a mile behind her question. "Right."

Chase hit the fastest speed she could reach on her tired muscles and swung over the shimmering water. Too fast, the drone was on top of them. She hit the brakes, and it flew by overhead so close that Chase heard the screech of metal on metal. She headed back into the atmosphere, shaking the drone a little bit off her tail before she had no choice but to come back down.

Down.

Too low. She had to pull back up, but the drone seemed to be waiting for her move. It engaged, nose to nose.

Chase fired, but the drone shot first.

A missile came at them in a blur.

At the cockpit.

Chase jammed the stick sideways. The jet jinked, and *Dragon*'s left wing exploded.

"Nyx!" Pippin cried out. They fell in a gut-twisting spin. Chase fought for control while the lake seemed to rise to meet the jet.

They were too low to eject.

She couldn't save the landing.

They skipped off the surface as though it were granite. *Dragon*'s right wing ripped off with a horrible screech. Chase's head whipped against her seat back, and they slammed to a stop near the sandy shore.

Smoke filled the cockpit. The canopy glass was somehow still holding shape, and yet it had been fractured like a net thrown over them. She hit the release and the canopy rose.

Chase got out of her seat, choking on each breath. "Pippin!" she tried to yell.

His head hung over his chest, and when she shook him, he didn't move.

Chase hauled Pippin onto her shoulder. They fell over the side of the jet, landing with a splash in the few inches of water. She dragged him away from *Dragon*. The wet sand swallowed each step, and she stumbled several times before they fell into a pile at the lapping edge of the lake.

Her helmet was gone, and she didn't know when she'd lost it. She pulled Pippin's off, finding a huge crack across the back of it. Bad sign. She checked his pulse, but her fingers were too cold from the water. She pressed her ear to his chest and listened for a beat.

He had one. Thank God.

"Wake up." She shook him. She knew she should be gentle, but she couldn't stop herself. "Pippin?"

His eyelids trembled before they opened. "My head," he said.

"You cracked it."

"*You* cracked it," he argued.

A bit of relief settled in. If he was joking, he was okay. She forced herself to breath, looking at the cloudless blue sky. "Where's *Phoenix*? Where'd that drone go? Will it come back?"

No one responded.

"Pip?" Chase pulled his body over her lap, and his head tilted at a harsh angle like he couldn't hold it up.

"I'm gonna—gonna—" He threw up, and she held his shoulders while the water turned gross. He collapsed onto her lap, and Chase found blood all over her hands. All down Pippin's flight suit.

"Your head is bleeding," she said. "I've got to get you out of the water."

"Doesn't matter. Cerebral edema. Brain filling with blood."

"Don't mess with me." She swore. "Rescue helos are on their way. It'll be any minute."

"They're hours away. We're in Nowhere, Canada. I'm the navigator, remember? You're the one failing geography." He sucked in breath. "I have a few minutes, maybe, before the pressure takes out my higher brain functions."

She ignored him. "We just have to stay chill to fight off shock. Okay?"

"Okay."

There was that word again. That god-awful word.

"Chase, I'm not going to make any sense in a…really soon. Hurts."

"You're not a doctor, and your head is fine." But it wasn't. His head felt heavier in her lap. It was *swelling* in her hands and—if Pippin was right—inside his skull.

An eerie calm fell over them as the water bloomed red. Chase forced herself to focus on him, but her fear was the wind and it was pulling her apart. "You just need some stitches and you'll be all right." She squeezed his uniform, pulled him tighter.

Pippin's eyes were glassy, bulging almost, but they were fastened to hers. "I hate these movies. They always kill the gay kid."

"Shut up. You're not dying."

"Why're you so sure?" he asked.

"Do you see me begging for forgiveness or spouting I love yous?"

"Indeed." He tried to smile, but his lips didn't quite make it. Blood lined his teeth. The panic spread from the corner of her mind and fractured inward at an alarming rate. Chase couldn't breathe. She couldn't lose Pippin.

Her breath rasped, and she glanced at the sky to hide her tears. "Where *are* they?"

"Lost my left eye. Confused," he said. "The bridge…cross it. The

Breaking Sky

right one." He started to gasp. His breath stalled out. "Respiratory center affected. *Confused*."

"Stop diagnosing yourself!" She shook him and then pressed her face to his hair. It was wet and gritty with sand. "Tell me about 'Ode to Joy.' What's it really about?"

"About joy. I was being…a…difficult." He cried out suddenly, his breath breaking apart. "Terrified," he said. "No legs."

"Your legs are fine," she said, choking on the words. The world was leaning in, shaking her, pushing her. She held Pippin even tighter. "Tell me something. Come on, Pip."

"Up, down, the notes. Up…and down." He closed his eyes. "Fools fly. No. Listen, *Chase*."

He gave her name his last tearing breath.

35

SMOKING HOLE

What's Left

C hase tripped down the shore, desperate to escape the waft of smoke.

She left Pippin's body. Her voice was broken from saying his name, and her flight suit was stained red from her stomach to her knees. When she could barely see *Dragon*, she sat hard and folded her legs into her chest.

Pippin was dead. The truth was too much, so she lost it. She let it go. It fled upward with the smoke, leaving her alone. And then she waited. She hoped Pippin wasn't right, that the rescue helos wouldn't be hours away.

But Pippin was always right. Even about his own failing body.

Chase checked the sky for the red drone. For *Phoenix*. All she found were a few large birds belatedly heading south for winter in a sluggish formation. It was too normal. Too picturesque for what had just happened. Her breath became erratic, cutting in her lungs with each seizing inhale.

The crystal canopy Chase kept over her for so long had fractured.

Fallen away. Now she was laid bare to a cruel wind. To feeling everything. The gust chapped the dried blood on her hands as she drew Ritz's heart circle in the rough sand.

She wrote *Henry* in its center.

And cried.

The helicopters came with a blast of furious sound. Two of them landed beside *Dragon* while a third hung in the air, making the surface of the lake turn white with chop. She saw the rescuers looking for her. Saw them sprinting down the beach. They were adults, not cadets. Real airmen, like everyone at the academy pretended to be.

Chase stood up, and one of the medics wrapped a reflective blanket around her. He led her to one of the helicopters, strapped her to a stretcher, her legs elevated. He swung a flashlight over her eyes and asked her questions. Many, many questions. She didn't bother to listen, let alone answer.

Through the open door, Chase watched *Dragon* being doused with white foam from the helicopter hovering over the crash site.

"You're going to be all right," the medic said. She started to laugh, a sick sound even in her own ears. "She's in shock," he yelled to the pilot. "Let's go!"

They took off just as an alarm pierced the helo. Chase thrashed, certain that the red drone had returned to finish her. "It's back! It's back!"

The medic held her down. "That's the military beacon," he said. "There are no bogies inbound." He pinned her arms and was leaning too close as he shouted to the pilot. His voice hit her like a smack. "What's happening?"

"Terror alert has been raised to 'severe.' President Grainor is addressing the nation. He's declared a state of emergency."

Chase's mind grasped at questions without understanding them. How could the president know? How long had she been on that beach? What was happening?

"What's coming from General Tourn?" the medic yelled to the pilot. "War?"

"Grainor says Congress is in session now," the pilot yelled back. "They'll declare soon."

Chase squeezed her eyes, confused and suddenly shivering. She felt *war*—such a small word—try to eclipse the crash, but it couldn't. It couldn't touch Pippin. She wouldn't let it.

"Where's my RIO?" she asked.

"In the other helo," the medic replied. He stuck a syringe in her arm without warning. Unconsciousness glided over her, and the rest of his words reached her unevenly.

"That's what...we get for...letting kids fly."

36

HARD DECK

The Lowest You Can Go

The tree line was too close. Riot yelled over and over, but his warnings were obvious. And wrong. Everything he said felt *wrong*.

"Shut up!" she screamed over him. Her outburst fed into her muscles, her nerves; she was jerky. Flailing.

Crashing.

Again.

Her wing caught the top of an emerald-green pine and spun out, clearing the woods with fire blazing as orange as a construction zone. Chase didn't have her visor on. Or her helmet. She wiped the sweat out of her eyes, shocked to find herself drenched, her hands shaking. "Get it together," she muttered. The U.S. was on the cusp of war with the New Eastern Bloc, and where was she? Stuck in the goddamn centrifuge simulator.

She shielded her vision from the neon blaze and threw the door open.

Riot got in her face. "How many times are you going to drop

too low? I warned you. I even gave you a countdown to the hard deck, which Sylph never needs by the way. HOW CAN I HELP YOU IF YOU WON'T LISTEN?"

Chase's head hung low but not in defeat. Or sadness. It was fury.

Poor Riot.

She reached back and slammed his face so hard that he crumbled to his knees, howling. Adrien tried to step in, but Chase flung the woman's kind arm away. "I can't fly in that stupid machine." Chase motioned to the Star City Centrifuge. "I have to get in a jet."

I need Dragon…*and Pippin.*

The words didn't come out, but they didn't stay deep either. They spotted her surface, tears coming on fast. Hands useless. Legs weak. She sat hard and covered her face, feeling the raw skin beneath her eyes and the weariness that now wrapped around her like a nightmare. It was exhausting to feel this much. If she could have unplugged every single emotion, she would have.

She was trying to do just that.

Riot got back on his feet, his nose bleeding. "I don't think you broke it."

"What is happening here?" Dr. Ritz stormed in, immediately inspecting Riot's face. "Did you do this?"

"He tripped into my fist," Chase said.

"Well, you've just set yourself back a week, Chase Harcourt."

Chase stood fast. "A week?! This is going to be over in a matter of days!"

Ritz spoke to Riot, ignoring Chase. "To the infirmary and then get some rest. How long until you're back in the air?"

Riot checked his watch. "Five hours."

"Go." Ritz turned to speak with Adrien, and Chase watched Riot leave.

He stumbled into two chairs on his way out, and it had nothing to do with his nose. He was leveled with exhaustion too. They all were, especially Sylph and Tristan. Tourn had ordered a permanent Streaker watch along the d-line. One jet wouldn't do much against an invading fleet, but with the radio humming nonsense and the satellite on the fritz, the Streaker's responsibility was to get back to the Star with a warning—a warning to send everyone to the bunkers...

Pegasus and *Phoenix* had been trading twelve-hour shifts over the last five days—since Pippin's death had turned the Second Cold War into an out and out conflict. And this time, there were no confidential statements. Everyone knew. About Ri Xiong Di, the drone, the crash.

About Pippin.

Chase glanced at Adrien's desk. The elderly engineer kept her handheld screen on mute, but Chase could still see the psychotic news coverage. The public's panic. Raids and hysteria, not to mention President Grainor's grim speeches and knuckle-white grip on the podium.

But this time, the screen showed a new terror.

Pippin's three brothers and mother had been squeezed onto a ratty couch. His mother kept her hand over her face.

"What is that?" Chase blurted, interrupting Ritz and Adrien's dispute. They followed Chase's glare, and Adrien touched the corner of the screen to turn on the sound.

The reporter leaned in like a predator. "Can you tell us about your son? What were his passions? His hobbies?"

"Nerd stuff," Pippin's oldest brother said.

Andrew, the youngest, squirrelliest, and inarguably dirtiest of the boys, sent an elbow into his eldest brother's side. "Henry loved flying. He was the best RIO in the Air Force. And the smartest. He had the best pilot too: Nyx."

Chase's heart bottomed out. She stopped breathing.

The reporter slid even closer, proving he wasn't a predator after all. He was a damn scavenger, and he was about to pick the family clean. "Mrs. Donnet, how do you feel about Henry's pilot? Are you angry that your son died while she lived? Do you blame her?"

Pippin's mom stared down.

Adrien made a move to shut off the screen.

"Leave it on," Ritz and Chase said in sync.

Chase needed to know. She certainly blamed herself. She should never have dropped so low with that drone on her tail. She should have let that missile take out their wing and ejected…

After a few long moments, Pippin's mother said, "They were attacked by Ri Xiong Di. We're lucky one of them survived."

The reporter didn't seem to hear her, launching into questions the family couldn't possibly know, including: "What can you tell me about the jet your son was flying in? Sources have led us to believe they're a new type of jet that has yet to be disclosed to the public."

Adrien put the screen on mute just as the image showed Chase's and Pippin's junior year cadet pictures side by side. Chase wavered and sat down. All the blood had left her brain.

"Hope they made a fortune from that interview," she murmured. "Enough to buy a real house." But that's not what she really hoped. She hoped it hadn't happened at all. No interview, because Pippin hadn't died, because there had been no accident. Her mind kept doing this sort of...rewind. She went backward, pulled the move differently, didn't head too low, bested the drone. Won the trials.

Then she celebrated with Pippin back in the chow hall. They ate cake. Well, he scooped up the icing and she ate the fluffy stuff beneath it. Like always.

Chase's mouth tasted bitter all of a sudden, and she came back to reality with more fury than she'd had after crashing in the simulator for the fortieth time. She locked eyes on the floor and made herself breathe, just like Kale had told her in the days following her accident. His words were loud through her thoughts, and she held on to them.

Focus, Harcourt. Breathe.

It might have worked if her eyes didn't catch on Ritz's low-heeled shoes and beside them, where a few drops of Riot's blood had smeared into a brilliant half rainbow on the tile.

Chase remembered Pippin's blood blooming and fading as it spread into the lake.

She gagged, and spit flew out in a long string. Ritz jumped back while Adrien came closer, holding on to Chase's shoulders.

Chase wiped her mouth and pushed herself toward clarity. Toward the pain. "Riot's going to get killed," she said to Ritz. "They all are. Sylph, Arrow, and Romeo. They're too tired! We need another pilot in the rotation, which means you need to give me my wings back!" Chase was in Ritz's face. She wasn't exactly sure when she'd charged forward, but she was there now, vomit breath and all. "Please."

The woman's narrowed expression, wire-rimmed glasses, and huge hair bun were different up close. Chase suddenly realized that Ritz wasn't forty-something but possibly early thirties.

"It's only been five days since the crash," the psychiatrist said carefully.

"Yeah. It's been five days!" Chase said right back. "Five days of 'any minute now' hostilities. They need me." Chase held back from adding that she needed the air. The speed. Flying was the only thing that could keep her from slipping backward. "You've seen the news. People are freaking out. They're afraid Ri Xiong Di is going to drop a thousand bombs on us at any moment. We have to do something." She shook her head. "*I* have to do something!"

"What is it you can do?" Adrien asked kindly.

Chase glanced away. "I'll figure it out when I get up there. That's what I always do."

Ritz exchanged a look with Adrien. "You have not yet proven

you will work well with another RIO. It would be dangerous to send you up there."

"Let me try with Romeo. Or better yet, let me go alone. If I get in *Pegasus* for ten minutes, I know I can get in the air. This stupid machine is messing up my concentration."

"Out of the question," Ritz said. "You've had too much trauma."

Adrien reached out a soft hand to Chase's elbow. "The Streakers weren't meant to be flown alone. You would only be able to take off and land. Even then, it's precarious to fly without a RIO to guide you."

Chase's chest turned to lead. Adrien was trying to help, but Chase heard it like a dare. Either way, she spun and left, making for the hangar so fast that the hallway blurred.

⚙ ④ ⚙

Chase found the Star eerily deserted. Cadets were shut up in their barracks, and classes had been canceled. She shot through the Green, glancing into the rec room. It was empty and shockingly smelled of old laundry.

A bold, red alert light pulsed overhead. Despite the pall it threw on the scene, the alarm hue was relieving. If red drones were inbound, if the whole Star were about to be blown to smithereens, the lights would go out completely. The dark of the Arctic could only protect them if they didn't cast a single beam—and *if* the missile defense software worked.

Chase's mouth went dry as she remembered JAFA's blaze, realizing for the tenth time that day how little of a chance they all stood against Ri Xiong Di. Tourn had been an idiot to wish for war. What could possibly stop the New Eastern Bloc from absorbing them into their empire? The only reason the Second Cold War had started in the first place was because of Tourn's bold nuclear strike on the Philippines. Ri Xiong Di did not think America would escalate so swiftly, and we'd scared them back a bit. But now? What could warn off the red drones before this turned into a last-man-standing kind of war?

Chase swallowed her doubt and misgivings and headed into the hangar. First things first, she had to get into the sky and clear her head…and her heart. But MPs stopped her inside the door.

"Cadets don't have permission to be in the hangar," they said together.

"I'm going to see Kale," she lied. They exchanged looks. "He's in the tower," she invented. "He sent for me."

"Let me see your pass," the smaller MP said.

"I might have forgotten it." She grabbed around in her pockets just to kill time, and that's when she caught sight of Sylph's boyfriend a few yards off. "Staff Sergeant Masters!" she called out. He stopped and eyed her cautiously, his arms stacked with paperwork. "Tell them Kale sent for me."

She could see the calculation in his expression. Masters knew Chase wanted this and that she knew about his big secret. "Kale wants her," he finally said. He turned briskly and took off through the cold concrete building.

352

"See?" Chase said. The MPs let her through, although one of them followed her until she ducked out of sight behind one of the older jets. She slid under the tarp and leaned against the cool metal of an F-14 Tomcat.

What was she doing? Was she really going to jump in *Pegasus* without permission?

"It was easier to break the rules when you were here, Pip," she admitted aloud. "Not so much fun without you pointing out all the ways in which things could go wrong."

Her hands spread over the Tomcat as her thoughts spun out of control. In truth, everything was *wrong* without Pippin. Wrong in the simulators. Wrong when Tristan tried to talk to her. Wrong when Kale looked at her like she was a shattered figurine. Wrong when she'd asked to meet with her father after the crash.

Wrong when Tourn had refused.

Chase's fingers snagged on a hole in the jet. Several of them. She pushed back the tarp and looked over a spray of bullet holes across the metal. They were rusted and leaning in. Crumbling with age—a mark of the nationwide fear of war that spectacularly outdated her own. She had to do *something*.

Tears prickled, but she shoved them down, running for *Pegasus* instead. She waited until she could move unseen, climbed up the wing, and sunk into the cockpit. It smelled of Sylph, and the pilot's chair was too far back. "Bird legs." Chase used the lever she'd found while in Tristan's cockpit to adjust the angle. "The girl has bird legs." She rubbed her cheeks, trying to get past the sudden rush of remembering how she and Tristan had somehow fit in one seat.

That felt like years ago, but it was only six days. *Six.*

She'd kept her distance from Tristan since the accident, and he'd given her that much, not that he had much time because he was in the air half of the day. Her face burned on those thoughts as she imagined him exhausted and flying the d-line. She should be the one up there toiling away. Not him.

She had been the one to screw up in the face of that drone.

Chase flipped the switch to close the canopy, and a ground crew member saw. "Hey!" the woman yelled. "Get out of there!"

Chaos erupted around her as people yelled. She ignored them. "I can do this."

Getting skyward would fix everything. Just a hop up and back again. Nothing dangerous. It would prove to Kale and Ritz that she should be in action—and silence her scream of fear that she'd never get skyward again.

As she powered up the jet, the whirl and swirl of crashing against the lake came back. In the endless sessions Chase had been subjected to over the last few days, Crackers had said this would happen. She set her teeth and steered out of the hangar and onto the snowy runway.

But that was it.

The jet coasted to a stop.

Chase's body was coated with sweat and her breath was a mess. *I* will *get in the air*, she told herself. Her body remembered how;

she just had to get her mind onboard. She looked out at the blue runway lights lining her path.

She drove the throttle and tightened her hand on the stick.

The first time she'd taken off on this runway, Pippin had been arguing with her. She'd done three passes without getting *Dragon's* nose off the ground, and her RIO had started to mock her. It had worked. The next pass, she had been so busy swearing at him that her nerves had stayed in check. And they had flown...

Now all Chase could remember was a very different sort of argument. Fighting with Pippin over whether or not he was dying. She remembered his strange smile and bulging eyes. She started to shake as she recalled the empty trust circle she'd doodled in the sand with fingers stained in his blood.

Chase pushed herself harder, faster, and the jet rose off the runway a few inches before her mind overflowed with painful images. Pippin was dead, and that meant Chase had no one. She was utterly alone in ways that finding a boy to kiss would never, ever fix.

Pegasus slammed down. Skidded out.

Chase was shaking so hard that she couldn't even steer back to the hangar. She opened the canopy, and a slapping wind filled the cockpit with shocking cold.

Everything hurt. Her joints, her legs, her head. But the worst pain was the gravity bearing down on her heart. She knew this pain beyond Pippin; it had always been with her. It was the loneliness that lived in her bones. It whispered that she was no good at loving. No good at being a friend or a daughter or a person. *She was no good.*

The sort of person who broke hearts because she didn't know what do with her own.

Snow touched down on her cheek, clung to her lashes, and melted into her tears.

"Harcourt." Kale's voice came over the shortwave like a whip crack.

Chase was finished now…expulsion for sure. She waited for it.

"Come home." His words hiccupped through her aching. She closed the canopy, turned the jet around, and followed orders.

37

WINGMEN

Those Who Stay with You

Listening to Kale had felt right. A little. So when he told her to go to her room and get some rest, she walked back through the barracks to the room she had shared with Pippin.

Chase couldn't keep her mind from rewinding. This time she went back to before the trials, to the conversation she and Pippin had about love. About each other. She hit pause there, letting Pippin stay alive in her mind.

She was so good at this that she'd nearly convinced herself that her RIO wasn't dead by the time she opened the door. After all, Pippin's headphones were still on his desk and his sheets were tucked in with tight corners, per regulation. His family pictures were on the bottom of the bunk overhead and his oily hair smell was on his pillow.

The bathroom door was closed, and the ugly fluorescent light reached beneath it. Pippin could be in there. She almost heard the toilet flush.

Wait a minute. She *had* heard it.

The sink was running—someone was in there. Chase jumped up and pushed the door open, suddenly flooded with happiness that felt equal parts desperate and dreamlike.

Sylph was rinsing her hands. "You always bust in on someone when they're in the can?"

Chase's hope evaporated. She slumped against the doorjamb. "What are *you* doing here?"

"Your door was unlocked." She held up a small plastic pterodactyl. "Why is there a dinosaur in your soap dish?"

Chase stole it from Sylph and held it tightly between both hands. "It's a pterosaur. Dinosaurs didn't have wings." Her heart felt strangled by the words.

"You're so weird." The tall blonde roughed up Chase's hair and sat on Pippin's bunk. "I'm not going to lie, Nyx. It smells like boy feet in here."

"Don't call me Nyx." Chase slid down the wall until she was sitting on the floor. She squeezed her knees to her chest, trying to hold herself together. "I'm not a pilot anymore."

"For now," Sylph said as though this information meant little to nothing.

"I just tried to fly, and I couldn't even lift off the apron. I'm on the Down List."

"That could be temporary, so let's not assemble the pity parade just yet." Sylph lay back on the bed. "Do you sleep on the top or the bottom bunk?"

"What are you doing?"

Breaking Sky

"I figured you needed a new roomie."

"I want to be alone," Chase lied.

"You never like being alone. I figure that's what all those boys are about. Thought I'd hustle in here before they find you hanging by your bootlaces." Sylph kicked her feet up. "I'm taking the bottom because I'm a bottom sort of person. You strike me as being a top person. Wink, wink."

"Did you just make a sex joke?"

"No."

Chase didn't know what to do. Sylph was in her room. Being sociable. Joking and talking about Chase like she actually knew her. *Dragon* had crashed, Pippin was dead, and yet this was suddenly the hardest reality to stomach. "We aren't friends, Sylph. You do remember that, right?"

"I don't have friends." Sylph's voice was matter-of-fact. "Liam says I am too imperious."

"The thought had occurred to me."

"Right, so, I'm imperious and you're unstable. But we got into the Streaker project together, and we'll get through the rest together." Sylph tugged her boots off and smoothed her shirt over her flat belly. "You are the closest thing I have to a 'girlfriend' and vice versa. There's no point arguing."

Chase stood and climbed the bunk, all the while looking over the edge at Sylph. "So let me get this straight. You're threatening to be my friend?"

"My plan is that you'll do this grieving thing, then—"

359

"Don't piss me off right now, Sylph. I've already corrected your RIO's face."

"Anger is good for you. It's one of the stages of grief," Sylph continued, as commanding as ever. "We'll get you back in the air soon. I'll let you fly *Pegasus* until *Dragon* is running again, but you'll have to be careful with my baby. Not. A. Scratch."

Chase couldn't help picturing the crash. Black smoke rising over that lake. *Dragon* in pieces. Pippin losing his words in fistfuls. The image was like a searing flare through her mind.

"I can't fly without him," she said lowly. And the truth of her words made her withdraw inside and shake like her whole body had been burned.

"Sure you can," Sylph dismissed. "Liam agrees with me that you'll be able to get your wings back. It'll mean practically living in the shrink's office. Kale has the final say—and Tourn—but you have some pull there. What are you thinking?"

"That I've phased into some parallel universe."

"That's also good. Denial and whatnot," Sylph said. "Another stage."

Denial? Was that what kept her mind rewinding, trying desperately to rewrite what had happened?

"I went through something similar when my grandmother died," Sylph continued.

Chase felt a pattern emerging. Kale had shared his backstory trauma earlier—about the wife he'd lost a few decades ago in child-birth—and now Sylph was throwing in hers. Apparently that's what people did when something terrible happened; they told you about something terrible that had happened to them. And while Chase could see why people would want to commiserate, it felt to her like tallying tragedy. No thanks.

"Grandmothers always die, Sylph. Old age is kind of a given."

"Do they *always* die from malnutrition, Nyx? From secretly starving themselves to save money for their granddaughter's training so that she might make it into her dream academy?" Sylph waited. The silence was so saturated with shame that Chase had to answer the rhetorical question.

"No, they don't."

"That's what I thought," Sylph said. "You wounded asshole."

"No wonder you're so serious all the time," Chase murmured.

Someone knocked loud and hard on the door. Chase had no clue who it could be. She and Pippin never had visitors.

The knock sounded again.

"Answer that," Sylph said. "This isn't my room."

Chase shimmied down from the bunk and opened the door. Riot stood in the hall. He shifted on his feet and rubbed his elbows. His nose was swollen and red. "Are you here for Sylph?" Chase asked.

He frowned. "Sylph's in there? I thought...well, I have to tell you something. Get it off my chest." They stared at each other for a long moment. Chase wondered if he had come to give his condolences. Or share his sob story. She was wrong on both accounts.

Riot spoke in a rush. "I told a few people about Tourn being your dad. The night before the trials. I was still mad at you." He waved his bandaged hand as though it gave him a pass.

Chase rested her forehead on the door. Closed her eyes. "So?"

"So I'm sorry. I wanted you to know that. I thought maybe that was why you hit me."

"Forget it. None of that matters now," Chase said, and she believed it.

"Trying to sleep here, Riot!" Sylph yelled. "You should be resting. We have to be airborne again in five hours."

Riot leaned against the door and whispered, "Are you all right?"

Chase wanted to lie, but she didn't have the fuel. That, and Riot looked like he really cared. It was as strange as Sylph lying across Pippin's bunk.

"No, I'm not all right," Chase admitted, feeling oddly relieved by the truth. "But I'm still here. Although I'm a little worried Sylph has decided to become my bosom buddy." Chase hadn't expected herself to joke, and it brought a goofy grin to Riot's face.

She said good-bye to him and shut the door, a little bit stunned.

"I know my RIO." Sylph put her feet on the bunk above and stretched her calves. "He doesn't really love you. He just gets crazy jealous of you and Arrow."

"Whatever you say, Sylph. I don't make a whole lot of sense out of love to begin with. You're the expert, with your airman boyfriend."

Sylph smiled a rare, secretive look. "You are the only one who knows about Liam. It actually makes me like you a little. I keep thinking that—" Another loud knock cut Sylph off. "Who is it now?"

Chase opened the door. It was Tanner. His eyes were centered on her as though he was getting ready to fire, but he pulled her into a hug first. Then he held her shoulders in both hands.

"Tell me it's not true. Tell me you don't know General Tourn."

"I don't know him." The truth came easily. "Not really. But he is my father. He made me take a DNA test twice just to be sure."

Chase's overshare caused Tanner to pause and stare her down even harder.

Sylph sat up in bed, making the springs creak. "Shove off, Arctic. We need sleep. I have a hop in a few hours."

Chase stepped into the quiet, red-lit hall and shut the door. "Apparently I'm bunking with Staff Sergeant Sylph."

Tanner scowled. "How'd that happen?"

"Luck of the Irish."

He almost smiled, and she almost felt like herself.

"Riot told me about *your father*," Tanner said.

For the second time, Chase felt herself trying to be cold and dismissive. But it didn't work. In fact, it was so much more work than just being true.

"It's as terrible as it seems," she owned up. "He doesn't want anything to do with me, and that's harder to swallow than it should be."

She watched Tanner weigh his next words.

"My grandfather was Filipino, Chase."

"I know." The minute he had told her that, she'd run so far that she was pretty sure something inside was still trekking. "I can't apologize for him. I'm not responsible for what he did. He isn't even responsible to be honest."

Tanner shook his head. "*I* would never have dropped that bomb. I would have said no, lost my commission, and been discharged."

Chase looked away. "I could have guessed that much about you."

"I'm telling you because you need to know what I think about him. And you need to know the truth about your dad doesn't change what I think about you."

"Oh, right. I'm a *love vampire*." Her hurt came with more energy than she thought she had left.

Tanner did that overly serious squint that made him look solemnly cute. "I wasn't mad you broke up with me, Chase. I was mad because I could tell you liked me—even while you were trying to get away from me. It made no sense, and I like things to make sense." He leveled his shoulders. "You were afraid of getting involved. Once I sorted that out, I wasn't so angry. I hoped you'd work it out. Preferably with someone other than Riot."

She surprised herself by feeling relieved. "You and me both."

When Tanner left, Chase returned to her room feeling stranger than ever. Both Tanner and Riot had seemed genuinely concerned for her. Why? She'd been terrible to them.

"Any more former suitors to worry about?" Sylph asked. "We could put up a sign."

"There were others, but most of them have graduated," Chase admitted. "There were a lot of them at one point."

"The Star's dirty little sexpot pilot," Sylph mocked. "I always wondered where you found the energy."

"Hey. I don't sleep with them. And I'm not the one who was dry humping a staff sergeant in the hangar."

"Not dry humping, Chase. We go all the way."

"Ew. Too much intel, Sylph."

"You really don't sleep with those boys who drool after you? Why not?"

Chase climbed onto the top bunk. "Because I don't love them, and they don't know me." It was simple. It was true.

"Virgin." Sylph chuckled, and it was as unusual as her smile. "That makes all my prior comments about you being STD-riddled rather hilarious."

"Oh, yes. Look at me. I can't stop laughing."

"What about Arrow? You'd sleep with him. I've seen the way you two hug on each other. It's all hips and arms."

"He knows me," Chase admitted. "And somehow he still likes me. It's weird."

Sylph kicked the bottom of the bunk, making Chase bounce. "He's a bit of a mess right now. He wants to comfort you. You should let him."

"I don't want... How do you know that?"

"Because he told me. Not everyone is a secret wrapped in a lockbox, Nyx. Some of us vent to each other. I'm going to tell him to head over here after he lands. Let him in the room, all right? And now sleep, Nyx, or I will put you to sleep."

Chase's heart pounded at the idea of being alone with Tristan. He *did* know her, and although it had felt good to speak openly with Sylph, Riot, and Tanner, Tristan was different. She covered her eyes, wondering how she could be brave enough to face a red drone but not strong enough to let one boy in.

38

INDIAN NIGHT NOISES

High-Altitude Moans

Another knock. Chase had been wrestling a black sleep, and it didn't let go easily. She heard someone come in, followed by the low murmur of voices.

When she felt a hand on her shoulder, she rolled on her side to look over the edge of the bunk, finding herself entirely too close to Sylph's beautiful face. "I've got to go relieve Arrow and Romeo on the d-line. Don't do anything crazy while I'm gone. Remember the plan."

"*Your* plan," Chase muttered.

"Arrow will come here after he lands. Play nice," Sylph said. Chase growled something, and Sylph flicked her in the forehead. Hard. "Let go, Nyx. Fall in love. It's fucking fantastic."

Chase heard Sylph leave. She wanted to roll back to sleep, but instead she slipped down from the bunk and peered out the door. Riot met Sylph in the hall. He was nervous, banging his fist against his thigh. Sylph ordered him to quit it in a way that proved she was nervous too.

Whatever was amassing just west of the d-line had the whole country scared out of their minds. Congress was set to declare war at any moment—waiting for the strike that felt so imminent that no one was catching a full breath.

Sylph and Riot might never come back from this hop. That was the naked truth. And all of a sudden, Chase was stricken by the idea of losing them. She had to get her wings back.

☉ ☉ ☉

When Tristan came in, he found her staring at him from the top bunk. He tried to smile and failed. "I thought you'd be asleep."

Chase looked over every inch of him. He was in his flight suit, sweat sticking it to him in places and his hair frayed. Half-asleep Pippin had called him manly gorgeous. Yeah, that was right. The almost-dark played with Tristan's profile, and she felt a hint of his magnetism.

She wanted to reach out, but she'd been right to worry about seeing him. He made everything heavy. He made the gravity crank up and her heart bear down.

Tristan kissed the back of her wrist. "I'm not here to seduce you, so stay up there." It was a good attempt at a tease. She could give him that much.

"You look beat."

"The sky was a traffic jam." He didn't have to say anything about drones. She could see it all over his face.

"I need to get back in the air," she said.

"You will. Give it a few weeks." He touched her cheek, his hand warm.

"But this standoff will be over in days or hours." Chase sat up, fired. "You're exhausted. Sylph is terrified. You need another pilot in the rotation. Now."

Tristan was going to say something, but he shook his head. "Patience, Chase."

"Yeah, well, that's never been a talent of mine." She jumped down from the bunk and glared at Tristan's vivid exhaustion. She knew she should be careful with him. But she couldn't; her own pain was too close to cresting. "You got right back up there after JAFA."

"I did, but it didn't feel right. I was on the edge. I could have killed myself." Now he was riled. "If I didn't have you, I wouldn't have been able to do it at all." He tossed his helmet at her. Hard. She caught it and almost threw it right back—but he was unzipping his flight suit. All the way.

"What are you doing?"

"I need a shower." Tristan pulled off his undershirt and let the top half of his uniform hang low on his hips. Chase's whole body went loose as he went into the bathroom and turned on the water. She dropped onto Pippin's bed, watching the edge of him through the cracked open door. He stepped out of his flight suit and pulled the curtain around him.

Tristan Router was in her shower.

"Christ."

She cradled his red helmet. Traced each letter of his stenciled call sign. Unbelievable. Tristan was in her shower, and she was feeling the lowest she'd ever been, and yet she didn't want to barge in and distract herself.

What happened to the girl who used skin to escape?

The water shut off, and she couldn't keep herself from watching through the crack as he dried off. Hints of pink-pale skin all over the place. He secured a towel around his waist. His hair dripped down his shoulders, seeming longer and blacker than usual. He sat on the bed. "I'll fight with you if it'll help, but I'd rather you trust me. I know this ache, Chase," he said. "Let me help like you helped me."

It took her forever, and it revved up her nerves in a way that ached, but she nodded.

He kissed her softly, and she pulled him, still a little wet, alongside her. When they lined up like that, it felt like nothing short of flying. His fingers wove with hers. "How do you feel?"

"Angry. Empty sometimes," she admitted. "Scared. That's the worst part."

His mouth pressed a kiss to her shoulder that made the whole room settle.

"What do you think about when you remember JAFA?" she asked.

"A leg." He leaned back and put a hand over his eyes. "When we heard the blasts, Romeo and I were asleep. By the time we made it out of our room, part of the building had collapsed. We found someone pinned under a bit of ceiling. One leg sticking out. I don't know who that was. It was just a leg, but whoever it was, I knew them. I knew everyone at JAFA."

He held her tighter, and she spilled her heaviest ache into the twisting silence.

"He didn't make sense," she said so quietly that she almost didn't hear herself. "Well, he told me he was confused. He was trying to diagnose himself. To joke even."

"That sounds like Pippin," Tristan said gently.

"He knew exactly what was happening, which was kind of annoying, and then his words got all mangled. That freaked out both of us."

Up...and down. Fools fly. No.

Listen, Chase.

The tears came. Heavy and ugly and unstoppable. It felt like drowning, and Tristan made her sit up and drink water. He shook her by the shoulders but nothing stemmed. Chase remembered the trials on repeat. No rewind this time. She saw the terrible, straightforward truth. The drone. The tight spin of the cockpit.

The sand and lake and that curse-blue sky.

She said Pippin's name, and it made her feel like she'd been set on fire.

When her heartbeat became a dragging limp, Chase felt his lips on hers. She pushed back with a mouth desperate for anything else. He pulled himself on top of her, and his weight held everything still.

He was real. The thought was a sole star in her gone-black sky.

And he was right there. Her hands found every inch of him. His back, arms, and neck—his long fingers and wide palms that opened like an invitation when she reached into them.

She didn't remember the breath when her lips finally left his or the moment she fell asleep. She didn't remember anything except his skin. His weight. The link of their bodies and the emotional back and forth that let her overflow.

39

BORESIGHT

Eye on Target

Romeo woke them far before she was willing to get up. He was in his flight suit, hair ruffled, with a crescent shading beneath each eye. He didn't seem at all surprised to find Chase and Tristan together in a semi-naked sort of way. He merely mumbled something about getting food before the hop and shut the door behind himself.

Chase saw the same shape of exhaustion in Tristan's face, only it was worse. How much sleep had he lost in the hours of comforting her? "You can't fly again. Not right now."

"Have to relieve Sylph." He stood, and his body popped at the joints.

"I could fly for you. Romeo's not as beat. Let me go." Chase watched him get dressed.

"You're on the Down List, Chase."

Every piece of her wanted to be Nyx. To take his comment as insult. To be hard and uncaring. But she stopped herself. She stood. "I'm going to get my wings back today."

He smiled. "Don't be impatient. Go to your appointments with the psychiatrist. Talk to Kale. Beat the simulator," he said. "Let Riot help you."

"Sounds like a lot of work." She tried a small smile, and although it felt stiff, it was real.

He wove his fingers through hers, and they left together.

In the hangar, Tristan met with the deck officer while Chase watched the state of high alert in action. The frigid concrete palace was half empty with so many jets out patrolling. Airmen hustled nonstop. The energy was shrill, taxing.

Romeo sidled up, gnawing on a banana with inhuman-sized bites. He looked like he had been beaten up, but his flirting skills were as intact as ever. "Hello, pretty lady. How's our boy holding up?"

"Is he ours?"

"*Oui*. You're the only girl I'd share him with."

"I suppose I can live with that." She didn't know what came over her, but she leaned into Romeo and hugged him.

"I knew it," he said when she let go. "You're totally into me. Am I right?"

"Not even a little." Chase watched Tristan from the other side of *Phoenix*. He flipped through a file and pointed something out to the deck officer.

"What's the chatter?" she asked Romeo.

"Base side says we're all about to die from Ri Xiong Di bombs. Academy side has been talking about Tourn being your dad. They've been saying he got you into the Star and you didn't earn your wings

Breaking Sky

and that's why you crashed. I think Riot the weasel let the cat out of the carton."

Her body turned as cold as the concrete floor.

"No one believes either side though," Romeo said. "Talk is just talk. Nerves and all."

She looked at him for a long moment. Pippin had *loved* him. It made Romeo seem more real all of a sudden. Someone who mattered. "I've been worried about people finding out about Tourn my whole time here, and now, well, it sucks." She paused. "It should be worse than that, right? But it's not. It just sucks."

"People will move on to other gossip. They always do."

"Pippin was afraid too," she started to admit. "He thought that if he was out, people would treat him differently. He was so afraid that he couldn't even tell you he had a crush on you."

"Really?" Romeo grinned.

She was shocked by his rather blissful reaction. "You liked him?"

"Nah. I like women, but it never feels bad to hear someone likes you." Romeo's face turned serious. A little sad. "Doesn't happen to me all that often to be perfectly honest." Chase needed a solid minute to do the math: although she'd seen Romeo flirt with practically every girl at the Star, Chase had never witnessed him having any success.

"I'm not that ugly, am I?" he asked.

Chase looked him over, boots to brow ridge. "You're not. But you should try not seeming so horny all the time. You don't send the right impression with your eyes on every girl in the room."

375

He smirked. "It's not that obvious."

"Oh, it is."

"*Sérieusement?*" He paled. "I mean, seriously?"

"And lose the call sign. It's not doing what you think it's doing. What's your real name?"

"Adam."

"Nice to meet you, Adam." She took his hand. It was weird, and she didn't care. "I'm Chase."

"In my hometown, we would say, '*Enchanté.*'" The moment stilled as Romeo gave her a long, sorrowful look that prepared her for his next words. "I'm sorry about the crash, Chase. I miss *Henri* already. He was my first friend at the Star." Romeo added something she didn't understand. It sounded mournful yet nice.

"Pippin told me you are sweeter in French. He was right."

Romeo looked at his boots. "Did he…what did he say when it happened? Did he suffer?"

"It wasn't long," she said. Her heart began to pound as she made herself remember. "His last words were…strange. I mean, he'd messed up his head, but I think it was more than that. I think he was telling me I shouldn't fly."

"What did he say?"

"Fools fly." Those words struck at her like something clawed, but Romeo started to laugh, and she stared at him with her mouth falling open. "You think that's funny?"

"*Oui.* I think he was having a little fun with you. Being too clever as always."

"How so?"

"It sounds like Gandalf's famous death line from *The Lord of the Rings*. He says—"

"Fly, you fools," Chase finished. Pippin had made her watch that old movie a dozen times. She shook her head. "There's no way that's what he meant."

Fools fly. No. Listen, Chase.

He had been trying so hard to, what? Make a joke?

Romeo put a hand on her shoulder. "It means, escape. Be free. Survive."

She ran her hands through her hair. "That does sound a little more like Pippin."

"Doesn't it?" Romeo's smile was kind, and it gave her the smallest lift. Small but necessary.

Tristan approached, and the solemn look on his face brought her back down. "Is it bad?"

"Yes," he said. "They haven't had any communication from Sylph. The radio, network—everything is jammed. No doubt she's too scared to open her signal and sneak a message through. They're pretty sure she's still in the sky and that the drones haven't crossed the d-line yet, but the satellite could be wrong. I'll be able to switch on the short-wave when I'm close enough and get her report on what's happening."

"The Streakers shouldn't be used as messenger pigeons," Chase said. "There's got to be more we can do."

"What I can do is blast back here in time to give everyone enough warning to seal themselves in the bunkers."

Romeo headed to the cockpit. "Come on, Arrow," he called back.

Tristan pinched her ear before pulling his helmet on. "This might seem superstitious, but I don't want to say good-bye."

"Deal," she said, forcing her chin up.

Chase watched *Phoenix* leave the hangar and sweep into the dark sky. She wrapped her arms around her chest and started back to the Green, but she could go no farther than a large tarp spread across the floor. It was covered in bits of wreckage.

Dragon.

The charred, smashed remains of her beloved bird. The emptiness that Tristan and her friends had helped hold back sprung forward, and she felt Pippin's absence all over again.

☉ ☉ ☉

Adrien was swearing in French, digging through a pile of *Dragon*'s smoke-stained parts. Her head was half inside a dismantled engine. "Socket wrench," she called out to no one.

Chase handed the wrench over. "Here it is."

"*Merci.*" Adrien glanced out at her.

"What are you doing with my baby?" Chase asked.

Adrien chuckled. "She was my baby first, Ms. Harcourt."

Chase put some ideas together that she hadn't bothered to before. "You built the Streakers in Canada and then shipped two of them here. And you worked with the Canadian Streaker team, but you never came here to see us. Why?"

"We weren't supposed to be working together, were we?" She tightened a bolt, huffing. "But now we're together for good and ill. What's left of us anyway."

The engineer seemed to be hinting at the larger picture. Pippin wasn't the only one who had been lost. JAFA was gone, its cadets and servicemen scattered or dead, and all because people like Tourn thought we could beat Ri Xiong Di at its own game.

"We can't win," Chase said.

Adrien looked at her. Grease had smeared along her face, and the red alarm light tinted her white hair to a soft pink. "We cannot. Not as we currently stand."

"How do we do it then?"

Adrien dipped back into her work. "You already know that answer. More Streakers means more strength. You have done your part on that front. Well, you did your best."

In light of the accident and the global uproar, the government board had yet to rule on the Streakers. Or so Chase thought. "Did the project pass? I haven't heard anything."

Adrien didn't answer, and that was answer enough. Of course the government board would have scratched the Streaker project after her abject failure in the face of that red drone.

Of course.

Adrien wiped her hands on a rag. "You haven't brought a knife with you, have you?"

Chase was taken back. "What?"

"I need a long knife to salvage some of the software." Adrien pointed to a hunk of jet guts. "To see if it is intact."

Looking over the wreckage, Chase remembered the crash with a shock of heat. She fell to her knees, and Adrien took hold of Chase's arm. "No tears," the woman commanded. "Help me take her for pieces. It will do your heart good."

The two of them struggled for over an hour, trying to get *Dragon*'s metal skin unbent from the machine's insides. Chase felt alive through the strain of the work. She enjoyed breaking parts of her jet away and swearing and sweating into her eyes.

When they were done, both of them seated on the tarp amid a few thousand tiny parts, Chase asked a question that felt strangely important. "What will you do with all this?"

"Put her back together. Fix some design flaws we learned from your crash. I only have a few weeks to quiet the government's doubters so that you might have your Streaker fleet."

"You still think you can change their minds?"

Adrien answer was a shrug. "They want Streakers without young pilots, but I cannot fix that. Only teenagers have the physical durability, impulse-fast reflexes, and mental agility to adjust to the demands of the engines. You learn with the *speed of heat*." The engineer looked proud of herself for using a jock pilot term. She even winked. "We will find a way to prove to our governments we need the money. We will keep moving forward." Adrien motioned to the parts around them. "We will rebuild."

Chase looked over *Dragon*'s remains. "When I left her on

the shore of that lake, she didn't look so mangled. She just looked…halved."

"They had to recover her fast to hold back Ri Xiong Di satellite interest. They knocked her into pieces to transport her."

Chase faced Adrien, feeling stronger for the first time since she woke in the infirmary. "You have to fix her. I need her."

"*Dragon* may yet be rebuilt. I have faith. She was my favorite, but…" Her voice tilted. "Will you fly her?"

"I…want to. But I don't know if I can fly without him. I'm going to try." Chase turned such a simple idea over in her hands and remembered something. "Pippin always asked, 'Where are we going, Nyx?' And I'd say, 'Anywhere.' It made flying feel like escaping, but I think it's not supposed to feel that way."

Adrien gave her a reassuring pat, but before they could exchange another word, the hangar door blasted open, and *Pegasus* roared in. Sylph pulled to a quick stop, and Chase rushed up the ramp stairs to help her out of the cockpit. Riot was unconscious in the back.

"Look at him!" Sylph yelled, although her voice was hoarse and quiet. "Knocked out on the way back and I couldn't wake him."

"Did he gray out?"

"No! He's asleep." Sylph got out of her chair on soft legs and hit her RIO in the helmet. "Idiot."

Riot jerked awake and looked around the hangar. "Shit."

"No kidding."

The deck officer rushed over for Sylph's report, and Chase helped Riot down the stairs.

381

"I'm all right," he said. "Man, I shouldn't have slept, but I feel so much better. It was nuts up there."

Chase *shhhed* him so she could listen to Sylph's report to the deck officer.

"They missile locked on me. Over and over again. Tell Kale I'm not going back up there without a dozen wingmen."

The deck officer ignored her. "Did any of the drones cross the d-line or attempt to hack your controls?"

"They stayed in their zone, and I never opened a channel to them."

"But you said they missile locked on you," Chase couldn't help but interrupt. "They're escalating."

Sylph thrust her helmet at Chase, and Chase saw how bad off Sylph was. The blonde looked like she'd been drained of life force. She wavered, and a staff sergeant caught her by the arm. Chase recognized Liam—but other than holding her up, he and Sylph acted like they didn't know each other. "They kept locking on me because they wanted to tire me out. They wanted to make me run evasive tactics until I didn't have any speed left."

"They want a Streaker," Chase said. "They were going to wear you down and then collect you."

Sylph nodded once, and then Liam half-walked, half-carried her out of the hangar.

Chase turned toward the deck officer. "Arrow is not going to last half as long as Sylph. He's exhausted." He had been up all night. "I have to relieve him."

The man turned and left. No word. Nothing. Chase wasn't

surprised. After all, she was on the Down List. And he clearly didn't know he shouldn't turn his back on Nyx.

Chase hooked her arm in Riot's and dragged him back up the stairs. She popped on Sylph's helmet. "Hope you had a nice catnap because we're going back out."

"What are you doing?" Riot asked.

"Skipping the hard work." She pushed him back in the cockpit and slid into the pilot's chair. The deck officer had come back yelling at her to get down, but she ignored him.

"How in the world do you expect to get Kale's permission?" Riot asked.

"Easy. I'll go higher." She flipped on the shortwave. Tourn might not want her as a daughter—that she'd learn to accept somehow—but he wanted her as a cadet. A pilot. "Tower, this is Nyx in *Pegasus* requesting to speak with General Tourn."

A long pause. Too long. Followed by a grunt.

"Cadet, what are you doing in that bird?"

"Trying to fly, General, but I need gas."

"What makes you think you can get off the ground?"

She bit her lip. "I don't know, but I have to try."

Another silence, but then she heard an order in the background for *Pegasus* to be refueled.

Tourn came back commanding. "Things are getting hot along the d-line. I want you to give it everything you got, but if the sky starts to break apart, you use that Streaker speed to get the hell out. Get back here. That's an order. Understood?"

"Understood, General Tourn." She was holding on to the throttle and stick as if they were her lifelines. "You're...you're really going to let me try?"

"No one so determined fails." It was one of his mottos, which she might have dismissed if it didn't feel like he was trying to tell her he had faith in her.

There were other words she wanted to say, but she chose the simplest ones. "Thank you."

When he spoke again, his voice was closer, as though he'd leaned into the mic. "Cadet, there are few people who can say what I'm about to say and know exactly what it means, but I am one of those people."

She waited.

"I'm sorry about your RIO."

40

DOWNTOWN

Enemy Territory

Chase shot *Pegasus* onto the runway. Her heart hammered at her chest and her doubts slid in. Could she do it?

She had to.

But how? Her mind slipped to Pippin's swelling, bleeding head, and their speed died out.

Riot began to ask questions. "You okay? What's happening?"

"I need a second," she snapped. "I'm getting my focus together."

The silence came with snow settling on the cockpit glass. She couldn't do it. Oh God, she couldn't...

"What do you think you're doing, Harcourt?" Kale's voice came over the shortwave. Despite the panic in his tone, his voice brought calm.

"I'm more stubborn than you are," Chase responded. "And I'm going to fly."

"This is almost over," he said, defeated. Resigned. "Harcourt, Donnet's death affected us all, but right now we don't need you to be suicidal."

"This isn't about Pippin. At least, it's not about his death. I have to get up there. For the other Streaker teams. For the Star." She was trying to convince herself as well as Kale. "I might not be able to do anything other than relieve *Phoenix*, but that in itself is important."

Kale sighed like he might relent, but an alarm went off in the tower, bleeding through the radio. Chase heard chaos erupt. "Everyone to the bunkers. That's an order!" Kale yelled at someone in the tower.

"Brigadier General? What's happening?" Chase's panic crested. "Kale?!"

"The drones have crossed the line. *Phoenix* is under attack!"

A blaring alarm sounded throughout the Star. Chase could hear it coming through the open hangar door. The lights were already going off.

Chase yelled above the racket on the radio. "Kale, what do I do?"

"*Phoenix* is beyond help. It looks like they're trying to bring him down over China. To collect the Streaker. Arrow doesn't have the fuel or energy to outfly them for long."

Her heart slammed around as she imagined Tristan taken as hostage. Tortured. Killed. "I'll get to him."

"You can't, Harcourt. You can't, and I don't want you taking his death on yourself."

"His death?" This time it was Riot.

"You can't help this time. I wish you could."

"What do you mean *his death*?" she yelled.

"If they succeed in getting *Phoenix* down, we're going to bomb the area. Ri Xiong Di cannot have a Streaker. You know that."

Chase fired up the jet's engines.

"Stand down, *Dragon*. That's an order."

"This is *Pegasus*." Chase leaned into the throttle. Sent them down the runway.

"Those drones are over the d-line, Harcourt. They could send firepower this way any minute. Turn around and get to the bunkers. That's an order!"

"I can get to Arrow, General. I can use the shortwave and talk him back to life."

He paused for far too long.

"Kale. *Please.*" Chase didn't know why she needed his approval so badly, but she asked for it nonetheless. "You have to trust me."

"Do not sacrifice yourself, Harcourt."

"Yeah, please don't," Riot agreed in a humor-hollow voice.

Kale sighed, a deep, tremulous breath that reached through her bones. "Be careful, my girl."

His words thrilled her and focused her mind on the runway. She breathed.

Chase felt as though she'd run the gauntlet, and yet she still wasn't in the air. They zipped across the apron at lightning speed, and all the while, she wondered at how her actions had felt so unattached before. Now, everything she did touched something else. All connected.

And if she failed again, she could kill Riot. Or herself. Or unwittingly give Ri Xiong Di a Streaker. She wouldn't mess up. Not again.

Chase's thoughts clung to Tristan being under attack. She had to get to him. There was no time to be afraid. To remember the crash. She closed her eyes long and tight before easing the stick into a lift.

And took to the dark sky.

As soon as she left the runway, the blue lights flicked off and the Star was lost in blackness.

She pushed forward, and the air welcomed her with almost-morning hues, spreading open at the same time it folded her in. *Dragon* may have been killed in action, but Chase could feel the memory of her bird between her palms. She applied the same sensation to the way she missed Pippin and found with a soft shock that it fit.

He was still there. Alive in her mind.

Chase held on to that feeling, wanting a few more minutes with the memory of her RIO's brilliance and its inherent quirk. His head half-swallowed by headphones. His boots always untied. She saw his face silhouetted through the small window in the Star City Centrifuge right before she lost her sight. He was always there, and she could take that with her.

Pegasus raced from the dawn. The eastern sky flamed with colors, orange-red hands reaching through the deep navy. Chase turned the network link off, and they popped Mach 3. Riot whooped into the strain. "Keep yourself tight!" she warned. "I'm not slowing down if you gray out." Her own body was so hard that she felt leaden.

Somewhere close to the Bering Strait, she passed a mass of old fighter jets heading west. *Pegasus* soared past them, out over the expanse of the Pacific Ocean.

"This is it," Riot said after a few minutes. "This is the demarcation line."

"Any bogies?"

"No. Looks like they're all on *Phoenix*."

Chase shot them over the invisible divide without a second thought. She heard Sylph's RIO swearing at his controls—at whatever he was picking up. "Talk to me, Riot."

"*Phoenix* is near China. Over land. There are hundreds of drones, Nyx. And I just got something from the Star." He paused like he was still working out the code. "The missile defense system has been hacked. Overridden. If those drones get through, nothing will stop them."

Chase's heart banged. Two Streakers against all those drones. The rest of the old fighter jets didn't stand a chance. She prayed they wouldn't join the fight—they'd only get killed.

She kicked up the speed.

"Why are we engaging?" Riot yelled. "What exactly are *we* going to do against hundreds of drones?"

"We've got missiles, don't we?"

"We've got *two* missiles, Nyx. *Two* against probably five hundred drones."

"Then we'll make them count."

Chase embraced the pinch of high-g. Her vision was still colored, and she wasn't backing down until she blacked out. Tristan needed her, and although the pressure pinned her back, her desperation to get to him drove her forward.

When they were deep in Ri Xiong Di airspace, she let off the throttle to catch her breath. Not a drone in sight. "Where's *Phoenix*, Riot?"

"Due west. He's close. We should see him soon."

Chase wanted to open the radio and call his name over and over. She wanted to be back in her bunk, tangled with him, letting every single one of his touches sink in. But instead, they were speeding over land, and not just any land—China.

"Look at that," Riot called. "Downtown Beijing. It's huge!"

Chase glanced at the ground, catching the expanse of a tightly built-up city huddled at the merge of northern and western mountain ranges. Beijing was a mess of metal and high buildings, but the mountains were green and tall.

"There he is!" Riot called out. "Mother of God, look at that."

The horizon was filled with a hive of blood-colored drones surrounding a pinprick of blue-silver. The drones darted like one huge net of red wasps, caging *Phoenix*'s every twist and turn.

Tristan wasn't flying very fast, and his wings dipped unevenly.

"Arrow," she said over the shortwave.

The pause was too long.

"*Dieu merci!* Nyx?" Romeo asked. "Is that you?"

"State your condition," she said.

"Arrow isn't talking anymore. He's going to pass out any minute," Romeo said shakily. "Me too. We're flying on vapes, Nyx."

Tristan wasn't talking, but he could hear her.

"Arrow, break right. I'll smash through and get their attention. If we're lucky, they'll confuse our birds and follow me." He didn't respond, and her heart slammed into the silence. "Come on, Arrow. On three. One, two, three."

Phoenix made no move.

"He's not going to let you guys take our place, Nyx," Romeo said.

"Yeah, well, in about a minute, I'm going to be too close to those drones, and they'll split and come after me too, so he better decide fast."

Phoenix didn't respond, and Chase started to worry he was too tired to escape.

"Arrow won't let you take the heat," Riot said, the jealous jab in his tone acceptable for once.

"He will or I'll never make out with him again. You hear that, Arrow?" She heard the surprised husk of Tristan's laugh. So he *was* listening. "I have a plan. You have to trust me."

The returning silence was too much.

"Tristan. Give me something."

She waited.

"*Okay.*"

The word was so small that it was mostly breath. In that moment, Chase couldn't help but remember Pippin's diatribe on *okay* being so inexact. And then her thoughts slipped to his odd and poetic last words on the melody of "Ode to Joy."

Up…and down.

"Right," she said. "On three. Arrow, you head up, and I'll go down. These drones have issues with breaking thin atmosphere. You'll be able to get away."

"How do you know that?" Riot asked.

"Because I've seen it."

"Ready?" She counted.

Tristan broke early, jerking and heading high, but Chase was ready. She dove through the cloud of drones, making several of them crumple and spin into a plummeting dive. Riot yelled, but Chase kept her eye on the sky. The drones were after her now, and she slowed just enough for them to cage her in like they had caught Tristan. "Is he clear, Riot?"

"He's headed back toward the d-line. I don't think they're following him, idiot machines." He groaned loudly. "But that's only because they're all over us."

It *was* quite a sight to see. The sky had turned red through the cockpit as the drones flew perilously close. They kept low and tight, trying to wear her down, force her to the earth.

Chase rushed the throttle. The blinding pressure in her muscles sent rivers of sweat down her cheeks and neck, but she only pushed the jet *faster*. The drone cloud started to thin as she passed Mach 3 and blasted out over the ocean.

"Shouldn't all the drones be the same?" Riot said in a tight voice. "Some are faster than others. Some are unevenly weighted. Is that because they're mass-produced?"

"Stop. Talking," Chase barked.

Even more drones fell back when she crossed Mach 4.

Four times the speed of sound.

She couldn't hold the pace much longer, and she knew that as soon as she lost it, they'd be all over *Pegasus* like a stinging swarm. "I can't keep this up," she admitted through her teeth.

And she didn't have to.

An alarm went off in the cockpit. The missile-lock alarm.

"They've gone to active missiles. *All of them!*" Riot yelled. She heard the controls as he punched them, attempting to map a getaway trajectory, no doubt. "They're going to shoot us down. I can't find a clear direction. Watch it!"

Chase jerked out of the way just as a missile screeched underneath them, hitting another drone and exploding it like a red-metal firework.

"You do have a plan, right?" Riot asked tensely. "You said you had a plan."

"I have an old trick." Chase took a deep breath and pointed the bird straight up, streaking toward the yellow orb of the sun.

"A *trick*? Are you serious?"

"We've got to get high. Real high."

Riot started to swear and didn't stop. The red drones chased them to the thinnest atmosphere, losing speed just like Chase had known they would. She pushed faster for a few seconds, turning back toward the earth with a flick of her wrists. Chase put every piece of herself into the throttle and threw them at the earth so fast that both cadets screamed with the engines.

The rushing speed was brilliant, and a cloud of mist burst behind them, announcing that the sound barrier had exploded. Riot must have been yelling, but she couldn't hear him anymore. To the right, China's coastline revealed its impressive naval force. To the left, she could make out the sky full of U.S. jets, waiting for whatever was about to happen.

Behind her, a few hundred drones raced to keep up. And below, the ocean swiftly magnified with stunning detail.

The deep blue.

The chop of waves.

She pulled up, braking at the split second before they smashed into the sea.

The drones were not so skilled.

They shattered against the cobalt surface as though it were a concrete wall.

"Boola-boola!" she called out through gasps. "Boola-fucking-boola!"

41

BRAVO ZULU

Well Done

Chase was breathing so hard that she could barely hear the cheering over the shortwave—the radio piping in from the fighter jets on the horizon. She steered *Pegasus* toward the demarcation line, leaving a sloshing sea of sinking red metal in her wake.

Chase knew how Tristan felt now, being too tired to respond. Words of affirmation came over the radio that she couldn't acknowledge. She was determined to make it back on her own power. She turned northeast. Toward the Star that called her home.

Riot was busy making sure no new drones had been launched in their wake, but it seemed that in an attempt to get a Streaker, Ri Xiong Di had gone full throttle.

Gone full throttle, and lost.

"This will change everything," Riot said. "A whole fleet of drones downed by one Streaker. They can't *not* take that seriously."

Chase's eyes stung with tears and her mind filled with images of Pippin. Of what he would have said in this moment. "Hobbits against Sauron. Am I right?"

"What the hell does that mean?" Riot asked.

"Indeed."

Somewhere over Alaska, Chase lapped *Phoenix*. Tristan took too long to be refueled and was now flying very, very slowly. Chase worried about the way his wings tilted—not in the cocky way she enjoyed. He was losing altitude and speed.

They weren't done yet.

Chase pulled *Pegasus* up beneath *Phoenix*, using her wing to ever so lightly lift his.

"How about a race, Arrow?"

She heard his breath over the radio, cool and growly. "On three," she said, but he pushed forward before she could count. She threw the throttle forward, catching up easily but holding back so he could keep a lead.

"Don't." Tristan's voice was a whisper. "Go easy. On me. Nyx."

She'd forgotten he always did his best when he was chasing her. She shot below him, crossing the icy water that led to Banks Island. He kept after her in a way that breezed right into her heart.

They were almost home.

When they reached the apron, Tristan landed in a spin, tilting the whole Streaker onto its side and bending its wing. Chase put down next to him. She was out in a shot, followed by Riot. *Phoenix*'s cockpit could only open halfway on its side, and Romeo struggled out.

Tristan hadn't moved.

"Whipped his head bad when we tipped just now. Knocked him

out, I think," Romeo said. He jerked Tristan's helmet off before she could warn him to be careful. Tristan looked dead. His skin was white and tight, and he'd burst a few blood vessels near his eyes.

A loud *pop* startled them, and *Phoenix* began to pump smoke.

No, no, no, Chase thought wildly. She struggled to lift him out of his seat, but she wasn't strong enough.

"Pippin!" Chase called out. "Help me!"

When she realized what she'd said, she froze in the smacking-cold air. Romeo's look was blank, and Riot moved forward like he might try to hug her. "Together!" she barked, and all three of them rushed forward. She counted down, and they hauled him free of the cockpit.

His body sprung free in a rush, coming down on top of Chase. Pain erupted all over her back as the air rushed from her lungs. She struggled for a few breaths without letting him go.

Now they had done it.

The emergency teams rushed out of the hangar amid their sirens and colored lights. They would be there within a moment. She gripped Tristan and told herself he was going to be okay, and then she told him the same.

Streaks of green blurred the navy sky. The northern lights danced above like her very own victory parade, and she kept her eyes on them for so long that when the medics pulled Tristan off, they thought she had passed out.

"I'm good." She waved them away. Riot helped her to her feet while the medics strapped Tristan to a stretcher. One of them listened to his heart, nodded to the others, and said one word.

"Stable."

Chase's tears froze to her cheeks in the blustering cold. The medics ran Tristan back to the hangar while Romeo tried to run with him, limping from exhaustion. She thought she saw him grip Tristan's hand.

She hadn't noticed Romeo's loyalty before. Maybe that's what Pippin had seen in him. After all, Pippin was the best at sensing people's hidden centers. She only wished that hadn't been because he'd spent years keeping his own heart a secret. Chase had always wished she knew more about Pippin. And now she knew she'd keep wishing that her whole life.

The bright square of the open hangar door seemed like an embrace waiting. Kale stood in the middle of the light. Chase could have recognized his silhouette from the clouds.

She ran toward him.

42

KICK THE TIRES, LIGHT THE FIRES

Let's Go

Sunlight leaned into Chase's room through her small window, bringing with it baby blue skies and hints of green life beneath the melting rivers on Banks Island.

Chase was bent over her political science textbook. She jotted notes and then rubbed her hands through her short hair. Tomorrow, her poli-sci teacher wouldn't be able to ask a question that she didn't know. That was satisfying in a new and surprising way.

"Kale wants us in the hangar ASAP," Sylph said from her door.

Chase glanced at the time and swore. She got up, zipping the rest of her flight suit and groaning as her spine popped as fluidly as her knuckles. It had been five months since she had faced off with the red drones, but she sometimes felt like she had aged ninety years in that heartbeat of a day.

"Where's the girl?" Sylph asked.

"Are we supposed to bring our RIOs? I thought it was just pilots."

"It is. I want to see if she's gotten my laundry done."

"Sylph."

"What? Starling wants to prove herself. Heaven forbid I stand in the way."

"Heaven forbid you don't benefit," Chase said just as Lin, call sign Starling, entered their room. The tiny yet solid girl balanced a mountainous pile of laundry, bending in ways that only a gymnast's body could get away with.

"Oh, hi, Sylph!" Lin said. "I'll have your clothes in your room in a few minutes."

"Don't forget to fold," Sylph said to Starling. "Be in the hangar in five, Nyx."

Chase shot a look at Sylph that made the tall girl blow a kiss sarcastically. Sylph really was learning how to be human. Maybe it was the intense chaos following the trials or just the fact that Sylph was attempting to be sociable—either way, Chase had to admit she enjoyed the perks of the girl's transformation. Sometimes it felt like they were becoming friends. Maybe *friend-like* was more accurate.

Starling watched Sylph go, awe in her expression.

"What'd I say, Starling?" Chase took the clothes and set them on the lower bunk. "Less enthusiasm for Sylph. Always less enthusiasm. That girl's head is big enough."

Chase's new RIO was every bit as daring as Pippin but not nearly as confident. The fact that Lin had been chosen to fill Chase's team had launched the sophomore as a celebrity at the Star. Lin treated her newfound fame like everything else: overwhelmed and blindingly sweet—until she got into the air and turned hard and sharp as a blade.

Chase watched Lin fold, her dark-skinned hands working fast and rhythmic. "You really shouldn't be doing that," Chase said. "Sylph's just trying to see what she can get away with. It's hazing."

"So what do I do?" Starling's nose scrunched up, and Chase pinched it.

"I'll tell you what I'd do. I'd throw all her clothes into the trees on the Green."

"That's wicked," Starling said. "You think I could?"

"Just be prepared for retaliation," Tristan said. He leaned in the open doorway, his arms hanging on the doorjamb in a way that flattered every piece of him. "You ready to head out, Chase?"

"Hi, Arrow!" Starling yelled.

"Seriously, Lin?" Chase rubbed the ringing out of her ear.

Tristan gave Lin a purposefully smoldery look. "Hey there, Starling Darling."

"All right already." Chase hooked her arm around Tristan's, leading him down the hall. "Be back for dinner, I think," she called to Lin. "Remember, don't do anything else for Sylph!"

Chase and Tristan walked fast together, shoulder to shoulder. It felt a little like flying. "You always have to tease the breath out of my RIO? You act like Romeo in front of her sometimes."

"It's funny. She seems to think we're movie stars."

"Don't encourage her."

He pressed a kiss on the side of her neck. "She knows I'm taken."

"You are."

Chase was somehow still comforted and thrilled that Tristan

was dedicated to her, and she to him. Sometimes she worried she'd wake up and they'd be over each other, and every day that didn't happen, she felt more and more.

"Did you hear the chatter?" he asked, switching to his serious tone, the one Chase had assigned to his more political thoughts. "Ri Xiong Di representatives agreed to a summit meeting. The first one in twenty-two years. Three European countries have agreed to come, including Britain. I bet several more are going to say yes."

"What will they talk about?"

"The Nuclear Response Act most likely. No one wants to worry about that kind of escalation. They're also going to insist on lifting the Atlantic trade restrictions."

"That sounds too good to be true. Ri Xiong Di isn't going to stand for the U.S. back in a fighting position."

"They don't have a choice. Allied strength." Tristan held her hand a little tighter. "Things are changing."

"Yeah, but for the better?"

"I don't know how long they'll be afraid of the Streakers. Adrien worries they'll figure out how to make one soon enough, and then…"

Chase squeezed his fingers and let him worry. After all, there was so much left uncertain. For one, her nightmares wouldn't leave her alone. Too often, she relived the way she had thrown herself down, down, down at the ocean.

And somehow missed.

She ached for Pippin in a soul-twisting kind of way, but she was learning how to air out her hurt when it came, to share it with people like Kale and Tristan. Even Sylph when she needed a more clinical ear. Venting made his loss feel like a real part of her, and she found that that was the only way she could live with it.

They double-timed it across the Green and toward the hangar. Cadets were everywhere, and Chase was still getting used to the other shade of blue uniforms that now spotted the Star, denoting the Canadian cadets.

"Any idea what Kale's surprise could be?" Tristan asked when they joined Sylph in the glass tunnel between buildings. Outside, the intense blue of the sky promised puffy clouds.

"No clue," Chase said.

"Morons." Sylph led the charge. "It's obvious."

The trio of Streaker pilots found the brigadier general outside of the hangar doors by one of the helicopters. "Get in," he ordered. Chase climbed in after Sylph and grabbed hold of Tristan's flight suit to bring him in behind her.

"Got to love a pushy woman," he muttered into Chase's ear as he took his seat beside her.

Sylph cocked a judging look at the way they sat close, hands entwined, but Chase didn't care. All of it, even the Sylph-mocking, felt kind of great.

The helo took them to the lower half of Banks Island, to a large camouflaged-white hangar. They set down outside and jumped out. Kale used a variety of security codes to open the door, and they ducked out of the chilled wind. When Chase lifted her head, she wasn't ready.

The hangar was full of Streakers.

Blue silver seemed to wink at her from every angle. "Holy hell."

"Language, Harcourt," Kale said.

"How many?" Tristan asked, his eyes huge.

"Sixty. The first batch. Fifty named for the states and ten for Canada's provinces." He waved his hand at the one stenciled with the name *Texas*, beside one bearing the incredibly long title *Saskatchewan*. "We're halfway to finding young pilots to start training. This is where you three come in."

Tristan and Chase exchanged looks.

Kale continued. "I know you won't graduate for a few semesters, but we need to get these jets in the air immediately. We need you to help with their instruction."

"Serious?" Chase almost fell over. "You want us to train Streaker pilots?"

"*Help* train them. You don't get to mold them into your demerit-riddled image, Harcourt." Kale squeezed her shoulder.

Tristan wore a cool sort of victory in his expression. "Sixty Streakers."

"Sixty-three, including your birds."

"You mean sixty-two, General," Chase corrected. She had to remind people too often. *Dragon* was gone.

Kale pointed to the last Streaker in the row. "I know it's been a while, Harcourt, but I think she'd be sore if you didn't recognize her."

Chase looked over the seamless silver metal and the sleek wings until she saw a recycled panel of metal on its side bearing a worn name:

DRAGON

"You rebuilt her." Chase's words were small.

"Of course we did. Well, I should say Adrien did."

Chase ran to the jet, touching every beautiful inch. She kissed her and rested her cheek on the dented metal panel.

"You're making me jealous," Tristan deadpanned.

Chase kept her eyes on *Dragon*. "You should be jealous. She was my first love."

"Well, she does remind me of you," he said. "Impulsive, fast... with very cute ears."

Chase checked to see that Kale's back was turned before she grabbed Tristan's uniform and brought him in for the kind of kiss that made him hold on to her hips.

"Give me a boost?" she asked.

"Course." He grabbed her leg and propelled her up and into her seat. She looked around as her hands trailed every dial, button, and control until she found something new. A small brass plaque bearing Pippin's name. Chase leaned back and closed her eyes. She traced the letters of his call sign and breathed.

⨀⨥⨀

Within a handful of hours, Chase was taxiing out of the secret hangar in *Dragon*.

Starling directed their takeoff through a strong headwind, chatting without stopping to breathe. She was shockingly good at that. "So then when Sylph saw that I hung her clothes in a tree, she stole all my underthings and put them in the rec room. Right on the pool table! Romeo was wearing a pair of my undies on his head by the time I found them."

"Turnabout is fair play, Lin," Chase said, trying to hide her laugh. "But I'd say you're in the clubhouse now." Chase pulled the Streaker up through the blue blanket of the heavens. They flew south in a blast, leaving *Pegasus* in *Dragon*'s wake.

Chase ducked below the clouds, feeling the strain evaporate as the thrill of flying took over. The sky opened, and the engines revved through her heart—willing and ready.

Phoenix darted above them in his flirting way.

Chase throttled forward.

The speed reached for her, connecting everything into one stretch of earth. One humanity. One wild pulse.

"Ah, Nyx," Starling started, "where are we going so fast?"

"Everywhere," she said through the mach rush.

Acknowledgments

First and foremost, I thank my grandfather, father, and brother for their inspiring service in the U.S. Air Force. Their dedication and skill have left me honored to say that I come from a military family.

Many loving thanks to **everyone** at the Writing for Children & Young Adults program at Vermont College of Fine Arts. Additionally, I offer thanks and call signs to the following flyboy friends and family who gave their enthusiasm to this story:

Kelly "Steam Queen" Barson

Nick "Awesome Neighbor" Borders

Winifred "Marathon" Conkling

Mary "Mermaid" Cronin

Anna "Princess" Drury

Tina "Steve" Elliget

Conor "Stinker" McCarthy

Evan "Beager" McCarthy

Mark "Poppy" McCarthy

Joan "Dynamite" McCarthy

Tara "Bat Mama" Nickerson
Christian "Scholar Hot" Peterson
Maverick "Winnie Pooh" Peterson
Tirzah "Mac" Price
and
Trent "Frost" Reedy

This book would not have been possible without my ever-supporting literary agent, Sarah "Wingbuilder" Davies, and my keen-eyed editor, Aubrey "Sherlock" Poole. A special thank-you to Leah Hultenschmidt for inviting me into the Sourcebooks family.

My fascination with the military sustained me during my toughest school years, and this story came straight from that struggle for direction. For that reason, an André the Giant–sized thank-you goes to Alissa (McFerren) Arnold for sleepovers, inside jokes, and innumerable viewings of *Top Gun*. Also, a blushing thank-you to the real Tristan, whose name proved too perfect to fictionalize.

I would not be a writer without the love, respect, and support of my parents, family, and friends. And most importantly (*!), I would not have had the courage for this story without the guidance of my RIO, Amy Rose "Aurora" Capetta.

Aim high. Fly, fight, *win*.

Love & cheers,
Cori "Sparks" McCarthy

> Can't get enough Cori McCarthy? Read on for a sneak peek of Cori's exciting new novel *You Were Here*.

Jaycee is about to accomplish what her older brother Jake couldn't: live past graduation.

Jaycee is dealing with her brother's death the only way she can—by re-creating Jake's daredevil stunts. The ones that got him killed. She's not crazy, okay? She just doesn't have a whole lot of respect for staying alive.

Jaycee doesn't expect to have help on her insane quest to remember Jake. But she's joined by a group of unlikely friends: the uptight, ex-best friend; the heartbroken poet; the slacker with Peter Pan syndrome; and...Mik. He doesn't talk, but somehow still challenges Jaycee to do the unthinkable—reveal the parts of herself that she buried with her brother.

From the petrifying ruins of an insane asylum to the skeletal remains of the world's largest amusement park, *You Were Here* is an emotionally taut page-turner told from multiple points of view—combined with stunning visual storytelling in the form of graphic novel panels and word art poetry.

CHAPTER 1

JAYCEE

I had been driving all afternoon, trying to get lost.

The road blurred. My foot was a stone on the gas pedal, and I took the turn too fast. Tires growled and spit gravel, almost sending my car sideways through the Saturday evening traffic.

I came to a slamming stop in the playground parking lot and pressed my head to the steering wheel, cursing. The pause was short-lived. I tightened my ponytail and got out.

Trudging toward the swing set, my face burned and my breath stung in my chest. That's what regret does well and grief does better: rips out your energy and leaves you feeling each and every heartbeat. Plus, well, I'd failed once again. Getting lost in my hometown was turning out to be as easy as disapparating—something I'd once wasted an entire lightning bolt–foreheaded summer attempting.

I sat hard on the swing. My endeavors to get lost were getting extreme. Just last week, I'd night-trekked into the woods where the cross-country team practices and chugged three inches of rum. I'd left the path behind, only to run into my equidrunk classmates, taking their idiotic dares to make out with a tree and underwear-roll through a patch of poison ivy. I emerged hours later on the road behind the middle school, the same spot where years earlier I used to pump my bike into dirt-sneezing speed, trying to spin out. In short, my earliest attempts at getting lost.

I itched the length of my arm. The poison ivy welts *were* starting to fade, even though a few hours earlier, my mom complained about how blotchy I would look in all my graduation pictures. "Photoshop," I had assured her following the ceremony. "I promise you won't have to remember me as rashy every time you marvel at my monumentous achievement in surviving standard education."

Surviving was the wrong word. My mom started to weep, and I ended up taking a three-hour drive on Easy Death Road. Which is exit 13 off Guilt Highway if you're curious. And then after all that, I surrendered to a seizure of loneliness and came here to the oddly placed Richland Avenue Park.

I scuffed my Chucks on the stubbly turf, drawn to the spot beneath the swing set where Jake died. Of course, it wasn't rubber back then. It had been good, old-fashioned, unforgiving blacktop. My mind hummed, and something inside me screamed *Run!* as if my worst memories were zombies, and if I were quick enough, I could outstrip them. But I stayed where I was, kicking into gear on the swing instead.

The sunset was taking forever to get over itself, and I pumped my legs like a ten-year-old. I could have been at any number of graduation parties, sneaking beer into Sprite cans and cheersing the end of high school. But no, I was here. Killing time. Waiting for dark, when I'd break into The Ridges and meet up with Mikivikious for our bizarro anniversary. It had been five years. That's something special, right? What's the traditional present for five years? Silverware? A couch? Flat screen?

The sun's blaring rays made me squeeze my eyes until the whole universe went orange-red. *Killing time.* What an expression. *How does one kill time? Anesthesia? Time travel? Lobotomy?*

The last one made me snicker as I stared up at The Ridges, the decrepit Victorian mansion on top of the hill. Until recently, it had been known as the Athens Insane Asylum, but the state had demanded a rebrand when they shut it down, as if a new name could erase a hundred years of inhumane abuse, death, and yes, copious amounts of lobotomies. I should know; I'd tried it once or twice. Not a lobotomy—changing my own name. Anything to escape being the infamous girl who'd had a front-row seat in watching her big brother snap his neck.

I would rather be known for frenching a tree.

My feelings flared as I imagined my mom on her way back to her own asylum, Stanwood Behavioral Hospital. She was most likely weeping for Xanax, a wreck because I wrecked her with my sarcasm. And my father was probably holding her hand and saying nice things, because that's how he dealt with Jake. My dad was a grade A deflector. Everything he said was ripe with the exact same sentiment: *So we don't have a son anymore, but hey, look at our daughter!* To be honest, I preferred my mother's tears.

I turned to the half-shadowed redbrick towers of The Ridges peeking over the tree line and wondered where I'd left off on my easier thoughts. Oh yeah: lobotomies. The guy who performed them, nicknamed Dr. Lobotomy, traveled from asylum to asylum in the '60s, living out of his *lobotomobile*—he seriously called it that—while banging out twenty procedures a day. Apparently it only takes a few minutes to destroy someone's frontal lobe. True story. Google it.

I kicked harder, faster, higher on the swing, and then turned into a board, locking my elbows and knees. I tracked the blue sky with each swinging pass, waiting for gravity to get predictable. To bring me back to earth.

When it finally did, I was no longer alone. A kid glared from a few feet away with that dog snarl only middle schoolers possess. Behind him, his buddies hung from the monkey bars, faux whispering. Clearly he'd been sent over. Chosen to poke fun at Jaycee Strangelove.

Yes, that's my name. No, you may not make fun of it.

I stared him down. "You're too old to be on the playground. Take off before you freak out the little kids," I said even though I was the only other person there.

The boy's hair was unevenly shaved on the sides, and he'd Sharpied rap lyrics up his ropey arms. "I dare you."

I exhaled for roughly ten years. "Dare me to do what, Eminem?"

He pointed to the top of the swing set, smirking.

"No."

"I can do the backflip," he bragged. "So can two of my friends."

I took the bait even though I knew better than to talk about the accident. "Jake could do it too, you snotwad. The flip that killed him was probably his thirtieth."

My thoughts went graphic. I couldn't stop imagining my big brother standing atop the swing set. He wore his cap and gown from graduation and was also half-drunk—a detail the coroner threw in later. Jake's classmates were cheering him on in a way that made me think he was the coolest human on the planet. I mean, I had only finished seventh grade, so that seemed entirely possible.

I remembered in slo-mo how he crouched and sprang backward. The flip was so fast that it had turned into one and a half flips, and then…

"Is it true that his head snapped off?" the Sharpie kid asked.

I glared.

"Well? Do the backflip," he said. "I dare you."

I got up and walked away.

"But you're supposed to do any dare," he yelled. "That's what everyone says."

"You've got the wrong Strangelove," I called back. "Jake was the one who did every dare." *I only do the ones that aren't suicidal*, I added in my thoughts. *Mostly.* I turned to walk backward and spoke my next words loud enough for him and his little thug friends. "Jake's head didn't snap off. His neck bent ninety degrees." I held my arm up, crooked. "Like an elbow."

Maybe that would keep them from mimicking the flip that broke Jake. But probably not. More likely, it'd make them even more interested. Middle schoolers make no freakin' sense.

I pretended like I was leaving, but I didn't go anywhere. Instead, I hooked around the small wooded area and back to the playground. To the swing set. Lil Eminem and his posse had bugged off, and I felt myself edging too close to the supermassive black hole inside that Jake had left behind.

Five years ago. Five. *Five.*

I eyed the playground like I might catch a glimpse of his ghost. He would probably be pissed to know that I imagined his spirit in that ridiculous cap and gown. Also barefoot, but then again, he never wore shoes.

I flipped off my bashed-up Converses and climbed the support beam of the swing set without another thought. The cool metal gripped my palms, and I looped my legs around the top bar and hauled myself into a sitting position. *Easier than it looks.* I wriggled my butt down the pole.

The sunset was lapsing into a cherry-stained twilight. A breeze came in from somewhere and set itself against my radical heart-beat. A few dozen people had watched Jake flip; none of them had tried to stop him, least of all me. And now I was alone. No one was going to stop me either. *I'm lost without you, Jake*, I thought, followed by, *What sentimental crap.*

"I'm always right here," I muttered. "How lost is that?"

Crazy and cursing, I stood up.

About the Author

Cori McCarthy was born in Guam, a military brat. She studied poetry and screenwriting before earning an MFA in Writing for Children & Young Adults from the Vermont College of Fine Arts. Kirkus called her debut YA novel, *The Color of Rain*, "[an] elegantly written and emotionally cathartic page-turner." Cori aspires to fly in a fighter, but until then, she sticks with roller coasters and skydiving. Find out more at www.CoriMcCarthy.com.